THE
AIR YOU
BREATHE

THE

AIR YOU

BREATHE

FRANCES

DE PONTES PEEBLES

RIVERHEAD BOOKS

New York

2018

RIVERHEAD BOOKS
An imprint of Penguin Random House LLC
375 Hudson Street
New York, New York 10014

Library of Congress Cataloging-in-Publication Data

Names: Peebles, Frances de Pontes, author.
Title: The air you breathe / by Frances de Pontes Peebles.
Description: New York : Riverhead Books, 2018.
Identifiers: LCCN 2017057494 | ISBN 9780735210998 (hardcover) |
ISBN 9780735211018 (ebook)
Subjects: LCSH: Female friendship—Fiction. | Dependency (Psychology)—Fiction. |
Identity (Psychology)—Fiction. | Psychological fiction.
Classification: LCC PS3616.E32 A47 2018 | DDC 813/.6—dc23
LC record available at https://lccn.loc.gov/2017057494
p.   cm.

International edition: 9780525540236

Printed in the United States of America
1   3   5   7   9   10   8   6   4   2

Book design by Gretchen Achilles

FOR EMÍLIA

THE
AIR YOU
BREATHE

Time is short and the water is rising.

This is what one of Sofia Salvador's directors—I can't recall his name—used to shout before he'd start filming. Each time he said it, I imagined all of us in a fishbowl, our hands sliding frantically along the glass sides as water crept above our necks, our noses, our eyes.

I fall asleep listening to our old records and wake with my mouth dry, my tongue as rough as a cat's. I pull the handle of my La-Z-Boy and, with a jolt, am sitting upright. A pile of photos rests in my lap.

I own the most famous photograph of Sofia Salvador—the Brazilian Bombshell, the Fruity Cutie Girl, the fast-talking, eye-popping nymph with her glittering costumes and pixie-cut hair who, depending on your age and nationality, is a joke, an icon of camp, a victim, a traitor, a great innovator, or even, as one researcher anointed her, "an object of serious study of Hollywood's Latinas." (Is that what they're calling us now?) I bought the original photo and its negative at auction, paying much more than they were worth. Money isn't an issue for me these days; I'm filthy rich and not ashamed to say so. When I was young, musicians had to pretend that success and money didn't matter. Ambition, in a sambista and especially in a woman, was seen as an unforgivable fault.

In the photo, taken in 1942, Sofia Salvador wears the pixie cut she made famous. Her eyes are wide. Her lips are parted. Her tongue flicks the roof of her mouth; it is unclear if she is singing or screaming. Earrings made to resemble life-sized hummingbirds—their jeweled eyes glinting, their golden beaks sharp—dangle from her ears. She was vain about her lobes, worried they would sag under the weight of her array of earrings, each pair more fantastical than the next. She was vain about everything, really; she had to be.

In the photograph she wears a gold choker, wrapped twice around her neck. Below it is strand upon strand of fake pearls, each one as large as an eyeball. Then there are the bracelets—bands of coral and gold—taking up most of her forearms. At the end of each day, when I'd take those necklaces and bracelets off her and she stopped being Sofia Salvador (for a moment, at least), Graça flapped her arms and said, "I feel so light. I could fly away!"

Graça drew Sofia's dark eyebrows arched so high she always looked surprised. The mouth—that famous red mouth—was what took her the longest to produce. She lined beyond her lips so that, like everything else, they were an exaggeration of the real thing. Who was the real thing? By the end of her short life, even Graça had trouble answering this question.

The picture was taken for *Life* magazine. The photographer stood Graça against a white backdrop. "Pretend you're singing," he ordered.

"Why pretend?" Graça replied.

"I thought that's all you knew how to do," the photographer shot back. He believed his fame gave him the right to be nasty.

Graça stared. She was very tired. We always were, even me, who signed Sofia Salvador's name to hundreds of glossy photos while Graça and the Blue Moon boys endured eighteen-hour days of filming, costume fittings, screen tests, dance rehearsals, and publicity shoots for whatever her latest movie musical was. It could have been worse; we could have been starving like in the old days. But at least in the old days we played real music, together.

"Then I will pretend to respect you," Graça said to that fool photographer. Then she opened her mouth and sang. People remember the haircut, the enormous earrings, the sequined skirts, the accent, but they forget her voice. When she sang for that photographer, his camera nearly fell from his hands.

I listen to her records—only our early recordings, when she sang Vinicius's and my songs—and it is as if she is still seventeen and sitting beside me. Graça, with all of her willfulness, her humor, her petty resistances, her pluck, her complete selfishness. This is how I want her, if only for the span of a three-minute song.

When the song ends, I'm exhausted and whimpering. I imagine her here, nudging me, bringing me back to my senses.

Why the hell are you upset, Dor? Graça chides. *At least you're still around.*

Her voice is so clear, I have to remind myself she isn't real. I have known Graça longer in my imagination than in real life.

Who wants real life? Graça asks, laughing at me. (She is always laughing at someone.)

I shake my head. After all this time—ninety-five years, to be exact—I still do not know the answer.

My current life is a dull jumble of walks along the beach chaperoned by a nurse; trips to the grocery store; afternoons in my office; evenings listening to records; tedious hours spent tolerating a steady stream of physical therapists and doctors with their proclamations and humorless devotion. I live in a vast house surrounded by paid help. Once, long ago, I wished for such ease.

Be careful what you wish for, Dor.

It's too late to be careful now, amor.

Now, I wish for the early, chaotic part of my life—those first thirty or so years—to return to me, even with its cruelty, its sacrifice, its missteps, its misdeeds. My misdeeds. If I could hear my life—if I could put it on a turntable like a worn-out LP—I'd hear samba. Not the boisterous kind they play during Carnaval. Not one of those silly marchinhas, as short-lived and vapid as bubbles. And not the soft-spoken, romantic sort, either. No. Mine would be the kind of samba you'd find in a roda: the kind we played in a circle after work and a few stiff drinks. It begins quite dire-sounding, perhaps with the lonely moan of a cuíca. Then, ever so slowly, others join the roda—voices, guitars, a tamborim drum, the scratch of a reco-reco—and the song begins to claw its way out of its lowly beginning and into something fuller, thicker, darker. It has all of the elements of a true samba (though not necessarily a great one). There is lament, humor, rebelliousness, lust, ambition, regret. And love. There is that, too. It is all improvisation, so if there are mistakes I must move past them and keep playing. Beneath it all, there is the ostinato—the main groove that never varies, never wavers. It keeps its stubborn pace; the beat that's always there. And here I am: the only one left in the circle, conjuring voices I have not heard in decades, listening to a chorus of arguments I should never have made. I have tried not to hear this song in full. I have tried to blot it out with drink and time and indifference. But it remains in my head, and will not stop until I recall all of its words. Until I sing it out loud, from beginning to end.

THE SWEET RIVER

Share this bottle with me,
share this song.
The years have hardened my heart.
Drink will loosen my tongue.
Come, walk with me,
to the places I once loved.

Man made the fire
to burn the fields of cane.
God made music
to take away my pain.

I come from a land
where sugar is king and the river is sweet.
They say a woman drowned there,
her ghost haunts the deep.

Sit beside me now, at the riverbank
hear my voice, loud and strong.
Wade into these sweet waters with me,
let me open your heart with a song.

Now we're both pulled under, friend,
singing the same refrain:
Dive back, again, to the place you once loved
and you'll find it's never the same.

Man made the fire
to burn the fields of cane.
God made music
to take away my pain.

THE SWEET RIVER

I t would be better to begin with Graça—with her arrival, with our first meeting. But life isn't as orderly as a story or a song; it does not always begin and end at compelling points. Even before Graça's arrival, even as a small child, I sensed that I'd been born into a role that didn't fit my ambitions, like a stalk of sugarcane crammed into a thimble.

I survived my own birth, a true feat in 1920 if you were born to a dirt-poor mother living on a sugar plantation. The midwife who delivered me told everyone how surprised she was that such a hearty girl could've come from my mother's tired womb. I was her fifth and final child. Most women who worked on the plantation had ten or twelve or even eighteen children, so my mother's womb was fresher and younger than most. But she was not married and never had been. All of my long-lost brothers and myself—I was the only girl in our lot—had different fathers. This made my mother worse than a puta in many people's minds, because at least a puta had the sense to charge for her services.

I didn't dare ask about my mother, afraid of what I might hear and not willing to risk a beating; I was not allowed to ask any questions at all, you see. No one spoke of her, except to insult me. They said I was big-boned, like her. They said I had a temper, like her. They said

I was ugly as sin, like her, except I did not have scars covering my arms and face from the cane. She was, for a little while at least, a sugarcane cutter—one of a handful of women who could stomach the work. But the insult that came up the most was the one about her easy way with men. If I didn't use enough salt to scrub blood from the plantation's cutting boards, or if I stopped stirring the infernally hot jam on the stove for even a second, or if I was too slow bringing Cook Nena or her staff ingredients from the pantry or garden, I was smacked with a wooden spoon and called "puta's girl." So I came to know my mother through all of the things people despised about her, and about me. And I realized, though I could not articulate it clearly as a child, that people hated what they feared, and so I was proud of her.

The midwife took pity on me, being such a healthy baby, and instead of smothering me, or throwing me in the cane for the vultures to pick at, or giving me to some plantation owner to raise like a pet or a slave (all common practices back then for girl children without families), she gave me to Nena, the head cook on the Riacho Doce plantation. There were hundreds of cane plantations along the coast of our state of Pernambuco, and Riacho Doce was one of the largest. In good times, when sugar prices were high, Cook Nena led a staff of ten kitchen maids and two houseboys. Nena was as full-breasted as a prize rooster and had hands as large and as lethal as her cast-iron frying pans. The Pimentel family owned Riacho Doce and were the masters of its Great House, but Nena ruled in the kitchen. This is why no one objected when, after the midwife brought me, naked and wailing, to Nena, the cook decided to raise me as her kitchen girl.

Everyone in the Great House—maids, laundresses, stable boys, houseboys—went to Nena's kitchen to get a look at me. They freely remarked on my rosy skin, my long legs, my perfect feet. A day later, I stopped drinking the goat's milk Nena gave me in a bottle. Nena visited a local wet nurse and I spat the woman's teats from my mouth. I was too young to eat manioc porridge but Nena tried to feed it to me anyway. I spat that out, too, and soon turned shriveled and yellow-skinned like an old crone. People said I'd been cursed by the evil eye. Olho mau, they called it, olho gordo. Both are different names for the same bad luck.

Nena went to Old Euclides for help. Euclides was wrinkled, gossipy, and the color of blackstrap scraped from the sugar mill's vats. He'd worked at Riacho Doce longer than Nena had, first as a stable boy and then as its groundskeeper. He had a donkey who'd given birth and lost her foal but not her milk. Nena took me to the stables and held me straight to that jega's teat, and I drank. I drank that jega's milk until I was fat and strong again. My color changed; I was less like a rose and more like that donkey's tan coat. My hair grew in thick. After that, I was called Jega.

In people's superstitious and backward minds, the girl I became was inextricably linked to the mother's milk I'd drunk.

"Jega's as dumb as an ass," the houseboys teased.

"Jega's as stubborn as an ass," the kitchen maids complained.

"Jega's as ugly as an ass," the stable boys said when they felt spiteful.

They all wanted me to believe it. They wanted me to become that Jega. I would never give them that satisfaction.

The Great House sat on a hill. You could stand on its pillared front porch and see nearly all of Riacho Doce's workings: the main gate, the mill with its blackened smokestack, the horse and donkey stables, the administrator's house, the carpenter's shed, the old manioc mill, a small square of pasture and corn, the distillery and warehouses with their thick iron doors. And you could see the brown line of water that gave Riacho Doce its name, although it was much wider than a creek and its waters were not sweet.

Every plantation had a ghost story and ours was no different: a woman had drowned in the river and lived there still. Some said she was killed by a lover, others said a master, others said she killed herself. They said you could hear her at night, under the waters, singing for her lost love or trying to lure people into the waters and drown them to keep her company; the story depended on whether you believed in the kind ghost or the vengeful one. Riacho Doce's mothers told their children this before bed, and it kept them away from the river. I heard the ghost's story from Nena.

Behind the Great House was an orchard, and behind that the low-roofed slaves' senzalas that had been converted into servants' quarters. Nena and I were the only staff allowed to sleep in the Great House itself, which set us apart from the rest of the servants. This special status didn't affect Nena as much as it did me. I was Jega—the lowest soul in the strict hierarchy of the Great House—and the maids and houseboys were determined to remind me of this fact. They slapped me, pinched my neck, cursed and spat at me. They thwacked me with wooden spoons and greased the staff doorway with lard to make me slip and fall. They locked me in the foul-smelling outhouse until I kicked my way out. Nena knew about these pranks but didn't stop them.

"That's the way a kitchen is," Nena said. "You're lucky the boys aren't trying to get under your skirts. They will soon enough. Better learn to fight them now."

Nena always issued such warnings to me:

Better keep your head down.

Better stay out of sight.

Better make yourself useful.

If I failed to heed her warnings she beat me with a wooden spoon, or an old bullwhip, or with her bare hands. And while I feared these beatings I didn't think them odd or bad; I knew no other kind of affection, and neither did Nena. She used her fists to teach me things she couldn't articulate, lessons that would keep me alive. Nena could keep me safe in her kitchen but nowhere else. I was a creature without family or money. I was another mouth to feed. And, even worse, I was a girl. At the owners' whim, I could be thrown out of the Great House and left to fend for myself in that sea of sugarcane. And what did an ugly little girl have to offer the world but her body? So I had to learn to defend that body ruthlessly against any stable boys or millworkers or others who might try to use it roughly. And, at the same time, I had to learn how to make myself useful within the house, to obey my patrons at all costs or, better yet, stay out of their sights completely. As long as I was invisible, I was safe.

So while little girls like Graça were playing with dolls and dresses, I learned to play other kinds of games. Games where force was power, and where cleverness meant survival.

When I was nine years old, the world's great financial crash hit Brazil and sugar became as valuable as dirt. Smaller plantations near Riacho Doce boarded up their Great Houses and put workers out of their gates. Riacho Doce's mill closed. After getting into crippling debt, the Pimentel family moved away. There were rumors of a sale. Soon afterward, the cane cutters left to work on other plantations that had weathered the crisis. The fields were abandoned. The distillery was locked. One by one, the housemaids and kitchen girls and stable boys left. Soon, only Nena, Old Euclides, and I were left.

"They'll be back," Nena said of the Pimentels. "No one leaves their land. And when they do come back, they'll remember who was loyal and who wasn't."

Nena was driven by loyalty and fear. She and Old Euclides had been born on Riacho Doce before slavery was banned in Brazil in 1888, and had stayed on even after they were freed. During the abandonment, Old Euclides took care of the grounds, making sure no one took animals from the stables or stole fruit from the orchard. Nena wouldn't let her copper pots and iron pans fall into the hands of looters or bill collectors, so she hid anything of value. Porcelain dining sets, silver platters and tureens, pure gold cutlery, a bowl made of mother-of-pearl were stashed under the Great House's floorboards. We ate whatever food was left in the pantry and then, because none of us had been paid since the Pimentels left, began to trade at the local market. Eggs for flour, star fruit from the orchard for a bit of salted meat, bottles of molasses for beans. These were lean times but not unhappy ones. Not for me.

For many months the Great House was empty and I spent my days inside it. I skipped across its stone floors. I slipped my hands under dust covers and felt cool marble, the slopes and curves of table legs, the gilded bevels of mirrors. I pulled books from shelves and opened them wide to hear their bindings snap. I walked proudly up and down the wide wooden staircase, like I imagined the lady of the house would. For the first time in my nine years of life, I had the luxury of time and freedom—to explore, to pretend, to play without fear of being hit or scolded, to live without the constant worry that I would be cast out of Riacho Doce for some small infraction. I was allowed to be a child, and began to believe that I would always have such freedom. I should have known better.

One day, as I sat in the library and tried to decode the mysterious symbols inside the Pimentels' books, I heard a terrible growling outside. It sounded as if there was a giant dog snarling at the Great House gate. I ran to Nena, who opened the front door.

A motorcar rumbled outside the front gate. Old Euclides scrambled, suddenly as spry as a puppy, down the drive and pushed open the gate. The car stopped and a man emerged from the driver's side. He wore a hat and a long canvas coat to protect his suit. He opened the passenger and back doors. Two women emerged: a pale one also wearing a driving coat, and another in a maid's striped uniform and lace cap. The maid attempted to tug something from the backseat. There was a hiss and a screech. For a moment, I believed there was an animal in the car—a cat or some kind of possum—until I saw the maid's hands wrapped around two tiny feet in patent leather boots. The boots kicked free of the maid's grip. The woman wedged herself deeper into the car's doorway. Then there were screams, grunts, a swirl of white petticoats and, finally, a cry. The maid jumped from the automobile's backseat, her eyes watering, her hand pressed to a fresh scratch on her face.

"Leave her inside!" the man snapped. "She's old enough to climb out herself."

The maid nodded, her hand still clamped to her face. The other woman sighed and unbuttoned her canvas driving coat, revealing a silk dress and a tangle of pearls at her neck.

A halo of red curls surrounded her face. Her skin was what we called "mill white" because that was the prized color of sugar. The sugar we used in the Great House kitchen was the mill's seconds—raw and muddy-colored, not white but not quite brown, just like me.

"It's better she doesn't come outside," the man said, staring at the dirt road. "She'll get herself filthy." He had darker coloring, a square jaw, and a Roman nose that sloped like an arrow pointing at his full mouth.

"We'll all have to get used to a little dirt from now on," the mill-white woman replied, and her lips pursed as if she was holding back laughter, as if she'd told herself a naughty joke.

At the mention of dirt, a girl my own age wiggled from the backseat. She wore a dress the color of butter, and white gloves. A bow sat crookedly atop her head; the girl snatched it from her hair and flung it to the ground. She kicked at the dirt, scuffing her boots, and then glared at the adults around her, daring them to tell her to stop. Then she saw me, and stood still. To her, I was not invisible.

Her eyes were the color of cork. Her mouth looked as if it had been painted onto her face, like a doll's. I don't know how long we stared at each other; I only remember not wanting to break first, determined not to let her win.

Still staring at me, the girl pressed her gloved hand to the car's body and dragged it across the entire side. Then she raised her hand. The glove's palm was as red as the earth under my bare feet. The girl smirked, as if sharing a joke, but I knew she didn't intend to amuse me. Gloves were for the rich. They were expensive and delicate. Some poor laundress would have the unenviable task of trying to clean that soiled glove, so small it would bunch in her hands and make her knuckles scrape against the washboard until they bled. But the girl didn't care about the glove, or the laundress, or anything. She would ruin something perfectly good, for no reason at all. I felt both respect and revulsion.

"Graça!" the man shouted.

The man and woman bickered. Nena, Old Euclides, and I kept very still, waiting for them to acknowledge our presence. Only when they needed help did we become flesh-and-blood to them—the man ordered Euclides to get the bags from the car's trunk; the pale woman dropped her driving coat into Nena's arms. This is when I knew that those people were not visitors but owners, come to claim Riacho Doce and the Great House for themselves.

They were also Pimentels—cousins of the previous owners. As we walked through the Great House together, Senhora Pimentel moved languidly alongside her husband, looking tired as she pointed out leaks and cracks, peeling paint and rotted wood. Her husband, Senhor Pimentel, yanked dust covers from the furniture, like a magician revealing his trick.

"I remember my grandfather using this desk!" he cried. And, later, "I was the one who spilled ink on this chair!"

The giddy freedom I'd felt over several months leaked away in the single hour after those new Pimentels arrived. All of the books I'd slipped from the shelves, all of the ivory and glass knickknacks I'd polished and stroked, all of the tables I'd hidden under, pretending I was in a tent in some exotic land, all of the mirrors in which I'd studied myself, would never again be mine to play with. I would once again have to be useful and invisible, to obey or be cast away. When her parents weren't looking, the cork-eyed girl stuck out her tongue at me. It was as pink and slick as a jambo fruit. I had the urge to bite off its tip.

Finally, the new Pimentels pulled the covers from two armchairs and sat, exhausted, in the formal sitting room. They ordered Nena to make coffee. We raced to the kitchen, where Nena grabbed my arm and told to get the last, precious beans she'd hidden under her cot. Back upstairs, I peeked through the slatted door of the sitting room as Nena served coffee to the new Pimentels. They waited to drink until she'd left the room; I did not follow her to the kitchen.

Senhor Pimentel took a sip from his cup and made a face. "Did she use an old sock to strain this?" he asked.

Senhora Pimentel shook her head. "We'll have to train a new staff. How exhausting."

"Nena's a good cook—you'll see. She's been here since I was a kid," Senhor Pimentel replied.

"You think she and the old man had that child together? Poor little ugly thing."

Senhor Pimentel laughed. "Nena's as old as the hills. And the girl's too light-skinned to be theirs. I bet she's not so ugly under all that dirt; she just needs a good scrubbing."

"She'll stay in the kitchen," Senhora Pimentel snapped. "If she grows up to be decent-looking she can serve the table."

Senhor Pimentel took his wife's hand. She fixed him with the same weary expression she'd had when she'd inspected the Great House. They discussed their plans for the house. Furniture that was upstairs would go downstairs. Rugs would be thrown out. Curtains replaced. Water pipes and a flush toilet installed, which meant hacking into the house's thick white walls.

There were footsteps behind me. Before I could hide, I felt a terrible stinging on the back of my arm. The cork-eyed Pimentel girl pinched the skin above my elbow. I glared and shook her loose.

"Marta always cried when I pinched her," the girl said.

"Who's Marta?"

"The kitchen girl at my other house, in Recife. It's a mansion. Better than this pigsty."

"This is the best house of any plantation," I said.

The girl shrugged. "You must die of boredom out here."

"Do I look dead?"

"It's a way of talking. Are you dumb?"

"Not half as dumb as you look."

The girl's eyes widened. "You can't talk to me like that."

She was right—I was risking my place in that Great House. I blame those many months of freedom for my boldness, and for what happened next.

"This is my house now," the girl said.

My hand made a crisp, exhilarating slap against her cheek. The girl gasped. I ran.

The kitchen pantry was an empty, cool space. I sat inside, waiting. My fingers throbbed from the slap I'd dealt. I had sickening thoughts of Nena finding me and giving me the worst thrashing of my life. Or, worse, Senhor Pimentel stalking into the kitchen and casting me out of the only home I'd ever known. After what felt like an eternity, there were footsteps and chatter, then the automobile growled again and the new Pimentels left with a promise to return and begin renovations.

I was impressed that the Pimentel girl hadn't snitched; it made her tolerable to me, but also dangerous. What would she want in return for her silence? What would I owe her? These were the questions I asked myself in the weeks before the new Pimentels returned, while carpenters and stonemasons and plumbers sawed and pounded and pressed copper pipes into the Great House's walls.

Years later, I asked Graça about the day we met and she laughed. I remembered it all wrong, she said. She'd slapped me.

I knew every dusty corner of that Great House, every empty armoire, every sideboard big enough to hide inside. When the new Pimentels finally moved to Riacho Doce, I waited for moments when Nena was distracted and left the kitchen. I hid and watched Graça dress and undress her dolls, biting her perfect pink lip when she couldn't match a dress to an apron. I watched the maid brush Graça's hair until it was as glossy as the melted chocolate that Nena poured over the Pimentels' cakes. I watched as Graça ate lunch at the formal dining table, her tiny foot kicking against the chair legs until her mother snapped at her to stop. Graça wore lace-lined socks and petticoats and dresses with frilled aprons. By the end of the day her starched clothes wilted from the heat. Once, I went into the laundry and found her dirty clothes. I held one of her dresses to my own body, and then to my face. The laundress caught me and, her chapped hand like a leather strap around my arm, dragged me to Nena. The laundress said I was trying to wear one of the Little Miss's dresses, which was a lie.

"I don't want her stupid dresses," I said, pleading my case to Nena. "I wanted to know what her sweat smelled like."

"And what does it smell like?" Nena asked, laughing. "Roses?"

"Just sweat," I replied.

Nena shook her head and then beat me with an old belt.

One afternoon, not long after the laundry incident, Graça sneaked into the kitchen. I was alone near the pantry, peeling potatoes. She tugged my braid. I was happy to see her, but did not smile.

"Come to my room," she ordered. "Now."

"I'm working."

"You have to do what I say."

I pressed a wet potato to her perfectly upturned nose. "I do what Nena says."

Graça stepped away, rubbing potato juice from her nose, and then ran.

I felt a secret thrill at having won that contest, and then immediately regretted it. This was not a match of equals; Graça was the Little Miss and could easily punish me in ways that I could never punish her. Yet denying Graça my company was the only power I had.

The next day, Senhora Pimentel appeared in the kitchen. She wove around the tables, pausing at each workstation and pretending to inspect each girl's work. Sternness did not come naturally to her. All of us working in the Great House had been born into our roles as servants, taught since childhood to be attuned to the habits and moods of our masters, so we sensed Senhora Pimentel's weakness before she ever issued a single order, and many used it to their advantage. Nena did not allow anyone working in her kitchen to shirk their duties, but the maids at the front of the house weren't under her command. They didn't dust behind armoires, left fingerprints on the silver, and sat on the Pimentels' furniture when no one was looking—all behaviors that a capable Senhora would have noticed and quickly punished. Senhora Pimentel was not capable. Like many women of her time, she'd been trained to be meek and decorous to everyone except servants, with whom one had to be forceful and self-assured. She was expected to be two women at once, which, I think, is what caused her frail health.

Thinking of the Senhora now, I can't recall her face exactly. Did she have brown eyes or blue? Did her front teeth overlap or were they as straight and even as a comb's? When I think of Senhora Pimentel, I think of a fado—its sadness obvious, but with such depth and volup- tuousness, you can't help but want the melody to wrap itself around you. Fado doesn't have the sly humor of the blues; its laments are pain- fully earnest. This makes some dislike fado, disgusted by its vulnerabil- ity. Others of us feel protective toward it.

Today, I'm sure a doctor would diagnose Senhora Pimentel with depression or anxiety or low self-esteem or any one of those mental ailments that have become so popular. She would be told to take pills, and read books about living her best life, and would pay someone to listen to her talk about her feelings. Maybe such things would have helped Senhora Pimentel, but they didn't exist when she was alive. Doctors visited Riacho Doce and each diagnosed Senhora Pimentel with a nervous disposition. Back then it was fashionable for women of a certain station to suffer from this kind of illness.

If the Great House's new Senhora was a living, breathing fado, then its Senhor was the opposite: he was a jingle. The kind of music made not to satisfy our deepest desires but to cajole us into buying a certain brand of chewing gum; the kind of tune whose catchiness and charm make you believe it is harmless at first, even as it worms its way inside you and coerces you into believing that you should want exactly what it tells you to want, that you should open yourself to it and let it stake its claim. And by the time you realize the jingle's intentions, it's too late. You can't escape it, even decades later, no matter how hard you try.

Senhor Pimentel was handsome for a married man of his status; he hadn't allowed rich meals and heavy drink to bloat him. Each morning he had Old Euclides polish his riding boots until they shone like mirrors, and, after allowing the old man the pleasure of tugging the boots onto his feet, Senhor Pimentel mounted his horse and rode the cane fields with his foreman, which made him seem industrious. He often kissed his wife's hand and helped her to the table for meals. If she was too tired to go downstairs to eat, he visited her rooms. He treated the Senhora as if she was an older, more powerful relation—ingratiating and kind while in her presence, and then, whenever she left, letting out a small sigh of relief. Maids gossiped that it was the Senhora's fortune that kept them afloat and allowed them to save Riacho Doce from ruin. But it was Senhor Pimentel, being the man of the family, who held the reins of the plantation. He had a smile for everyone, even me, and especially for the young housemaids. More than once, I spotted Senhor Pimentel chatting with the youngest of them—farm girls of thirteen and fourteen who were awed by his fancy clothes and, most of all, his interest in them. He made them giggle and blush.

"Better keep out of the Senhor's way," Nena warned me.

I believed her warning was simply a repetition of what she'd already hammered into me: keep to yourself, stay out of sight. And later, when Senhora Pimentel insisted that all maids work in pairs—one older, one younger—I thought she was simply trying to show us all who was boss.

On the day Senhora Pimentel appeared in the kitchen, we kept our heads down and continued our peeling, scraping, mixing, or washing. But we kept track of her as she wove past the stoves and the cutting tables, and finally stood beside me. She watched for what seemed like hours as I sorted dried beans, removing pebbles and shriveled sours. Then she did something I did not expect—she reached out and held my braid in her pale hand, as if she were weighing a length of rope.

I froze; until that point, the gentlest touch I could remember was Nena prodding me with a wooden spoon. The fact that the Senhora did not yank me backward confused and startled me.

"Hair as straight as a little Indian's," she said, smoothing the end of my braid with her fingers. "Girls in Recife would pay a fortune for hair like this."

Senhora Pimentel stepped away from me and spoke quietly with Nena.

"Jega!" Nena called as soon as Senhora Pimentel had left. "Wash your hands and behind your ears and go put on your good dress. The Senhora wants you in the front of the house."

My hand fluttered to my braid and held it. "Why?"

"There's no 'why,' girl," Nena replied. "The Senhora wants you. That's that."

"Is she going to steal my hair?" I blurted.

Next to us, a kitchen girl let out a whoop. Another giggled. Nena shook her head. I was never particularly attached to my hair, but it was mine and I wanted to keep it that way.

"Go before I beat you black and blue, and cut off your hair myself!" she barked.

The front of the house was silent. The maids spoke in whispers. From the front hall I could hear Old Tita plumping pillows in the sitting room. When she saw me in the doorway, Tita sighed, stopped her work, and led me upstairs, to the playroom. Graça was there. With grim determination, she dressed and undressed a series of glass-headed dolls.

"Here," she said, flinging one at me. "Change her clothes."

I'd never held a doll before. Her painted eyes were wide, her red mouth open in a dumb kind of awe.

"Why do they call you Jega?" Graça asked.

I met her eyes. "Because I kick and bite."

Graça stared back, unimpressed. "It's a stupid name. Probably the stupidest I've ever heard."

I looked down at the doll in my lap so that Graça wouldn't see me smile. "Do you like these dolls?"

"No," Graça replied. "I used to play in Mamãe's closet. I could try on her evening dresses. Her tiaras. But she didn't bring any of her fine things here."

I put down the doll and headed toward the playroom door. "Come on," I said.

"Where?"

"Outside."

Graça stood. "We can't go there."

"Why not?"

"Because I didn't say we could."

"So say it. Tell me we're going outside."

Graça stared at the limp doll in her hands, then at me. "Tell me your real name first."

Nena had told me my name—my given name—when I was old enough to remember it. Before she'd died, my mother told the midwife what she'd wanted me to be called. It was the only thing she ever gave me, besides my life.

"Maria das Dores," I said.

Graça threw her doll into a pile of toys. "Dores, I'm bored. We're going outside."

I surprised both myself and Graça then by taking her hand. It was soft and warm, like a small ball of dough that I could easily work between my fingers.

S he was Maria das Graças and I was Maria das Dores. Pick any name, starting with any letter of the alphabet, and add Maria in front of it and you'd name three-quarters of the girls from our generation, rich and poor—Maria Emília, Maria Augusta, Maria Benedita, Maria do Carmo, Maria das Neves, and on and on. There were so many Marias that no one ever actually called us Maria. We used our second names instead. So Graça was always Graça, until she became Sofia Salvador, and I was always Jega until she called me Dores.

Americans make my name rhyme with *kiss* or *bliss*. There's no helping it. I try to teach people how to say it properly, the way it is said in Portuguese. "Do-res," I say, "like *dough*. And then *riche*, very soft." When they ask what it means I tell them without flinching. "Pain," I say, "hurt." There is always a frown after this. I understand why; everyone wants a name to mean something lovely. As if our names are our destinies.

Graça and Dores—grace and pain—what a perfect pair. The plantation was our kingdom. I taught Graça how to climb trees in the orchard, how to throw rotten acerola berries at the houseboys, how to sneak oats to the donkeys and pet their soft snouts. She taught me how to play marbles and jacks, how to tie a bow, how to sit straight with our ankles crossed. We stood on barrels and peeked inside the mill, watching the men, their chests glistening with sweat, make the cane into sugar. We stayed away from the fields because the cane leaves were as sharp as Nena's knives; all the cane cutters had scars across their arms. But after harvest the land was brown and bare like a cake without icing and Graça and I roamed wherever we pleased. Sometimes we escaped to the river for secret swims and returned sunburned and sweating to the Great House, where Senhora Pimentel stood on the back porch (I was not allowed to use the front door) waiting for us.

"Where have you been?" Senhora Pimentel asked Graça. "You can't play too long in the sun! You'll brown your face and never be married."

This was the threat Senhora Pimentel used against Graça in her feeble attempts to discipline her daughter: *Don't chew your nails or you'll never be married! Don't scrape your legs on trees or you'll never be married! Mind your manners or you'll never be married!*

Graça was a Little Miss, and a Little Miss's destiny was to be married and have a Great House of her own. Riacho Doce's Great House and all of its lands weren't meant to be Graça's; they were destined for her brother, who, much to Senhor Pimentel's frustration, did not yet exist. During their frequent arguments, Senhor Pimentel asked his wife why, after months exposed to the fresh air and tranquility of the countryside, she wasn't feeling better. Senhora Pimentel would respond that their move to Riacho Doce hadn't been for her sake, and she wished her husband would stop pretending it was. They had, she insisted, moved away from the capital for him, and his misguided dreams of becoming a sugar baron. If they'd stayed in Recife, the Senhora yelled, Graça would be in a proper school, have proper friends, learn manners, wear hats and gloves, and, later, be surrounded by a dozen young gentlemen who would want Graça as their wife. "She has the Pimentel name," the Senhor inevitably responded. "Even if she's as dull as a post, boys will line up for her. What's in her head doesn't matter, querida."

"My daughter will never be dull," the Senhora replied.

If Senhor Pimentel believed that, by virtue of Graça's being a girl child, she was insignificant and therefore invisible, then the Senhora believed it was her duty to give Graça substance and make her be seen. Back then being a woman of substance meant you were charming but never flirtatious, funny but not frivolous, likable but not desperate to be liked, and pious but not self-righteous, and, most important, if you lacked beauty then you had to have grace. A fine family and plenty of money were also requirements, but weren't things you could be taught; they were prerequisites. I, of course, had neither family nor money, but this didn't stop Senhora Pimentel from including me in her daughter's lessons. She expected both Graça and me to excel, but for different reasons: one day, Graça would be a Senhora, and (if I was lucky and smart) I would run her house.

Senhora Pimentel staged elaborate make-believe parties for the three of us, placing a dizzying number of utensils around our place settings and making us memorize which fork was for fish and which for oysters, which glass was for sherry and which goblet for water. Other days, the three of us took long walks together, far from the Great House. To protect their skin, Senhora Pimentel and Graça wore large straw hats that made them look like cane cutters. During these walks, the Senhora taught Graça and me to count in English: *one, two, three* . . . Then she taught us English words for all the things we saw during our walks: *bird, sugar, man, tree, knife, donkey, cart, mill, smoke.*

In those days, proper young ladies were required to learn either British English or French. Brazilians from Senhora Pimentel's set considered anything European the pinnacle of good taste. In Recife, our capital city, the British ran a railroad company, operated enormous textile mills, and even had their own country club and private cemetery. In her youth, Senhora Pimentel had attended a British school and spoke passable, if a bit labored, English. Those English words she taught us entered my brain and stayed there, caught, as if I'd been hungry and had set a trap for them. But they escaped Graça's memory quite easily, and by the end of our walks both she and her mother pouted and sighed in frustration.

When the Senhora wasn't feeling well (which was more often as time went by), Graça and I visited her room, where she lay in bed and read us fairy tales from a book she kept at her bedside. Soon, Graça and I were reenacting them. I was the woodcutter, the prince, the old crone, the frog, the troll. Graça was always the princess. Sometimes Senhora Pimentel braided our hair and I liked feeling her cool, pale fingers on my scalp. Once, after I delivered her food tray, she asked me to brush her red hair and my hands grew so slick that the brush fell and startled us both.

The tales Senhora Pimentel read to us and the stories she told of her own childhood contained words I'd never heard before. Big words.

Words with so many syllables they seemed like incantations. *Petulant. Vanquished. Verdant. Perambulate.* I asked Senhora Pimentel to please repeat those new words, and then to define them. She seemed happy to help me. At night, in my bed across from Nena's, in our tiny room attached to the kitchen, I whispered the words I'd learned that day again and again, as if casting spells of my own. I knew I could never use them outside Senhora Pimentel's room for fear of being slapped by Nena and told I was acting too fancy for my own good, but how I loved them! Loved the sound of them, and most of all the possibility that they represented: that there was a word for every idea and emotion I could ever fathom, no matter how difficult or strange. I wanted to collect them all. Then, one day, in front of Graça, the Senhora handed me a little notebook—one that fit inside my apron pocket—and a pencil.

"For you to remember our words, Dores," the Senhora said.

Our words. They belonged to us both.

It was a simple little book with a cloth cover. The pencil was stubby and poorly sharpened. But I held them so tightly in my hand—afraid they would be snatched away—that my fingers ached. It is said that no love can compare to your first love, and I also believe that no gift can compare to your first gift, no matter how small and insignificant it might have seemed to the giver.

I kept my head down and shut my eyes but a hot, fat tear escaped and ran down my cheek. The Senhora clucked. She pressed a soft hand to my face. In that moment I hoped, in the silly way a child does, to exert power over time and make it stop completely.

"I'm bored," Graça snapped. "This room has no air."

The Senhora's hand left my cheek. "Ask Nena for some water and a slice of cake," she said.

I reluctantly followed Graça out of the room and down the stairs, but she did not go to the kitchen. Instead, she left the Great House and headed to the river.

There, we both stripped off our dresses and waded into the cool water, but never too far, for fear of being carried away by the current.

"Tell me about the ghost again," Graça ordered.

I obliged, telling Graça the legend of the drowned woman leading people into the river with her songs. She listened intently, then shook her head.

"She doesn't want company," Graça said, staring into the murky water around us. "She wants to be rescued. Someone put her here, someone terrible, and she wants people to save her, but no one pays attention."

"That's not the story," I said.

"It's the story I want," Graça replied.

"You can't do that. You can't change a story just because you want to. That's not how it goes."

"Yes it is," Graça yelled, slapping the water. "Because I say so. Because I'm the Little Miss, not you, no matter how many stupid words you know! You don't even need a notebook. You don't even know how to write."

She'd had schooling before Riacho Doce. I hadn't. But that wasn't what bothered me about Graça's outburst. It was the first time she'd called herself "Little Miss" in front of me. Before that, we'd laughed at the name. We'd mocked it, as if the Little Miss was another girl and we'd run away from her to play by ourselves.

We had our first fight there, in the water. Graça pushed me. I pushed back. We grappled and snatched at each other, our hands sliding over our wet arms. We pulled hair and tugged each other's soggy camisoles. By the time we stomped back onto the shore, we were both crying, our arms red, our scalps sore. Side by side, we sat in the red dirt of the riverbank, catching our breath. I put my head between my knees and covered my neck with my arms, the way I sometimes did when Nena hit me. Usually in those moments with Nena I felt a calm determination to wait her out, to see things through to the finish. I tried to find that same calm with Graça as we sat on the riverbank, but instead I felt an extraordinary loneliness. She'd called herself Little Miss, and I saw the hopelessness of our friendship.

The sun was bright; I felt its heat on my shoulders. Then there was another kind of heat, along my left side. Graça scooted beside me, her leg pressed against my leg, her hip against my hip.

"I can't write, either," she said. "I had a tutor in Recife but it was no good. I'm dumb as a rock."

I lifted my head. Graça squinted at me, her cheeks and nose bright pink.

"Your face is burned," I said. "Now you'll never be married."

Graça smiled. She threaded her fingers through mine and we squeezed our sweaty palms tight. Then we both leaned back, closed our eyes, and sat in the sun, together.

T he little notebook Senhora Pimentel gifted me remained in my pocket, its pages empty. Graça and I didn't fight again, but our visits to her mother's room weren't the same. Graça shifted and sighed, stared out the window, fidgeted with her dress and the buckles of her shoes. After a few weeks, she announced that Senhora Pimentel's stories were boring and her hair-braiding annoying, and her room smelled of mothballs. One day, after a morning gallivanting around Riacho Doce, instead of returning to see her mother in the Great House as we always did, Graça insisted we visit the mill.

With its smokestack that rose thirty meters above the cane fields, the mill was the tallest building in Riacho Doce and, as far as I knew, the tallest in the world. Only in the weeks after harvest did smoke pour from that narrow brick tower. No one from the Great House was allowed near the mill when it was sugar-making time, and none of us complained about this rule. In the weeks after harvest, the mill ran night and day, turning cane into sugar, and even from the Great House we heard the groan of gears, the snap of logs bursting in huge fires, and the songs of the men who worked in four-hour shifts because the heat was intolerable otherwise. They stirred the copper cauldrons filled with liquid sugar that vomited foam hotter than fire. Sometimes there were screams. Then a group of men, slick with sweat and eyes wide with panic, would appear at the kitchen door holding one of their own and shouting for Nena. Some burns Nena could treat with her herbs and poultices. Others required a doctor's attention, or a gravedigger's. One poor soul died right there, in the kitchen in front of us, his skin as charred and papery as a husk of corn placed in the fire.

The day Graça and I went to the mill, Riacho Doce's cane still grew tall in the hills around us. The mill's giant wheel was quiet and its cauldrons empty, their copper a sickly greenish hue. Graça moved past the worn tools and ancient-looking machines like a dog following a scent, disinterested in whatever human contraptions surrounded her. At the office door, Graça did not bother to knock. I contemplated running away—invading the empty mill was one thing, but disturbing Senhor Pimentel in his office was quite another. There was no time for me to disappear; Graça strode inside his office and I shut my eyes, prepared to hear Senhor Pimentel's yells. Instead there was laughter. He opened his arms wide and swung Graça onto his lap.

"To what do I owe this honor?" Senhor Pimentel asked his daughter. His shirtsleeves were rolled up, exposing muscled forearms.

Graça regaled her father with stories about our morning: how we ran through the orchard, climbed trees, sucked on star fruits until our mouths puckered. Neither of them acknowledged my presence at the door. After only a few minutes, however, Senhor Pimentel's smile faded and he shifted his knees. Graça tumbled from his lap.

"Time to go," he said. "Little girls can play all day. Men must work."

Graça frowned. "But I didn't tell you the best part!" she said. "We saw a bright red fish jump out of the river and into the air!"

Senhor Pimentel raised his eyebrows.

"We saw it, didn't we?" Graça asked, staring at me.

Senhor Pimentel looked in my direction. He did not smile or nod, did not say "Hello" or ask me to enter. Yet he kept his eyes fixed on me, acknowledging, for the first time, my very existence.

"Tell us, Jega," he said. "Is it true what the Little Miss says?"

What is truth? Someone can be completely sincere in their belief of what they saw and when. But another person, seeing the same thing, has a different vision. A red fish becomes purple at sunset, black at night. An ant would call Riacho Doce's river an ocean. A giant would say it was a trickle. What we see in the world depends so much on who we are at the moment of seeing. Such stories may turn out to be gifts, like bread crumbs leading us out of a dark forest; or they may be terrible diversions, leading deeper into a maze we can never escape.

Graça and I hadn't gone near the river that morning, but that didn't matter. Graça stared at me, her eyes pleading. And Senhor Pimentel stared, too, his jaw rigid, his gaze unflinching.

"Yes," I replied. "We saw it."

Senhor Pimentel nodded. Graça smiled and turned to her father. I was, once again, forgotten.

"I bet he jumped out of the water to see your pretty face," Senhor Pimentel said, kissing Graça's forehead. "Suitors will line up to kiss this face! And you'll marry the richest man of them all. Rich enough to buy every plantation from here to Paraíba!"

We went to the mill office every day after that. Every day, Graça was coddled and kissed for a few minutes until Senhor Pimentel tired of her and tried to push her off his lap. Graça gripped his neck to stay on. She told taller and taller tales. As long as Graça was entertaining, she would be held.

"We saw a two-headed hawk!" she said. Or, "There was a ghost in the river!"

After such stories, Senhor Pimentel shook his head and, inevitably, looked at me. Both he and Graça waited for my obedient nod. No matter how ridiculous the tale, I always agreed. We went on with these terrible visits for months; as long as I never contradicted the Little Miss, I would be allowed to stay. But Senhor Pimentel always pushed Graça from his lap and shooed her away, declaring he was too busy.

"I can help you, Papai," Graça said, pointing to the papers on his desk. "I can sort things. I can stamp those papers, or fill your ink pot."

Senhor Pimentel shook his head. "You'd make a mess of things, querida. Go tell your mother to give you a little brother. He can help me, and you can help take care of him."

I began to despise Senhor Pimentel then, not for making me lie but for taking Graça's attentions and then throwing them away. Still, Graça persisted in her visits. In the weeks before the sugar harvest, bills piled high on his desk and workers began to crowd the mill. One day, Senhor Pimentel yelled at Graça as soon as she opened the office door, screaming at her to leave, calling her a useless nuisance.

We ran to the river. There, on the banks, Graça gulped back sobs and declared that we would never, ever set foot in the mill again.

I was happy; she had said "we."

After a year of letting Graça run wild alongside me, Senhora Pimentel hired a private tutor. The woman was a widow who wore only black dresses and thick-soled shoes. Graça and I nicknamed her Bruxa, though she did not look like the witches in Senhora Pimentel's fairy-tale books, with their warty noses and knobby fingers. As a child I believed she was ancient, but I realize now that she must have been in her thirties, with dark hair pulled into a tight bun, and eyes so large and brown they resembled those of a horse. She might have been pretty, if she hadn't had a witch's spitefulness.

When Graça discovered I wasn't included in the lessons she shouted, cried, flung a set of porcelain angels to the floor, and stomped them to bits under her boots.

I quickly became the second pupil in Bruxa's class.

I received seven new dresses (one for each day of the week) and was taken off kitchen duty during lessons, but Bruxa never let me forget that I came from the kitchen. I was not allowed to speak during lessons. During the midmorning snack, I watched Graça and Bruxa drink coffee and eat cookies but was never allowed to have any myself. And if I had a question I had to whisper it to Graça, who would then ask Bruxa.

The tutor occupied a small, airless guest bedroom in the Great House. Bruxa was not allowed to dine with Graça and her family, but was allowed to have meals in her bedroom, delivered on a tray. This made her different from the other servants, and any variation in Riacho Doce's hierarchy was met with suspicion. The laundresses were expected to wash and iron Bruxa's clothes, and they often put extra starch on the tutor's black dresses and laughed at her yellowed camisoles and ratty underwear. The kitchen maids who delivered her food trays tried to engage Bruxa in conversation, but could not and quickly proclaimed her "high and mighty." There were rumors, most of them vicious, about why Bruxa wore only black shoes and dresses: she was in mourning for a husband who'd jumped off a bridge to escape her; she'd poisoned her entire family and gotten away with it, and continued to wear black as a kind of penance. Nena warned me never to eat food offered to me by Bruxa, as if the tutor even acknowledged my existence. But I was happy to endure Bruxa's slights if it meant I could be a part of her lessons. Unlike Graça, I liked learning to count and write and speak proper English and Portuguese. I liked how each letter of the alphabet had sounds that, when joined with others, became words. And how English words were short and to the point, while Portuguese had more melody to it, with words that had seven and even eight syllables, and masculine and feminine words (the moon is a woman, the sun a man; the land is woman, the sky a man; and on and on without logic or neutrality).

Mathematics came easily to me and I began to help Nena by keeping track of the pantry's stock—counting jars of jam, bottles of palm oil, the hundreds of onions and carrots and other vegetables. I counted each morning and each evening, and this way we knew if we had to order more supplies and, more important, if any had been filched during the day by the housemaids. As long as my learning was applied to something practical—inventory, reading the labels of the fancy flavored oils Senhora Pimentel brought from Recife, adding the butcher's bill to see if he was cheating us—it was accepted, praised even. Each time I double-checked a bill, or challenged a peddler for charging us too much, Nena's chest puffed up and she patted my back with her enormous hand, nearly making me fall forward. "Can't fool this one!" Nena said, smiling, while the kitchen girls stared, openmouthed, as if I'd just been nominated as president of the Republic.

Whenever I kneaded bread I wrote in the layer of flour that coated the table: *Maria das Dores.* I shaped the leftover bits of dough into *M*s and *D*s. Each time I stirred jam and the syrup thickened, I wrote my real name over and over again in the jam with my spoon. Once, in the orchard, I took a rock and carved my name into the trunk of a lime tree. When Nena found out, she took a branch from that tree and whipped me, but I didn't care. For months afterward, each time I walked by that tree, I saw myself there. I was not Jega, the puta's girl, the kitchen maid who would live and die forgotten in Riacho Doce. I was Maria das Dores, a girl who would leave her mark on the world. A girl who would be remembered.

I began to copy many-syllabled words into my little notebook. Some of their ending sounds corresponded: *consummate, negate, infatuate, consecrate, innovate, undulate.* I had known about rhyme before, of course. I'd heard the housemaids singing love songs with simple, rhyming verses. And it is human instinct to try to match things, to attempt to find likeness where there may be none. But this rhyming felt different to me; I was understanding the music held within words before I truly understood music itself.

After a year of lessons, I could read whole passages aloud from Bruxa's books better than Graça could. During class, Graça looked to me for help with her lessons and I'd whisper her the answers. Then I watched as Graça was praised for my cleverness.

One afternoon, Senhora Pimentel left her bed, collected Graça and me from the playroom, and escorted us across the Great House lawn to the mill, where Senhor Pimentel kept his office. Senhora Pimentel had put on a dress and pearls, and pinned her hair for the occasion, and the effort of making herself presentable coupled with walking across the lawn sapped her strength; the minute Senhor Pimentel opened his office door, she sank into a chair.

Senhor Pimentel greeted her stiffly. He wore a tie and, dimpling its center, a golden sugar cube encrusted with diamonds. It was new, a gift to himself I suppose, to make him feel like a real sugar baron despite the plantation's steady losses. Senhor Pimentel spoke again to his wife but I did not register what was said. I watched the tie pin shimmer with each rise and fall of Senhor Pimentel's chest.

What did a diamond mean to me then? If someone had asked me what a diamond was, I wouldn't have known. But seeing that cube with its hundreds of glimmering stones, white like real sugar but shinier, more lovely, made me want to reach across Senhor Pimentel's massive desk and snatch it, put it in my mouth and see if it was sweet, if it would break apart on my tongue. Thankfully, before I could act on this urge, Senhora Pimentel spoke.

"I'm taking the girls to a concert," she announced. "In Recife."

"The girls?" Senhor Pimentel asked.

Senhora Pimentel sighed. "You can't expect me to entertain Graça the entire ride to Recife and back? She and Dores will play."

"You mean old Jega there?" Senhor Pimentel said.

"Nicknames are vulgar, Miguel," Senhora Pimentel replied.

Senhor Pimentel's smile disappeared. "What kind of concert?"

"The kind with music. Real music, not the lunduns the maids sing."

"Can you make the trip?" Senhor Pimentel asked.

Senhora Pimentel straightened herself in her chair. "Of course. Graça needs to be exposed to art."

"So have that tutor show her some books, or make her draw a few sketches of flowers in a vase. What use is a concert?"

"Not everything has to be useful," the Senhora said.

"It does if I'm paying for it," Senhor Pimentel replied.

His wife shuddered. People in their set, no matter how indebted they were, never spoke of money. But the money was originally hers, not his, which is why, I think, the Senhor suddenly softened his tone.

"She's growing up with fresh air and hearty food, without any of the distractions of the city," he said. "She's as pure as a little flower bud. That's what'll matter to her husband, not all those other things that those so-called sophisticated girls have. She's our little flower."

Senhor Pimentel cupped his hand to Graça's cheek. She closed her eyes, as if she was about to swoon.

"She'll turn into a heathen out here if we're not careful," Senhora Pimentel said. "Any husband worthy of her will move her to a city, and she'll be a laughingstock who doesn't know a symphony from a cantiga. They'll call her a matuta behind her back."

Art, to me, was the dark oil painting that hung in the Great House parlor. It was strange that Senhora Pimentel believed that little girls needed such a thing. Even stranger that Senhor Pimentel finally agreed with her.

That was how, at twelve years old, I left Riacho Doce for the first time and found myself in Recife, the capital of our state. We stayed in the Pimentels' former home. They'd left the place closed and its furniture dust-sheeted, with only one maid to care for it all. On the day of the concert, this maid clumsily unpacked our formal dresses. Senhora Pimentel had a fancy dress made for me—a simple sheath of blue silk, which was quite plain compared with the tiered, ruffled creation Senhor Pimentel had bought for Graça as a surprise. Despite my dress's simplicity, I'd never worn something so fine and was petrified of wrinkling or staining the dress before we arrived at the theater.

A famous fado singer from Portugal was touring Brazil and had stopped in Recife to play at the Saint Isabel Theater. Until that night, I'd believed the Riacho Doce mill the largest building on earth. The Saint Isabel made the mill seem as small and decrepit as a cane cutter's shack. Walking through the theater's crowded lobby, with its staircases as wide as roadways, I felt dizzy and afraid. How could such a structure stay upright? How could the ceilings hold such massive chandeliers? My heart beat as fast as a bird's. Surely the theater walls would buckle and collapse at any moment under the weight of so much glass and stone, I thought. I grabbed Graça's gloved hand and did not let go until we found our seats.

I wasn't a complete heathen—I'd heard singing and instruments before, at Riacho Doce. Once a year on Saint John's Day the Pimentels allowed a bonfire and asked workers to play tunes on wheezy accordions. And every night, there was the sound of drums and faraway voices from the cane cutters' shacks. They had circles there, I knew, but no one from the Great House was allowed to fraternize with the cutters, much less sneak off in the middle of the night to hear them sing. Some nights I woke to their drumming and believed it was the beating of my own heart.

The theater's lights dimmed. There was applause. A woman waddled onto the stage, lifting the heavy skirt of her evening gown so she would not trip over its hem. Her ankles were as thick as my thighs. Her tiny, heeled shoes seemed as if they might snap under her weight. A lone guitarist accompanied her. As soon as the applause finished, the guitarist plucked his first notes. The singer's voice rang like a bell— sharp, powerful, alarming—across the theater.

"At the end of my street,
  the ocean laps,
  the ocean laps.
  Above it I see a piece of the moon,
  a sliver of my destiny."

I closed my eyes. I saw an ocean as dark as the cane fields at night. I saw stars sparkling more than the diamonds on Senhor Pimentel's sugar cube pin. The singer continued.

"Where is my destiny?
  Where is my home?
  Will I never have a place in this world?
  Will I always be alone?"

I felt as if a hand had wrapped itself around my heart. With each note of the singer's song, the hand squeezed harder.

"Oh, dear," Senhora Pimentel whispered. "Let's clean you up."

She removed a handkerchief from her beaded purse and stuffed it into my hands. When I did not wipe my wet cheeks or the snot running down my chin, Senhora Pimentel took the handkerchief and wiped for me. She was gentle, but I hated her for distracting me from the singer. I hated Graça for shuffling in her seat. I hated the man behind us for coughing. I hated my life up until that point—to think of all of those evenings I'd wasted peeling potatoes or listening to maids' gossip when someone, somewhere, was singing such music! Why hadn't I heard this music before? And when would I ever hear it again? My insides felt very heavy, as if I'd drunk a pitcher full of concrete and it was hardening within me.

I eventually learned to identify this feeling as regret. But at the time I was twelve years old and believed I was deathly ill. Music had triggered this sickness but it was also my only cure. Sitting on the edge of that red velvet seat, I believed my condition was grave—I would die as soon as the concert was over, as soon as the music stopped.

To my surprise, I lived. At the end of the show Senhora Pimentel led us through the crowds and into our hired car. There, she removed her gloves and placed a cool hand on my forehead.

"She's not sick," Graça said.

Senhora Pimentel shook her head. "I should've known the city would overwhelm her, poor thing."

"It's the songs, Mother," Graça snapped. "The songs are still inside her."

Senhora Pimentel looked at her daughter as if Graça had spoken in tongues. But Graça's words—her complete understanding of how I felt—made my eyes well up again. Ashamed, I covered my face in my hands.

"She's having a nervous attack," Senhora Pimentel said. "If you have to vomit don't do it in the automobile."

During the ride back to the Pimentel house, Senhora Pimentel shut her eyes, a sign that the trip to the theater had worn her out and she could pay me no further attention. Graça squeezed beside me. She smoothed my hair. My head fell into her lap. Her hands were soft, her dress slippery under my cheek. My ear fit perfectly in the hollow between her legs. I fell asleep listening to the ruffles of her dress shift beneath me.

That night, Graça insisted I sleep in her room and not in the servants' area behind the kitchen. As soon as Senhora Pimentel bid us goodnight, Graça crawled out of her bed and onto my small mattress on the floor. She wore a scarf over her hair to keep her curls springy. Her arm felt very warm against mine.

"I'm going to sing on a stage like that," Graça said. "I'm going to make people swallow my songs and hold them inside. I'm going to be known. I'm going to be seen."

"Me too," I said, and steeled myself for Graça to make fun, to tell me I could never do such a thing.

"We'll have to get a phonograph," she said.

"A what?" I asked.

"A machine that plays records. I'll ask Mamãe for one. She gets me whatever I want."

"All right," I said, as if I understood Graça's plan.

I'd never even seen a record, much less heard one, but I was giddy despite my ignorance.

That night, I barely slept. Even then, I knew that there are few certainties in this life—one action can have a dozen interpretations, one word a dozen meanings depending on how it's spoken. Everything can be questioned, picked at, and scrutinized, even one's own feelings. How miraculous then to hear something and know, without any doubt, that it is beautiful.

I was luckier than most orphaned bastards: I hadn't been thrown into the cane to die; I'd had Nena as teacher and protector; I'd become the Little Miss's favorite and was given an education. But if the winds shifted and Graça grew bored with me, or the Pimentels tired of feeding and clothing me, or if I made a mistake that would bring disfavor, I would lose any good fortune I'd gained. Nothing in my life was certain, and nothing was mine alone. How incredible then that, despite the precariousness of my existence, despite the coarseness and violence that always threatened to suffocate me, there was this beauty, this grace, that had found me through music, and that no one could take from me. This was the gift that music gave to Graça and me that night, and every night afterward: we had something of our own to truly love, and we had each other to share it with.

Senhora Pimentel's health worsened after our trip to Recife. She stayed in bed as she had before, but didn't have the energy to braid our hair or tell us stories. The tiny gold bell the Senhora kept beside her bed and rang constantly to call the housemaids and order them to bring her water, or a new book, or lunch on a tray, stayed silent. The bell was too heavy to pick up, Senhora Pimentel complained. A doctor visited, locking the bedroom door behind him. When he left, Graça sprang into action, slipping into her mother's room before a maid or her father could stop her.

Inside, Graça gripped her mother's fingers so hard I saw Senhora Pimentel flinch. "I need that phonograph," she said, as if she'd made the request to her mother many times before. Senhora Pimentel smiled.

A week later, the machine arrived at Riacho Doce. It sat in a tall wooden cabinet in the Great House parlor. A box of records arrived with it. Graça and I took each record from its paper sheath and put them, one by one, on the phonograph's turntable. That first day, we listened to the *Moonlight* Sonata, Enrico Caruso, Heitor Villa-Lobos, and others. We played that first batch of records so often, Senhor Pimentel complained about the noise. But he could not keep us from that mournful fado, or from Caruso's bottomless, unyielding voice, or from the guitar concertos where the ringing of the plucked strings felt as crisp as biting into a ripe star fruit.

We all have the same basic body parts: lips, teeth, tongues, palates, all leading to a series of tiny muscles in our throats covered in mucus the same consistency as hospital Jell-O. We take a breath, air hits the tiny folds of these muscles, they vibrate and produce sound. If we are lucky, they can produce song. It's more complicated than this, of course; we might all have the same body parts, the same ability to make sound, but not every voice is made equal.

For Graça, singing was as natural as breathing. For me, singing was like attempting to lift a thirty-kilo sack of sugar over my head—something I could certainly do, with time, but not without great practice and effort. This didn't discourage me. My twelve-year-old brain did not consider the fact of raw talent, of having a natural gift, of Graça's vocal cords being somehow better made than my own. Instead, it seemed natural that I had to work at singing while Graça did not—she was a Little Miss, after all, and Little Misses worked for nothing. I, on the other hand, had been raised to believe that anything worthwhile came through struggle.

Each day after our interminable lessons with Bruxa, we ran to the parlor and argued over which record to place on the turntable. One afternoon, Graça and I froze at the parlor door; the Senhora sat in a cushioned chair beside the phonograph, a blanket over her shoulders, her red hair freshly washed and wound into a thick braid.

"I ask Tita to keep my door open, so I can hear you girls," Senhora Pimentel said. "But today I wanted to watch you."

Graça and I shuffled toward the phonograph. It didn't seem proper to argue in front of the Senhora, so I let Graça choose the first record. She picked the Caruso—the most difficult to sing—of course. When we were alone, I often closed my eyes when I sang, while Graça liked to leap and twirl and open her arms to the sky. Sometimes I copied her and we dropped into a fit of giggles by song's end. That day, with the Senhora watching us, we stood shoulder to shoulder as we did at the beginning of Bruxa's lessons when she inspected behind our ears and under our nails for dirt. Behind us, the record began spinning. There was Caruso starting out at a sprint, hurdling over the notes of "Nessun dorma." Graça and I sang in whispers at first, but then our favorite part of the song arrived—when Caruso's voice becomes pleading, but not in a weak way. It is as if he is shouting to the stars, asking the world for the help he deserves. I didn't know Italian, and neither did Graça; the song's lyrics were nonsense to us. It was only decades later that I discovered what Graça and I attempted to sing each day in the Great House parlor:

> "But the mystery of me is locked inside me.
> No one will know my name!
> No, no, I will say it on your mouth,
> when the light will shine!
> And my kiss will melt the silence
> that makes you mine."

I closed my eyes and held fast to Graça's hand as my voice tried desperately to keep up with hers. Then the song was over, the record silently spinning, and Senhora Pimentel clapped. I opened my eyes.

"Bravo!" the Senhora cried.

Warmth moved from my chest to my neck, and into my ears, which pulsed and burned.

"Now you must curtsy and bow," the Senhora said. "It's how you tell your audience you are grateful to them for listening. You are in their service, after all."

I looked at Graça for guidance. She shrugged. Senhora Pimentel stood and the blanket slid from her shoulders. She held her silk robe, placed one foot in front of the other, and dipped down, bowing her head. Her hair fell over her shoulder, a red rope with a ribbon at its end. Then the Senhora straightened and collapsed back into her chair.

After this day, we always found Senhora Pimentel waiting for us in the parlor, ready to listen. She was our first audience, and our best.

When we are young, we give ourselves completely. We allow our first friends or first lovers or first songs inside us, to become a part of our unformed being, without ever thinking of the consequences, or of their permanence within us. This is one of the beauties of youth, and one of its burdens.

A few months after our first performance for the Senhora, a doctor arrived from Recife. His motorcar shot through the Great House gate and screeched to a stop at the front door, where Senhor Pimentel waited. In the kitchen there was shouting, scurrying, prayers. Nena, her face so sweaty it looked like glazed clay, poured boiling water into tin pans that the maids hoisted upstairs.

"Jega!" Nena called, after spotting me. "Wipe the sleep out of your eyes and help your Senhora."

"What's wrong with her?" I asked.

"The baby's trying to come early."

"Baby?"

Nena shook her head. Sweat dripped onto her apron. "She should never have taken you girls to the city. All those bumpy roads. And then coming downstairs every day to listen to that Devil machine's music! Well now . . ."

Nena wiped her face and ordered me to the laundry, to get clean rags and carry them upstairs. I did as I was told, but all I could think was: *There is a baby inside of her.* I knew how such things happened; to a child growing up in the countryside, sex is as common as the sun rising and setting. I'd seen Old Euclides breeding his donkeys. The stable boys made sport of it, betting how many times a jenny would buck a jack before he got his way. I'd seen billy goats piss themselves all over before mounting a nanny, and roosters fight each other bloody for the chance at a hen. But the thought of Senhor Pimentel—tanned, muscled, and thin-lipped—doing such things to the Senhora was reprehensible to me. No wonder she was dying.

Senhora Pimentel fought that baby for many hours. She was stubborn, like Graça. The Recife doctor sometimes left the Senhora's room and stood in the hall to smoke or gulp down a mug of coffee. Each time he appeared the doctor looked different: first his suit jacket was gone, then his vest, then his shirt's buttons were open, then his sleeves rolled up past his elbows. Senhor Pimentel paced the hallway and smoked. Each time the doctor appeared, he ran to the man and asked: "Is it a boy?"

Graça and I hid at the end of the hall, crammed under a credenza.

"The doctor hasn't left yet," I whispered. "What's he doing to her?"

"The baby's killing her," Graça said. "I wish I could kill it."

"You knew about the baby?" I asked.

"You didn't?" Graça replied.

Without a word between us, we sneaked out of the Great House, past the orchard, where I led Graça to the henhouse. Inside, I slipped eggs out from under the hens' warm bottoms as I'd done hundreds of times before, for Nena. This time, as soon as we were out of the henhouse, I handed Graça the full basket.

We flung most against a tree. Others we stomped. A few Graça hurled to the ground with such force that bits of shell and yolk spattered my chin. When there were no more eggs, Graça pitched the basket against the henhouse wall and we sat under a tree in the orchard, too afraid to walk back inside.

The child was a boy, a fact that Senhor Pimentel lamented to the maids and kitchen staff and, later, to the handful of relatives who traveled from Recife for the funerals. Senhora Pimentel and Graça's unborn sibling were buried in the mausoleum in Riacho Doce's chapel, only fifty meters from the Great House, but a distance I was not allowed to cross. Servants did not attend funerals.

In an interview many years later, when a reporter asked Sofia Salvador what was the saddest moment of her life thus far she'd said, without hesitation and to my great surprise, "Losing my mother when I was a child. Being motherless is a burden I wouldn't wish on my worst enemy."

Sometimes I feel like a motherless child. I once watched T-Bone Walker sing this spiritual in a ratty little Los Angeles club with sloped floors and yellowed dollar bills pinned to the walls. I sat in the dark, at the bar, and heard him sing the same line over and over again. At first I didn't understand his lament and was annoyed by it. Aren't we all motherless, eventually? Isn't it the point for children to outlive their parents? But the power of the song is in one word: *Sometimes.* As if this feeling is too hard to bear all of the time. As if there are other times, more hopeful times, no matter how brief, when the singer remembers the unassailable comfort of being completely loved.

Listening to T-Bone, I realized that his song wasn't about losing a mother's love, but about the feeling of never experiencing it in the first place. If passion is deeply entwined with uncertainty, then a mother's love is the opposite: it never wavers, never depends on performance, never requires an equal amount of love in return. You have the luxury of brushing off a mother's love, knowing your scorn or indifference will never make it go away. It is like air—you can forget it exists, and that it is essential to your life. There are those of us, though, who can't forget; who have never had the sweet reprieve of "sometimes." My mother was a rumor, a shadow, a bit of dirty gossip, a way for others to insult me. So while I understood Graça's grief at losing Senhora Pimentel, there was also something about her sadness that made me bitterly angry. Graça had experienced twelve years of buoying love—she'd known what it felt like to breathe in that sweet air, and could therefore carry it within her for the rest of her days. The Senhora was not my mother and I never, not for a second, pretended she was. But she had been kind to me when others were not. Hers were small kindnesses— little whims one bestows on a favored servant—but they were kindnesses all the same. So I grieved for her, too, in my own way.

During the funeral, Nena ordered me out of the kitchen, where she and the girls were preparing the post-funeral meal, and to the orchard to collect limes. It was an easy task, one I could finish in minutes. I left the full fruit basket in the kitchen and tiptoed to the parlor, where the Senhora's chair sat, empty. I slipped a record from its sleeve. I ran my fingers across its ridges, then slid one into its empty center. How I wanted to hear that music! How I wanted to set the needle on that record and turn the phonograph's volume to full blast until the house shook with its vibrations! Until the mourners at the chapel, in their black suits and lace mantillas, heard the sound and raised their heads! Until the cane cutters, given the day off out of respect for the Senhora, wandered out of their shacks and wondered where that magnificent sound was coming from! Instead, I held that shellac record in both hands and bent it until it shattered like glass.

"What are you crying for?" Graça stood in the doorway, her black dress wrinkled, her lace mantilla bunched in her fist.

I wiped my eyes with the heels of my palms and answered her question with another: "What are you doing here?"

"That chapel smells like rotten eggs. No one notices if I come or go." Graça walked into the room and stared at the shards of record at my feet. "We're running away."

"To where?" I asked.

"To Rio. Where else?"

"You should go to Recife first. It's closer," I said.

Graça shook her head. "Rio's the only place to be. It's where they make radio shows. And my aunt said they have movies there. A movie's a moving picture, Dor. They put them on a screen bigger than a cane field and you see the actors moving on it, playing their parts."

"Like a theater show?"

"No. It's not the real people playing the parts. It's moving pictures of them. So they can be lots of places at once."

"Like ghosts?" I asked, thinking of the chapel's mausoleum and Senhora Pimentel within it, stuffed into a cold stone drawer. "Sounds like a bunch of macumba to me."

"Well it's not. You'll see."

"How?"

"We'll hop on a boat. Ride a train. There're plenty of ways to get down to Rio."

"We'd need tickets," I said. "We'd have to buy them."

"Mamãe left me all sorts of jewelry. It's in her closet. We'll take that and sell it along the way."

"Sell it to who?"

"Stop being such a bore! Who cares *how* we get there?"

"I do," I said.

"You're as dull as dirt!" Graça shrieked. Then she stomped away.

We reconciled eventually; we always did back then. After this argument Graça stopped talking about running away from Riacho Doce, but I knew the idea was within her like a seed in the earth, patiently taking root.

Each year on the sugar plantation there was a great fire. Harvest was always in the summer, the dry time. The river grew narrow, the roads cracked and dusty, the water tasted of earth. But the cane stayed green and thick, its leaves as long and sharp as machetes. If a cutter were to take his cane knife and hack into an unburned paddock, it would be like doing battle with a thousand men. He'd be sliced apart if he wasn't bitten and killed by a poisonous snake first. So, at the beginning of every harvest, an army of cutters carried cans of gasoline to the edges of the cane fields. It was always dusk, when the temperatures cooled and the winds died down. And the cutters walked in lines, pouring gas onto the brown bottoms of the cane stalks, and then lighting them.

Graça and Senhora Pimentel, when she was alive, always left for Recife during the burnings. Staying was unpleasant. The fires were never near the Great House, but their heat pushed through the house's walls and made us feel as if we were trapped in an oven. Everyone at Riacho Doce, even Senhor Pimentel, who pretended to supervise the burnings, had to wear wet handkerchiefs over our noses and mouths because of the smoke. Our eyes stung. Our clothes smelled of soot for weeks after the fires died. Ashes floated in the air as if a thousand gray birds had lost their feathers. And in the sky there were probably more than a thousand birds, swooping along the burning cane's edges and catching the snakes, rats, skunks, and possums that fled the fires.

If the wind shifted suddenly, cutters could be trapped between burning paddocks. Men died. Not every year, but often enough to make the burnings an uneasy time at Riacho Doce. Those of us at the Great House were told to keep away from the fields.

In the months after Senhora Pimentel died, when Graça and I turned thirteen, she was sent away during the cane fires to stay with an aunt in Recife. Senhor Pimentel sent the aunt enough money to buy Graça a new wardrobe. The buttons of Graça's old blouses strained against her growing bust. Her skirts hugged her thighs. A Recife seamstress could make a dozen loose-fitting dresses for Graça, but even a jute sack would not hide her newly ample figure. It was hard for everyone at Riacho Doce—maids, houseboys, even Old Euclides himself—not to stare when she passed.

Graça was not beautiful; at least, not in the way we've been taught to see beauty, as something that provokes either desire or a need to protect. Graça was not sultry or delicate. There was nothing truly extraordinary about her mouth or her eyes or her figure. But when you combined all of her features with her voice, her laughter, her raw and unflappable energy and glimmering motion, Graça made you believe she was beautiful. Being beside her made you feel a part of a great adventure, a fate loaded with meaning and purpose. Her beauty was not a physical trait. Her beauty was an influence you fell under—like a stiff drink or a line of sweet flour—infusing you with bravery and wit and affability that you never knew existed inside yourself until she coaxed it out.

I didn't know this when we were children, of course. I realized it many years later, when I saw Graça in her coffin. It was surrounded by flowers, and Graça lay inside with her eyes closed and arms crossed over her chest. She wore a red evening gown and her signature red lipstick, yet she looked disturbingly plain—a schoolmarm in an actress's costume. I leaned over her and pinched her, hard. "Graça, stop joking! Get up. Please?" I whispered until Vinicius pulled me away.

Unlike Graça, during our teenage years I grew tall, not curved. My blouses were too short for my torso; my skirts could not cover my suddenly gangly and uncooperative legs. I had to duck through the kitchen's low doorways. Stable boys, millworkers, even Senhor Pimentel himself, had to tilt their heads to meet my eyes. Many years later, when we moved to Los Angeles, being five-foot-ten wasn't odd among those Amazonian movie starlets and strapping leading men, but in Brazil I was positively massive. As a teenager, my height did not bother me as much as other changes in my body. My chest was tender to the touch, and, to my horror, dark hairs sprouted under my arms and between my legs. The housemaids and kitchen girls had hair in these places, but on them it seemed natural, beautiful even.

At the end of the day, Nena always ordered a few of the kitchen

maids back to their stations because they'd forgotten to clean something properly. During the cane fires, Nena sent me to the women's
changing area to fetch the delinquent kitchen girls. A gaggle of them
were there, gossiping and taking off their uniforms and aprons so that
the laundresses could wash them. I hid in the doorway, dizzy with the
smell of cheap perfume mixed with smoke from the cane fires, and
watched those glorious country girls wiggle out of their starched uniforms. It was a mystery how those girls, once bullies and annoyances to
me, suddenly became the most fascinating creatures I'd ever seen. I
tried to stay out of sight as long as I could, just to watch them unbutton
their uniforms and lift their long arms over their heads, their underarms fluffy with hair, their bellies taut, their breasts hanging round and
soft like perfectly ripe fruits.

One of the maids caught me in the doorway.

"Little spy," she hissed. "Don't you tell Nena what I said about
meeting Rodrigo behind the henhouse."

"Are you kidding," another maid said. "Jega wasn't paying attention to a word you were saying!" And she cupped her bare bosoms in
her hands and shook them at me.

I stared at the floorboards. The maids laughed. They were a crude,
mean lot, and were hoping I'd run off without delivering Nena's orders. I took a deep breath and faced the shirtless one again.

"Nena wants you back in kitchen. You didn't scrub the cutting
boards right."

She smiled. "When're you going to get a boyfriend, Jega?"

"Never," I snarled.

The maids laughed.

"You'll change your mind. Or one of the boys will change it
for you."

"Who can we pay to tame Jega!" another girl screeched. "She'll bite
and kick, but she'll get ridden!"

I left those girls, cackling and coughing in the changing room, and ran to the orchard. The sun had set, but a cane fire lit the western horizon. The orchard's trees were furry with fallen ash. I wove around them.

I had no intention of being mounted by a stable boy, or a houseboy, or any boy for that matter. Nena was head cook and had no husband, no children, no desire deeper than to serve the Pimentels. I always believed that would be my fate, until Graça arrived. I wished she was there, in that orchard with me and not in Recife, buying silly dresses. I tried to conjure her, tried to hear her voice convincing me that the housemaids were dimwitted bores, and that larger, grander dreams than being a plantation cook were possible. Sick with loneliness for Graça, I stared at the burning cane along the horizon.

Then I disobeyed the harvest-time rule and went to see the fire.

After what felt like hours of walking, I hid behind a cart the cutters used to carry their gasoline canisters and watched as they started a fire at the edge of a paddock. The fire was timid at first. It lapped at the cane's stalks and fallen leaves. Then it climbed, steady and determined, gaining confidence, until finally it flooded upward and flared, a fountain of light and heat.

I went back to the Great House covered in soot and so giddy I felt drunk, before I even knew what being drunk was. Nena beat me. She was particularly stern that night, caning my legs and backside until their skin was red and raw.

"Are you soft in the head!" she said, breathless from hitting me. "That fire doesn't care if you're a little girl or a bunch of cane; it won't stop for you. It wants everything it touches."

All of my brief life I'd felt a perpetual ache, like a rotten tooth I could never cure. Like a broken bone that would never set. Jega was not allowed to want anything beyond the most base desires of the human condition: a meal, a bed, survival. But Dores? She'd been granted a notebook and a pencil, lessons, books, and words. She'd been granted music and an audience. She'd been granted a friend.

Beyond that kitchen and those cane fields was a world of possibilities that I couldn't fathom, but wanted to. I was awed by the avarice of that cane fire. It was beautiful in its constant need, in its unbridled hunger. I watched it burn, its heat pounding against my skin, and knew that we were alike, that fire and me. We wanted more than we'd been given, and we always would.

ESCAPE

Do you remember, my love,
when you convinced me to escape?
We were like hand and glove,
our future about to take shape.

We hatched our plan,
we flew.
We left everyone behind.
Then you said I didn't love you.

But I can't lose my mind, girl,
    when there're bills to pay.
My love is washing your clothes.
My love is cooking dinner every
    day.
My love is sweeping our steps.
My love is putting our children to
    sleep.
My love is never getting rest.
My love is fathoms deep.

We hatched our plan,
we flew.
We left everyone behind.
Then you said I didn't love you.

Don't you know by now, querida,
that other kind of love, that
    storm,
won't keep the lamps lit, my vida,
it won't keep the house warm?

My love is washing our windows.
My love is fixing our doors.
My love is doing our dishes.
My love is scouring our floors.

But you hatched your plan,
you flew.
You left me in our tidy home.
You said I never loved you.

efore she became Sofia Salvador and I became Dores de Oliveira, Graça and I had our records at Riacho Doce. We believed music magically emerged from those albums. Later, when we recorded our own songs onto LPs, we learned the truth: the records' ridges were a code read by the player's needle; low notes were thick grooves on the record's face, high notes were thin ones. The needle, vibrating a thousand times a second, drops into those peaks and valleys and, miraculously, deciphers music.

What is sound but vibration carried over air? An endless and invisible tide that strikes our eardrums throughout our entire lives. It is overwhelming to think of the cacophony around us. Even the womb isn't quiet; we hear the whoosh of our mother's blood, the drumming of her heart, the growl of her stomach, and her voice—reverberated by fluid—until it vibrates inside each of our tiny bones.

For our sanity, we train ourselves to distinguish which sounds are important and which we must ignore. We memorize the difference between a whisper and a shout, a purr and a roar. We accumulate within us a great index of sound, until we hear the creak of a step and know, by its depth and tone, how much weight is being placed on the wood and who is coming up the stairs to greet us. An inhale and the soft crackle of paper make us crave a cigarette. And when a lover sighs we learn to distinguish between long and high-pitched and short and huffy, and we know whether they are satisfied or disappointed. So, you see, sound is never simply sound. Sound is memory.

My memory is long-playing, but like that very first generation of LPs, there are kinks: sustained notes that waver slightly; sometimes a warp, or a dull sound; and the pre-echo, when a part of the music made a faint and untimely appearance ahead of the beat. It's not supposed to be there. It's not supposed to reveal what comes later, much later, if it comes at all. You're never sure if the pre-echo is real or imagined.

Here's one for you:

We sit at the Desert Inn's bar—Vinicius and I—sipping whiskeys and waiting for the blast. The Desert Inn has a vast picture window that looks out on the Strip and the desert. Sixty-five miles outside Vegas, in the Mohave, the government is going to detonate an A-bomb. Some hotels hired limousines to take special guests near the blast site, to have a better view. But at the Desert Inn there is an Atomic Party.

Graça is onstage. She wears an electric-green dress and a white fur stole. Her hair is freshly dyed black and so short it is like a pelt. She sings "Escape," an old favorite of mine, at a slower pace than the song allows. The lyrics are supposed to be sung quickly, so the audience understands the frantic nature of the words and their lament. But Graça drags the tempo, pausing after each word. She smiles and makes sweeping gestures with her arms, but her legs stay planted in the middle of the stage. Her eyes are glassy. The audience, like Vinicius and me, divide their attention between Sofia Salvador and the picture window, waiting for the blast.

The Strip is a carnival of neon. I doubt if we'll be able to see the blast from so far away and with so much illumination already around us, but before I can say this, Vinicius nods at the picture window.

"There she goes," he says.

On the horizon is a small flash. Then there is a rumble, like thunder. Only instead of traveling above us, the sound moves beneath us. The Desert Inn's picture window shakes. Our drinks tremble on the bar. Night turns into day. The Strip disappears in a blaze of white light that moves toward us, brighter than any spotlight. Vinicius grabs my hand. I turn away from the picture window and stare at Graça. She's stopped her song but her mouth is open. Her eyes have lost their foggy look. She stares at the horizon—so bright and dazzling—and smiles as if she's facing a great, clapping crowd. Then the light finally reaches us and Graça, the stage, Vinicius, the bar and all of its patrons, including myself, are awash in light, and then obliterated by it.

I remember this. I remember the ice clinking against my whiskey glass as the bar shook. I remember the look of vague panic on Vinicius's face, the color of Graça's dress, the bright light—and yet none of it can be true. The Desert Inn never scheduled performers during its atomic viewing parties; the bomb itself was enough entertainment. Most detonations were at four a.m., so we would have been asleep at that time, after a long night of shows on the Strip. During those shows, Vinicius played alongside other exiled musicians, so he would've been onstage and not beside me at the bar. I would have been drunk—too drunk to be allowed in the audience. And Graça? She never set foot in Vegas. She was long dead by then, and yet here she is in my mind, in my memory, stubbornly inserting herself where she shouldn't.

Can something be called a memory if it is untrue?

It's my fault Graça's here; I spent so many years conjuring her that now she appears of her own accord, and in places where her physical presence is an impossibility.

In the years after Graça died, anytime Vinicius and I ate an incredible meal, or saw a terrible show, or listened to an up-and-coming musician's album, we'd ask each other: *Can you imagine what Graça would say about this?* And then we re-created her for each other in a kind of competition.

"Graça would've despised that little tart of a singer," I'd say.

And Vinicius would shake his head and counter: "She would've loved her."

Sometimes these little disagreements turned into genuine arguments, depending on our moods. "You didn't know her like I did" was the cruelest insult Vinicius and I could inflict on each other.

Did we know her? Who was this Graça we created between the two of us? She was always young, always beautiful, always cussing and laughing with her head tossed back. Our Graça never had to endure the indignities of age: the aching bones, the sagging flesh, the fading memory.

A lifetime later, when Vinicius's Alzheimer's progressed, it became harder for him to conjure her concretely, yet Graça persisted. The days when his face was a mask—the Lion Face, the nurses called it—impassive and emotionless, as if Vinicius had disappeared inside himself, he would sometimes return for a few moments, his eyes brightening, his mouth open in a tiny gasp, as if he'd just swum back to the surface of himself.

"What beat are you?" he asked.

"Beat?"

"Are you *bim bim bim*, or *barrum pum pum*, or *dum dum dum*?"

I laughed. "I'm *dum dum dum*."

Vinicius nodded very seriously. "What beat am I?"

"You? Well, let me see. You're a complicated one: *ba para para ba ba ba ba ba parum pa!*"

He smiled. "The boys are gone, but she knows where to find them."

"She does?" I asked, knowing exactly who he meant.

Vinicius nodded.

"What beat is she?" I asked.

He flinched as if in pain. Then his face went slack and he disappeared again beneath the surface.

What is it like, to feel yourself slipping away?

I close my eyes and see Graça again on that Las Vegas stage, staring wide-eyed at the atomic blast. Am I losing my grip? Or am I simply doing what I've always done: holding on too tightly?

ESCAPE

I n the weeks after the cane fires died and the stalks were harvested to
make sugar and Graça returned from Recife, I lay on my cot and
dreamed of cruel kitchen maids, with their dusty feet and chapped
hands, their perfect bodies and sharp tongues, until I felt a painful
burning on my arm. Graça pinched me awake.

"Let's go," she hissed.

Nena was fast asleep on her cot.

"Where?" I whispered, but Graça was already tiptoeing out the
door. I tugged a shawl over my nightgown and followed her.

The night was warm, the Great House quiet. Graça led me to the
parlor. There, she unlocked one of the glass-paneled doors that led to
the porch. Outside, she hiked up her nightgown and climbed over the
porch's railing. I followed her, too confused to speak.

There was a breeze. The smell of charred cane still lingered in the
air, mixed now with the scent of burned sugar that bubbled in the mill's
vats each day. The garden's grass was wet under my bare feet. From the
cane cutter's shacks, I heard the steady and familiar beat of drums.

Graça walked out of the Great House gate and toward the river,
toward that drumming. I tugged her arm.

"We can't," I said. "Not there."

"Listen," Graça whispered. A chorus of voices, male and female, rose above the low thump of the drum. "I want to hear them."

"We can do that right here."

Graça shook loose from my grip. "I'm going, Dor."

"I'll tell," I said. "I'll wake up the whole house."

Graça froze. "Do it," she said. "You're the one they'll whip for being out at night. For corrupting me."

"They'll never let us listen to our records again," I said.

"So what?"

"Please," I said, clasping her hand. It was limp between my fingers. "Let's go back."

"I'd rather die," Graça said.

She would often make this threat during our years together, but that night was the first time Graça said such a thing to me. I pictured Graça stuffed in a tiny coffin. My stomach cramped. I winced and Graça grabbed my hands so that we were mirror images of each other in our white nightgowns and shawls.

"You want to stay in that house," she said. "If you're not careful you'll stay there all your life. But I have to *see* things, Dor. I have to hear them. Real-life things, not just songs on a bunch of records. Don't you want to know what they're singing? Don't you want to feel it? If we're going to be real performers, real artists, we have to feel!"

Graça had a heroine's determined breathlessness; she believed she was our savior, and her self-infatuation was enveloping. All her life, she was able to convince others that they were brave heroes in her story— always in her story. That night, she convinced me.

A fire brightened the rows of cane cutters' shacks. Men and women sat cross-legged on the ground around it. Graça and I squatted in the shadows near the river.

Four cutters sat on stools. Their arms shone with scars. One man hunched over a drum. Two other cutters held empty tin cans and hit them with the tips of their machetes. The fourth man rested a small drum on his lap. Like the other drums, this one had a dried hide stretched across its top, but an open bottom. In the middle of the hide, piercing its center, was a thin bamboo stick. Instead of hitting the little drum, the man took a wet cloth, slipped his hand inside the drum, and massaged the stick up and down until it moaned. Then one of the cutters began to sing:

"Love, I want to tap on your window.
Maybe then you'll see me?
And I'll beg a cup of water.
Maybe then you'll hear my plea?
Fill that cup, quickly.
Bring it to me.
Just so I might brush your hand.
Love, you make me thirsty.
Your touch stings me like a brand."

The classical songs on our records had been, for many years, my main understanding of music. I loved those songs the way a child loves an old relative, seeing them as sweet and benign, without any notion of how long they've endured and why. The cane cutters' songs were different. They contained cryptic messages about adult life that I wanted to decode as much as Graça did.

Later, we'd learn that the little moaning drum was called a cuíca. Graça said that its sound made her want to cry.

"But you didn't cry," I pointed out.

Graça rolled her eyes. "Well I *wanted* to, Dor. But I wasn't going to make noise and get caught. It would've ruined the song. We have to go back. We can't skip a night. Those circles are going to save us."

"Save us from what?" I asked.

"From everything," Graça replied.

Each night we listened for the drumbeat. Whenever we heard it, Graça and I sneaked downriver and crouched closer and closer to the cutters' circles. To my great surprise, I recognized faces I saw each day around the Great House. The kitchen maids I hated and admired stood beside the fire and held hands with stable boys. The thick-necked laundress Clara sang alongside the cutters. Old Euclides sat on an overturned bucket and nodded in time to the music. All of them were fraternizing with cane cutters, and disobeying rules I'd thought were ironclad.

"A house without a Senhora is a house full of trouble," Nena muttered, though she'd become the Great House's temporary commander. "Don't bother me! Ask Nena," was Senhor Pimentel's refrain in the year after his wife's death.

The pantry grew emptier each time I counted supplies. Gone were the fancy spices from Recife, the barrels of cake flour, the crystallized fruits used to decorate puddings. The daily servings of manioc and beans Nena doled to me and the kitchen girls grew smaller and smaller. She began bargaining with the butcher again, buying tiny portions of the finest cuts and saving them for Graça and Senhor Pimentel. When Bruxa complained about her meager portions, Nena ordered the tutor out of her kitchen. When Graça complained about not having a different dessert each day, Nena banged about the kitchen, searching for a stray can of condensed milk.

"Tell your little friend that her daddy better stop wasting the last of the Senhora's money on nonsense!" Nena growled.

She never expected me to tell Graça such things, and I never did. Masters know little about their servants, but the reverse is never true. When you work in a house, you see every stained bedsheet, every pillowcase flecked with hardened snot from a night's tears, every article of trash, every bit of food left uneaten on its plate, every pill in a medicine cabinet, every book left open at the last page read. You learn your masters' habits and routines because you must. And, in doing so, you learn when these routines go unfollowed, or when new habits are acquired.

Senhor Pimentel let his beard grow and his boots go unpolished. He emptied half a bottle of cane rum at each meal, then stumbled to his mill office. He visited the little chapel and returned red-eyed and sharp-tongued, snapping at whichever maid or stable boy was unlucky enough to cross his path. Some maids he followed relentlessly, courting them with words and caresses until they capitulated to him; without the Senhora around to curb his appetites, the Senhor had free rein. Sometimes he led a maid into a linen closet, or his private sitting room. Most of the maids were at least eighteen, if not older. But some were fourteen—the same age as Graça and me. It was an unspoken rule in the Great House that we open no door without knocking first, even if it was to the pantry or a broom closet.

Mornings were the safest times to be in the Senhor's company; though he was groggy, he hadn't had a drop to drink. These were the moments when he was patient and even kind to his daughter. At breakfast he asked Graça to tell stories and listened with rapt attention. He said she was beautiful and called her his treasure. Evenings were less predictable. At dusk he ordered Graça to the parlor and told her to sing.

I was not allowed to join them, but watched whenever I could, cramming myself into one of my old hiding spots. I sat wedged between the phonograph and the wall, my shoulders hunched, my legs going numb beneath me. Usually, Graça sang and the Senhor put down his drink and closed his eyes. Sometimes he fell asleep and Graça tiptoed away. Other times he woke from his trance and had harsh words ready, as if he'd been dreaming them.

"You bored me right to sleep," he'd say. Or: "I'm not sure why your mother encouraged you."

On those nights, Graça retreated to her room and cried behind her locked door, with me on the other side, waiting. Then she would open the door, wipe her eyes, and take my hand, our fingers intertwined, and we would tiptoe to the cutters' circles. There were other nights, however, when the Senhor gave her compliments and, upon leaving the parlor, Graça was giddy and flushed. When we sneaked to the cutters' circles later in the night, she nearly skipped down the dirt path without me.

"Your mother was right," Senhor Pimentel said once. "You have a beautiful voice. I'm going to miss it."

Graça stood very still before him. "Where are you going, Papai?"

"I'm not going anywhere, querida. You're getting married."

M arriage was an inevitability that loomed over Graça's future but never with an exact date or time, like death. We knew it would happen but convinced ourselves that it wouldn't happen anytime soon.

A year after the Senhora's funeral, Senhor Pimentel traveled to Recife and stayed a week. When he returned, he'd shaved his beard and parted his hair differently. On another Recife trip, he ordered a dozen new suits in the latest fashion. One day he returned to Riacho Doce driving a new automobile with a convertible top.

"The rooster's out of the coop," Nena said each time Senhor Pimentel's car bounded out of the Great House gates. The kitchen girls whispered rumors about Senhor Pimentel's finances. Sugar's price hadn't risen after the Depression, and even the best planters were struggling and deep in debt. Some had burned their crops to try to drive the value up. A few maids wondered if they should leave Riacho Doce and trek to Recife to find work before the Senhor went bust, or before a new, meaner Senhora arrived. The rumor was that the Senhor was sniffing around for a rich young wife.

Graça and I didn't mind Senhor Pimentel's absences, and when he returned from Recife he drank less and was more cheerful. But a new Senhora meant trouble—no young wife would want a surly teenage daughter, a sourpuss governess, and an overeducated kitchen girl to contend with. She would want to populate the Great House with new children and trusted servants, and expel any reminders of her husband's former life. But after many trips to Recife, a prospective wife never appeared. Instead, Senhor Pimentel began to lavish his attentions (and whatever remained of his money) onto Graça. He returned from his trips with silk gloves, gold pendants, and expensive dresses. One day, a large truck barreled through the Great House gates and stopped at the front door. Two millworkers carried from the truck a machine wrapped in blankets and tied to a board, like some kind of beast. Unwrapped, the machine was made of wood and arched on top like a doorway. Senhor Pimentel slapped its side as if testing the fitness of an animal. Then he looked at Graça and said:

"Every respectable house in Recife has one of these. We must show our guests that we're keeping up with the times."

Graça and I were so entranced with the delivery that we failed to ask which guests Senhor Pimentel hoped to impress. I'd heard the word *radio* many times—the Pimentels' cousins visiting from Recife had boasted about being members of the Recife Radio Club, with monthly subscriptions that let them hear shows and music. The idea of voices moving through the air and finding their way into a wooden box seemed like one of the biblical miracles that Old Euclides talked about. Except that this miracle was happening every day, all around us.

After the radio arrived in the Pimentels' parlor, the staff was allowed to gather and watch Senhor Pimentel turn on the machine for the first time. The buzzing that erupted from the speakers sounded like a swarm of angry bees. I later learned that this noise was static. Then Senhor Pimentel slowly turned the knob, and a woman's faraway voice sang through the mesh speaker:

"Oh! Baker on the corner,
who rolls dough every hour,
don't bake me bread
unless you use Bragança Flour!"

Everyone crammed into that parlor disappeared. I closed my eyes and felt only the presence of that radio woman, her voice, and my own questions: What exotic place was this where flour was called not simply "flour" but "Bragança flour"? Where did such things make a difference? Where did people notice these differences enough to sing about them? Graça grabbed my hand. I opened my eyes and saw her beside me, her mouth open, her cheeks flushed, her breath heavy. She looked as if she'd just raced up and down the Great House steps a dozen times, but she hadn't moved an inch since the radio had been unveiled.

Now, instead of our records we had the five-o'clock radio hour. Each evening Graça and I raced to the parlor, Bruxa at our heels telling us to slow down, and clicked on the machine.

The five-o'clock program consisted of a news segment, a few dramatic skits, jingles for the Radio Club, and a music interval. The music was the only part of the show that I truly liked, but Graça loved it all. Each time we sat in front of the radio, Graça gripped my hand and shut her eyes very tightly, as if she were willing herself away from Riacho Doce and to the Mayrink radio station in Rio de Janeiro. My hand seemed to be the only thing keeping her grounded beside me. I held on tight.

I went to sleep thinking of the radio and its music and woke every day excited for five p.m. Nothing else felt important. Even Bruxa's lessons, which I'd once loved, became agonizingly boring. I felt obligated to mask my impatience and boredom during lessons, but Graça did not. She daydreamed, raced through her homework haphazardly, made no effort to learn. Bruxa called Graça impertinent and spoiled. The tutor flicked Graça's forehead hard with her finger each time she neglected to answer correctly. One afternoon, Bruxa boxed Graça's ears.

Graça ran to the mill office, where she burst into tears and showed Senhor Pimentel her red ears. He shook his head. "It's time you learned to respect your teacher, Maria das Graças. You'll have to respect a husband soon, and he'll do much worse if you don't listen."

Graça stumbled from the mill office, her face pale and eyes glazed. We walked together to the river and sat on its bank.

"I hate this place," she cried.

"Me too," I said, even though I had nothing better to compare it with, and no real hope of ever leaving. My only escape was the music we heard in the Great House parlor by day, and the cutters' circles at night.

One night, at the circles, Graça and I crouched so close to the cutters' fire we could almost feel its heat. In the middle of a song, Old Euclides was suddenly beside us. He grabbed my arm roughly and pulled me from my hiding spot.

"Jega! Take her back," he ordered, nodding at Graça. "She can't be here."

"You're not supposed to be here, either," I replied.

Euclides raised his withered hand. I pressed my eyes shut, steadying myself for the blow. But before he struck me, Graça spoke.

"Go away," she ordered. "You're ruining the music."

The cutters had stopped their singing. The group stared in our direction. Several housemaids stepped away from the fire and ran back to their quarters behind the Great House, afraid Graça would snitch.

Euclides released my arm. He smiled at Graça. "I'm sorry. Is the noise bothering you, Miss? We'll quiet down so you can sleep."

"I don't want to sleep," Graça said. "I want to hear them." She adjusted her shawl and strode next to the fire. "Go on," she said to those cutters, their wives and children. "Pretend I'm not here."

The cutters obeyed. They chose songs with boring lyrics praising their work and God. They sang stiffly, as if in a church. The circle broke up earlier than usual. As we walked back to the Great House, Graça knotted her shawl tightly around her shoulders.

"I hate that stupid Euclides," she said. "Now we have to sit and listen to church music. They'll never sing like they used to."

"Maybe we don't just sit there," I said.

"I can't stop going now, Dor. It'll look like I got scared off by that old donkey."

I shook my head. "We'll still go. But maybe we don't sit there like little spies. Maybe we sing, too."

Graça stopped walking. "Every night they do different songs. I can't remember them well enough to sing along."

"We don't do their songs," I said. "They sing for us, give us what we want. And then we give them something they want."

"Like what?"

"The radio hour," I replied.

The Great House staff was not allowed to sit in the Pimentel parlor and listen to the nightly radio show. Some of them hid near the parlor door, hoping to overhear a segment or two. Others accosted me in the kitchen and asked about the day's news segments: *Was it true women would get to vote soon? How many had perished in the landslides down south? Were the stories of an underground metro in São Paulo real?* The cane cutters were even farther removed from the Great House's radio, but they knew of its existence and had just as many questions about the world outside Riacho Doce.

The next day, Graça and I listened to the radio hour more intently than ever before. Then we went to the cutters' circle and re-created as much as we could remember: the dramatic monologues, the jingles for Dr. Ross's Vitamin Pills, the news segment, which we repeated like real newscasters, and the musical interludes. During these songs, my and Graça's voices were an odd mix of hard and soft, of ease and exertion. I closed my eyes and pretended Senhora Pimentel was there, sitting beside the fire, gathering all of her energy to stand up at the end of our song and cry, "Bravo!"

After a few weeks, others from the Great House—maids, house-boys, kitchen helpers—who hadn't been to the circles before began to appear beside the fire. Whether they came for the novelty of seeing the Little Miss and Jega perform, or simply to hear the radio hour, I wasn't sure. And I didn't care. They clapped for us. They asked us questions. They did not make fun of me for performing beside the Little Miss. I belonged in front of that crowd as much as Graça did. The heat of the cane cutters' bonfire shone on my face like a thousand stage lights. I never wanted to leave it.

That summer, Graça and I took refuge in the cutters' circles at night and in Senhora Pimentel's abandoned room by day. Senhor Pimentel hadn't bothered to sort or pack any of the Senhora's things, so Graça and I were free to try on her veiled hats, silk gloves, and beaded bags. Once, Graça tugged a tin of red lip paint from her dress pocket.

"Turn to me," she ordered.

"Where'd you get that?" I asked.

"I paid one of the maids for it. Pucker up, Dor."

I shook my head. "Only loose women paint their lips."

Graça sighed. "Don't be a bore. In real cities, all the ladies paint their faces. Especially if they're going to be radio stars, like us."

Graça peeled off her mother's gloves. She rubbed a finger in the lip paint and then dotted my mouth with the red stuff. Her breath felt warm and smelled of coffee. She rubbed some paint onto my cheeks, then onto hers. We kept our backs to the room's door; when we heard it open, we believed a maid had come to dust.

Graça rolled her eyes. "Not now!" she called. "We're busy."

The door did not shut. We heard heels click against the stone floor. "Your father has asked me to prepare you for lunch," Bruxa announced. When we turned toward her, her mouth fell open. "Wipe your faces! You look like common hussies."

Graça laughed. "Are there uncommon hussies?"

Bruxa grabbed her arm and tugged her to standing. "You will have an important visitor today."

Graça's eyes widened. I hopped up from the floor. Neither of us had expected a Senhora candidate.

"Dores, you will stay in the kitchen," Bruxa said. "And don't even think of cramming into one of your hiding places."

Curiosity made us obedient. We washed the rouge and lip paint from our faces, and Bruxa riffled through Graça's armoire and made her try on several of the fancy dresses the Senhor had bought her in Recife. Each time I helped Graça button the back of a gown, Bruxa shook her head.

"Too tight," she declared after the fifth attempt. "Your figure could make a nun's smock look vulgar. What is your largest dress?"

I found a boxy sheath in powder blue at the back of the closet. Graça reluctantly slipped it on and Bruxa approved. After tying a ribbon in her hair and spraying her with lavender water, our tutor ordered me to the kitchen and escorted Graça downstairs.

A few minutes later, I crept out the back door and leaned against the Great House's far wall, closest to the gate. Senhor Pimentel waved from the porch; an automobile had arrived. As soon as the motor cut off, a young man emerged from the driver's seat and peeled off his leather driving gloves. A watch chain glimmered at his midsection. His hair was slicked back with so much Brilliantine, he could have oiled every machine in the mill. I suppose he was handsome, insofar as he didn't look ill or bloated or prone to drink. Graça appeared on the porch beside her father, her gloved hands clasped chastely at her waist. Her cheeks were very pink, and any fool might have mistaken this for a rise in her color upon seeing a young man. But I knew it was the rouge I'd wiped away with a rough towel.

There was pressure on my shoulder. It wasn't painful, so I knew the touch could not be Nena's.

"I told you not to spy," Bruxa said. The noonday sun made her squint. Her upper lip glistened.

"You told me to go to the kitchen," I replied. "Not to stay there."

She could have boxed my ears for speaking to her this way. Instead, she ordered me back upstairs, to help her straighten the schoolroom.

"We won't study today," she said, arranging the books on her desk. "Does that disappoint you?"

She had never asked me a direct question before.

"I don't like missing lessons," I replied.

Bruxa nodded. "You'll be wasted working in a kitchen. I've said as much to Senhor Pimentel."

Bruxa's cheeks had color and her eyes shone; she almost looked excited.

"You're a bright girl," Bruxa said. "That is a rare gift. It has been rewarding, teaching you these past years. I used to think it wasn't right, letting you have lessons, giving you hope when there was none. I thought it was cruel of the Senhora. But she must have sensed you were sharper than most. Certainly brighter than the Little Miss, who is spoiled beyond comprehension. I pity the man that marries her. But I suppose most men want a pretty wife, not a bright one. That's how it was in my day; pretty girls could get away with any vice, while the rest of us had to have talent."

"She's got talent," I said. "She sings. We both do."

"Singing is a useful skill for parties and entertaining guests," Bruxa replied. "If her husband provides some musical training, I'm sure she'll be a hit in Recife's parlors."

"She doesn't want a husband," I said, my voice so loud it made Bruxa's eyes widen.

"Who does?" the tutor snapped. "The Little Miss gets everything she wants, but in this case, the choice isn't up to her. You have a choice. You were brought up in the kitchen, and that gives you certain advantages even a Little Miss doesn't have. No one expects *you* to wed or make a family. I hope you don't expect that of yourself."

I shook my head.

Bruxa allowed herself a smile. "There are many capable young women becoming clerks and typists now. There are typing courses in Recife. The Senhor could pay for your coursework, and you could return and work in the mill's office until your debt's been paid. After that, you'd have a profession. You could move to Recife if you wanted. You don't have to follow the Little Miss when she leaves."

"Where's she going?"

"She's fourteen. She could stand to mature a bit more, but the Senhor . . . Well, I'm sure you know the price of sugar isn't what it used to be. He has hundreds of employees to think about. I've been . . .

Well, I must leave here to work with another family in Recife, one that can pay me what I'm worth. It isn't wise to let the Little Miss stay idle here. Young girls like the Little Miss can find trouble quite easily if left to their own devices. If her father waits much longer, she might not find a proper suitor like that young man downstairs."

My stomach felt hollow, as if my insides had been scooped out with the spiked spoon Nena used to scrape coconut meat from its shell. The playroom door was open and I wanted to push past Bruxa and downstairs, into the parlor, to warn Graça, to tell her to run.

When Graça and I were girls trapped in the cane fields of northeast Brazil, marriage was a way for the rich to keep their fortunes within a tiny, acceptable group. And love? Love was only something you heard about in songs.

Growing up far from any city had its advantages in Graça's case— suitors could be led to believe that she wasn't exposed to temptations or tainted by modern notions. And she was quite pretty. I suppose this was how Senhor Pimentel advertised Graça to her suitors: an innocent girl, a bud ready to bloom. Whether he did this for her sake or for his own, we'd never know. If Graça married well, Senhor Pimentel would certainly benefit, whether by loans from his wealthy new son-in-law, or by being able to start his own marriage search, this time with an empty house and fancy new family connections. Or, as Graça came to believe years later, after she forgave Senhor Pimentel, maybe her father intended to care for her in the only way he knew how: by placing her in a wealthy house. But even the best intentions can be born of selfishness. Mine were.

A part of me has always believed in suffering: that suffering is a duty, and we are made stronger for it, like clay in the fire. But losing Graça to a husband was a blow I was not willing to bear. She could not leave Riacho Doce on a stranger's arm. She could not become a wife, and therefore be lost to me forever. Even though the notion of our running away together to become radio stars seemed as impossible to me as building a ladder to the moon, I wasn't ready to relinquish our shared dream, or our shared life.

So, that afternoon as Graça had lunch with her first suitor, I lingered upstairs in the schoolroom. I straightened books and shaved countless pencils. All the while hoping to hear a racket downstairs in the dining room: the breaking of glass and toppling of chairs; Senhor Pimentel yelling; Graça talking back to him, protesting her fate, recreating our radio heroines in her most dramatic fashion. But all was sickeningly quiet.

When it was time for the radio hour, after the young man had left and the lunch plates had been cleared, Graça was not in the parlor. I found her in her mother's room, a blue velvet baggie in her hands.

"He gave me this," she said, opening the bag's drawstring mouth and removing a strand of pearls. Graça examined the necklace, eyeing each creamy circle.

"And you kept it," I said.

Graça looked at me, surprised. "Sure. It's nice."

"So you liked him?" I asked, feeling short of breath.

She eyed the pearls again. "His hands were like frog's skin—so sweaty and cold. But he said I was a real beauty. He's coming back next week."

"Do you want him to?" I asked.

Graça looked up. "It's a way out of here," she said. "Papai thinks it's the only thing I'm meant for. Do you think so, Dor?"

We stared at each other until it seemed as though the room, the Great House, and all of the fields of Riacho Doce dimmed and disappeared, leaving only the two of us in that moment, which felt so wide and so deep it has lasted for decades in my memory, so that if I close my eyes I can still see that Graça of fourteen in front of me, her face round, her eyebrows thick and unplucked, and her gaze electric in its ferocity.

"No," I whispered.

Graça dropped the necklace into its bag and shut the mouth tight.

A week later, that suitor returned to Riacho Doce with a valise under his arm. He would stay overnight. Graça was serious and unsmiling in his presence. That night, after the suitor had retired to his guest room, I watched from my hiding spot in the parlor as Senhor Pimentel caught Graça's arm.

"Show him some charm," he coaxed. "Let him see that smile of yours. Next week we'll host another guest and get them fighting over you. So give him a little something to fight for, querida."

Graça nodded, then excused herself. Later, when the Great House was dark and the cane cutters' drums sounded, I waited in our usual meeting spot on the porch. She arrived wearing her mother's old driving coat.

"You taking the car for a spin?" I whispered, nervous.

"It can't be hard. It's just pressing a few pedals," she replied. Then, seeing what must have been panic on my face, Graça shook her head. "The gates are all locked and Euclides has the keys. Even if I knew how to drive, we couldn't bust through them. Come on."

She took my hand and we walked away from the Great House and toward the cutters' fire. But instead of going to the circle, Graça continued down a different path, away from the music.

"Where are you going?" I asked.

She tugged me down the dark trail. "To the river."

There was a sliver of moon suspended above us. The river was a wide, glossy ribbon. At its bank, Graça let go of my hand and began collecting rocks—big ones—and dumping them into the driving coat's deep pockets. Behind us, the cutters' drums pounded.

"Those stones are too big to skip," I said. "They'll sink right away."

"That's what I want," she replied.

Frogs hooted to each other from opposite ends of the river, their calls high-pitched and frantic. Graça stopped searching for stones. She looked at me, then at the water.

"Remember that ghost you told me about? The one who lives in the water. She was real once. She was a girl, living here, just like us. And people still talk about her. She's a story, and I will be, too."

"What kind of story?"

Graça smiled, her teeth gray in the dark. "The crazy Little Miss—a nervous girl, like her mother—who walked into the river with rocks in her pockets."

"You'll drown."

"I won't," Graça said. "You'll save me."

I shook my head. Graça sighed, exasperated, as if we'd already gone over this plan a dozen times.

"You followed me down here because you were worried about me. You saw what I was doing and dove in. You pulled me to safety! Make sure to scream and make a big event of it, Dor, so the cutters can hear. I'll scream, too. We'll wake up the Great House."

"Why?" I asked.

Graça crossed her arms. "Everyone says you're so smart, but you act like a numbskull. Don't you see who's sniffing around today?"

Numbskull. Sniffing around. We'd heard those words on the radio, said by smart-aleck heroines with more pluck than sense.

"I'm not some ninny. I've been thinking about this a lot," Graça continued. "No one wants to buy a bruised fruit. Well, now we've got to put some bruises on me. If we really want to nip this marriage business in the bud, I've either got to be crazy or a puta. And I sure don't feel like opening my legs for some stable boy or cane cutter. So this is it, Dor. This is our chance. No man wants to marry a loony, no matter how pretty she is. Gossip gets to Recife, and I'm as good as a spinster."

"Can't you just splash around and scream?" I asked. "Without the coat. Without the rocks?"

Graça shook her head. "They won't buy it. I won't go in too deep. And you're as strong as an ox."

"And if I'm not?"

"Then we're both goners," Graça said. "Either way, we'll be the talk of Riacho Doce for a long time."

I shook my head. "I can't."

"You have to," Graça said, her voice suddenly stern. "I'll leave this rathole no matter what, whether it's on some dumb husband's arm, or all on my own. But you won't. You need me to drag you out of here. You save me now, and I save you later."

So that was how I found myself wading waist-deep into Riacho Doce's namesake, hand in hand with Graça. If I hesitated, she pushed forward.

"A little farther now," she said, fighting the weight of her coat. "Then scream and tug me out."

Graça looked back at me and smiled. I smiled back, gripping her hand so hard my fingers ached. She lost her footing. Water rushed over her neck, her hair. Her eyes were wide with panic. The river's current was stronger than I expected. I held fast to her, but the weight made my knees buckle, tugging me under, too. Graça clawed at my night-gown, my neck, my arms. I heaved her up and she gagged, then frantically tried to tug off the coat before sinking again. I pulled her up again and tried to move toward shore but made no progress. I was wading in concrete. I gnashed my teeth and took one step, then another, my toes barely touching the bottom. All the while I kept my grip on Graça, who'd calmed enough to take deep, gulping breaths. The shore was not far, but in the dark we'd waded deeper than we'd imagined. A stone under my foot shifted. My legs gave out. Water slapped my face. I didn't know which way was up, which was down. I held Graça under her armpits and paddled, frantic, until we surfaced. I heard the cutters' drums. I thought of that fado singer onstage in Recife and how her song had reached so far, so fast. I took a breath and cried out until my voice filled the darkness.

There was a splash, a groan, a gurgling breath. I was no longer burdened by my body or Graça's. There was no grasping or fighting. I was weightless. Was I ascending? Was I making my way, like a saint or a cherub, into the heavens? I opened my eyes and saw a cane cutter's face. Then I was on the muddy bank, where I rolled onto my hands and knees and vomited river water and bile.

My nightgown stuck to my chest like a wet napkin. My stomach ached from so much heaving. How long had I been on that bank? I looked around then, frantic, remembering Graça.

"They've got her," the cutter said.

Ahead of us, far up the dirt path, a dark knot of cane cutters carried Graça to the Great House. Many hands held her, as if she was a saint's statue in a parade, or a coffin.

The lone cutter held my arm to steady me as I stumbled up the path, after Graça. Before us, an automobile growled to life. Its headlights made me squint and stop just before the Great House gate. The suitor, in his pajamas, held the steering wheel with both hands as if he was just learning to operate the machine. Old Euclides occupied the passenger seat beside him, pointing at the road like a nervous teacher. Behind the car was Nena—in her nightgown and shawl, a cloth knotted tightly around her hair. She strode past the open gate, toward me.

"Now you've done it," she said, taking my arm from the cane cutter, like guards handing off a prisoner.

The Great House was alight as if the Pimentels were hosting a ball. Nena tugged me around back, to the kitchen.

"Euclides was in the car," I whispered, my throat raw. "With that man."

Nena kept walking, her wide hand encircling my arm. "To get the doctor. That city boy made a fuss of helping and the Senhor wanted him out of the house. Euclides is showing him the way."

I stopped. "The doctor?"

Nena tightened her grip on me. "She's still on two feet. No thanks to her, or to you. She wanted attention and now she's got it."

Stable boys lingered out back, near the chopping block. Inside, all the maids and kitchen girls stood shoulder to shoulder in bare feet and nightgowns, whispering. As soon as Nena walked in with me, they quieted. My nightgown was still wet and clinging. I covered my chest with my free arm and stared straight ahead, believing that Nena would take me to our shared room and beat me. No one was treating me like a hero, like the Little Miss's savior, the brave kitchen girl who'd stopped a tragedy, because I hadn't stopped it, the cutters had. I was, if anything, a failure. The maids would stay outside our room and listen to my punishment. I resolved not to make a peep.

I was confused when Nena pulled me out of the kitchen and into the main hall, under the blazing lights of the front of the house. My nightgown was streaked brown. Mud on my elbows and forearms had dried to an itchy crust. Outside the parlor's closed doors, Nena took off her shawl and covered me with it.

"If you have any good sense left, you'll keep quiet," Nena whispered. "Everyone knows you follow her like a lamb."

Then she made a fist and rapped on the parlor door. Senhor Pimentel opened it.

His hair was uncombed. The top three buttons of his shirt were undone, its tail untucked, as if he'd dressed hastily. As soon as he saw Nena and me he turned on his heel and walked to the other side of the room, beside the radio. Atop the machine was a half-empty bottle of cane rum.

Graça sat in the Senhora's old chair with her knees tucked under her chin, a wool blanket wrapped around her so only her head appeared. Her hair was wet and matted, making her face and eyes look enormous, like a cat that had been dunked in a bath. Beside her chair was a chamber pot filled, almost to the brim, with watery vomit.

Senhor Pimentel closed his eyes and massaged the lids with his fingertips. "Whose idea was it?" he asked.

Graça and I glanced at each other.

Senhor Pimentel opened his eyes. "Speak up!"

My hands shook though I wasn't cold. The parlor pulsed with color: Graça's blue blanket, the footstool's green velvet, Senhor Pimentel's blindingly white shirt, the radio's chocolate wood. Every corner seemed sharper, every curve more swollen. I felt a crackling, restless energy within me, making it hard to keep my thoughts straight. Years later I'd feel this again, only it wasn't the remnants of adrenaline that caused it but pure Benzedrine from the bennies we swallowed to pep ourselves up for long movie shoots. I shifted my feet. The Senhor looked at me.

"This is your repayment for everything I've given you?" he asked. "You encourage her schemes instead of doing your duty and stopping her, or telling someone?"

"Dor saved me," Graça said.

"The cutters saved you," the Senhor snapped. "Old Euclides saw you two walking into the water. Holding hands."

His cheeks flushed. Nena's grip tightened around my arm. The Senhor stared at Graça.

"So you've disgraced yourself—is that what you wanted? Every cutter saw you practically naked in that wet gown. Everyone thinks you're a half-wit who can't even drown herself."

Graça wrapped the blanket tighter around herself. "I don't care what anyone here thinks. I won't be here much longer."

"No," the Senhor replied. "You won't. Recife isn't the only city in the world, and that man"—he pointed to the ceiling, as if the suitor was still asleep in the guest room above us—"isn't the last husband on earth. But he was the best you could do. All those weeks I spent in Recife courting him for you, convincing him to travel here and meet my sweet daughter. And then you go and act like a lunatic. All you've done with this stunt is make your life harder."

"I'm not marrying any dumb lug!" Graça shouted. "I'm going to be a radio singer."

The Senhor laughed.

Entertainers weren't respected then as they are now. Radio singers, circus people, showgirls, cabaret dancers were all considered to be the same kind of people: transient, licentious tricksters. For a Little Miss to want such a life was so incomprehensible it was comical. Senhor Pimentel's laughter filled the parlor and seemed to smear itself across us like mud from the riverbank.

"Did you hear that, Nena?" the Senhor said, chuckling. "My only child wants to sing jingles about butter and face powder."

Graça's cheeks were wet, her upper lip slick with snot. "Mamãe said I have a magnificent voice."

The Senhor sighed. "Every mother tells her children they're exceptional even when they're not."

His mention of Senhora Pimentel brought her back as if she was still there, sitting where Graça now sat, ready to hear our voices.

"She is exceptional," I called out, startling myself. "We are."

The Senhor looked in my direction, appraising me as if seeing me for the first time. If, prior to that night, I was simply an ugly foundling who followed his daughter everywhere, then, on that night, I became something else to the Senhor, something more. Nena's grip on my arm was so tight my fingers tingled.

"Jega," she said. "Be quiet."

The Senhor held up his hand, palm out, as if taking an oath. Nena hushed. The Senhor moved toward us.

Behind me, Nena held my arm and pressed the toes of her feet hard against my heels, ready to prop me up from whatever blow he might administer. The Senhor extended his hand and stomped his foot. I squeezed my eyes shut, ready for him to strike. I was the trunk of a tree, thick and rooted, my skin a bark that grew in rings around me. I was the steel toe of a boot, impenetrable. I was Jega, and she had been beaten many times before.

I waited to feel the sting of his hands against me, triumphant, as if I'd already won. But there was no slap, no punch, no knock to the head. I opened my eyes.

The Senhor laughed again, louder this time.

"You think I'm some brute?" he asked. "Punishing kitchen girls is Nena's job, and I'm sure she will fulfill her duties. She always does. You know, your mother was a hanger-on, too."

I wobbled. Nena held me straight.

"She worked in the kitchen; didn't Nena ever tell you? I'd spend summers here, with my cousins, and she'd try to be a part of our games. A gangly thing she was, like you—always following us. When we were older, we used to trade little trinkets—gloves, a marble, a lost charm on a necklace; trash really—to go behind the chicken hutch with her. Then Nena kicked her out; she didn't belong in a decent house. I warned my wife a dozen times that the fruit never falls far from the tree. And I was right."

I could withstand a thousand blows from any fist, but words? Words would always undo me.

The tiniest, most treacherous sob began to bubble up in the back of my throat and tried very hard to push itself out. Graça watched me. She uncurled from her blanket and stood. Then, behind her father's back, like the pluckiest heroine in a great caper, she winked at me. As if this was all part of our plan. As if she and I were playing our roles to their fullest, and this was not the end of our story but the very beginning.

We were separated—me hidden in Nena's little room in the bowels of the kitchen, and Graça upstairs, in her massive bedroom, her door locked from the outside to avoid any more escapes.

After we left the parlor, my eyes felt dry in their sockets. My legs and arms and neck pounded in time to my heartbeat, as if my body was one large, quivering organ. "River fever," Nena said, and forced tea between my cracked lips.

When the Pimentels' doctor finally arrived to examine Graça, he popped downstairs to check on me. I pretended to sleep and, in this way, I was privy to the gossip between the doctor and Nena. This was how I discovered that Graça would be shipped to a convent school in Petrópolis, some two thousand kilometers south.

"Thank the good Lord the Senhora wasn't here to see her in that river," Nena said.

"Her mother had a nervous disposition," Dr. Aurélio said, lowering his voice. "I'm sad to say they are cut from the same cloth."

"The Little Miss wants to be onstage," Nena whispered. "A singer."

The doctor sighed. "Mental unsteadiness. I've told the Senhor she needs guidance. The nuns will sort her out."

My pillow felt strangely wet beneath my face. I did not know if it was sweat or tears that had soaked it. I shivered.

"Well, look who's awake," Nena said.

Dr. Aurélio patted my head. "Jega, my girl. Welcome back."

The Petrópolis Sion School was the place where the wealthy sent wayward daughters to be forgotten—if not forever, then at least until their tarnished reputations had been sufficiently mended. Even the fanciest boarding schools in those days required students to supply everything but food. Senhor Pimentel grumbled about the cost of fabrics to make Graça's bedsheets, towels, uniforms, and underclothes. Each student at the prestigious school was also required to bring one servant to wash her clothes and prepare her food. These servants were called "helpers" and they lived in the school, under the watchful eyes of the nuns, and received food, lodging, and religious instruction. Most helpers went on to become nuns themselves. Everyone believed Senhor Pimentel would send a housemaid to Petrópolis with Graça, and the girls whispered nervously at the back of the house, fretting over who might have to go. I was on my feet by then, limping around the kitchen, forbidden by Nena from going anywhere near the front of the house or even outside for fear that the Senhor might see me and cast me out for good. The maids, who had always teased me, now shot me icy stares, as if I had caused all of their troubles. Even the girls who ached to leave Riacho Doce wanted no part in convent life, at the mercy of nuns, who, in those days, were known to be particularly vicious.

Three days after the doctor's visit, Senhor Pimentel called Nena and me back to the parlor. I could not look at his face, and instead stared at his shoes, so polished that they seemed to glow in the morning light. I suppose Senhor Pimentel understood my reticence as obedience, but Nena knew better. She kept her massive hand around my arm like a vise, making certain I didn't move any closer to the Senhor as he spoke.

"Nena has been here since I was a boy, and I have the greatest respect for her," he announced. "She is a part of this house, just like the front door or the columns. It wouldn't function without her. Because of her, and her attachment to you, I am giving you a great opportunity, Jega. The Sisters at Sion will cure you of your disobedience better than I ever could. You will find your place there. And when Graça has finished her studies and returns to be married, you will stay on."

Nena gave my arm a rough squeeze. I remembered Senhor Pimentel and how Sion was supposed to be a punishment, not a prize. I kept my eyes cast down and mumbled thanks. Back in our room, Nena finally let me go.

"I should've stopped you going to those circles," she said.

"You knew we went?"

"Everybody knew. Except the Senhor. I didn't think it'd do you harm, to sing a little. The Little Miss can think she's meant to be a radio star, but I thought you had the good sense to know better, not to get caught up in fantasy."

"It's not a fantasy," I said. "I can sing, too."

"Did you hit your head, Jega? Because your brain's as scrambled as an egg. If Euclides weren't such a snoop, you'd have gotten yourself drowned. And for what? For that Little Miss?"

"I wasn't going to drown. I was going to save her. Those cutters interrupted."

"Oh, they interrupted?" Nena said. "Well, excuse me, Your Highness." She crossed her muscled arms. "You're too old to be holding hands with that girl."

My skin tingled, as if the fever was returning.

Nena smoothed her apron. "I didn't raise you to be a daydreamer like the Senhora—God rest her soul—or some loose woman like your mother. Bruxa said you have a quick mind. It'd be a shame to waste it. So I told the Senhor you had to go to that nuns' school, or else I'd leave this house. I'd walk right out the front gate and let him run this place into the ground. That scared him enough to give you a chance in Petrópolis. Those nuns down there, they eat. They have kitchens. You've been watching me, you can cook better than most. Show them what you can do, Jega. Forget that Little Miss. Don't carry her troubles on your back. You keep saving that one, and you'll be saving her all your life."

"I don't want to be a cook," I said. "Or a nun."

"Who told you we get to choose what we are?"

"I told myself."

Before I could raise my arms to protect myself, Nena swept across the room and clapped my face between her massive hands, yanking me toward her. It was the closest thing to a hug she'd ever given me.

"You think you know the world, Jega?" Nena asked, shaking her head. "The world will eat you up."

The next day, I sneaked into the Great House library and looked up Petrópolis in an atlas; it was in the south near Rio de Janeiro. We would get there by boat—one of the massive passenger liners that left each day from Recife's port. All of it seemed so strange and exciting to me, I might as well have been going to Jupiter on a rocket ship. Graça was also excited, but not about the voyage.

The day before our trip, I bribed a maid to give me the key to Graça's room.

She sat atop her bed, the sheets kicked aside and tangled as if she'd spent the night wrestling them. Her face was pale. When she saw me at the door, she scrambled from bed and kissed me on the cheek.

"They lock you in here all day?" I asked. My cheek throbbed where Graça had kissed it.

Graça nodded. "I'm so bored I even picked up a book. I don't know how you like those things," she said, and pressed a hand to my face. "I'll give you all my books if you want."

I shook my head. "Someone'll say I stole them."

"You mean Papai will," Graça said, pursing her lips. "We're going to show him."

"Show him what?"

"We're running away as soon as we dock in Rio," she whispered, as if we weren't alone in the room. "I'm going to be on the radio."

Our trip to Sion School is, in my memory, like an album with many forgettable tracks but a few persistent ones. I recall seeing our mammoth passenger liner at Recife's docks and being mystified that such a ship didn't sink. I recall holding tightly to my little note-book of words—the only possession I'd taken from Riacho Doce, aside from my helper's uniforms—as I followed Graça and Senhor Pimentel up the gangplank. I remember my throat being raw from vomiting into a bucket because of seasickness. I recall holding very tightly to Graça's hand as Rio de Janeiro first came into view. We saw mountains rising out of the water, with a city tucked into the land's curves as if held firmly in its bosom. (There is a reason why so many love songs are dedicated to Rio.) I recall those strange trees on the road to Petrópolis—they were shaped like triangles with millions of green branches instead of leaves. I'd eventually learn that these were pine trees and were common in cooler places, but on that day the sight of those trees worried me very much. If the trees in Petrópolis were this strange, certainly everything else would be, too. But the sharpest memory from that trip—the one that has remained clear even in the fog of age—happened before we ever set foot in Rio. Our ship made a stop in Salvador, Bahia, and Graça strode into my third-class cabin and dragged me from bed, almost knocking over my vomit bucket.

"You have to see this," she said, and pulled me outside and off the boat.

On Salvador's docks first-class passengers bypassed the crowded, foul-smelling areas by walking across a private bridge. At the end of the bridge was a tidy little square with benches, potted palms, a ticket office, and a line of porters ready to receive passengers' bags. Behind the porters were the Baianas.

White turbans hid their hair. Ruffled white blouses fell off their shoulders. Full white hoop skirts puffed around them, covering their feet and concealing the stools on which they sat, making it seem as if the skirts themselves held those women up. The fabric of their clothes was covered with webs of white lace so detailed and stiff, it seemed as if the dresses had been iced like wedding cakes. Around their necks and wrists were dozens of strands of colored beads and gold chains.

Most of the women were as dark-skinned as Old Euclides. They sold food—in front of each woman was a table covered with ingredients and, on one side, a pot of bubbling palm oil atop a small fire. As the women fried dumplings for the ship's curious passengers, their bracelets clinked and chimed. Graça and I stood slack-jawed, jostled by the crowd but unable to move.

"Holy moly," I breathed.

Graça reached for my hand.

We'd heard about Baianas but had never actually seen them. To wealthy and lighter-skinned Brazilians, the Baiana was a figure associated with the past, with the end of slavery, with the streets, with voodoo and mystery, much like samba itself. At Riacho Doce, the most prized sugar was mill-white, as was the Camellia Rice Powder Girl, the smiling boys in ads for vitamin powder, the saints' statues on every church pedestal. Most Brazilians didn't fit such strict criteria—even magnates of industry, politicians, plantation owners like Senhor Pimentel and Little Misses like Graça. There were shades of acceptance: if you wore fine clothes or had a good family name, then you'd be forgiven your darker skin or your thicker hair. Or, if you were mill-white but had a northeastern accent in Brazil's south, then you were considered riffraff. Only one standard was certain: If you were as dark as Nena, Old Euclides, or those Baianas, you wouldn't be barred from fine shops, theaters, or first-class cabins if you could afford them, but you'd never be allowed to reach that point in the first place.

To understand the extent of my and Graça's amazement at seeing those Baianas, you must understand the limits that had been imposed on our imaginations. Color photographs did not yet exist. We had never seen a moving image on a screen. Fashion magazines like *Shimmy!* were considered vulgar among Graça's class, and impossibly expensive among mine. We religiously flipped through old sewing catalogues abandoned in Senhora Pimentel's room, but the women pictured in those yellowed pages were illustrations: line drawings in black and white. And the women we saw in real life? At Riacho Doce they were maids, cooks, and the drab Bruxa. During my single trip to Recife, I'd seen women in the Saint Isabel Theater, yes, but their ideas of elegance were tightly bound by rules of propriety. Even in Recife's heat, women wore gloves, stockings, and undergarments that pinched waists and bound breasts. If there was lace, it was on a wedding gown or reserved to a tiny scrap of collar. If there were jewels, they were worn sparingly: ears were not pierced; bracelets were nuisances; necklaces had crosses on them; pendants were reserved for balls and the theater. For those women, elegance meant blending in. These were not the women Graça and I pictured when we listened to our radio plays. These were not the heroines we hoped to emulate. But we hadn't yet been given an idea of *who* to picture. We had no living example of the kind of women we hoped to be. We knew only one thing: we wanted nothing to do with blending in—we wanted to stand out.

For me, that day on the docks, the allure of the Baianas wasn't their clothing but their confidence. They wore rings on every finger! They wore bracelets up to their elbows! They did not cover their mouths when they laughed! They glistened with sweat and wore no makeup!

They kept their backs straight and their gazes even straighter! It was as if Graça and I had escaped a country of dowagers and had suddenly found ourselves in a foreign land, surrounded by queens.

Soon enough, we would be surrounded by their opposite.

Nearly every wealthy Brazilian woman my age has a nun story. Nuns were as common as bread back then. Convent schools were prestigious. The church used rich girls' tuitions to allow less fortunate girls like me to have an education. Most poor pupils became nuns themselves, while the rich pupils became wives. So our story was no different from those of thousands of other girls dropped off by their parents at the gates of a convent school. Graça and I were not special, and this realization was hard for her to bear.

Until then, Graça had been the Little Miss, the sole girl-heir with the best dresses and finest toys. At Sion, owning a struggling sugar mill in northeast Brazil was not considered a noble background. Graça's Sion classmates were heiresses to fortunes much larger than that of the Pimentels. The girls in Graça's dormitory had softer sheets, lacier underclothes, sterling-silver hairbrushes, gold rosaries. They had eiderdowns imported from Germany, which made me ashamed for Graça of the thin, scratchy wool blankets Tita had placed in her trunk. What bothered Graça most, however, were the nuns' constant refrains of humbleness and simplicity. Graça was neither humble nor simple.

As Graça's helper at Sion, I was responsible for washing and ironing her clothes, sheets, underwear, slips, socks, and school aprons. I didn't mind. Every time I scrubbed the yellow rings on the armpits of her school shirts, or smelled the sweet sweatiness of Graça's nightgowns, I felt a thrilling heat rise in me at the thought that Graça's arms and legs had touched those clothes. Once, one of the snobbish helpers made fun of Graça's uniform, saying, "Look how rough that cotton is! Your girl must be as poor as you are!" I pummeled her, bruising her eye and thwacking her arms and legs with the strings of my apron. Sister Edwiges, the stocky nun in charge of the helpers, caned me for the fight and stopped feeding me dinner for two nights. But afterward, no one dared give me lip.

Apart from sleeping in separate areas of the school, the students weren't very different from the helpers. All girls slept in dormitories separated according to age, so older girls couldn't corrupt younger ones. Petrópolis was cold and the school was drafty. All of our belongings went into small trunks at the feet of our beds, and, once a week, a nun checked the trunks. If Sister found a poorly folded apron or a set of mismatched underclothes, she turned the trunk over and everything inside it—clothes, pictures, contraband items like gum or lipstick—spilled out. The trunk's owner was required to clean the mess, and to go without lunch or dinner. On my first week at Sion, Sister Edwiges searched my trunk and found my little notebook tucked in a stack of underwear. The Sister flipped through the book's pages, moving quickly through my list of Portuguese words and stopping at the English ones. Her pale brows knit together.

"What is this, Maria das Dores?" she asked.

"It is English, Sister," I said, nervous she might take the book, but also delighted to know something the nun did not. "My mistress spoke it. She gave me lessons."

The nun set her blue eyes on me and I could not tell if she was suspicious or impressed. "Do you like languages?" Edwiges asked.

"Yes, Sister."

"We teach the pupils Latin. A few helpers are allowed to learn each term, if you are a quick study and a good candidate to take your vows."

I nodded. If I looked eager, it was only because I didn't want her to confiscate my notebook, and because the little Latin I'd heard in my first week at Sion seemed strangely beautiful. The Sister dropped the book back into my trunk and moved on to the next girl.

Every morning, Sister Edwiges blew her whistle and walked up and down the narrow rows of beds.

"*Salvator mundi,*" she said.

"*Salva nos,*" we were required to reply.

Those who didn't respond fast enough went without breakfast. That was how they punished us at Sion—denying food for little infractions, caning for more serious ones.

I enjoyed Sion's strict schedules, its uniforms, our morning prayers, and the habit of bowing to the Mother Superior each time she passed. I enjoyed the predictability of life there. No day was different from another. Masses were tedious, but the Latin chants! The way the entire chapel seemed to vibrate with all of our voices made me feel the way a bird must feel when it sings with its flock.

The unforgivable part of Sion was that I barely saw Graça. I held her dirty skirts and slips and blouses to my nose, hoping to smell her on them. I noticed the shiny crust of dried snot on the sleeves of her nightgowns, and knew that she'd been crying. Lots of Sion helpers cried into their pillows. Our beds were set close together, close enough that some girls reached out to one another and held hands. Some nights, I heard the creak of bedsprings and the wet clicks of kisses. I missed Graça terribly then, and wondered if she missed me. I pictured her asleep in the student dormitory, and then I pictured her awake, moving across the room at night, into another girl's bed. Then there was always a horrible knotting in my stomach and I could not stop my tears.

We changed clothes under the covers and bathed in our nightgowns, reaching under the wet cloth to soap ourselves properly. There were rows of shower spigots that spat out cold water. It was only afterward, as we toweled off, that I paid attention to how the nightgowns stuck to skin and how, through the cloth, you could detect dark patches of hair, the twin points of breasts. Many of the girls in my dormitory talked about "melting"—how they could make themselves melt, and make others, too. Soon enough I discovered what this melting business was, and tried it for myself at night, in the dark privacy of my bed. What a wonder our bodies are! What pride I had that I could give myself such feeling! And what odd shyness I felt each morning, believing the girls in the beds beside mine knew what I was doing under my blankets. The only person I wanted to share this discovery with was Graça. Did she know how to melt? Had she done it, too?

All of her life, Graça made people overlook her tiny stature, her strangely upturned nose, her lack of formal music and dance training, her accent, her tantrums, her addictions. At Sion, she somehow made those snobbish students overlook her origins and want to befriend her. Once, I walked down Sion's main hall and saw Graça in the courtyard, holding court over a group of Sion girls. Graça spoke and they listened. She laughed and they laughed. The girl who sat the closest to her and laughed the loudest was a thick-ankled blonde. I wanted to rush into the courtyard and pull out that girl's yellow hair.

On Sundays, helpers and students celebrated mass together. We sat in different sections of the chapel, but filed in and out together in neat lines. One Sunday in September, Graça's blonde friend walked beside me as we left the chapel. Before I could quicken my pace, the girl grabbed my hand. If the Sisters caught her, we would both be caned. The girl's grip was tight, her fingers as wet and firm as peeled carrots. She pressed a bit of paper into my palm. Half an hour later, alone in the toilet stall where no one could see me, I opened the note and recognized Graça's round, curly script. *Pray at 5*, the note said, in English.

I nearly swooned inside the wooden box of that toilet stall. Not only had Graça sought me out, but she'd done it in a language most of the Sion girls and the nuns themselves could not decipher. I couldn't bring myself to throw the note away. From that day forward, our stilted and paltry English became a code between us—a puzzle that, until we found ourselves in Los Angeles many years later, Graça and I believed only we could decipher.

S ion's only common area was the chapel, where students and help-ers were supposed to perform thirty minutes of daily, solitary prayer. At five p.m. I met Graça in the chapel. Her brown eyes bulged; her cheeks were concave as if she was constantly sucking them in. She had clearly been punished, her food taken away, but for what?

"We're leaving," she said.

"Who's we?" I asked, my mouth suddenly dry. *Graça and the blonde girl will run away*, I thought, *and she's telling me first, so I won't be surprised when they're gone.*

"You and me," Graça said, threading her fingers through mine. My hands were as rough as oranges from doing her laundry. "You're not a maid, Dor! And I'm not a nun. I'm an artist. I'll die if I stay here!"

I nodded. Did I truly think Graça and I could make our way past every watchful nun, scale Sion's brick fence, navigate the pine forest, and somehow arrive in Rio, unscathed? As Nena would say, a dog that's been beaten enough knows how to walk without a leash. So I felt teth-ered to Sion, but could not see the harm in joining Graça in the chapel each day to plan an escape. Even if the Sisters caught us whispering and not praying, even if I had all of my meals taken away for the next year, it wouldn't have mattered, because Graça had chosen me and no one else.

Every day afterward we knelt side by side in the chapel and spoke into our cupped hands, as if we were praying. The more we met, the more our imaginary escape became a very real possibility, and the more I realized how much trouble we would find ourselves in if we were caught. Actually, I'd be the one in trouble. The Little Miss might get her food taken away or her hands caned, but an unruly helper would be turned out on the street, with no objections from Senhor Pimentel. Meanwhile Graça talked about getting to Rio and finding the Mayrink radio station, and which songs we'd sing once we got there. The radio station's owner would hear our voices and sign us up immediately to sing jingles, Graça said. With a job on the radio, we'd be set. Before long, we'd be the stars of the daily radio hour.

I was the one who steered us out of dreams and back to Sion, who talked about the kitchen door and the deliveries that came each day. Could we hide in a truck? Could we use the pocket money Senhor Pimentel sent her to bribe the boy who delivered milk to take us away in his donkey cart? Could we steal the gardener's ladder and prop it against the school fence in order to climb over? Could we save bits of bread from lunch and hide them in our coats, so we'd have food after our escape? On and on I went, while Graça yawned into her hands.

"Should we sing a tango? Or a fado?" she asked. "A fado might be too dull. We need something peppy."

"Are you listening to me?"

"Yes, but I want to talk about the important stuff."

"Getting out isn't important?" I asked.

"You're like one of those girls that only thinks about pushing a baby out and how much it'll hurt," Graça said. "But I'm thinking about after. I'm thinking about taking care of the baby, Baby."

"This isn't funny."

"I'm not laughing. We can yak all day long about locks and bribes and fences, but what we really need to do is be ready. One of these days, a nun's going to take a nap at the wrong time, or a door's going to be left open, or the gardener's going to forget to lock the gate, and we're going to have to be quick. Opportunity's going to knock, and we're going to have to answer."

"What if it doesn't knock? What if we have to make it ourselves?"

Graça glanced at the nun at the back of the chapel, then leaned ever so slightly toward me and planted a kiss on my knuckles. "We're not supposed to be here. We're meant for greater things," Graça said, and cocked her head toward the Jesus on the cross before us. "Even He knows that."

A few weeks later, Graça practically skipped into chapel. As she knelt to pray, she pressed her elbow into mine, knocking my arm from the pew.

"You hear that, Dor?" she asked.

"Hear what?"

She tapped her foot against the floor, making three quiet knocks on the tile. "Opportunity's knocking. The Holy Sisters are taking us on a trip."

The Sisters planned an excursion to Rio to see the famous Christ the Redeemer statue. Back when Graça and I were still going to the cutters' circles in Riacho Doce, a new president had taken over the country. We were too young to care, but the adults around us seemed worried. Getúlio Vargas was the president's name, and though he'd lost the official election, he'd banded together military friends and popular support to oust the rightful winner. It was a revolution, although at Riacho Doce we were too far away to feel its effects. This revolution lasted only four days; by the time we heard the news out in Riacho Doce, fighting in the capital cities was over and Getúlio was president.

Everyone, even the Sisters at Sion, called our self-made president by his first name, as if he were a long-lost brother or cousin. After he installed himself in the presidential palace, Getúlio ordered a flurry of public works projects to put people at ease. One of these projects (started years before Getúlio took power but which he, wisely, took all the credit for) was a thirty-eight-meter-tall statue of Christ set on Rio's Corcovado Mountain, in the middle of Tijuca Forest.

The trip to Corcovado was considered very important to the nuns at Sion. Only older girls were invited on field trips, but helpers were also allowed to go. There would be seventy-five of us going to see Christ the Redeemer with only five nuns as chaperones.

"This is our chance," Graça said, nearly squealing. "We'll be in Rio. It's like they're delivering us there."

"We'll be in a forest, on top of a mountain. Rio's kilometers away," I said.

"Well, it'll be closer than it is now."

"How would we even get down the mountain by ourselves? Hike? It'll take days. We'd need food."

"Stop it," Graça whispered. "You're complicating everything. We go, and then we ditch them. That's all."

I laughed.

Graça looked up at the chapel's Christ. Her hands were clenched together so firmly, the knuckles were white.

"You think you're so smart," she said. "Well, you weren't smart enough to get yourself out of Riacho Doce. I had to nearly drown us in the river to do that. So stop treating me like a pea-brain and questioning every little thing I say. Just follow orders like you're supposed to, and I'll get us out of here, too."

"Like I'm supposed to?" I asked.

"That's right," Graça said.

"You didn't get me here, Nena did," I said. "The only reason I'm in this chapel is because Nena said she'd leave the Great House if I didn't get to go to school, too. Your papai doesn't care if you're two thousand kilometers away from him. He doesn't even notice you're gone. But he sure didn't want to lose his cook."

Graça looked at me, startled. Then she stood, made a great show of crossing herself, and left the chapel.

The next day she didn't appear for five o'clock prayers, or the next, or the day after that. I knelt alone in the chapel's front pew, groggy from sleepless nights thinking of Graça and if she would really run and, when she did, if she would take me along. On the day of the Redeemer trip, I could barely spoon breakfast's watery oats into my mouth, my hands shook so badly. Before we left Sion, I grabbed my little notebook from my trunk and slipped it into my skirt's pocket; it was the one thing I wouldn't leave behind.

At Corcovado's base, there was an electric railway that took visitors up and down the steep slope to the Redeemer. We rode up in separate cars—students and Sisters in the first few, helpers on the last. The train lurched through the thick tangle of trees and palms that was Tijuca Forest. Every year, hikers and tourists were lost in that forest. Many died.

Near the top of the track, we saw Rio in the distance. There was the semicircle of Guanabara Bay, the white dots of passenger ships arriving at port, the domed roof of the Senate, the glinting bronze eagles of Catete Palace. My palms sweated, making the handrail rail slick. I was in the last car, the conductor barely visible in the first. Near him, staring placidly at the mountains, was Graça.

At the statue's base, the Sisters made us all kneel and pray. The Redeemer statue was made of white soapstone. He was so impossibly tall it made me dizzy to stare into His calm face. After prayers we had thirty minutes to roam around the statue.

I watched as Graça and Rosa, the blonde girl, sidled up to each other. The girl spoke. Graça nodded, her expression grave. I felt my insides go as cold as that statue's soapstone. *They are escaping without me*, I thought. And then, without a moment's hesitation, I turned to find one of the Sisters.

I was going to snitch. Better Graça captive in Sion with me than wandering Rio without. Before I could find a nun, Graça blocked my path.

"Ready?" she asked, in English.

Back at Sion, she'd traded her blonde friend three silk camisoles in exchange for a favor: blondie would hide a bottle of castor oil in her school bag, then drink half of it before they boarded the train. Ten minutes after prayers at the top of the mountain, the blonde doubled over howling. She was sick in the bushes near the statue's feet. Our five chaperone Sisters blew their whistles and ran to her aid.

Graça grabbed my hand. "Now!"

Together we ran toward the empty train.

The contraption was attached to electrified cables, with ascending and descending cars counterbalanced. This meant that one set of cars regularly went up the mountain while the other set always went down, whether there were passengers or not. Without the conductor registering our presence, Graça and I slipped into the last, empty car and crouched behind its wooden benches.

She'd stuffed the little spending money her father had sent her into her brassiere. And she'd worn an extra blouse under the Sion uniform's shirt, which had the school's patch affixed to it. Halfway down the mountain, Graça unbuttoned her school shirt and flung it off the train and into the forest. She ordered me to take off my school shirt and turn it inside out; this way, no one could immediately associate us with Sion.

I fumbled with the buttons, my fingers bumbling, my breath short, my legs already burning from their awkward crouch.

"Here," Graça sighed, and began to undo my blouse for me.

The train groaned. We swayed back and forth. Graça's fingers were quick and steady. She bit her bottom lip, concentrating. When she was done, my blouse flapped open. Graça held both sides and gently tugged it off my shoulders. Then she smiled.

In that moment, only Graça and I existed. We were the first and the last of our kind. We were all of creation. Of course she would be a star. Of course she would find her way to Rio. Of course she would make the seemingly impossible possible. How could I not be taken hold by such confidence, by such unbridled belief?

I put my blouse back on, inside out. The train lumbered down the mountain. Graça and I held each other close. Around us was jungle. Before us was Rio de Janeiro, the sprawling capital of Brazil. We were fifteen years old; runaways who had never lived in a city. We had never been without the protection of adults. Was I afraid? Did I have doubts? I don't remember. All I can recall is feeling Graça's warmth against me and thinking of Riacho Doce, of the cane fires and the way hawks would circle the burning paddocks, waiting for mice and snakes and any other animal that tried to escape the flames. The birds swooped in and carried their catches away. They wouldn't kill them immediately; they'd fly with them first. So the animal's final moments were in the air, far from the world it had known, suddenly seeing everything from above. How terrifying that must be! How wonderful. I felt like that, on the train—caught in the grips of something larger, wiser, more powerful than myself, flying toward a fate that was frightening, yes, but now that I'd caught a glimpse of the world from above, how could I possibly go back to living in the dirt?

THE AIR YOU BREATHE

Here I am, Love.
Always by your side.
I buy your food.
I make your bed.
I place the pillow
under your head.

But you don't notice.
You don't care.
You seem to think,
I'll always be there.
What would happen if I were to leave?
No one notices the air they breathe.

What do feelings matter,
as long as your stockings are new?
As long as your baths are hot,
and every door's opened for you?
What would happen if I were to leave?
No one notices the air they breathe.

We all take for granted
things that come too easily.
That's why I can't let you go—
you're always a challenge to me.
Here's my vow to you, here's all I believe:
For you, I'll stay invisible. I'll be the air you breathe.

Her costumes occupy an entire room in my house. I'm still surprised by how heavy the dresses are; I no longer have the strength to remove them from their bags. All of those rhinestones and beading make some weigh as much as six kilos, some twelve. It's a wonder how Graça ever danced in them, let alone stood for hours on set, propped up by an ironing board at her back so she would not be tempted to sit and possibly ruin her costume.

What's astonishing wasn't the costumes, but the fact that Graça was not swallowed up by them. Any other woman would have seemed invisible beneath the sequins and stones, but Sofia Salvador made them seem natural, almost necessary—the glittering carapace that protected everything vulnerable underneath.

Being a woman is always a performance; only the very old and very young are allowed to bow out of it. The rest must play our parts with vigor but seemingly without effort. Our bodies must be forms molded to fit the requirements of our times: pinched, plucked, painted, not painted, covered, uncovered, perfumed, dyed, squeezed, injected, powdered, snipped, sloughed, moisturized, fed or unfed, and on and on, until such costumes seem innate. Everywhere, you are observed and assessed: walking down the street, riding a bus, driving a car, eating in a café. You must smile, but not too widely. You must be pleasant, but not forward. You must accommodate and ingratiate but never offer too much of yourself, and never for your own pleasure. If you do this, it must be in secret.

Any deviance from this role has the potential for disaster: shun the part and you are trying to be a man; you are a bitch; you are angry; you are pitiful; you are a dyke or, as they used to call us in my day, a "Big Foot." Embrace the role with too much gusto and you are a puta, like my mother. Either extreme can get you beaten, or defiled, or simply killed and dumped in a ditch. If you think I am exaggerating, or that I am trapped in a harsh past and times have changed, then listen carefully to what I am telling you now: when you have no power in this world you must create your own, you must adapt to your environment and try to foil the many dangers around you, so a woman's pleasantness—her smile, her grace, her cheer, her sweetness, her perfumed body, her carefully made-up face—isn't some silly by-product of fashions or tastes; it is a means of survival. The performance may cripple us, but it keeps us alive.

When I think of our first months in Rio's Lapa neighborhood, it's a wonder Graça and I didn't end up dead and floating in Rodrigo de Freitas Lagoon. You could say we had luck on our side, but I prefer to think of it as the economies of scale. When cicadas leave the safety of the earth every seventeen years and crawl into the light, they have no stingers or barbs or poisons to protect them from their predators. Their only defense is their sheer number. So it was in Lapa in 1935—there were girls everywhere. Shopgirls, good-time girls, cleaning girls, cigarette girls, errand girls, candy girls, showgirls, butterfly girls, and girls like Graça and me, who refused to be anything but ourselves. This is, of course, the most dangerous thing any girl can be.

It was easy to disappear. In those days, a regular phone line was a great luxury. Even automobiles were rare. For the police to be notified of a disappearance, someone had to physically run to a station and tell them. It must have taken the Sion Sisters the better part of the afternoon to realize Graça and I were gone, and then to lumber down from Corcovado on the train and fetch the authorities. Senhor Pimentel would have been informed of Graça's disappearance the next day, by telegram.

Riacho Doce was twenty-three hundred kilometers north, in what may as well have been a different country. And what could a northeastern sugar planter know about Rio and its convoluted workings, its dozens of neighborhoods, its lazy police always sniffing for bribes? Plus, President Getúlio wasn't loved by all Brazilians; in São Paulo there'd been a bloody revolt against him, and then the communists tried to lead uprisings in four major cities. With so many threats, Getúlio's police didn't have the manpower or the desire to find a piddly sugar planter's daughter. And if no one could look for Graça, they certainly wouldn't look for me. I was no one's daughter. I was no one's heir. You can't disappear if you've never existed.

We were found eventually, but by then Graça and I had already transformed ourselves. Or, I should say, Lapa transformed us. Sweet, decadent, rotten Lapa! A neighborhood of musicians and thugs, of tourists and pickpockets, and girls—heaps of girls—most of them like Graça and me: so full of hope and naive illusions that we ached inside. Lapa either ruined girls like us or saved them; there were no in-betweens.

Tour company brochures billed Rio de Janeiro as "The City of Splendor." These advertisements never mentioned Lapa, but plenty of visitors—men especially—found the neighborhood. In Lapa's maze of cabarets and juke joints you could find senators listening to foreign jazz bands; handsome young bucks flashing vials of cocaine inside their suit jackets and whispering "Sweet flour!" to any passerby; rebellious debutantes from Rio's best families holding fast to their boyfriends' arms and laughing wildly, masking their fear with giddiness. In Lapa there were rooms you could rent by the hour, and hotels with brass doors as shiny as mirrors opened by white-gloved doormen; restaurants that served Beef Wellington next door to dives with sticky tables and bloodstained floors; boardinghouses with so many residents their hallways were as crowded as cabarets, and apartment buildings with electric lighting and gated elevators where an army of "kept girls" lived in stylish prison, locked inside their rooms until their rich patrons—men and women alike—visited bearing food and department store gifts.

In Lapa you heard the heart-bracing rhythms of samba and the slow, thunderous drums of candomblé rituals, and if you wanted to keep breathing you didn't dare interrupt, either, because both were a religion. At night there were always nervous foreigners alongside Rio's well-dressed elite traipsing through Lapa's alleys, attempting with all their might to escape their privileged lives by doing whatever they pleased with whomever they pleased, and always for a price. Nothing was free in Lapa except for music, and even that changed, eventually.

Graça and I changed, too. I suppose you could say we lost our innocence in Lapa. By innocence I do not mean some silly notion of purity; depending on your definition of virtue, that kind of innocence could end as swiftly as a peck on the cheek. What is more difficult to lose—and terrible when it is lost—is the belief that the dreams you'd nourished as a child are attainable, the idea that hard work can make up for lack of talent, the silly conviction that life doles out her rewards and challenges fairly among us. What is fairness, after all, but an illusion?

Illusions, Vinicius sings in one of our songs, *aren't terrible. They are what make exile, and love, bearable.*

THE AIR YOU BREATHE

Our first night in Lapa, Graça and I ended up at a rooming house run by a square-jawed matron who looked like one of our stern Sion nuns, only without a habit. This was probably why we chose her place; it seemed the safest.

"Pay on time or I give away your room," she barked. "And no male visitors. This isn't that kind of establishment."

Graça nodded and I took the brass room key. I had no idea how we would pay our new landlady at the end of the week, but I kept quiet and followed Graça upstairs. Our room had a sagging bed, a rusted sink, and a dark, unfortunate stain on the floor. Graça sat gingerly on the bed, as if afraid the frame would collapse. She sniffed the air, then leaned and smelled the bedcover. She immediately stood.

"These sheets smell like other people," she said.

"At least they don't smell like dogs," I said, trying to cheer her. Graça covered her face in her hands.

I kept quiet, knowing better than to console. We were exhausted. After taking a tourist taxi from Corcovado to Mayrink—the only radio station in the city—we'd spent the rest of the day on our feet, in front of the station's doors. Graça and I sang for every person who moved in and out of Mayrink. The station's employees laughed at us. They patted our heads. One man gave us a coin, which Graça threw furiously into the gutter. Later, at the boardinghouse, I wished she hadn't done that. With our braided hair and plain white blouses and Sion skirts—mine brown, Graça's blue—we looked like what we were, or what we had been until we escaped: simple schoolgirls. No one took us seriously, but, I later realized, the men were careful not to proposition us because it seemed like we had homes and families. By evening Graça and I were ravenous. Our throats were sore and our feet ached. I was secretly thankful when a security guard at the radio station finally shooed us away.

I took the last of our money (the tourist taxi, we'd later find out, had greatly overcharged us) and bought us a bottle of Coca-Cola and a fried meat pie, food we were never allowed to eat at Sion or Riacho Doce. The soda was warm and terribly sweet. The pie leaked oil.

"Should we go back to school?" I asked, dreaming of our tidy Sion beds.

Graça's lip curled. "Never."

So we found our way into Lapa.

The next morning I woke to find Graça in her camisole, hunched over the edge of the bed. I thought she was sick or possibly crying until I heard ripping. Her school skirt sat on her lap. Using the metal tip of her crucifix, Graça ripped away the threads of her skirt's school patch, the Sion crest.

"They'll be looking for us," she said. "The sooner we get rid of these uniforms the better."

When she finished she admired her work, then lit a match and burned the detached patch, throwing the blackened remnants out the window and into the alley below, along with her crucifix. At the sink, Graça splashed water onto her face and wove her shiny brown hair into a braid. Then she dressed.

"I'm going down the hall to use the toilet," she announced. "Then I'm heading back to Mayrink."

My eyes were crusted with sleep. My stomach ached. Even Sion's breakfast of watery oats and a hard-boiled egg sounded lovely to me. Graça shut the door loudly behind her. I heard her short, purposeful steps to the hall toilet and realized she would not wait for me. She would head to Mayrink alone if I wasn't ready to go. I scrambled from bed and washed my face, using the front of my Sion skirt as a towel.

We were careful to take the same route to Mayrink as we had the evening before, so we wouldn't get lost. Halfway there, Graça stopped walking.

"I'm hungry," she said.

"Me too."

Graça looked impatient. "I need breakfast. I can't sing all day like this."

"We used all our mil-réis yesterday, on the cab and dinner," I said.

Graça stared, confused.

"To buy food we need money," I said.

People pushed past us on the crooked sidewalk. There were sharp screeches of metal against metal as a barber and a café owner lifted the gates from the fronts of their businesses. Near us, an old woman washed vomit from her front steps. She eyed us and upturned a bucket. Water slapped the stone and splashed against our legs, soaking our shoes. Graça jumped toward me and grabbed my hands, as if she was afraid she might be swept away.

"But I'm starving, Dor," she said again, as if this might change things, as if I controlled whether we ate or not.

"We have to get jobs," I said.

"At the radio station?"

I shook my head. "Maybe one day, soon. But in the meantime we'll have to look for something else. To get us by."

"Get us by," Graça repeated. "And once we're by, I can start singing."

"We can," I corrected.

During those first miserable days when Graça and I begged for work, we discovered that our accents alerted people immediately that we were from the northeast, which made us both—even Graça with her lighter skin and her good looks—considered inferior. We also discovered that Lapa was not one neighborhood but two, each with its own tribes, customs, and rules. There was daytime Lapa with its profusion of bakeries, pharmacies, barbershops, fruit peddlers, flower vendors, window washers, shoeshine boys, and countless little factories that made tourist trinkets for foreigners to buy at the docks. This was the Lapa of hustlers and enterprise. Everywhere you looked, there were deals and trades and gossip. Everyone you saw lived in the neighborhood. Nighttime was when outsiders arrived. Shoe repair shops turned into bars, cafés into dance parlors. Newspaper boys reappeared on the streets selling cigarettes and hits of ether. Girls with painted lips lingered in doorways. Neighborhood toughs carried knives and staked out street corners.

At dusk on our second, dismal day in the city, just as daytime Lapa and nighttime Lapa were trading places, Graça and I returned to our boardinghouse without work and faint with empty stomachs.

"Oh, baby girl, you're stoppin' my heart," a man shouted to Graça. He wore a tie as thin as a ribbon.

Graça stared intently at the sidewalk. The man's buddy tipped his fedora and blew kisses. We weren't at Riacho Doce anymore, where all the men were forced to look away from the Little Miss or lose their jobs.

"Hey, Stretch!" the buddy called. I glanced up at him. "Yeah, you!"

he persisted. "Hot damn! Look at those long thighs of yours. What lapas!"

The Sion skirt was the same one I'd had since we first arrived at the convent school the year before and, by the time we ran away, its hem barely covered my knees. On Graça, the skirt accentuated her tiny waist and full hips. Her lace camisole was easily visible under her white blouse and, under that, there was no hiding the fullness of her chest.

"You girls look hungry," the fedora man said. "How 'bout we get you some grub?"

Graça glanced at me. I threaded my arm through hers and walked faster, nearly dragging her along. Those boys weren't harmless and we both knew it; if we were unable to pay for our little room we'd be on the street, at their mercy.

Across from our boardinghouse, a man had set up a little fire and grate where he grilled corn and sold it for five tostões. Graça stared at the fire, then closed her eyes, as if the food was too painful to see.

"I'm going back," she said, her eyes shut tight.

"To Sion?"

Graça shook her head, impatient. "To those malandros. I'm telling them to buy us dinner."

"But they'll want things from us."

"I don't care," Graça said, sinking onto the boardinghouse stoop. "I'll give them anything."

Graça was always a creature of the present—she wanted what she wanted in that moment, without regard to future sacrifices. I slumped beside Graça.

"Someone will give us a break tomorrow," I said. "And we'll buy a huge lunch. You can eat a whole steak if you want."

"Shut up, Dor!" Graça said. "The closest we're getting to a steak is if we steal one off a table, like two street mutts." She hid her head between her knees. She sniffled and let out little moans. The smell of corn and butter grew stronger; my stomach knotted. I pressed my palms to my eyes and tried to think of a plan. Someone kicked the toe of my shoe.

A boy stood before us. His clothes were made of sturdy fabric, though they looked like they hadn't been washed in weeks. His knees were gray, their skin strangely thick. Under one arm he cradled a shoeshine box. In his other hand—its nails rimmed black—he held out a corncob.

"Take it," he ordered.

I hesitated. Graça looked up, her face blotched pink, and snatched the cob from his hand. She ate quickly, her little teeth gnawing until half the cob was white and empty. Before she could eat it all, I grabbed the cob and finished it off.

Hunger sharpens memory. I still recall the smoky taste of that corn; the way the butter slid across my lips; the way each kernel popped between my teeth! As soon as I'd finished, Graça took the cob from me and sucked the last of its butter off.

"We can't pay you back," I said, wiping my mouth with my arm.

"If you could, you would've bought dinner yourself," the boy replied. "I shine shoes on the corner. I saw you gals leaving this morning. Lapa's not easy for new folks. Especially rich ones."

"We're not rich," I said.

The boy looked us up and down. "Some fancy schoolgirl went missing. She got lost in Tijuca Forest a few days back. Wandered off from her school's group. People around Corcovado are still looking for her on the mountain."

Graça forgot the cob in her hands. "Where'd you hear that?" she asked.

"It's in the papers. I can't read, but the men whose shoes I shine sure can."

My chest felt very tight, as if my lungs had been sewn shut and no air could pass in or out of them.

"But you're two schoolgirls and the papers say only one's gone missing," the boy said, then tapped my shoe with his toe again. "Those are real nice. Patent leather. I can sell them—they'll get you a good price."

"We can't go barefoot," Graça said.

The boy smiled, his teeth yellow. A pack of cigarettes peeked from his shirt pocket. "You can get some sandals, real cheap. You've got to pay your landlady, don't you? She's as nice as a dog with rabies."

Graça laughed.

"And listen," the boy said, lowering his voice. "Those outfits aren't doing you two any favors. You look like gals whose families will send police to find you, and no one here likes police, if you catch my drift. You can sell those outfits, too. There's places around here where girls are paid to dress up," he said, and wiggled his eyebrows. "Rich folks that visit at night like some weird shit, I tell you. I know a house where they might want to buy some schoolgirl threads. I can take you there in the morning."

"Why?" I asked.

The boy looked surprised. "You'll give me a cut of whatever you sell. And you'll pay me back for the corn."

"You're a real businessman," I said.

The boy smiled. "Querida, in Lapa that's the only way to be. So, we have a deal?"

Graça and I looked at each other. It was the only offer we'd heard all day. She nodded at me and I at her, as if we were doing business with each other. Then we agreed to meet the boy the next morning to sell the clothes off our backs.

Wearing cheap sandals and secondhand dresses, Graça and I blended in with daytime Lapa, and began to learn its ropes. We got odd jobs sweeping front stoops, husking corn for the vendor on our corner, fetching drinking water from the local pump for our landlady, plucking chickens for a little lunch place, washing dishes, scrubbing windows. Or, rather, I did these things and Graça lagged behind, complaining that her broom was too heavy, the chickens too smelly, the dishwater too hot, the buckets too hard to carry. Still, each morning we set out like explorers, learning Lapa's streets, its alleys, its rhythms.

Carmelita's Alley was where the snobby French girls lived and worked. (In those days anything French was considered high-class.) Joaquim Silva Street was where you found the Poles—blonde and pale with a dour look to them. (I suppose I'd be dour, too, if I was always considered second-rate to a French girl.) Morais e Vale Street was where local good-time girls worked. The borders of Lapa near the Senate, Catete Palace, and the House of Representatives had wide streets, smooth sidewalks, and better shops. Lapa's best cabarets were around there, too. They had marquees with real electric lights, and ticket booths out front where snooty-looking girls sat behind glass and collected money. Inside were second-string vaudeville acts shipped in from the USA and foreign bands, because anything from outside Brazil was considered chic. If you wanted to find real music, you had to risk going deeper inside Lapa.

Of course, Graça and I didn't know what samba was until Lapa. At the time, tango was so popular that Brazilian singers were putting out their own versions in badly accented Spanish. But Lapa's music was different—it had none of tango's toughness or sharp tones. From our boardinghouse window we heard guitars, the metallic clang of agogô bells, the cry of cuícas. There were homemade instruments, too: beans in a tin can, hollow gourds, forks moving back and forth across the sharp teeth of coconut scrapers, the shaking of matches in a box. These were what people called the batucada—sounds that were common by themselves but that, together, became distinct. The batucada moved like a school of fish, always keeping pace with one another whether they were diving forward or pulling back.

Doormen, bellhops, waiters, sweet-flour pushers, street toughs, barbers, and others came together at the end of each day and played for one another, and everyone in Lapa listened. These were not the lighthearted, silly marchinhas that Odeon and Victor later recorded and sold each year during Carnaval. Samba was never truly about happiness.

"I sing to find you.
Hoping my voice will carry
through your window
to your bed
and my words will touch you where I can't."

In our boardinghouse room each night I lay bone-tired beside Graça, her breath on my neck, and listened to those men's laments. Hearing them, I felt slippery inside, as if something had spilled within me.

Those first months in Lapa were, for me, a kind of paradise. Every night Graça and I curled side by side in our sagging bed, holding hands and laughing about our day's adventures. We learned how to use the little money we made, how to bargain, how to wash properly without having a bathtub full of water at our disposal. We learned how to swear. *Porra, asshole, boceta, creep, piroca,* and many other, more colorful words became things we said with relish. We'd also learned Lapa's language: a "hoofer" was a dancer, and we did not wear shoes but "ground grippers." If something or someone was batatas, they were the best around. We did not say good-bye but "Gotta fly!" We called friends and workmates "nêgo" or "nêga." We addressed the shopkeeper on the corner, the butcher, the trolley driver all as "querido" and we giggled each time we did this, thrilled to be calling perfect strangers the endearment that a wife would use for her husband. And I wrote all of it down in my little notebook—the one the Senhora had gifted me long ago—making lists of new words and scenes and smells, until the book's pages began to fill.

During these weeks, Graça and I were together like nail and finger, as we say in Portuguese. In Lapa, we weren't Little Miss and Jega. We weren't Sion Student and Helper. We were, finally, just Graça and Dores.

Years later, Graça told people that this was the worst time in her life. I was surprised every time she said this. Sure, we were dirt poor and learning to navigate a new city, but we were together and surrounded by music. It was foolish to believe that this was enough to make Graça content.

One evening, after Graça and I had finished sweeping the hair from a barbershop floor, she refused the coins the owner offered us.

"We'll get paid in cuts," Graça said, plopping into his chair and holding up her braid. "Lop it off. I'll take one of those Marlene Dietrich bobs. And she will, too."

We couldn't afford tickets to the cinema, but we admired Marlene Dietrich in movie posters plastered around Lapa. Other girls in the neighborhood had taken to wearing Dietrich's risqué hairstyle, cut just below the chin and leaving their necks exposed. Graça, of course, wouldn't be outdone. The bobbed style made her look older and, at the same time, mischievous, like a little girl about to make trouble.

I'd never gotten a haircut in my life. When it was my turn to sit in the barber's chair, I held tightly to my long, heavy braid and thought of Senhora Pimentel—how, years before, she'd brushed and styled my

"Indian's hair," as if it was something to be cared for and admired. I rose from the chair.

"I'm not cutting mine," I announced.

"Why not?" Graça asked.

"I don't want to."

Graça's eyes narrowed. "You look like a goddamn milkmaid. It's embarrassing. If we want to move up, we need new looks."

"Move up where?"

"I'm not working these piddly jobs forever. We're getting our hair cut, and then we're getting a regular gig at one of the tourist shops, where they really pay. First chance we get, we're buying new dresses— no more of these god-awful potato sacks—and we're going back to Mayrink. I didn't come here to sweep, I came here to sing. What about you?"

I returned to the chair. The barber, a quiet old man, wasn't used to cutting women's hair. He held my braid gingerly, then took his largest scissors, the blades cool against my neck, and sliced hard. The braid fell to the floor and lay there, a dark, limp snake at Graça's feet. I looked into the mirror and saw eyes that startled me with their blackness; the sharp line of a jaw; jutting cheekbones made more severe from a diet of coffee and bread; a neck, long and almost beautiful in its nakedness.

The most popular tourist trinkets were tea trays, bonbon boxes, and pencil cups covered with iridescent scenes of Rio and Sugarloaf Mountain. These scenes weren't made with paint. They were made with butterfly wings—detached from their bodies and glued strategically onto any surface to resemble Rio's skyline. Yellow and orange wings for sunsets, blue wings for the sky, black for Sugarloaf, brown for beach sand. Girls like Graça and me did the gluing. A few days after debuting our new haircuts, we were hired to work in a souvenir shop blocks from the Senate.

There were twenty girls in Mr. Souza's shop, each of us paid by the piece. Some girls were better at gluing the wings; their pieces sold for more money. The pay was much better than at our previous odd jobs, but it was tedious work. The glue made me dizzy. The shop's work-room was humid and cramped. The butterfly wings tore easily in my hands. (We had to pay one vintém for every wing we broke!) Graça was worse than I was at our new job. The butterfly wings were very pretty and Graça liked to hold them up in the room's weak light.

"Will you look at this color, Dor?" she asked. "I didn't even know these colors existed."

Graça worked slowly, which made Mr. Souza, the shop's owner, impatient. He often hunched over us while we glued, pretending to look at our work but really letting his hands wander. The first time I felt his fingers brush the side of my breast I nearly knocked my glue pot over. After a few of these brushings, Mr. Souza realized, I think, that there was nothing much on me to feel and moved his attentions to the better-endowed girls. Graça liked to sing while she worked, and, hear-ing her voice, the other girls encouraged her. Mr. Souza didn't com-plain on our first day, but by day three whenever Mr. Souza came close to Graça and his fat little hands tried to cup her bosom, she stopped singing. The silence made us raise our heads in her direction and Mr. Souza backed away.

"No more singing," he announced. "I want work, not chirping!"

At the end of each workday, Graça and I left our table in a great rush, hoping to get to Mayrink before six p.m., when the evening's ra-dio announcers arrived. Graça and I sang for them as they walked into the station's doors, often until our voices were hoarse. There were other street performers—comedians, singers, a ventriloquist—also hoping to land a radio gig, so Graça and I had to rush to Mayrink to beat the pack and grab our corner. But before we could leave the butterfly shop, we had to wait for Mr. Souza to pay us our day's wages, counting our finished pieces and then dropping coins into our hands.

Mr. Souza never had a particular order in which he paid us, but no one ever wanted to be last. Sometimes the last girl was paid like everyone else and allowed to leave the butterfly shop. But every few weeks, when the mood struck Souza, he called the last girl for her payment and made a great show of searching his pockets for more change, quickly declaring that they were empty. The last girl had to receive her payment in his office. He never chose the prettiest girls, but the quietest ones. At the time, I didn't let myself speculate why Mr. Souza took a girl into his office and closed the door in order to pay her. I believed that those girls were no concern of mine or of Graça's. They weren't us, and we weren't them.

After a pleasant month of work, Graça and I were able to pay rent, buy decent food, even put down payment on two new dresses with belted waists and fluttering sleeves, the latest style. Every day after work, on our way to Rádio Mayrink, we walked by the seamstress's shop and admired the dresses in her window, knowing that, soon, we'd be wearing them.

One evening, Mr. Souza paid girl after girl, weaving between the worktables to inspect their pieces. Graça and I waited, shifting impatiently behind our table. After a few minutes, only she and I were left. The other girls lingered around us, pretending to count their money or tie their shoes. Really, they were waiting to see which of us would be last.

Mr. Souza counted our finished butterfly pieces, then turned around and dropped several coins into Graça's hands. My eyes burned from the glue's fumes. I felt dizzy as Mr. Souza shoved his thick hands into his pockets.

"Let's see here," he said to me, then shook his head. "What's your name again?"

"Dores."

Mr. Souza cocked his head in the direction of his office. I glanced at Graça. She pursed her lips and bugged her eyes, trying to warn me. But I'd had a particularly productive day—I'd finished nearly twenty pieces—and if we didn't get my wages, we wouldn't be able to pay our landlady in full for the week, or buy our dresses.

I felt Mr. Souza's hand on my shoulder, guiding me to his office door. I felt the other girls' eyes on my back, watching me just as I had watched some of them follow Mr. Souza into that dark little room with the warped wooden door.

Before we reached the threshold, there was a loud clang. I turned around. So did Mr. Souza. Graça ran from worktable to worktable, collecting jars of glue and tins of wings and throwing them all into the air. The glue jars shattered on the workroom floor. Some of the tins opened before they reached the floor, releasing a cloud of blue and orange and red and black wings. The remaining girls squealed and hooted and held out their hands to catch the floating wings.

"What the hell are you doing?" Mr. Souza yelled, knocking me aside and rushing toward Graça. There were whispers, then the click-clack of heels. The other butterfly girls—who'd lived in Lapa long enough to know when to make a quick exit—pushed through the front door. Souza caught Graça's arm. She threw a tin at his face. He twisted her wrist until Graça staggered toward him, her back against his chest. She yelped.

I felt as if I had been pushed underwater. Sounds seemed faraway and distorted. My vision was a blur. I seemed to move slowly—as if the air had thickened to liquid—taking one stride, then another, using my arms to propel me forward, toward Souza, then leaning, picking up a wooden work stool, and lifting it high over my head.

When the stool came down, sound returned. There was a satisfying crack. Souza slumped to his knees, then fell, face-first, pinning Graça underneath him. She screamed. I dropped the stool, then dragged her out.

Souza stayed quiet on the floor in front of us, a knot the size of a plum on the back of his head. I held on to the rickety worktable so I would not fall, but my body shook so violently that the table wobbled under my grip.

Graça slipped her hand into Souza's back pocket, removed a wad of bills, then stood and grabbed my arm, dragging me across that sticky floor and out the back door.

We ran so fast, everything around us blurred. We ducked into alleyways and wove around fruit hawkers and sweet-flour boys. The butterfly wings were how I kept Graça in my sights as we ran—her curls were dotted with iridescent blues and yellows.

After what seemed like an eternity of running, we ducked into the dark doorway of a shoe repair shop. Graça rested her hands on her knees and leaned over, catching her breath. My lungs felt too big for my chest. My sides cramped. I felt a terrible heat rising in my stomach and worried I was going to be sick. Graça stared at me. I expected her to boast about how fast we'd gotten away, or to congratulate herself for her quick thinking about the money. Instead, Graça took a long breath and asked: "Are you dumb or something?"

"No."

"Well you sure act like it. Don't you know what he does in that office?"

"I wasn't going to let him do it to me."

"So you were going to fight him in there but not out in the open, in front of the other girls?"

My head ached as if I was the one hit by the stool. Why had I let Souza steer me toward that door? Would I have allowed him to touch me for a few measly mil-réis? Why had I stood up for Graça, but not for myself?

"I wanted my money," I said. "How else were we going to pay for our room?"

Graça shook her head. "Well you didn't have to crack his skull."

"You think I cracked his skull?"

"I'm not a fucking doctor! You could've just stepped on his foot. Or kicked his shins. Or kneed him in the pinto. But you always take things too far, Dor. One second you're a little housemaid about to let him drag you into some closet, the next you're a fucking lunatic."

"I was never a maid," I said.

"What were you, then?" Graça asked.

The saliva in my mouth felt too warm; I held my stomach. I wanted Graça to answer her own question: to say that I was her friend. That I was Dor.

"Maybe I'm used to seeing girls get dragged into closets," I said. "It's nothing new to us."

Graça was quiet. Blood leached from her face in patches, leaving a jagged, pale line that ran from her nose to her forehead and disappeared in her hair. "Papai was lonely after Mamãe. He drank too much. He was never like that butterfly pervert."

"If you miss him so much, you should go back."

"Maybe I will. Maybe I'll leave you here to get arrested."

I pictured Souza on the floor, blood leaking from his head. Then I doubled over and vomited on Graça's sandaled feet.

She gasped and staggered backward. "Aw, hell, Dor," she said. Then she moved next to me and tucked my loose hair behind my ears. "It's okay," she said, her voice soft. "All the police care about is arresting commies. And anyway, he's not dead."

"How do you know?"

"Because he's not," she snapped.

"You can't just decide he's alive."

"Why can't I? You can groan and moan and worry all you want, but I'm telling you: he's not dead."

Graça grabbed my shoulders as if she was about to shake me. Instead, she brought her mouth very close to mine and spoke slowly, as if I was a child. "That's not possible. That's not how things are going to turn out for us. We're here to make it big. And you don't have to follow anybody's orders. Not ever again."

The money she'd swiped was stuffed inside her camisole. Graça patted the bulge under her shirt.

"Now let's go home and buy ourselves a real bath in the landlady's tub. With bubbles. I can't smell like vomit for weeks on end, and we've got to get these butterflies off us. Just in case."

I used to wonder what would've happened if I'd had the better voice and Graça the lesser one. Would I have become Sofia Salvador? Would I have been able to withstand the rigors of fame? Would Graça have lived past her twenty-sixth birthday if she hadn't become Sofia Salvador and I had? I realize now that none of these questions matter. Graça would have been a performer no matter what. And I would never be a star—not a real one. Not because I had the lesser talent, but because I had the lesser imagination. I knew how to work, how to avoid going hungry, how to survive. But I always needed Graça to teach me about possibility.

Souza was not dead, just hurt. Another butterfly girl saw us singing outside Mayrink and told us this news, congratulating us for "knocking his block off." The girl didn't mention anything about the money we'd stolen, but this didn't bring relief. When we returned to our singing on the street corner, I fumbled my lyrics and lost harmony with Graça. She glared at me, but I could not regain my focus. Every time I looked into the little crowd gathered around us, I believed I caught sight of Souza's beady eyes or, worse, of Senhor Pimentel's dark hair and arrow nose, and my stomach clenched.

Even before our fight with Souza, Graça and I picked old newspapers out of trash bins and looked for articles about the missing schoolgirl. In the beginning, there was news: police had found Graça's extra Sion shirt (the one she'd flung off during our train ride) in the trees, and this was seen as a bad sign. A group of hobos camping in the forest nearby were questioned and released. The search was suspended due to lack of funds and manpower. There was an article about Sion School and the bad publicity it endured; a few of the Sisters were transferred to faraway convents. There was a petition to make the Tijuca Forest safer. There was mention of Senhor Pimentel and how he held out hope to find his daughter.

After we read this brief article, buried deep inside the Local section, Graça balled up the newspaper and flung it into the trash.

"There's not even a crummy reward!" she said. "He didn't even travel down here to help the search party. If I were a boy, he would've clawed through that forest day and night to find me."

"Do you want to be found?" I asked.

Graça looked in the opposite direction from me. Her chin trembled. "Just wait until we're famous," she said. "Wait until he hears me on the radio! He'll be real sorry he laughed at me then."

At dawn, in our sagging bed, Graça wove stories about how one day she'd ride into Riacho Doce in her own automobile, with furs at her neck and jewels on her wrists, and announce that we were performing shows in Rio! It was easy to get caught up in such vengeful imaginings: I pictured how the kitchen girls who'd once mocked and hit me would stare openmouthed as they served me coffee in the Great House's finest china. I imagined slipping Nena a stack of mil-réis and watching as she removed her apron and announced she was quitting the kitchen for good. Graça only imagined her father—how he would weep, hug her, and beg for her forgiveness. Such things were possible only in our imaginations; as long as the Senhor was alive, we could never return to Riacho Doce. Nor could we live completely in peace anywhere in Brazil.

In 1935, a girl was not simply a girl—she was property. First you belonged to your father, then to your husband. For as long as those men lived you were their ward, on par with a child or a mental invalid. Your emancipation came only after their deaths. As long as Senhor Pimentel walked the earth and Graça remained unmarried, she was his, no matter her age or her success. He could swoop in and claim her and any riches she might have, and every police officer, every law, every judge and jury, would be on his side.

Souza was a simpler matter. Worried he'd want his money back, Graça and I took the route many in Lapa took to avoid being caught for transgressions: we traded daytime for nighttime. Instead of going home after singing at Mayrink, we went to work. We were hired as Candy Girls, hanging wooden trays from our necks with a thick strap and selling chewing gum, cigarettes, mints, handkerchiefs, and glass vials of ether to the posh crowds outside Lapa's best cabarets. Each morning we returned to our boardinghouse feeling empty-headed and exhausted. One such morning, our sour-faced matron waited for us at the door.

"A man came by last night," the woman said. "Asking questions. Wanting to know if I had any girls living here. He showed me a photograph of a little girl, dressed fancy. He said she was the daughter of a planter up north. He wanted to know if I'd seen anyone like her."

My stomach cramped. I wrapped my arms around my midsection. "What did you tell him?" I asked.

The matron straightened. "I don't talk to strange men looking for little girls." She handed me a calling card. "He left this."

On the card was the name and address of a private detective based in Recife. Graça grabbed the card and stared at it for a long time, her eyes very wide, as if she'd taken a hit of ether.

I took her arm and guided her upstairs, to our room. There, I tugged our few dresses from their hangers and stuffed them, along with our tangle of camisoles and underwear, into a canvas laundry sack. As I hunched over that sack, I recalled Senhor Pimentel laughing in my face, his breath sour and hot. Pinpricks of sweat needled my forehead.

"What're you doing?" Graça asked, still holding the card.

"We're leaving."

"Why?"

I stopped packing. "He'll come back."

Graça stared at the calling card. "Detectives cost a bundle. I wonder how long Papai's had him looking?"

"Too long," I said, and tried to pull the card from her hands. Graça snatched it back.

"He's not looking for you," I said. "He's looking for the Little Miss to marry off. And she's rotting in that Tijuca Forest. There's no more Graça Pimentel and no more Jega. Those girls are dead and gone. Right?"

Graça's eyes examined our little room, taking in its yellowed mattress, its stained floor, its crooked window that looked out onto an alley. She moved toward that window and banged it open, then tore the detective's card to pieces and let them fall—one by one—into the street.

L apa's web of alleys and its seemingly endless supply of girls made it easy for Graça and me to believe we could disappear. Our new boardinghouse wasn't any better than our first, but escaping there made us feel as if we'd foiled both Senhor Pimentel and Mr. Souza. We quickly learned, however, that Lapa was smaller than it seemed, and we were more conspicuous than we'd hoped.

The part of our routine that did not change was singing at Mayrink. Every afternoon we stood on the corner and performed tangos and fados until dusk. Few showed us sympathy. Radio announcers got accustomed to our presence and sometimes smiled in our direction, giving us false hopes. (We were too naive to understand the way radio, still in its nascent stage, worked; how announcers had little power; how jingle singers and radio performers paid bribes or performed all kinds of favors to get their parts.) At best, passersby dropped a few coins at our feet. The money was enough to buy hot coffees to soothe our sore throats. I'm sure we would have given up on Mayrink sooner or later and found a different way to get ourselves noticed, but fate—combined with our own stupidity—intervened. Turns out, we'd already been noticed, just not by the people we'd hoped.

One evening, as Graça and I prepared to leave our Mayrink corner, a boy who'd listened to us the entire afternoon walked in our direction. His shirt was crisp with starch; his shorts had two stiff creases down their front from a hot iron. He smiled at us and clapped.

"You're like two little birds! No wonder Madame Lucifer wants to see you," he said.

"Who's that?" Graça asked.

The boy looked surprised. "Well, if you don't know, you're about to find out." He held out his arms as if he was a gentleman escorting us to a dance. "Ready?"

"We've got work," I replied.

"Skip it," the boy said.

"You going to pay our rent?" I asked.

The boy's smile disappeared. "I was sent here to get you kittens, that's my job. And if I don't do it, somebody else will. Somebody not so nice. Seems like you're new here, so I'll get you wise: when Madame Lucifer asks to see you, you don't say no."

Graça and I looked at each other. We could not plot or weigh our options in front of the boy, but we didn't have to. I was curious, and so was she. The boy seemed respectable, and this Madame—whoever she was—did something few had done since we'd arrived in Lapa: she'd picked us out of the crowd. Maybe she owned a cabaret? Maybe she liked our singing? Whatever the reason, in that moment running away from Lucifer's boy seemed more trouble than it was worth, and the last thing Graça and I needed was more trouble.

The boy led us to Morais e Vale Street, where the tall houses, shut-tered during the day, were beginning to open their windows and turn on their lights. An older woman received us at the door to one of these houses. She wore slippers and a silk robe, and ordered us to keep quiet because her girls were asleep. Months earlier I would've thought she meant her children, but after our brief residence in Lapa, I knew better.

The boy remained outside. Graça and I followed the woman through a series of parlors with gauzy yellowed curtains and worn vel-vet sofas. A stooped girl swept cigarette butts and used matches from the floor. In her dustpan were stray buttons and feathers, which the robed matron ordered her to collect and hand over as soon as she'd finished. In the deepest part of the house, the woman opened two glass-paneled doors and motioned for Graça and me to move through them. We obeyed and the woman left, shutting the doors behind us. I remember feeling quite nervous, but then noticing that, in front of us, there was a record player with a large brass horn atop it. Graça and I looked at each other, curious about which record was on the turntable. We walked slowly toward the machine, but before we reached it, I saw movement in the room's far corner.

A man sat in a plush chair, his face in shadow, his legs crossed at the knee. His suit pants were white, his shoes a gleaming black patent, his socks lavender. I'd never seen that color on a man before. He was long-limbed, making the chair beneath him seem cramped. His thin brown fingers tapped the chair's arms.

"You ever seen a record player in your lives?" he asked. His voice was as deep and luxurious as a radio announcer's.

Graça straightened her shoulders. "Sure we have!" she replied.

"Lucky for you," he said, still in shadow. "You look scrawnier than I pictured. Just goes to show that even the tiniest bees can sting. You girls know who I am?"

Graça and I shook our heads.

"I'm the Queen Bee."

The man laughed, tilting his head so we could better see his face. His lips were glossed pink. Graça let out a little gasp. I poked her with my elbow. Never in my short life had I imagined that a man could make himself up; novelty can often be more impressive than sheer force. The man lifted himself from his chair and walked toward us. His long legs carried him gracefully across the room, as if he were on wheels.

"You girls ever hear of a man named Souza?" He fixed his gaze on me, his stare as languid and indifferent as a cat's. His eyebrows were plucked into perfect arches, his lashes as long as a film star's. Before Graça or I could make a sound, the man spoke again, as if our reply didn't matter.

"This Souza, he runs a shop—makes horrible little boxes and things for the gringos to carry back home. He pays me to protect that shop. Lapa's the kind of place where you need a friend like me. Well, a few weeks back, Souza couldn't pay what he owed. He says some girls he hired bopped him on the head and picked his pockets. An ugly girl and a pretty one, he says. Well, stealing from him is as good as stealing from me. So I ask around, talk to some of the gals that work at Souza's place, and, wouldn't you know it? Two girls like the ones Souza talked about sing over at Mayrink every afternoon."

A tinny whine filled my head. My heart beat fast. I felt hot with rage.

"He's a pervert," I said. "We were defending ourselves."

The man nodded. "And you took the opportunity to steal his money?"

"He didn't pay her salary," Graça said.

"That's a hell of a salary!" he said, laughing. "You must have quick hands to earn that much. Which of you bopped him?"

Graça and I were silent. The man sighed and moved back into his chair.

"The boy that brought you here, he's been watching your little corner show a few days now. He said you two can hold a note. Why're you over at Mayrink, collecting coins like little beggars?"

"We're going to be radio stars," Graça said.

The man laughed. "Aren't we all, baby? Now, do me the honor of singing a tune."

We stared at him, then at each other.

"We're supposed to be quiet," I replied. "That's what the Senhora said."

The man waved his long-fingered hand. "A Carnaval parade could make its way through here and those girls upstairs would keep sleeping. Besides, it's time for them to get up and work. Now, sing."

He sat back in his chair.

"Let's do the tango then," Graça whispered. "The one we like from the radio."

I nodded. It was a romantic duet that we'd memorized at Riacho Doce; I always sang the man's part. Graça brushed her hair from her face. She moved her fist near her mouth, as if she was holding an invisible microphone.

"I've returned from the land of forgetting,
   I wasn't a good citizen there.
   I would not give up the memories of our love.
   I refused to let go the sweet agony of my despair."

And then it was my turn. I closed my eyes and forgot the room, the cat-eyed man, the sleeping girls above us.

"I was a slave to your heart,
   to your whims and cruel demands.
   And you repaid me with betrayal
   putting yourself in another's hands."

Our time at Sion had improved the way Graça and I sang together. Being in a chorus of girls had forced Graça to become a better listener, and made me less shy about releasing my voice, flaws and all. In that dark Lapa room, during each solo verse, Graça and I let our voices move around and then, finally, embrace in the last chorus. Together, we produced a sound both delicate and urgent. The room became thick with our layered voices, like the air just before an afternoon thunderstorm.

When we finished, I opened my eyes to see the man on the edge of his chair, elbows on his knees, hands woven together under his chin. The robed woman who'd received us stood in the doorway, her eyes wide. The man stood, slipped his hand into his pocket, and produced a thick wad of bills. He counted several bills—more than we would have made in three months as butterfly girls—and held them in front of us.

"Go buy yourselves some new threads," he said. "And some closed shoes. Those rope sandals make you look like urchins."

Graça and I made no motion to take the money. The man raised his perfectly arched brows and shook the bills at us. I glanced at the robed matron still in the doorway, then back at the man.

"Why are you paying us?"

"I'm not paying you," he replied. "Paying means you've done me a service, and that hasn't happened yet. I'm making you girls a loan. And I'm considering the money you stole from Souza a loan, too—taking out the wages he owed you, of course. Congratulations, girls. You've got new jobs."

"What'll we do?" Graça asked, her voice a whisper.

"I'm not going to waste you two upstairs, if that's what you're worried about. But I'll tell you what you won't do: you won't be singing on street corners anymore. And you won't be bopping people on their heads," he said, chuckling. "You can read and write, can't you? Do arithmetic?"

Graça and I nodded. The man took my hand and pressed the money inside it.

"Good. Now, go to the dress shop on Conde de Lages Street and be sure to tell them I sent you. You'll get more butter on your bread that way."

"What name should we give them at the shop?" I asked. "Who should we say sent us?"

"My proper name's Francisco Marcelino," the man replied, smiling, "but around here they call me Madame Lucifer."

At the dress shop, Graça and I were fitted for three gowns apiece. Upon hearing the name "Madame Lucifer," the seamstress put a rush on our order, and our first new dresses were ready the very next day. At a nearby diner, when we mentioned we were Madame Lucifer's girls, we got double portions of eggs and bread. Graça and I smiled and shoveled the food into our mouths; we hadn't eaten so well since Riacho Doce. And as soon as our landlady discovered we worked for Madame L., she gave us a room with a window that faced the street and not the alley, and with a private bathroom.

Before we'd even started our new jobs, Graça and I discovered what everyone in Lapa already seemed to know: Madame Lucifer was a successful businessman who also offered loans and protection to most merchants in Lapa. Protection from what, we weren't sure. But we learned that he always kept a gold-handled knife tucked into his belt, even when he slept. Just two years before, he'd used that knife to gut a longshoreman in the cramped booth of a bar because the man had called Madame L. a bicha. Each year during Lapa's raucous Carnaval parades, there was a costume contest. Francisco Marcelino always dressed as Madame Lucifer—a temptress and witch in elaborate gowns and enormous wigs. He'd won the contest ten years in a row, and the temptress's name became his own.

Madame L. didn't read or write well, so we became his secretaries. Each morning Graça read him the newspaper (he liked her voice better) and I wrote his correspondence (he preferred my handwriting). He sent letters to the editor and looked for them in the papers each day, though they were never printed. He sent dispatches to his tailor requesting new suits, and cryptic notes to merchants around Lapa, which Graça and I delivered. The notes seemed harmless enough when Madame L. dictated them to me, but as soon as the merchants read Lucifer's cards, many grew pale and immediately handed Graça and me thick envelopes of their own. What was inside these envelopes we could only guess; we'd been instructed never to open them. Another one of our duties was to find the large black Studebaker always dutifully parked on Lapa Street, just at the border with the Glória neighborhood, and rap on its window. The driver always took us to the Royal Bakery, where three kilos of French bread were waiting for us. This much bread filled four enormous paper bags, which Graça and I carried—as warm as babies in our arms—back to the cab. Then the driver took us around Lapa and we delivered loaves to places Madame L. had specified. As ordered, we always saved a loaf for our driver and gave it to him at the end of the ride. Once, one of the drivers broke open his bread in front of us and inside was a vial of white powder. Another driver once forced two loaves from my hands. I explained this to Madame L., who did not chastise me for the loss. A week later, we overheard the good-time girls in Madame L.'s house gossiping: that driver had turned up drowned in Rodrigo de Freitas Lagoon.

Fortunately, the only money Graça and I handled was our salary, which was more than enough for our weekly room and board. Graça was still ogled on the street, but there were no more propositions and no more lewd jokes. Being Madame L.'s girls gave us a sense of freedom, and wealth, that we hadn't had before. When a model in *Shimmy!* magazine appeared in wide-legged trousers, Graça and I went straight to the tailor's shop and put a stack of bills on his counter.

"Pants?" the old man asked. "Those are for the spiky-haired Big Foots. Not for girls like you."

"Big Foots"—that's what Lapans called women with short hair who liked to wear men's shoes and suits, and who liked to keep the company of good-time girls as much as men did.

"Look here, sonny," Graça said, "slacks are the latest. You'd better get ready to make them for all the girls."

We plucked our eyebrows until they were nearly gone, then bought a makeup pencil and darkened them into dramatic arches, just like Marlene Dietrich's. We went to the cinema once a week, and our favorite picture was still Dietrich's *Shanghai Express*. I didn't think I'd be impressed by movies—especially the silent ones—but when Dietrich strutted and laughed and pouted her dark lips on that enormous screen, I felt short of breath.

"Look at her, Dor," Graça whispered. Then she turned in her seat to stare at the other patrons in the smoky movie hall. "Look how everyone looks at her!"

Instead of staying in bed most nights and reading together (Graça with her copies of *Shimmy!* magazine and me with my dime-store novels, which I bought by the dozen), we began to go out on the town. We saw several vaudeville shows that featured jugglers or ugly little dogs balancing plates on their snouts. We went to jazz clubs, which thrilled me. But the music was always cut short by Graça's flirting. There was always a boy in the crowd—either a dapper university student, or a broad-shouldered rower, or a tubercular-looking artist—that caught Graça's eye and offered to buy her drinks. These boys inevitably had friends who were stuck with me each night. While Graça and her boys laughed and nuzzled each other, me and my boys ended up talking. Some could hold decent conversations; others were as dull as rocks. On our walks home, Graça and I made fun of the boys—hers and mine— and called them "knuckle draggers."

"You think we'll ever have real boyfriends?" Graça asked late one night as we lay side by side in bed, trying, unsuccessfully, to fall asleep.

"I don't want one," I replied.

"Every girl wants one."

"Not me," I said, turning away from her.

"Poor Dor. You haven't kissed any boys yet."

"No," I replied, annoyed. I'd seen kissing in the movies, and it looked like a violent smashing together of faces.

"Well, you'd better learn," she said.

"Why?"

"Because! Around here, you have to be able to handle yourself. You have to know how you want to be kissed and how you don't."

"I don't," I replied.

Graça rolled her eyes. "Everyone wants to be kissed, Dor."

"Do you?"

"Sure," she said. "But I don't want bad kisses, like the kind these knuckle draggers we're stuck with around here dole out. Yuck!"

"They're bad?" I asked, happy that Graça disliked all of them.

"They're terrible!" Graça replied. "You could tell they never practiced a day in their lives."

"Practiced?"

Graça sighed at my ignorance. "Even movie actors have to practice, to make their kisses just right. I read it in *Shimmy!* They don't just walk onto a set and slobber all over each other."

"Disgusting."

"Yeah. But not if you do it right. You have to practice, Dor. So you don't embarrass yourself."

"All right," I said.

Graça sat up in bed. My stomach did a somersault.

"First, you have to look into each other's eyes," she said. Graça stared at me, tilting her head. A soft smile spread across her face. My heart pounded as if it would split the skin and bones of my chest. Graça's smile quickly turned into a frown.

"No," she said, frustrated. "This isn't right."

"No?" I croaked.

"First," she said, "you have to have a horrible fight. You have to hate each other."

"But then why would you want to kiss each other?"

"God, Dor! Keep up! You don't *really* hate each other. Here, I'll be the man." Graça straightened her shoulders and crossed her arms. She glared at me. "You're a silly girl!" she said, and then in a whisper, "Come on, Dor. Tell me you hate me."

"I hate you?"

"Say it like you mean it."

"All right," I said, trying to channel the film actresses Graça admired. "I hate you!"

Graça flew toward me. She became a blur. I smelled the rose soap she used on her hair, the slight sourness of her breath. Her mouth pressed hard against mine. I kept my lips closed tight, holding my breath until my chest burned and my eyes grew watery. Graça pulled away.

"That was terrible," she said. "You've got to put some action into it, Dor. Otherwise it's like kissing a lamppost."

"You weren't so great, either," I said, rubbing my top lip. "I felt like you were swooping in to eat my tongue."

Graça rolled her eyes. "That's called *emotion*, Dor."

"Well, can there be a little less emotion? I don't want a split lip."

"Fine," Graça said. "We'll do it your way."

"Fine," I replied. I quickly replayed movie scenes in my head, but none satisfied me; we'd look ridiculous acting out such scenes. Surely life was not like those movies. I thought of my dime-store novels. I thought of Capitu—a heroine in one of those books—and her long, thick hair, and how her boyfriend, Bentinho, must have felt the first time he touched it.

"Close your eyes," I said, worried Graça would laugh at me. She obeyed.

I moved my hand to Graça's hair, stroking it carefully, so my fingers didn't get caught in the curls. I let my fingers run around her ear, then down her neck. Before she could open her eyes, I let my mouth rest on hers. Things came naturally then—more naturally than I could have guessed. Our mouths moved softly. A bit of saliva escaped our lips, making them glide easily across each other. Then, without my realizing it, my tongue moved ever so slightly. Its tip grazed the tip of Graça's. I felt a jolt, as if I'd touched a live wire. Graça must have felt it, too, because she jerked back. Her eyes were wide. She looked at me as if seeing me for the first time. Then she looked away.

"That was all right," she said. "Now you be the girl."

We practiced this way, on and off, for months. After work and before our forays into Lapa's cabarets, I tried to rush us back to our little boardinghouse room. But often Graça wanted to go shopping, or she'd dillydally at the magazine stand while I paced and sighed.

"You need a bathroom or something?" she'd say, and shoot me a withering look.

So I learned to hide my eagerness for our practice sessions, believing Graça was also hiding hers, because once we started she was never reluctant. I realize now that Graça had always been, and would always be, undaunted by her body's needs. Satisfying them was the same as eating a meal when she was hungry, or gulping water when she was thirsty. Once satiated, Graça plowed through the rest of her day without a thought to what had happened before. After our kissing practices, Graça fell dead asleep beside me but I could not shut my eyes. She'd uncovered in me a depth and an urgency of feeling that I never knew existed. I stared at my feet, my rough hands, my flat stomach and even flatter chest as if seeing them for the first time. Before, they'd been tools. They functioned as servants to my mind, allowing me to stir a pot, or to curl up tightly when fists fell on me, or to run through a maze of alleys. It took Graça's hands and teeth and tongue to bring me into myself, to show me that my body was not a shell built to withstand beatings, or a device made to follow my mind's orders. It was not an "it"—it was me.

I wanted more: to explore further, to move deeper. Graça would not have it. We could kiss until our lips were numb but I had to constantly remind myself not to hold her too tightly or let my hands stray below her stomach. If I did, Graça pushed away and the session was over. Each night was a gift and a struggle.

One morning as we sipped coffee at the corner bakery, Graça said something funny and, before I could stop myself, my hand shot out and stroked hers. She pulled away as if I'd burned her.

"Stop," she whispered. "You want people to think we're Big Foots?"

It's said that Adam and Eve felt no shame in the Garden. Only when they were exiled did they look at themselves, at their nakedness, and feel the need to cover up. Many young girls do this sort of "practicing," as we called it. But back then I was foolish. I felt no shame because I was convinced that Graça and I were our own invention. I believed that we were different—that no two before us and no two after would do as we did together, during our practices. We *were* different, certainly, from those kept girls with their wealthy patronesses. We were different from Lapa's rumored spiky-haired "Big Foots." No girl dreamed of becoming either of those kinds of women, and neither did I.

What kind of women did we want to become? I had, in my memory, an image of Nena's authority and Senhora Pimentel's grace. I recalled the queenly dignity of the Baianas we'd seen in Salvador. I watched Marlene Dietrich's shimmering, electric energy on-screen. But these were images and recollections, not flesh-and-blood.

In Lapa, girls in the limelight shimmied and danced in skimpy costumes; they stood in line in identical dresses and sang background vocals; they were magician's assistants, holding scarves and hats; they appeared, kicking their legs into the air, as a distraction before the main act. Women didn't sing samba or tango or jazz. They didn't compose songs or play instruments. They weren't part of the band. Sure, in candomblé terreiros there were priestesses who sang to their gods. And in opera houses there were women sopranos and fado singers, but in Lapa's nitty-gritty? Women were, at best, muses for composers and, at worst, locked inside places like Madame Lucifer's until their bodies wore out.

We steered clear of Madame L.'s place in the evenings, but one night the well-dressed boy found us again and told us we'd been called. When we arrived at Lucifer's there was music playing in the parlor and a gaggle of girls, still in their robes, scattered about playing checkers, reading *Shimmy!* magazine, and devouring bowls of rice.

"Hey! It's the daytime gals!" one of them shouted. "You two get a promotion?"

Graça and I heard the others laugh as we trudged upstairs, to Madame L.'s fourth-floor office. The room smelled of citrus cologne. Lucifer sat behind his desk, his suit impeccably pressed, gold cuff links glimmering at his wrists, and a mole carefully drawn above his glossed lips. He did not smile or ask us to sit.

"You little canaries ready to start paying me back?" he asked.

"We're working for you," I said. "Haven't we already started?"

"You'd have to run errands the rest of your lives to pay what you owe," he replied. "Luckily you didn't come here to make deliveries and read newspapers. You girls ever been on a stage before?"

"We've done plenty of singing," Graça said.

"That's not what I asked," Madame L. said. "I'm not talking about street corners."

"Not a real stage, no," I replied.

Madame L. leaned back into his chair. "Near the Grand Hotel, number fifty-two," he said. "Go there tomorrow after you finish your work for me. Ask for Anaïs. Tell her I sent you."

The Grand Hotel was in the ritzy part of Lapa. Graça and I spent the night speculating which fancy cabaret had the name "Number 52." But when we arrived at the street Madame Lucifer had indicated, number 52 was not a name but an address, and it was not a cabaret but a shop. The store's display windows were shuttered, the glass doors locked. A small brass plate above the door read: "La Femme Chic."

Graça knocked. A woman poked her head outside. She looked like a heroine from a silent film—long-necked and pale, with enormous black eyes and mauve lipstick so perfectly applied it looked as if it had been stamped onto her mouth.

"What?" she asked.

Madame Lucifer's instructions came into my mind but I could not make my mouth speak them. Anaïs raised her penciled brows.

"Madame Lucifer sent us," Graça said, impatient. "I'm a singer."

"Me too," I added.

The woman rolled her lovely eyes. "Lu-ci-fer," she purred in accented Portuguese. "Of course he sends me more singers."

She opened the door just wide enough for us to squeeze inside. What did I expect to find at La Femme Chic? In Lapa, I'd quickly learned that places and people took various forms—men could look like women and women like men; a shoe repair shop also served as a bar; a piece of bread was a place to stow sweet flour; a bellhop by day was a great musician by night. From the moment we knocked on Anaïs's door, I held out hope that number 52 was secretly a great cabaret, but also steeled myself for it to be another brothel. Turned out, Lapa could always surprise me. As soon as Graça and I stepped inside, we both gasped.

Propped upon wooden perches like dozens of bright, exotic birds were the most incredible hats we'd ever seen. There were button plate hats with clusters of red satin cherries. There were berets in colors I'd never known existed. There were little Robin Hood–style numbers with sprays of green feathers along their sides. There were veiled styles that had hundreds of tiny, sparkling stones glued to the netting, making it look as if the hat had been brushed with dew.

In those days, if a classy woman left her house without wearing a hat, it was as if she was wandering around barefoot. Even I was a fan of hats, though I could never afford one. La Femme Chic, it turned out, was the most exclusive hat shop in all of Rio, and Anaïs was its creator.

She inspected our little belted dresses and our bare heads. Then, suddenly indignant, she said: "Come with me if you must."

Anaïs led us out of the showroom and into a cramped and dark parlor. The milliner stood very close to Graça. She pressed a pale hand to Graça's stomach and, for an instant, I thought of Mr. Souza and his back room. But instead of feeling afraid, I felt jealous.

"Breath is a singer's fuel!" Anaïs shouted.

Graça and I jumped.

Once again, she pressed her hand to Graça's stomach.

"Relax here," she ordered. "Breathe in. No, no! Do not gulp air. It is not the quantity that matters, but where the air travels. Breathe again. Again. Again . . ."

We spent that evening, and many others, learning how to breathe. Long before she was a milliner, Anaïs had been a singer. She'd taken classes in France and had even been onstage at several opera houses, as a part of the chorus.

"Voice—it is a mysterious entity," Anaïs said during our lessons. "It is invisible, yet all around us. It must envelop. It must fill a theater, a concert hall! It must communicate every emotion ever known. It must expand, never contract! Expand your voices, my dears, and you expand your souls!"

We did very little actual singing during Anaïs's lessons. She made us practice yawning to relax our throats. She made us stand before a mirror and say "EEEEEE-AHHHHH-EEEEEEE-AHHHHHH" without moving our jaws. She taught us how to expand our rib cages, and what our diaphragms were. She taught us how to walk onto a stage with our chins up and shoulders back, how to smile, how to bow, how to project our voices to reach the farthest listeners, how to keep singing even if we forgot a lyric or botched a note. Outside La Femme Chic, Anaïs required us to drink eight glasses of water a day and prohibited cigarettes. Graça and I obeyed because we respected not only Anaïs's teaching but also her sense of style. If Anaïs said smoking was gauche, or capped sleeves were childish, or bobbed hair was passé, we submitted as though we'd heard a decree straight from the heavens.

Our daily lessons satisfied—for a short while at least—our dreams of becoming performers. From Anaïs, Graça got uninterrupted attention, which she loved, and I—ever the obedient pupil—got a sense of working hard at something I cherished. Anaïs was the first real singer we had ever known. We assumed (correctly as it turned out) that she gave us those lessons because she, like many in Lapa, owed Madame Lucifer a favor. He'd sent other girls to her in the past but, according to Anaïs, those girls had neither the discipline nor the talent to truly succeed. When we asked her what became of those girls, Anaïs's expression darkened. "They found other ways to entertain," she said. "Lucifer, he always puts people to use, one way or another."

The fact that Anaïs continued teaching us gave us hope that we had what those other girls lacked. We weren't the first entertainers Madame Lucifer had taken under his wing but, as far as Graça and I were concerned, we would be the best.

One night, Madame L. appeared at La Femme Chic after our lessons and said he was taking us to a cabaret. We expected a fancy place, with a marquee out front and champagne on the menu. When we arrived, we found a small show house on one of Lapa's side streets. Outside was a wooden sign with the words "Tonight! Miss Lúcia & Her Twin Wonders!"

The club was hazy with smoke. A few men in sagging suspenders watched the stage. A large woman occupied the wooden platform. She wore scuffed heels, purple stockings, and a corset that made her waist unnaturally pinched. Spilling from the top of the corset, covered in a shiny metallic cloth, were the woman's breasts. They dwarfed her head and neck. As she minced across the stage, singing and waving her arms lethargically, the breasts quivered and shook.

Behind her, a tall man played guitar. He hunched over his instrument, his eyes closed, as if trying to imagine himself somewhere else. His body was still but his fingers moved wildly across the guitar strings. Hearing him play, I forgot about the shabby bar and Miss Lúcia's twin wonders. The sound that came from his guitar was crisp and bracing, like walking outside on a cool morning.

He had dark eyebrows, hound-dog eyes, and a mouth twisted in a sly grin, making a dimple appear on his right cheek. Most Lapa musicians at the time looked tubercular and wore their hair slicked back. He wore his without pomade, and had sideburns before they were ever popular. Halfway through the song, the guitar player looked up, and directly at me. It seemed as if everyone in that club had disappeared except for the two of us; I could not look away from him. He looked like a brawler sizing up an opponent. My neck felt hot. Warmth seeped down into my chest, then into the pit of my stomach. I had never taken notice of a man in this way before, and it confused and frightened me. I remember telling myself not to be afraid; that I was a brawler as well.

"Close your mouth," Madame L. said, tapping my arm. "You'll let the flies in."

He guided Graça and me to the bar. At the other end, a very short man in a red suit moved in our direction.

"Lucifer," the man said. "These the girls?"

"Why else would I bring them?" Madame L. replied.

The man nodded. His arms were so short he could barely cross them. He extended a hand to Graça. "Little Tony," he said. "Lucifer tells me you've got quite a voice. But I didn't expect you to be so pretty." Little Tony looked at me and furrowed his forehead. "And you're a whopper! But you've got to get some meat on those bones. You gals ate yet? How about a steak?"

Behind the bar was a small kitchen where the bartender began to cook for us. The smell of meat drowned out all other scents—smoke, cigarette ash, liquor, a faint note of vomit. Madame Lucifer's voice shook me from my trance; he was talking money.

"These girls will bring in a big crowd," Madame L. said. "More people mean more drink sales. I want a cut of that action."

Tony gritted his teeth and nodded.

Onstage, Miss Lúcia bowed deeply, finishing her act. The men around us whistled and banged their rough hands against tabletops. Those weren't the obedient cane cutters from Riacho Doce. They were painters, bricklayers, drunks, and street sweepers. Those men wanted spectacle. They wanted winks and laughter and shaking bosoms. They wanted to forget their grueling workdays by drowning themselves in drink and watching girls cavort onstage. And if they didn't like an act, they wouldn't keep quiet.

"But we're just singers," I said. "It seems like they want showgirls."

Graça glared at me. Madame L.'s heavy-lidded eyes met mine.

"If you've got what it takes, you can win over a pride of hungry lions," Madame L. said. "You want to be entertainers? Well, this is where you prove it. There's a thousand good voices out there, but not everyone can charm a crowd."

The steak arrived, sizzling and fatty, accompanied by two frosty beers. I'd lost my appetite, but Graça chewed large mouthfuls of meat and washed it down with beer, finishing her portion and mine.

Every great performer in Rio had a stage name; Graça and I decided early on that we would be no different. Long before we stepped into Little Tony's joint, on hot evenings when we walked home from our lessons at La Femme Chic, or mornings when we huddled in bakeries and sipped coffees, Graça and I imagined the women we would become onstage. We needed names that were elegant; names that gave us confidence; names that, Graça insisted, had pizzazz. She found her name first.

Of all of Anaïs's clients, a woman named Sofia was La Femme Chic's best customer, buying a hat for each day of the year. Graça was impressed by such self-indulgence.

"Sofia," she said, as we swept pins from the showroom floor. "It sounds like a queen's name."

Another customer—a woman who was less extravagant but more cultivated, in my opinion, than Graça's namesake—was Lorena. I liked her name well enough. Since the first halves of our stage names came from elegant women, the second halves, we decided, would come from places we admired. Graça chose the city where we'd stopped during our first boat ride, while I chose Lapa.

"Sofia Salvador," Graça sighed. "Playing exclusively at the Copacabana Palace!"

"And Lorena Lapa," I added.

Our debut wouldn't be on the Copa's illustrious stage, but as far as we were concerned, Little Tony's ramshackle show house was as good as Rio's finest theater. When we arrived on our first night as performers, the wooden board outside Tony's had changed.

TONIGHT! MISS LÚCIA & HER TWIN WONDERS
AND THE NYMPHETTES

Graça gripped my hand. "That's us," she said. "We're on a board at a real club!"

Backstage was a dark, stuffy area infested with mosquitoes. Miss Lúcia took Graça into the club's tiny dressing area while I searched for the guitar player. Little Tony didn't care what we sang, so Graça and I had decided to perform two of the most popular tangos at the time: one upbeat and the other slow and sad. We had to let the guitar player know our choices before the show began, so he could properly accompany us onstage. That night, the musician was nowhere to be found.

I fretted and paced behind the stage's curtain. On the other side of that stained velvet, Little Tony's patrons ordered drinks and dragged chairs near the stage. It was a weekend night and the house was packed. Soon, it would be time for Miss Lúcia to entertain the crowd, and I was still in my street clothes.

When the guitar player finally appeared backstage, a cigarette dangled from his mouth. A curtain of dark hair obscured his eyes. He walked quickly past me. The guitar case he carried bumped my leg.

"Excuse me!" I called.

"Sorry," he mumbled, and continued walking.

I blocked his path. "You're the accompanist?"

With his free hand, the man removed the cigarette stub from his lips and flicked it away.

"What do I look like, a senator?" he asked. "Who're you?"

The cigarette landed near my feet, which were stuffed uncomfortably into the open-toed heels Graça had forced me to wear. I teetered away from the lit butt.

"I'm one of the Nymphettes," I replied.

"What's that?"

"The new act."

The man sighed. "The new Baby Doll, you mean."

"No, the Nymphettes."

"That's just a new name for the same kind of girl," he said. "The Baby Dolls, the Bonecas, the Nenês, the Bebês. Tony's had them all, thanks to Madame Lucifer. I think Lucifer wants to be onstage more than the girls he sends over. I bet he could sing better than them, anyway."

"We can sing better than anybody," I said.

The man laughed. "I'll believe it when I hear it, querida."

"I don't know who your querida is, but she sure isn't me," I replied. Then I told him the songs in our act. "Do you even know how to play them? Or do you need some help?"

The guitar player grinned. "Everybody knows those songs. They're not exactly original choices. I could play them with one hand behind my back."

"I'll believe it when I hear it, querido."

The guitar player laughed. Behind him, Little Tony ambled backstage. His presence made the small space even more cramped. The guitar player's arm pressed against mine.

"Vinicius," Little Tony said. "Get out there. Play a little ditty before Lúcia goes on. The crowd's getting restless. And you," Tony said, eyeing my street clothes. "For God's sake get dressed. You look like you're here to bus tables, not sing onstage."

In the dressing room, Graça was already transformed into a Nymphette—hair in pigtails, freckles painted across her rouged cheeks. Her dress was gone and in its place was a body stocking that Miss Lúcia called the "Eve suit." There were two suits, both of them pink and pale, even compared with Graça's skin. Graça's hands and feet stood out, and mine were so much darker than the suit that it looked like I was wearing tan gloves and socks. Sewn onto the front of the flesh-colored stocking were small green leaves that were supposed to cover our "private bits," as Little Tony called them. The suits, soiled at the elbows and knees from previous performers, had been sized for different girls. Graça was busty, which made the suit pinch and pucker up top. I was straight as a rail, so my suit sagged in several unfortunate places. The little green leaves sat either too high or too low on both of us, making even Graça's perfect body look strangely lumpy and uneven.

As we waited in the wings for our act to begin, beads of sweat pushed their way through the thick layer of makeup on Graça's face. Her forehead glistened.

"I'm going to vomit," she said.

"Here?"

"Of course here!" she snapped, then nodded toward the stage, where Miss Lúcia traipsed back and forth. "I can't do it out there!"

"All right," I replied, and grabbed a garbage bin. "Go ahead."

Graça took the bin and eyed me. She expected some kind of reassurance, but what could I give? If I told her we'd be a hit on that stage, she would hear the hesitation in my voice. The only crowd we'd ever performed for were her father's employees; even if we'd been awful, they would have clapped for us. I thought of Vinicius, the guitar player, and what he'd said about the previous Nymphettes and Baby Dolls: they weren't singers at all. I imagined those Nymphettes wearing our Eve suits and kicking up their legs, giggling, and shaking their rumps for the crowd. They were not artists and probably hadn't pretended to be. What, then, was Madame Lucifer thinking, putting us in front of that gang of Lapa men?

I took Graça's clammy hand in mine and told her the one thing I did believe: "Pretend those men don't exist. We don't need them. We sing for ourselves."

Graça tilted her head, confused. "But Dor, we *do* need them. There's no point in singing if no one hears you."

Miss Lúcia left the stage. Vinicius began to pluck the first notes of our tango. Without any introductions or welcomes, Graça ran onto the stage. I scurried behind her.

There were catcalls, whistles, and drunk hoots. My hands grew numb. Beside us onstage, Vinicius stubbornly continued to play the first notes of our song, but Graça and I were silent. In the back, at the bar, I caught sight of Madame Lucifer's finger-waved hair, his watchful gaze. A tingling sensation crept over my scalp. I felt as if someone was tugging my hair by the root, pulling me offstage. My breath came too quickly. I opened my mouth but no sound came.

There were boos. Stomping feet.

Come on, girlies! Give us a twirl!

Someone gripped my hand. With more force than I'd ever expected from her, Graça tugged me close, until we faced each other.

Woo hoo! Fiu fiu! Now we're talking!

Graça's eyes locked on mine. Her neck lengthened, her chest puffed out, she opened her mouth, and her voice—so sure and sweet—worked its way into me, parting my lips until my own mouth opened and released the same song.

"I was your heart's slave.
I bowed to your whims, O Love!
With you I came to know,
love's intoxicating delights.
But then you left me, little girl.
And I feel my soul shrinking, little by little."

Our voices poured into every dark corner of that miserable club. There was no more whistling, no more chatter, no more sound except our own. And Vinicius's playing, of course. As we sang, his guitar buoyed us. His notes pressed Graça and me forward when the song demanded it, then pulled us back to be softer and milder in the tune's more tender moments. We sang the song's chorus over and over, but each time it sounded different, and better, than before.

Nena used to say: "God protects drunks, fools, and dogs." That night, Graça and I were the fools. We walked onto that dimly lit stage without any kind of rehearsal, wearing dirty and ill-fitting jumpsuits, and faced an audience who wanted things we could not deliver. Or so we thought. Something I learned that night—and would recall forever afterward—was to never underestimate your audience. Those lowly bricklayers, clerks, trolley drivers, and shoe shiners that crowded Tony's bar were born-and-bred Lapans, and in Lapa, music was faith, it was a healing balm, it was how you spoke to your gods and your lovers, it was how you respected your dead loves and courted your living ones, it was what you turned to in your darkest moments, and how you celebrated your best ones.

Those men may have been expecting two silly and lewd girls with poor voices, but they did not object when they got two serious ones. Of course, if we'd been mediocre, they would have pelted us with limes and bottles. But Graça's voice was perfection and mine was imperfection. Hers was triumph and mine was loss. Together with Vinicius's guitar playing, there was a perfect synchronicity among the three of us.

At the end of our set, there were no catcalls, no whistles, only clapping.

"One more!" a gruff voice cried. The applause grew louder.

There was a saying in Lapa that went like this: As long as you have a song inside you, you are never alone. That night, so many songs rose within me they felt as necessary and unwavering as a heartbeat. On one side of me was Graça, flushed and glowing with confidence. On the other was Vinicius, gentle and wise. Until that moment, I had never had a home or a family. I hadn't even known I'd wanted such things. But that night I found my place in the world—there, on that stage, alongside Vinicius and Graça. I believed my loneliest days were behind me.

WE ARE FROM SAMBA

Before we can get serious, girl,
you'll have to meet my family.
So I'll take you to a roda,
to see who raised me.

I'm not from Santa Teresa or
    Lapa,
Copacabana or Tijuca,
I'm not from Botafogo,
Praça Onze or Urca.

I am from samba, my love.
She was my only mother.
My father may have been the
    batacuda,
but she could have had others.

In the circle you'll meet my
    brothers
and some sisters, too.
There's Tiny playing his
    cavaquinho,
he'll try to flirt with you.

That's handsome Bonito on the
    cuíca.
And ugly Noel, beating his
    pandeiro drum.
Kitchen can hit the agogô bells,
and scrape the reco-reco with his
    thumb!

The serious girl is Dores,
who can make lyrics for any tune.
The smiling one is Graçinha,
her voice will send you to the
    moon.

Banana is the snappy dresser,
who plays the guitar with seven
    strings.
The tall one's the Professor,
who can play anything.

We're not from Santa Teresa or
    Lapa,
Copacabana or Tijuca.
We're not from Botafogo,
Praça Onze or Urca.

We are from samba,
she is our only mother.
And the roda is our family,
we'll never have another.

All of the songs we have ever heard and all we will ever hear are
made of twelve simple notes. Complexity comes when these
notes are put together in an infinite number of combinations and then
played slower or faster, repeated or not. Music is highly organized
sound. It is a language we learn without even realizing it. We hear our
first song and decipher its repetitions, its orderliness. The song teaches
us what to expect and when to expect it. We learn to associate low notes
with sadness and high ones with pep. Soon, we hear a brand-new song
and its notes collide with our memories of past tunes. We have expectations for this new song. Even if we don't entirely know what is coming next, our instincts tell us where the song might take us, and what
memories it might unearth.

The year before Vinicius turned seventy-six and became house-
bound because of his illness, we took a trip to the Grand Canyon. By
then we were living in Miami, married to each other for nearly twelve
years and mourning Graça for forty-two.

At the canyon, there was a viewpoint with a man-made stone bar-
rier; Vinicius and I stood at the edge and stared into the crevasse, at the
many layers of rock and the blue shadows of clouds. The other side of

the canyon was visible, but well beyond our reach. Vinicius set his hand on my shoulder. "Makes me feel small," he said. "Insignificant in the story of the world."

I put my hand over his. "It makes me feel right at home."

There is a gap between our reality and our desires. If we are lucky, we live safely on one side and spy the other. Sometimes, we are able to bridge the gap, to cross the void, but only for a short while. When Vinicius and I made music, when we forgot the world and were lost inside our songs, it was as if we'd held hands and jumped the divide, together.

After Graça died, the leap was too wide. We both fell into the void, though Vinicius would never admit it. In his mind, he was left behind and dutifully tried to clean the mess. And me? I was the mess.

I walked through the world as if I was wading through concrete. Food had no appeal to me. Attraction to another human being never crossed my mind. I grew skinny and unkempt in middle age. I drank too much. I tried the patience of the few loyal people who still considered me a friend. Vinicius was one of them. We both lived in Las Vegas during those years, but not together. When I was kicked out of an apartment he always got me a new one. He paid my rent. He visited. During his first visits Vinicius turned on the radio, trying to get me to hear some newfangled music or other. I'd tell him to shut it off. One day he arrived carrying an old record player. I told him I didn't want it. He told me to throw it in the trash myself then. The machine was heavy, so it stayed.

During his visits Vinicius brought records: bossa from Brazil; a few Motown albums; Aretha Franklin; Patsy Cline; and later Dolly Parton and James Brown. We'd listen together at first, starting off with a song or two and eventually building up to listening to an entire album together. We'd talk afterward about the tracks, the voices, the songs' merits and flaws. Vinicius started leaving those records at my place until they sat in a stack beside the player and I couldn't help but put them on the turntable when he wasn't around. One night he asked me to leave my squalid apartment and go with him to a club—a hole-in-the-wall off the Vegas Strip—to hear some blues. We sat in back so I could make a quick escape. The place was dark and nearly empty, which was a relief. The kid that played was good but not a revelation. But, Vinicius liked to point out, for the hour we were there listening, I didn't touch the drink I'd ordered. After this, we went to music clubs regularly and on those days I drank a little less, so I could enjoy the shows.

One day, Vinicius picked me up and took me to a studio.

"I've got some songs to record," he said. "A couple young cats from Rio are staying with us. I thought you could help us pick our set list."

He was always trying to make me feel like a help and not a burden. It was a little game of his during my drinking years, before we were married. That day, I played along. It was 1972. Graça had been dead for twenty-seven years by then—nearly as long as she'd been alive. Brazil was in the grips of another, much more brutal military dictatorship. When musicians from Brazil came to visit, it meant they'd been exiled for their music. Vinicius gave them places to stay, food to eat, and a network of musicians to call upon in the States. In exchange, Vinicius recorded albums with those young, long-haired bucks who didn't look like men or women but something in between. They called their sound Tropicália.

That day, the young man in the studio with Vinicius was a kinder-looking version of an old bandmate of ours named Kitchen, who was now long dead. The boy was twenty-five with an Afro and bell-bottomed pants and high-heeled boots. I was fifty-two years old and felt ancient beside him. I hid in the back of the studio, behind the glass, but the boy found me.

"You're Dores Pimentel," he said. "It's a real honor to meet you."

"Why's that?"

"You're . . . well, you're the other half of Sal e Pimenta. Yours and Vinicius's songs are classics. My mother used to listen to 'Without Regret or Virtue' so much she wore out the record. She saw you two play your first show in Ipanema."

"Our only show."

"I'd love to record a track with you and the Professor. It'd be the privilege of my life."

"Did Vinicius put you up to this?" I asked.

The boy shook his head.

This was how the three of us—Vinicius, the boy, and me—ended up in the dark recording studio together, on the other side of the glass. I hadn't sung in decades, since our first and last show in Ipanema, the night before Graça died. Both Vinicius and the boy promised that it was just a practice session, just for fun. So they played their guitars, and the boy and I alternated verses. We sang "We Are from Samba." My voice had become deep and husky from years of smoking and alcohol. It was like a shadow voice to the boy's bright and crisp one. The song returned to me easily. I felt, for that moment, that we were in Lapa again.

Vinicius liked the sound of the boy and me together, so we spent the afternoon recording one old song after another. I didn't need a drink until we'd finished. The next day, we recorded more.

I realize now that his visits, the radio, the record player, and the clubs were all bread crumbs Vinicius put in my path to help lead me out of the void, to where he was waiting.

That boy is a great star now. He comes to Miami to play shows and visits me each time. His hair is short and gray. He wears glasses and tailored suits, but he is still a boy to me. Our record together still sells well and is considered a classic fusion of samba and Tropicália. Each time I listen to it I do not hear the genres or the words or the songs themselves as much as I hear myself, calling out from the darkness, emerging from my nothingness with a song.

WE ARE FROM SAMBA

At sixteen I believed I was a musician. I believed our act at Little Tony's made Graça and me important in the world. And what a tiny world ours was! We didn't see beyond our little corner of Lapa, our boardinghouse room, and our place on Tony's rickety stage. We were, like many girls that age, blind to history unfolding around us. What did it matter that women had been granted the right to vote when elections were constantly postponed? What did it matter that Old Gegê (as we Lapans called President Getúlio) had ousted every elected governor in the country and replaced them with his own men, calling them "Interventores"? What did it matter that, thanks to Gegê's new National Security Law, police jailed so many dissenters and suspected communists that old cruise ships were refurbished into floating prisons in Guanabara Bay? What did it matter that these men and women would never see a judge or jury, and their fates would be decided by the Supreme Security Tribunal of Gegê's military men? These were concerns for university firebrands, or newspaper editors, or wealthy intellectuals in their Santa Teresa mansions—not for us Lapans, who'd always been ignored, who never cared for doctrines (communist or otherwise), and whose only concerns were music and making a buck.

By 1936—six months into our run at Little Tony's—the crowd

there came to depend on Graça and me, just as they depended on their shots of sugarcane rum. Thanks to the Nymphettes, ticket sales doubled, then tripled. Madame Lucifer was happy. Little Tony placed a new sign outside the club's door where the Nymphettes got top billing. When Graça and I took the stage each night, the rowdy club fell as silent as church. Even Gegê's "Tomato Heads"—a special regiment of police who wore red berets and were notorious for strong-arming their way into Lapa cabarets and ruining shows with their rowdiness—sat respectfully during our shows, as quiet and reverential as altar boys.

Something important was happening in Lapa. No one spoke of it, but there was a charge in the air, a buzz you felt in your bones. Radios became cheaper, so every corner bakery suddenly blasted music. You heard less tango and jazz and a lot more samba—not the real kind, just the idiotic marchinhas people sang during Carnaval: songs about parties and pretty girls. Songs that the clueless listeners outside Lapa—the ones who believed that samba was the music of voodoo and violence and lust—could stomach. Three recording companies—Columbia, Victor, and Odeon—set up studios downtown, just close enough to Lapa to be "authentic." And, at night, if you wandered Lapa's alleys, you saw many respectable university boys speaking our slang and looking to hear "real music," whatever they believed that was.

Who was I to judge? What on earth did Graça and I know about real music, either? At the time, thanks to our lessons with Anaïs, we thought ourselves experts. Those lessons, like our role as the Nymphettes, consumed us. I'd never seen Graça take any study, before or since, more seriously than our daily appointments with Anaïs, though our young teacher seemed to take little pleasure in hearing us sing. Anaïs sighed. She shook her head in frustration. She often told us that our voices were wild and needed taming. But she continued teaching us, which meant that Graça and I had talent. It meant that Sofia Salvador and Lorena Lapa had great potential together.

You see, I only thought of us as a duo.

Our lessons with Anaïs grew longer but my time with her grew shorter. It was Graça's stomach that Anaïs pushed and prodded. It was Graça's breathing she complained about, and Graça's vocal range she chastised. More and more I sat in the back of the parlor, watching Graça and Anaïs work. I chewed my nails in frustration, then tapped my foot against my chair until Anaïs was forced to notice me.

"This is not a roda, Dores," our teacher said. "We do not need your improvised instruments."

"If I'm not going to sing I need to do something," I said. "When will it be my turn to do the breath work? How will I get better if I don't practice, too?"

Graça rolled her eyes. Anaïs stared at me, her usual look of frustration replaced by what seemed like concern. She ordered Graça into the empty hat shop to perform one hundred vocal exercises. "And do not try to cheat," Anaïs warned her. "Dores and I will be here listening."

Graça obeyed. Anaïs sat in the chair beside me, her leg touching mine. She was older than me by ten years at least, but because she was not married or burdened with children like most women her age, I saw Anaïs not as a matron but as an ideal. She wore a pencil skirt that clung to her hips and exposed her long, pale calves. My palms were clammy; it took great effort on my part to sit still. *Finally!* I thought. *I am getting the same attention as Graça!* I'd spoken my mind, and Anaïs had realized that both of us—Graça and I—deserved equal time! The look of concern she'd shown me minutes before was real.

"You love music, yes?" Anaïs asked.

I nodded.

"So do I," she said. "When I am at my worst, it is my only comfort. Music, not performing. Music is much more than performing. You must understand this difference, Dores."

I snorted. "Of course I know the difference."

"A singer is not like a composer or a conductor or even a player in a band," she continued. "Singers cannot turn their backs on the audience. They cannot hide behind an instrument. They must face us. They must surrender themselves to the song and take that journey of the words. They must be impressive. To the audience, the song and the person are one. I was a singer for a bit, but only in a chorus. I was never alone on-stage. My voice could not sustain it. It is dangerous to be onstage, so vulnerable, and not have a voice to protect you. So it is for the best that I did not become a singer. It was quite sad for me, to realize that my talent was not enough. But it was better this way. Graça, she has a talent. Her voice, it can protect her onstage. It can sustain being alone."

"She won't ever have to be alone," I said. "She has me. We're an act."

"An act is what you find at a circus," Anaïs spat. "When people hear a true voice, they forget themselves. This is what all of us want, even if it is just for the length of a song."

"I can make people forget themselves," I said, cutting Anaïs off. "I can work harder. I can practice more. But I can't do anything if you make me sit here and listen to Graça all day. I need to sing, too."

Anaïs's large, liquid eyes met mine. There were the finest wrinkles around her mouth and eyes, like tiny cracks in smooth sand. She was so young, but to me, in that moment, Anaïs seemed ancient and danger-ously wise, like one of those goddesses the candomblé worshippers paid tribute to, a flawed deity who could be selfish and vengeful if she wasn't praised. I felt both angry and afraid of what she would tell me next.

"All of the practice and intelligence in the world can't make a singer, my darling," Anaïs said. "Voice, it is a wild thing. There is no justice to it. Either we are born with it, or we are not. Do not try to force what cannot be. That is the saddest waste of a life."

I picked at the tip of one of my fingernails until it loosened. Then, with great purpose, I ripped the tip from the nail, until my finger bled.

Anaïs rested a hand on my cheek. "I am sorry, my flower," she whispered.

At every lesson I'd wanted her hand on my stomach, her fingers lifting my chin. But in that moment I couldn't bear Anaïs's touch or her pity. I shook her away.

Graça had always been the better singer; I'd never denied it. But that didn't mean my voice wasn't worth hearing. Singing was something Graça and I had always done together, and until that moment, I'd believed we would always share the spotlight. Anaïs had wounded me. Like an animal, I bit back.

"You like Graça, not her voice," I said. "I see you looking at her."

"Oh," Anaïs said, surprised. "No. She is lovely, but she is not my type of beach, as you Brazilians say."

We stared at each other. Anaïs was the first to look away.

"When I came here, to Brazil, oh, how many hopes I had! I was your age—still a child—and gloomy because I had not become a singer in France. I had been studying since I was a tiny girl. My family had pinned many hopes onto me. And so I escaped from them, and from my failure. Some of us love music. Some of us can make music. And some, if we are lucky, can teach others how to make it. You girls are not the first Lucifer has brought to me. But Graça, she is the best. She can be on a real stage one day. Lucifer knows this. So I must focus on Graça now, in our lessons. Lucifer can be a very loyal friend, but he is not a man to anger."

"*It* isn't my beach," I said. "That's how we'd say it. You don't have to say 'she.' I already know what you're talking about."

"Do you, Dores?"

Warmth crept up my neck, rising to the tips of my ears. "Girls . . . I mean, women, aren't your beach."

Anaïs shook her head. She cupped my chin in her hand. Then, very gently, she moved her thumb across my lips, tracing them again and again, until her finger was wet with my saliva.

"*She's* not my beach," Anaïs said.

Graça finished her round of exercises and came bounding into the room, ready for praise. Anaïs stood. I looked down at my hands. My ripped nail was bloody, but it was my mouth that throbbed.

What was I to do? I was sixteen and an adult had told me a painful truth. Of course I did not accept it gracefully.

On our walk home from that terrible lesson at Anaïs's, Graça chatted endlessly about boys and new songs and other nonsense. My head ached. I could not bring myself to tell her what Anaïs had said. A few hours later, when Tony introduced the Nymphettes onto his stage, Graça and I held hands and stared at each other as we always did, but my eyes became blurry with tears. Graça furrowed her brow and kept singing, her voice soaring above mine. I tried to catch up, to be louder, more powerful, more graceful, but was left a wheezing and red-faced mess. After the show, I bought a pack of cigarettes and matches.

"Who're those for?" Graça asked.

"Me."

Graça snatched the cigarettes from my hands. "You can't have these. Anaïs says so. They'll make you sound like you've got gravel in your throat."

I twisted the pack from Graça's grip. "I don't care what that French snob says."

"Since when?"

"Since she told me I'm not good enough to take lessons with her." My voice cracked.

Gently, Graça held my hand. "What the hell does she know?"

"Everything."

"We've got our gig at Tony's, and we'll have plenty more after that," Graça said. "So throw those goddamn cigarettes away. Or whatever's left of them."

The pack was a mangled lump in my fist. I laughed and wiped my eyes. Graça laughed, too. I recalled our practice sessions, her mouth warm and wet against mine, the way we pressed together with such urgency it was as if we wanted to inhabit each other. I wanted to feel that right there, in the middle of that Lapa street, with her. Without thinking, I wrapped an arm around her waist and brought her closer. Graça stiffened. She glanced around the dark alley.

"Stop," she whispered. "That's not how I want things."

It seemed to me that Graça and I had always wanted similar things—music, escape, being more than anyone thought we could be—and we'd always wanted them voraciously, and with each other. But now I was in front of Anaïs all over again, listening to proclamations I couldn't bear to hear.

I backed away from her, my hands up like a criminal. "Don't be a prude," I spat. "It's just a hug. You're not my beach."

She winced as if I'd struck her, and my shame ebbed.

We walked to our boardinghouse in silence. Over the next few days, when we did speak to each other, our talk was overly polite, as if we were roommates who had just met the day before. Meanwhile, I broke all of Anaïs's rules: I drank, I yelled, I smoked so many cigarettes I hardly had enough breath to get from my bed to the bathroom in the mornings. I spoke harshly of Anaïs to anyone who might listen, calling her a snob and a Big Foot. I skipped her afternoon voice lessons even though she'd insisted that I could, at least, learn more about music by listening to Graça sing. Instead, I spent many horrible afternoons in bookstores, huddling in back aisles, pretending to look though novels while crying and wiping my nose on my sleeve. Each time the store's bell rang, I looked up, hoping to see Graça weaving through the crowded stacks of books in search of me. I imagined us holding hands and begging each other's forgiveness. I imagined her telling me that she'd quit Anaïs's classes, too.

It was only onstage, as the Nymphettes, that we truly came together, and only for the course of our show. During this long and polite fight, Graça went on dates with university knuckle draggers. They took her out until dawn, when she'd return to our boardinghouse trailing sand across the floor and flop into bed next to me without even washing her face. I was always awake, waiting, although I pretended not to be. Graça slept with her back to me, and after her nights out she smelled of smoke and yeast, salt water and wind. Part of me wanted to press my mouth to her bare shoulder, to taste the salt on her skin. Another part wanted to slip my hands around her throat and twist.

After our shows, Graça tugged off her Nymphette costume and ran to meet some knuckle dragger who was always lurking near the bar. I took my time in the dressing room, rubbing off my Nymphette freckles and rouge and steeling myself for my walk home, alone. I often grabbed a drink at the bar before nodding goodnight to Vinicius, who always nodded back. One night, however, he made his way to the bar and stood in front of me, the tip of his battered guitar case brushing my knee.

"I'm heading to Auntie Ciata's," he said. "Want to come?"

I stood, looped my arm through Vinicius's (startling him and me), and said with confidence, as if I knew exactly what Auntie Ciata's was, "I'd love to."

Vinicius loped toward the door. He was in his late twenties like Anaïs but I considered Vinicius ancient. I suppose it was because of the way he carried himself; each time I saw him I remembered Bruxa's lessons on gravity and wondered if that invisible weight pressed him more than the rest of us.

I let go of his arm as soon as we left Tony's, but as Vinicius and I walked along Lapa's dark alleyways, I felt triumphant; Graça wouldn't find me waiting pathetically at home after her date.

"Hold this, would you?" Vinicius asked, handing me his guitar case. It was heavy but I obliged. He slipped a metal cigarette case from his jacket pocket. "Want a smoke?"

"Yes," I said, not knowing what I was accepting.

Back then, Vinicius smoked hand-rolled cigarettes made with Onyx tobacco that made me dizzy after just two puffs. (Even now I get a craving for those cigarettes, a craving for those first few puffs that made my lungs burn and my ears buzz.) Vinicius pulled two from his case and placed them both in his mouth. He passed me a lit cigarette, its end wet from his lips, and I felt a secret thrill to be placing that cigarette between mine. Vinicius took his guitar case back. We continued walking.

"So how'd Lucifer get his hooks into you two?" Vinicius asked. "What do you owe him?"

"Why do you think we owe him anything?"

Vinicius shrugged. "Everybody's got a debt to pay."

I remembered the cigarette Vinicius had given me and took a long drag. My chest felt as if it was on fire. "Madame L. heard us sing and liked us," I replied. "Simple as that."

"Nothing's simple around here," Vinicius said. "Except for those tangos you sing. You girls ever hear a proper samba in your lives?"

"What's a proper samba?" I asked. "Why's that any better than our music?"

Vinicius laughed. "No offense, but the ditties you sing at Tony's aren't music, they're shit. Graça's got a heck of a voice, though. Plenty of girls want to be cabaret stars, but it's not enough to be a good singer, you know. You've got to have something different. I hear that in her voice. It's like she wants something but can't have it."

"You can hear that?" I asked, slowing my stride.

"Sure," Vinicius said. "Your voice is different—sadder, rougher—but not in a bad way. It's like you've been around longer than seventeen years, or however old you are. Everyone hears different things in different singers. When a singer's really good, you hear yourself in them. You know what I mean."

He said the last sentence not as a question, but as a statement. And it was flattering, to be held in such regard, to have him believe I understood.

We were quiet for the rest of our walk. It wasn't an awkward quiet but a reassuring one, as if we knew all there was to know about each other and didn't need conversation to draw it out.

When Vinicius arrived at Ciata's with me in tow, the men in her yard exchanged smiles.

Years after Auntie Ciata's place was torn down, some fools claimed that her house was the birthplace of samba. Others said it was a ter-reiro, where pagans went to practice their candomblé religion. And some historians even claimed that Auntie Ciata never existed—that she and her house were representative of many houses and many Baianas who allowed samba to evolve in Rio. I can quash all of those theories: samba was not born in Auntie Ciata's house, but she did exist and she never separated music from faith.

Every night Ciata sat outside her front door in full Baiana garb: white turban, white blouse lined with lace at the sleeves and neck, white hoop skirt, and so much beaded jewelry around her neck and wrists one wondered how she could walk with all of that weight on her small frame. Ciata did a brisk business frying acarajé on her front stoop and selling the bean fritters to late-night revelers who craved salty foods, and to those tourists who wanted to prove they'd had an adventurous night in Lapa that ended in meeting a "real" Baiana. (A "real" Baiana still evoked a sense of danger and magic in the minds of those who did not understand the tradition. In an attempt to disguise this fear, people mocked the Baiana once a year, during Carnaval. Wealthy revelers who invaded Lapa during Carnaval's four days and nights often chose the Baiana as their costume, and hundreds of "fake" Baianas— both men and women—drunkenly danced in hoop skirts and crooked turbans.) Rain and shine Auntie Ciata sat, as quiet and watchful as an ancient tortoise, and cooked for drunks and tourists. Some visitors, however, didn't come to Ciata's for food. They carried instruments and liquor, and they kissed the old woman's sunken cheek before entering her backyard, which she'd set up as a makeshift bar. These men had finished their shifts as waiters, doormen, busboys, bellhops, and cabaret players, but did not return home to their families or their beds, if they had such comforts.

"You're late, Professor," said a heavy man with bulging eyes.

Vinicius set down his guitar. "Since when do we worry about time?"

"Time is a figment of the imagination," said a young man with so many dark freckles scattered across his face, it looked as if his skin had ripened like the peel of a banana.

"Tell that to my boss!" the heavy one said, and laughed. His whole body jiggled.

"This is Dores," Vinicius said. "I thought she should hear us play."

His choice of words surprised me. I *should* hear them play—as if their music would be good for me, or I would be good for it.

A few of the men nodded but did not make room in their circle of chairs.

"I thought you said no girlfriends," the freckled boy said.

"I'm nobody's girlfriend," I said.

The hefty man with the frog's eyes smiled. "Well then, pull up a seat, sister."

They called him Tiny. His sheer bulk, his easygoing authority, and the fact that, outside the roda, there were always women on his arms made Tiny seem like the impresario of some secret casino. He was Auntie Ciata's actual nephew, and he played the cavaquinho, a little guitar similar to a ukulele. Despite his bulk, Tiny had small, deft hands that moved quickly across his instrument's strings.

The Brothers, Banana and Bonito, were from Bahia. Banana was the freckled one, and played the six-string guitar. Bonito was, as his nickname implied, dashingly handsome. He was the color of Banana's freckles and had a long, regal nose and dark, soulful eyes like a puppy dog's. Bonito played the cuíca, that mix of drum and percussion instrument that I'd first seen in the cane cutters' circles. Tiny called Bonito "the decoy" because while his good looks drew in the ladies, his shyness made it hard for them to stay interested. This is when Tiny swooped in with his charm and humor.

The very tall man in the corner with the sharp cheekbones and stern expression called himself Kitchen. He played percussion—the agogô, tambourine, reco-reco, and anything else that made the shaking and rattling sounds he needed. He got his nickname because, he said: "I'm always the cat in back, sweating, cooking, giving this band its flavor." If Tiny was the band's jolly showman and the Brothers its shy princes, then Kitchen was its warrior. His shirt collars were always crisp and his shoes always polished. He liked to shuffle cards in his long fingers and he carried a stiletto strapped to his calf, though I never saw him use it.

The band's last member was Little Noel, the earnest youngster of the group. A birth defect had mildly stunted the growth of his lower jaw, making it seem as if he had no chin, just neck. It was difficult for Little Noel to chew certain foods, which made his meals consist of soft fruits and porridge. This diet gave him a pale, tubercular look associated with tortured artists and, consequentially, considered very chic in those days. Little Noel occasionally played the banjo, but his true love was the small tamborim drum.

Over the years, all of us in the Blue Moon Band changed—some for better, most for worse. But when I think of the boys, I always see them as they were that first night at Auntie Ciata's. They had no set list. No rehearsals or costumes. No audience to please, except for me. And I was forgotten as soon as they played their first note.

I'd heard samba day and night since arriving in Lapa. But nothing was like the samba the Blue Moon boys played in their circle. Their music was lush yet controlled. It frolicked and soared and then glided, like the huge birds that floated around Sugarloaf Mountain, opening their wings and coasting on air. The boys' music carried me far from Lapa and from Anaïs and from Graça and even from my own, sickening dread that my talents were paltry and unremarkable, and that I was, too. Caught in the drift of their music, I was without boundaries or burdens. I was everything and I was nothing at all. This, I learned, was the effect of the roda.

The roda was a ritual. It was an event, not a show. What's the difference? A show's done for those watching. The roda was done for those of us playing and singing and composing. If you weren't part of the roda, you didn't exist. The roda was a conversation among musicians, into which you had to be invited. There were hundreds, maybe even thousands, of rodas in Lapa every night. But every samba roda had the same rules.

Newcomers were always treated with indifference. Even if you were the best guitar player, or cuíca player, or composer, or cavaquinho player, in the world, you had to be invited to join the circle. Don't even think about joining and fighting to set the pace right away—newcomers only follow. The batucada—that glorious, improvised roda sound—was like a school of fish, sometimes floating serenely together, sometimes darting faster than you could keep up with, but you had to earn the right to lead that school. And the songs? Don't even think about playing a lighthearted marchinha—those were for once a year, for Carnaval, for outsiders. Samba in the roda had mirth but it wasn't a party; it was a lament. When you play samba in the roda, you laugh at your own misery. You and your loneliness hold hands and traipse through the music, in awe of how pathetic and glorious you both are.

Even after the record deals and radio play and endorsement contracts; even after samba was declared Brazil's national music, the roda remained a sacred space. There, it was blasphemy to speak of a song's catchiness, or to call it a hit. In order to be a "true sambista" you were required to pretend that samba was not a product. Sure, individual songs could be recorded and sold, but samba itself could not be soiled by such mundane transactions. If you were true to your art, you did not seek success but stumbled upon it.

I was allowed into the roda's embrace each night, but not into the roda itself.

The boys poured me beers, offered me smokes, pulled a chair behind Vinicius for me each night, and then shut me out of the circle. They played long instrumentals, making up songs as they went along. Occasionally they toyed around with the lyrics of a few traditional sambas that everyone already knew. Vinicius always sang the leads, and his voice was clear and plain, as if he'd sat his listeners down for a frank talk.

One night, after a week of visiting Ciata's, I tapped my nails against the metal table in time to the boys' music. Another night, I clinked the tip of a beer bottle against my empty glass. On another night, I shook a box of matches. Each night I pulled my chair closer to the circle, then closer still. Until, one day, I wasn't sitting behind Vinicius anymore but beside him, ticking away the beat, moving in time with the men around me. No one looked up from their instruments. The music did not stop, the boys did not complain. To mask my elation, I focused even harder on keeping the beat.

I'd felt this same, giddy happiness only a few times before: after hearing our first concert in Saint Isabel; at the cutters' circles, when workers applauded my imitation of the radio hour; and during our first Nymphette show. Graça had shared each of those moments with me, but the roda was mine alone. Mine, and Vinicius's.

One night, we stayed so late at Ciata's that Lapa grew quiet. There were only four of us left outside: me, Vinicius, Tiny, and Kitchen. My backside ached from the wooden folding chair. My throat stung from all of the cigarettes I'd smoked. Tiny snored in his chair. Kitchen rolled us a fat cigarette filled with what he called "his herbs." Vinicius strummed a tune on his guitar. In the early-morning quiet, the notes sounded crisp and startling. I closed my eyes. In my head, those notes formed words:

I'm here, they said. *Always by your side. I buy your food. I make your bed. I place the pillow under your head. But you don't notice. You don't care. You seem to think I'll always be there. What would happen, if I were to leave? No one notices the air they breathe.*

"What's wrong?" Vinicius asked. He stopping playing and placed a cool hand over mine. I opened my eyes.

"You don't like it?" he asked. "The tune's no good."

"No, it *is* good," I whispered, hoping Kitchen wouldn't hear. "It's just . . . I heard something in it." I shook my head, embarrassed. "It's nothing. Keep going."

"No," Vinicius said, quite stern. "Tell me what you hear."

I glanced at Tiny and Kitchen, then at my hands. Vinicius put down his guitar, stood, and loped to the bar, where he found a scrap of paper and a pencil.

"Put it here," he ordered.

Vinicius played the tune again and I wrote down the words I'd heard in his notes. The boys looked on. When I showed Vinicius the paper, he stuck out his bottom lip and bopped his head from one side to the other.

"It could be a chorus," Vinicius said. "*No one notices the air they breathe.* That's pretty good, kid."

Of the few compliments I've ever received in my life, this remains the finest. Sure, years later, when Vinicius came up with a heart-stopping beat or an incredible melody for our songs, I'd nudge him and joke: *That's pretty good, kid!* And we'd both laugh. But in that moment in Ciata's yard, there was no joking. Tiny, Kitchen, the house, the street, even Lapa itself disappeared. The universe was made of only Vinicius and me. Staring at him, I knew he didn't see a kid, or a hanger-on, or some girl he could woo with pretty words. He saw me. He saw what I'd just made, and what we could make, together.

That is how our first song was born.

In the beginning, composing was like this for us: I'd listen to Vinicius play the initial bits of a tune and look for the emotion behind the sound—some tunes were angry, some hurt, some malicious, some pleased with themselves, some trying hard to be convincing. By listening, words came to me. With those words, I made stories. With those stories, Vinicius and I began to make songs. Night and day I carried the little notebook Senhora Pimentel had given me, filling it with images of things I saw around Lapa, with lines the Blue Moon boys used about pretty girls, with feelings I had but could never say aloud. They went into our songs.

Some songs were easy to work with—we took the lyrics and hung them on the melody like decorating a tree for Christmas. Others were thrilling and frustrating at the same time, like trying to undress a gorgeous dame who won't stop dancing. Some songs were like pouring ether on a hankie and taking a sniff: an amazing high that was over too quickly, and didn't satisfy. And some songs were like having honey poured all over you—sweet, but a goddamn mess.

After we made that first song, it was hard not to tempt fate and make more. It was a temptation because there was something illicit and slightly dangerous about our working together—girls weren't composers. Tiny and Kitchen never talked about that morning at Ciata's, when Vinicius praised my lyrics. I suppose they thought (in the beginning at least) that those lyrics were a fluke, or a bit of silliness brought on by Kitchen's herbal cigarette. If Blue Moon or any other musician got wind that Vinicius was actually writing music with a dame, he'd be the butt of every joke.

I stopped spending my afternoons in dark bookstores, nursing my wounds about my poor voice and Graça's late nights. Instead, I met Vinicius. We went to cafés and talked about things we couldn't share at Ciata's in front of the other Blue Moon boys. Vinicius asked questions about Graça's and my old life. Where was Riacho Doce, exactly? What did the air smell like when cane was boiled in the mill? What were the Pimentels like? What was Graça like as a little girl? Did she always want to be a singer?

I asked questions about Vinicius, too. Like me, he was an orphan, growing up in the care of his aunt Carmen. She played piano in the Odeon cinema, providing sound tracks for silent films as they played. Vinicius spent his childhood in that dark theater, watching heroes and heroines with glossed lips and kohl-lined eyes move on the screen, in time to his aunt's piano. Later, he was the one who played the piano, with his stern aunt watching him.

"It was in the dark that I learned to love music," he liked to say.

Eventually, he escaped his strict aunt and stumbled upon Auntie Ciata's little house.

"That was where I heard my first true samba," he said.

Samba; it always came back to that. During our talks, I would inevitably say, "That's a hell of a line for a song." Then Vinicius would start to whistle. Vinicius had a lovely whistle; smoother and richer than a bird's. Or he clinked a glass with his knife. Some days, he even brought Tiny's little cavaquinho and plucked at its strings while I drummed softly on the café's table. We moved tentatively, afraid of making too much noise. We whispered the song's words like secrets shared between us.

The only other person I'd shared secrets with was Graça. If she wondered where I spent my afternoons and nights during those weeks, she pretended not to care. And I pretended that this didn't sting terribly. I told myself that Graça had her knuckle draggers and her lessons with Anaïs, which she'd refused to give up. It was only fair for me to have something of my own, too. And it was thrilling to have such independence; each morning just before sunrise when I left Ciata's, I felt buoyed, as if a balloon had been inflated inside me. And yet, as I stumbled home I realized that I couldn't joke with Graça about Tiny's flirting or Kitchen's sternness, because she didn't know them. I couldn't tell her all of the new curse words I'd learned, or about the herbal cigarettes I'd smoked. I certainly couldn't describe our new music to her, because words would never do it justice. This inability to share the sound with Graça made the music itself seem a little less alive, and this left me infuriated—that Graça could dampen my music's life just by her absence. So, by the time I pushed open the door to our room each morning, I was exhausted and yet wide awake. I lay down beside Graça and listened to her little snores, and I imagined leading her to Ciata's and offering her a chair, not so she could be in the roda, but so she could see *me* in it, and bring it all back to life.

One night, just as we'd started the roda, Auntie Ciata's gate creaked. I looked up from my place in the circle and there was Graça, smiling and breathless, balancing a package in the palm of her hand as if she was a waitress. She wore a red dress. She'd done a shabby job of wiping away her Nymphette makeup; there was still a scattering of penciled freckles across her nose.

She dropped the package—wrapped in waxed paper spotted with oil—on the table in front of us and untied its twine. Inside were three steaks, brown and glistening and still warm.

"The grude's arrived, queridos!" Graça announced, as if we'd been waiting all night for this delivery, and for her.

"What are you doing here?" I whispered.

"Bringing you food," Graça replied loudly. "You're skinny as a rail and now I know why. These handsome bucks are working you too hard every night. Shame on you, Vinicius, for not giving her dinner after our shows! Dor's a growing girl. She deserves a gentleman taking care of her."

"Dor doesn't need anybody to take care of her," Vinicius replied.

Graça flashed her teeth at Vinicius, her smile achingly wide. "You don't get to tell me about Dor. Dor and me have been a team since we were kids."

"What're you now? Wise old women?" Vinicius interrupted. The other boys laughed.

"If we're old women, then you're a dinosaur," Graça replied.

"Owwwww," the Blue Moon boys moaned.

"The Dinosaur!" Kitchen said. "I think I like that name better than 'Professor.' It's got a ring to it."

Tiny fixed his gaze on Graça. "You fry up those steaks all by yourself, sweetheart?"

"I haven't touched a stove in my life and don't plan to," Graça replied. "I swiped them from Little Tony's. I couldn't swipe knives, though."

"We wouldn't want you to, querida," Tiny said. "A girl like you's dangerous enough. You put a knife in my heart as soon as you walked in."

Graça laughed. Tiny heaved himself up and offered Graça his chair, right next to mine inside the circle.

"I couldn't," she said.

"Sure you can," Tiny said. "It'd be a crime to let those legs of yours get tired."

"Graça's got a date," I said, my mouth very dry. "She can't stay."

Graça eyed me. "Sure I can."

The Blue Moon boys watched intently as Graça sat and crossed her legs. Tiny scrambled inside Auntie Ciata's house to get forks and knives.

"You think I could get one of those cigarettes, querido?" Graça turned to Little Noel, who fumbled for the pack in his shirt pocket. Tiny returned, dropping utensils with a clatter onto the metal table.

"Good. Let's eat them while they're hot," Graça said, facing me. "I got them bloody, just like you like them."

Her voice was soft, her look expectant. Were the steaks a peace offering to me, or simply a way to ingratiate herself with the band? Part of me felt pleased that Graça had made this effort, and that she'd ditched whatever knuckle dragger was hoping to have her company that night. The other part was furious that she'd invaded the roda so easily when it had taken me weeks to be allowed into the circle.

While the boys shoveled meat into their mouths, Graça laughed at Tiny's crude jokes. She held a whispered conversation with Banana and Bonito, and later egged on Little Noel's grand ideas of future success. Some, like Kitchen, seemed to tolerate her. Others, like Noel, fell head over heels, blushing each time she touched his hand. I could not pick up my fork and knife; my arms felt as if they were made of concrete. I felt a strange kind of resignation as I watched Graça with the Blue Moon boys: it was no use vying for their attentions; how could a sparrow compete with a peacock? How could a shrub compete with a bloom?

Across from me, Vinicius also stayed quiet and stern, watching

Graça as if studying an alien species. Only when the music began did he shift his gaze away from her, to me.

The boys played a few neighborhood songs, fiddling with the tempos and changing a few lines of the choruses. I used my fork to tap the bottle in my lap, but I couldn't disappear into the music like I had before. Next to me, Graça sighed. She crossed and uncrossed her legs. She studied her nails.

One song flowed into another until it seemed there was no difference between them. We found ourselves playing an old street samba—"Servant to Your Love"—a song everyone in Lapa, young and old, had heard in bakeries or rodas or as they walked down the street. Vinicius sang, as always.

"I'll wash your windows.
I'll polish your doors.
I'll do your dishes.
I'll scour your floors.
I'll clean all the bad feelings
out of your heart.
So you can open it to me again
and we'll have a fresh start."

Graça eyed me. She wiggled her brows. I ignored her. She elbowed me and leaned in so close, her mouth was nearly pressed to my ear.

"He sounds like a fucking librarian reading a dictionary. What does this band do: put people to sleep? Don't you ever pipe in?"

I glanced nervously at the boys. "You're not supposed to talk," I whispered into Graça's ear. "They haven't let me sing yet."

"What do you mean they haven't let you?" she whispered back.

"Vinicius sings. He's the leader. It's the way the roda works."

"Your voice is better. They should give you a shot."

The music stopped. Vinicius, nearly shouting, looked at Graça and asked: "Is there a problem over there?"

I felt annoyed at Graça's lecturing me about the roda, as if she was an old-time sambista, but I was also buoyed by her support: my voice was better; I deserved a shot. Even after weeks of fighting, she was on my side. Or maybe she was on her own side, fighting for her own shot. It was always hard to tell with Graça.

Graça gave Vinicius a withering look. She put her hands on the arms of her chair and straightened her body, as if she was about to stand and walk out of the roda. Instead, she lifted her head and let her voice pour out.

"I'll be your maid,
I'll be your butler,
I'll be your cook,
your chimney sweep,
if only you'd stay
just one more day."

The boys stared. I turned in my chair to face her. Who did she think she was? A girl, singing in a roda, interrupting the leader on her first night, and without invitation! Despite the silence, she kept singing. Then Little Noel began to beat his small hand drum, making it *rat-tat-tat*, and Graça did the same with her voice, drawing out every percussive syllable and accenting them, so her voice was like an instrument, too. She dove deeper into the song with each verse. Slowly, the boys picked their instruments off their laps and began to play again. With her.

The Blue Moon boys and I didn't have tin ears. We all knew the truth from the moment Graça opened her mouth to sing: the roda was better with her in it. Our laughter was louder, our joking rowdier, our rhythms more synchronized, our songs more beautiful. It didn't matter that Graça was a girl, a chatterbox, a terrible card player, a cigarette stealer, a conversation hog. What mattered was that she could sing and, more important, she knew how to make people love her. Eventually, everyone did.

So the Blue Moon boys accepted her singing, and mine, too. We didn't hog the roda—Vinicius continued to sing, and even the other boys got in on the act. We shared the spotlight and the music, and things continued this way for a few weeks, until, one night, Graça sat back in her chair and asked:

"Why do we sing the same worn-out tunes as everyone else in the neighborhood? It's like we're eating beans and rice for three squares every day."

Tiny smiled. "You like a little sausage in your stew?"

Bonito chuckled. Graça rolled her eyes. "I like variety. Who doesn't?"

"These are classics," Vinicius said. "If you don't know these tunes, you don't know shit."

"We know them inside and out," Graça replied. "Seems like we need to make some classics of our own."

"It's not a bad idea," Little Noel said. "Other rodas write their own stuff."

Tiny nodded at Vinicius. "You and Dor wrote something a few weeks back."

"You were sound asleep!" Vinicius said.

Tiny smiled. "I guess your tune woke me up."

"These two have a whole bunch of songs they're keeping to themselves," Graça said. "Seems selfish not to share them."

Vinicius looked at me, his eyes wide as if I'd just fingered him for a crime. I glared back at him.

"I told Graça we write in the afternoons," I said. "It doesn't have to be a big secret."

Banana raised his eyebrows. "You're writing with *her*?"

"You got a problem with that?" I asked.

Graça smiled and leaned forward in her seat, as if she was at the cinema.

Banana turned to Vinicius. "We got them singing, and now we got them writing?"

Vinicius stayed quiet. My hands balled into fists.

"What's it to you?" I growled at Banana. "Songs are songs."

"Let's hear one!" Tiny said.

"Oh, boy," Banana muttered, and shook his head. "We're going down a slippery hole."

"There's nothing I like better," Tiny said. Graça howled with laughter.

"Keep joking," Banana said. "It won't be so funny come Carnaval, when the whole neighborhood's laughing."

"Fuck the neighborhood," Vinicius shouted. "If the songs are good, it doesn't matter who wrote them."

Samba has a two-four rhythm. I discovered this years later, in New York City, when some cats from the New York Musicians' Union joked that they could play any samba or rumba or cha-cha; they all sounded the same to North American ears. But when those New York musicians heard Blue Moon play, they realized their ears had been mistaken.

"That's really a two-four?" one of those swing band musicians asked after our first rehearsal. "It's the other percussion, with the drum, that makes it seem faster, like eighths?"

Vinicius nodded.

"What did he mean?" I asked after the musician had left.

"Nothing," Vinicius said. "He's trying to understand without feeling."

We never talked about music in quarters or eighths or sixteenths.

When Vinicius corrected one of us in the roda, he never spoke of notes or measures.

"Your cuíca, Bonito!" he'd shout. "Listen to your cuíca, man! It's got to plead, not whine."

"It's not slick enough," Vinicius said when the boys couldn't find the groove. "It sounds too snappy. This isn't a goddamn pep rally. It's got to be greasy. It's got to get on your fingers and your lips. It's got to make you feel slippery."

We all understood what Vinicius meant. We all listened to him. If Tiny was the band's showman, then Vinicius was its curandeiro, its high priest, its mediator between the known and unknown. So, that night in the roda, after Vinicius made his proclamation about our songs, the boys and Graça grew quiet, giving us the floor.

Vinicius plucked the strings of his guitar. His eyes met mine. I nodded, recognizing the tune we'd created for "Air You Breathe." I sang the first verse, then the second. We heard the scratch of a reco-reco; Kitchen held it in his lap and played. Little Noel flicked the wand against his tamborim drum. Tiny strummed his cavaquinho. Then Bonito and Banana joined in with their cuíca and guitar, making the song deeper, thicker, and sadder in a way it hadn't been before. After the last verse I rounded back to the beginning, starting again and looking at Graça, who watched me with such focus, such rapt concentration I almost stumbled over my own words.

One morning in 1937, after only a few hours of sleep, I woke to a barrage of knocks on our rented room's door. Next to me, the bed was empty. Graça hadn't come home. She'd left the roda early for a date and Vinicius had argued with her, saying it was disrespectful. Graça had laughed in his face.

The knocking persisted. I squinted at my wristwatch; it was seven a.m. I flung open our door, ready to hurl a string of my saltiest curses at Graça for forgetting her keys. But it was the boardinghouse matron in a nightgown and shawl, her face stern. There was a telephone call for me. I stumbled downstairs and picked up the phone's heavy black receiver. A voice—reedy and weak, but immediately recognizable—called from the other end of the line before breaking off into muffled sobs. "Dor!"

She was on Copacabana Beach. Some bakery had let her use their telephone. I asked for its name and told her to wait right there.

As I rode the trolley, the streets seemed empty. A line of soldiers surrounded the outskirts of Catete Palace. A young man behind me whispered to his seatmate:

"I tried going to the university, but the gates were locked. Gegê's pulled off another coup."

When I arrived at Copacabana, the sun made the beach a furnace. The Copacabana Palace Hotel and Casino stood like a white fortress along the strip. With its ivory turrets and enormous balconies, it was the tallest building on the beach, and the grandest in all of Rio. Thick-necked doormen guarded its entrance.

Graça was not waiting in front of the bakery, as we'd agreed. I found her in the sand, staring not at the ocean but at the Palace Hotel. The sleeve of her dress was ripped, her neck scratched. Her right eye was swollen and purple; a red streak slashed the white of its eyeball.

"What the hell happened?" I cried, rushing to Graça's side.

"Don't be a Nervous Nellie," she said, her eyes still locked on the Copacabana Palace. "Please tell me you brought a drink."

I patted my trousers and produced a flask, still half full with rum. I handed it to Graça. She took a long gulp, then gnashed her teeth together and stared back at the Copa.

"They always show pictures of the Palace in *Shimmy!*" she said. "Their stage is the biggest in Brazil. Greta Garbo saw a show there.

And the president of the USA, too." She took another swig from my flask. "I should be in there, singing on that stage. Instead I'm stuck with a bunch of drunks at Tony's every night."

I was almost as surprised to hear this as I was to see her bruised face. Tony's still felt like a dream to me—we were loved and accepted there; the clients depended on us; and no matter how much Graça and I bickered offstage, at Tony's we forgot our cares, held hands, and sang freely, together.

"We'll get on a better stage," I said. "We just have to keep working."

"Working with who? With that band you ditched me for? If you think they're our ticket to the moon then you're not half as smart as everyone thinks you are."

"I ditched you?" I asked. "You didn't want my company, you had your dates every night."

"Who the hell cares about dates?" Graça said. "All those weeks you were playing music with a band—a real band—and you never even told me. You never even invited me to tag along. I had to barge in on my own, and when I did, you and Vinicius looked at me like I had the fucking pox."

Blood bubbled from the cut on her upper lip. Graça hid her face in her palms.

I wrapped my arm around her shoulders. "What happened to your face?"

Graça looked up at the Palace again. "That knuckle dragger last night, he was a rower for the Flamengo Club. A real hotshot. He told me he was taking me to the Copa. Turns out, he wasn't taking me to a show, he just wanted to roll around on the beach. So I told him *No, sir*. I told him I was respectable. I told him I was going to be a real goddamn star, and that one day he'd beg for my autograph. You know what he did, Dor?"

I shook my head.

"He laughed."

A fat tear wiggled down Graça's bruised cheek. She wiped it with the back of her hand. "He tried to make me roll around with him anyway. He was so strong! I almost got tired of pushing him off, but then I thought about you. I thought about how you cracked Souza's skull. I thought: *What would Dor do to this blockhead?* And it was almost like you were there with me, punching that knuckle dragger until he let me go."

My ears rang. My voice sounded far away. "I'll kill him."

Graça grabbed my hand and squeezed it tight. "Who cares about him? Who cares about any of those idiots? I don't."

I thought of the two of us in that dark alley, weeks before—how I'd tried to bring her to me and how she'd pushed away. "Then why do you give them the time of day?"

Graça stared back at the Palace. "When I'm not singing, I feel like people look right through me. I don't matter. The littlest breath will blow me away," she said, her voice very small. "You don't see the way those boys look at me, at first, when they're wooing me. When someone looks at you like that, Dor, it's like you've got a spotlight on you. You feel real."

"You are real. To me."

Graça smiled. She placed a hand on the underside of my chin, then pressed her bloodied mouth to the tip of my nose.

"Then don't ever ditch me again," she breathed, her lips brushing mine.

That evening, Graça and I went to Tony's early in the hopes of finding Miss Lúcia and asking her to hide Graça's bruises under a layer of makeup. When we arrived, Tony had his radio on. Graça and

I stood shoulder to shoulder with him, the bartender, and Miss Lúcia, and listened as Gegê addressed the nation. His words tumbled out of the radio's speaker, his voice earnest and dull, like a teacher struggling to give a lesson. Congress and the Senate were shut down. There was a new constitution, giving all power to the president. Brazil was not a ragtag collection of states but a unified republic. There would be no pretense of elections, not that year or any other; Gegê would continue to serve the nation—his nation—indefinitely. The military was (momentarily) on his side; historians later called it a dictatorship born of bureaucrats. But that night, Gegê called it the Estado Novo.

After the address, Tony's filled up with regulars like any other night. (It was, we later discovered, a sign of things to come: the Estado Novo would be a relatively mild-mannered tyranny, and Gegê was less tyrant and more magician, making freedoms disappear without our even noticing.) Graça and I played the Nymphettes for our loyal audience and planned to go to Auntie Ciata's after the show. It seemed like nothing had changed, except for Graça's face. Even under a thick layer of makeup, you saw the shadows of bruises. When Vinicius asked what happened, we said she tripped and fell. Under Little Tony's weak stage lights, as Graça and I sang our tragic love songs to each other, I stared at the red slash that ran across her left eye and my chest burned.

Near the end of our show, Graça faced the audience and, for an instant, lost the rhythm of our song. It was an imperceptible error to most, but one that made me stare out into the crowd where Graça was looking. I saw him from the stage. He lingered at the bar and held a little bundle of flowers in his rower's mitts. His suit was expensive. His hair slicked back. On his cheek were several raised red lines, as if a large cat had clawed him.

My hands shook. The words to our tango became jumbled and then forgotten. Graça kept singing but took my hands in hers and squeezed, trying to bring me back to our act. I pulled away. Keeping my eyes on the knuckle dragger, I walked to the edge of the stage and jumped down, into the crowd. The drunks were so startled they didn't whoop or complain or attempt to grab me. Graça stopped singing and Vinicius stopped playing. I made my way toward the rower.

"What's this?" I asked, pointing to the wilted bouquet in his hand.

"Flowers," he said stupidly.

"What're those?" I asked, pointing to the scratches on his face. He glanced back at the stage, at Graça.

I grabbed the rower's hand in mine. His fingers were as thick and rigid as the handles of Nena's wooden spoons. I thought of how those fingers had moved against Graça, of all the secret places they'd tried to enter. I bent the rower's fingers backward.

There was a crack and then a yell—a howl, really—that sounded quite far away to me, as if it had happened onstage. I fell back, pushed. The floor under me was sticky. Onstage, Graça screamed. The bartender jumped the bar and was suddenly standing between the rower and me. I felt other, gentler hands on my shoulders, lifting me up.

"You okay?" Vinicius asked me.

"She broke my fucking finger!" the rower spat, squeezing his hand to his chest as Tony's massive bartender threw him out of the club.

Graça knelt beside me. I recognized her perfume—a rose scent she'd bought at the apothecary. There were fierce yells from the crowd. The drunks stomped their feet. Little Tony appeared.

"You can't leave in the middle of your set!" he yelled. "Get back up there before there's a fucking riot."

"No," Graça said, wrapping her arm around mine. "We're not going back on. Dor's hurt."

"He didn't hurt me," I said, pushing myself to standing.

"Get back up there," Little Tony said, "or get the hell out."

Graça pulled out her pigtails and threw the ribbons on the floor. Little Tony yelled but was drowned out by the crowd. A fight had erupted near the stage. A wave of men moved toward us. Vinicius grabbed his guitar and pushed the three of us outside, where we ran all the way to Ciata's.

I t was still early by Lapa standards: Ciata's was empty. We wandered into the backyard and caught our breath.

"You want to tell me what happened back there?" Vinicius asked.

Graça and I stared at each other. Sweat had smeared her makeup, revealing her bruises. The Nymphette costume's vines curled up her legs, looking strangely sinister, as if they could bind her to that dirt floor forever. She gave me the smallest shake of her head.

"I guess Dor doesn't like bouquets from admirers," she said.

Vinicius smiled at me. "Is that how you treat your fans?"

"Don't you know?" Graça replied. "A good punch is Dor's idea of romance."

"I'll remember that next time a fella asks about her," Vinicius said.

Graça giggled. "You've actually had fellas ask about her? I sure hope you warned the weak ones away."

Vinicius laughed as if Graça had just shared the best joke he'd ever heard. I moved to stuff my hands into my trouser pockets when I realized I had no pockets—I was still in my Eve suit. I ripped out my ridiculous pigtails and walked toward Ciata's gate.

"You two have fun making jokes about me," I said. "You could start a comedy routine."

"Hey, Dor! Come on," Vinicius said, catching up with me. "Let's have a drink."

I snorted. "I'd rather jump off Christ the Redeemer."

"I'll jump with you," he said. "But it's a long way down. Let's get a few drinks in us first. I don't want to feel it when I spill my brains."

"There's nothing to spill," I said.

"True," Vinicius replied, then lowered his voice. "Who was that cat you hurt? He bother you?"

I shook my head. "He's just a rower for Flamengo."

A smile spread across Vinicius's face. "I guess he won't be rowing in the championships this weekend. Can you hold an oar with a broken finger?"

I smiled back. "I've always hated the fucking Flamengo Club."

"Well, that's one way to show your passion for the sport," he said, his face crumpling.

Vinicius laughed. I laughed harder. It was hard to stop; every time we looked at each other giggles poured out. Before long we were doubled over, cackling like two drunks. Tears ran down our faces. I rested my forehead on Vinicius's shoulder. I leaned my face into his neck. It smelled of aftershave and smoke. Why did my heart feel as if it was caught in my throat, beating hard against the tendons of my neck?

"Wait'll we tell the boys what happened," Vinicius said. "They'll love you forever."

There was a scraping noise. Graça pulled a rusted trash barrel into the center of the yard. Then she grabbed a book of matches from a nearby table, lit them all, and flicked the entire book into the barrel.

Vinicius moved away from me. "What are you doing?" he asked.

Fed by greasy newspapers and oily rags, the fire grew fast. The insides of the barrel glowed orange. Flames found their way over the barrel's metal lip.

Graça eyed me, her mouth twisted in what looked like a smirk. She held a hand under her armpit, caught the catsuit's zipper between her fingers, and pulled. The suit loosened. She moved one arm out, then another, as if shedding a dirty skin. The Eve suit pooled at her feet.

Elastic didn't exist back then. We wore camisoles—sheer little tops with straps as thin as angel hair—and little shorts held in place by a drawstring. Graça's camisole was pale blue with scalloped edges, its fabric worn so thin you could see her curved outline underneath, made plain by the firelight. The tips of her breasts were two hard, round points under the gauze of her shirt. Her belly button was a tiny smudge, like a single drop of water had landed there. Her hips swelled and in the dip between them, where her legs met, there was deep shadow.

Vinicius let a sigh escape him. "What . . . what are you doing?"

Graça hopped out of the Eve suit, scooped it up with one hand, and threw it into the fire.

"I'm done with small potatoes," she said, staring into the barrel.

Vinicius looked back at the gate, then again at Graça. His forehead shone. "The boys will see you."

"So what?" Graça asked, smiling now. "Girls around here wear less than this to the beach."

The fine hairs of her arms and legs glowed in the firelight, making her look like she was covered in thousands of golden threads. On her thigh were five dark spots—bruises in the shape of ovals. An ache rose in me. I held my stomach, worried I'd been hit, afraid the rower had gotten a punch in without my realizing it.

"You can't be like this," Vinicius said, his voice thick.

"So give me your jacket," Graça replied.

He didn't move immediately. They were quiet for a beat, staring at each other until I wondered if there'd been a bit of conversation I'd missed, an exchange I didn't hear. Then Vinicius took off his suit jacket, walked toward Graça, and dropped it, quickly, onto her shoulders.

Graça smiled. "Dor, are you going to join the fun?" she asked, nodding at my Eve suit.

I shook my head.

She wrapped Vinicius's jacket tighter around her. "If you change your mind, ask one of the other boys for his coat. This one's all mine."

The next evening, Madame L. sent for me. When Graça tried to go, too, Lucifer's messenger boy shook his head. "Just the tall one. Madame L.'s orders."

It was early—only seven p.m.—but music came from the record player and a few girls sat on the room's velvet sofas and chatted with the night's first customers. I made my way past them, to Lucifer's office. He sat cross-legged in his favorite chair, the velvet along its arms worn and ripping. He ordered me to sit down in the chair beside his.

"Tony got rid of you," he said. "Every cabaret owner from here to the Senate knows the story. The two of you fighting in front of the audience over a boy from Flamengo."

"We weren't fighting over him," I said. "He beat up Graça."

Lucifer clucked like a disappointed mother. "So you break his hand in front of everyone? And in costume? Oh, Miss Dores. Revenge and sex are two things you never do in front of a crowd."

"So I should've let him waltz in there like nothing happened?"

Lucifer's smile disappeared. "You should have come to me. But it's too late for that. Now I have to deal with Little Tony."

I forced myself to meet Lucifer's eyes. "You'll get our act back?"

"Tony was right to fire you, but he was wrong to do it without my permission. And you two? No club in Lapa will hire your friend now, unless I twist a few arms for her."

"And for me?" I asked.

Madame Lucifer sighed. He uncrossed his legs and bent forward, resting his elbows on his knees.

"Graça's got the better voice," he said. "And she sure knows how to work a crowd. Don't look so sad, puppy dog. You've got more useful talents."

"Like what?" I asked, gritting my teeth. Of course Graça was better; I was tired of Lucifer and Anaïs pointing out the obvious to me, as if I didn't have the courage to see it for myself. But I'd always believed that "better" or "worse" didn't do our duo justice; Graça and I were different, and in our differences we each made up for what the other lacked. My voice—growling, deep, strange—gave hers weight and mystery. Her voice—lush, enveloping, bold—took away my edge. Now I'd lost my role as the Nymphette and my rightful place beside Graça.

"Why do you think I let you do my deliveries?" Madame L. asked. "Graçinha just went along for the ride. You, Miss Dores, never came up short. You never lost a loaf. You never let people charm you into giving them extra. You didn't let anybody bully you, either. You can count, Miss Dores, you can make a buck. What's the use of talent if you can't make a living off it?"

I shrugged.

Madame L. stared at me, his eyes steely. "So your childhood dreams didn't pan out? Whose do? I thought I'd be onstage once, a long time ago, but that wasn't in the cards. If I'd pushed too hard with that dream, I'd have been nothing but a dead black boy in a gutter. All those malandros outside that tip their hats to me today, Miss Dores, you think if I didn't have the reputation I've made for myself, they wouldn't slit my throat with a broken bottle? Even here, in naughty little Lapa, people only put up with me because I *make* them. They can call me a bicha behind my back all they want, but I'm still a man, Miss Dores. And I don't let anybody forget that. Use *your* talents, don't chase after ones you'll never have."

"So you'll get Graça a new act, but not me?"

Madame L. sat back. "No. You'll get Graça a new act."

"But you said no one will hire us . . . her . . . now. I can't twist arms like you can."

"I have businesses to run. You girls made me good money at Tony's, and you, Miss Dores, lost that. If I didn't like you, I wouldn't give you the chance to earn it back. You have three weeks, no interest; after that I want my cut again. Get me the same amount you girls got me at Tony's, and we'll be straight."

The tips of my fingers felt cold. I gripped the arms of my chair.

"And if I can't?" I asked.

"I always get paid, one way or another," Madame L. said, and smiled. "Don't worry, Miss Dores. I have great faith in you."

Downstairs, the music grew louder. Girls laughed. Madame L. lifted himself from his chair and buttoned his suit coat. "I'll see you out," he said. "Before the night really starts."

People who attribute success to luck have never truly been successful. Luck may place an opportunity in your lap, but only a constant, obsessive attention transforms that opportunity into some kind of meaningful success.

I suppose it was lucky that, a few weeks before my talk with Madame L., good old Gegê used his weekly radio address to announce sweeping changes to the country's "cultural policies." Foreign-language newspapers would be banned. Only Portuguese was allowed to be spoken in schools and public buildings. "I don't believe in foreign influences over our melodies," Gegê said. "We are a new people, and new people triumph over the older ones. Brazil has its own music, a new music."

No Argentine tangos or American jazz or European operas could be played on national radio, or in Rio's best casinos, or anywhere the government thought foreign tourists might frequent. Visitors and Brazilians alike would be exposed to Brazil's "new music," whether they liked it or not. That music was samba. Though Getúlio didn't call it samba at first. Radio announcers and Brazil's new cultural minister called it "folk," and its players "folklorists," as if their songs were ancient and respectable.

Graça and I hadn't yet figured out how to repackage ourselves the way Gegê had suddenly repackaged samba. Lucifer was right—no cabarets or show houses would hire us. Most had heard about the brawl at Tony's. Others simply didn't like Graça's attitude; she refused to stand in line with dozens of other pretty hopefuls for auditions. Plenty of doors were shut in our faces, mine in particular. Anaïs paid us for odd jobs around her shop, so we were able to make the week's rent, but eating was a challenge. I got so desperate I returned to Tony's place, in secret, to beg for our jobs back. That's when I discovered that Little Tony was in Saint Mary's Hospital with half his face burned off. Days after Graça and I were fired, Madame L.'s errand boy—the same kid who'd found Graça and me at Mayrink—had entered the bar, thrown lye in Tony's face, and run away.

Miss Lúcia broke the news to me. Afterward, I stumbled from the empty bar and threw up in the alley.

I wiped off my shoes with some newspaper, bought a Coca-Cola, and sipped it as I wove through Lapa's alleys to meet Vinicius. He'd found a job playing guitar at another cabaret, but we still had our afternoon writing sessions. Aside from our roda at Ciata's, my afternoons with Vinicius were the only things I looked forward to. I liked the gentle way Vinicius held my arm, steering me into a café. Or how he took a handkerchief from his pocket and wiped my chair down before I sat. Or how intently he listened each time I gave my thoughts about a song.

That day, after I'd visited Tony's, I didn't have any thoughts worth sharing. Vinicius played some new tunes on his guitar and tried to coax me into coming up with lyrics, but no words came. The songs refused to speak to me.

"What's wrong?" he finally asked. "Got someplace better to be?"

Behind Vinicius, at the café's counter, the owner turned the radio's volume dial. A silly samba with a fast pace and irreverent lyrics filled the café's patio.

"Can you believe this folk shit?" Vinicius asked. "Some milk-fed motherfucker up in Santa Teresa picks up a cavaquinho for the first time, calls himself a folklorist, and rakes in the dough thanks to Daddy Gegê."

"How much do you think they make off recording those songs?" I asked.

Vinicius shrugged. "Enough to keep making them. People are eating them up. Would you look at this café cat? I have a mind to tell him to turn the radio off."

"People don't know better," I said.

"That's a damn shame."

My heart beat wildly, a bird trapped in my chest. "We could let people hear some real samba," I said. "We could cut a record."

Vinicius cocked his head. "I don't write songs to make records. It doesn't work like that."

"So everything we're doing, all these songs we're writing, what're they for?"

"They're for the roda."

"For the boys and Ciata to hear?"

"Sure. Why not? That's the way it's always been."

"Because there weren't records before, or the radio. We could have a lot of people listening to our sambas. To real sambas."

"Why would I want that?" Vinicius asked.

"You'd rather have people think samba's this folk shit?"

"The people that believe this is samba? Hell, I don't care what they think," Vinicius replied.

"But you care about Graça, don't you? And about me?"

Vinicius moved a callused hand through his hair. Waiting for his answer, I felt both giddy and petrified, as if I was back in that Corcovado train, riding away from one life and into another.

"Sure," he said. "Of course I care."

"Then help us."

"By recording a samba?"

"Madame L.'s a businessman—remember you told me that? He wants his cut, whether we're working at Tony's or not. If we record a song with you and the boys, and it gets on the radio, people will beg us to perform at their clubs. Nobody else plays samba like us. Nobody else has girls in their band. This can be good for all of us: we can be a real band, and show people what real sambas are."

Vinicius stared at me for what felt like hours. "I'll have to convince the boys."

"They'd follow you off Sugarloaf if you told them you were jumping."

"I don't know, Dor. What if people don't want our kind of music?"

I pulled Vinicius's hand into mine. "No one knows what they really want. We just pick what's easiest. So let's make it easy for them."

A week later we were in a cramped recording studio in downtown Rio. Yellowed mattresses were nailed to the walls and ceiling. The air was foggy with smoke. Two technicians—their shirts stained at the collars and armpits, a bored expression on their faces—sat behind a pane of glass. The name "Victor Recording Company" was painted on the wall behind them. Between them was a glass ashtray, piled high with the smashed ends of cigarettes.

No musician expected to get rich cutting records; it was radio play that brought gigs, and those gigs brought money. Before our recording session, Vinicius signed a contract making our song, "My Mutt," the sole property of Victor Recording Company. In return, they paid us the equivalent of fifty U.S. dollars and the honor of cutting a record. At the time, we thought this was something to celebrate.

When Graça and I squeezed into the studio alongside Vinicius and the boys, a technician left his seat and moved to the doorway. He wore a pair of thick-framed glasses, their lenses smudged.

"You gals wait outside," he ordered. "Your boyfriends are working here."

"We're the singers," I said.

The producer shook his head. "I didn't hear about any girl singers. What are you, backup?"

Graça gripped my arm before I could reply.

"Something like that," she said, and flashed him her sweetest smile.

The technician stared through his bottle-cap glasses, then nodded and went back to his chair. "Let's do a few practice rounds," he shouted from behind the glass. "Because once I hit 'record' you only get one chance, you hear me? There's five more bands scheduled after you."

To cut a record there were only two takes allowed. The first was to get the timing of the song. There was a clock on the studio's wall whose hands ticked off the time limit of three and a half minutes, which was all a ten-inch disk could hold.

We'd rewritten one of our sambas—a fun, snappy number—to fit the three-minute record requirement. A song's second take would be the real thing. If any of us messed up, the producer made it clear that we'd never be invited back.

There was a single microphone at the front of the studio. We'd never seen a microphone before—in Lapa's cabarets, a singer relied only on her voice. This particular mike was very wide and covered in holes, like a metal sieve. I pictured my voice falling right through it and dripping onto the record's wax.

We arranged ourselves. When the singers' parts were over, the producer explained, we would have to jump back very quietly and press ourselves against the studio wall, getting out of the way so the mike could pick up the band's sound.

Noel's tamborim drum went *bump, bump, bump*. Kitchen scraped his reco-reco: *cricka-crack, cricka-crack, cricka-crack*. Tiny's cavaquinho went *plink plink, plink plinka plink*, like tiny raindrops. Then came the sweet whimper of Bonito's cuíca: *ooo, ah, ooo, ah, ooo*. Vinicius's and Banana's guitars came in fast and low, tethering all of the sounds together. Graça nodded, and she and I moved quickly toward the microphone, afraid of being pulled away if we didn't hurry.

"I like mutts!
They live without owners,
free to roam.
They don't have a time,
when they have to come home.
I like mutts!
Scrappy and free.
Sniffing out the best sambas.
I wish my mutt would find me."

"Stop!" the producer shouted.

The boys obeyed. I moved away from the mike. We'd been caught— Graça and me—we weren't backups and never intended to be.

Once again, the eyeglassed technician came to the doorway.

"I don't care if you cats hire a fucking goat to sing on your track, as long as it sounds right," he said. "You gals are canceling each other out. You've got two singers duking it out on a song that needs one. It's 'I like mutts,' not 'We like mutts.' Let's do this again, with one of you. Who's it going to be?"

Graça and I looked at each other, then at Vinicius. He glanced at Tiny. Banana and Bonito wouldn't meet my eyes. Little Noel blushed. Kitchen stared at his instruments. When I shifted my gaze back to Vinicius, he looked stricken, as if I was a puppy dog he'd just run over.

I realized in that moment just how much I wanted my voice on a record. I wanted to be imprinted in wax and copied again and again, to invade parlors and cafés, to wind my way into people's ears and stake a claim in their memories. I wanted to be heard. And hadn't I been the one to insist on recording? Hadn't I written "My Mutt"? None of that mattered, of course; we all knew whose voice was the strongest. I resolved to save myself the embarrassment of being asked to step away from the mike.

"Graça will do it," I said, and moved to the back of the studio.

Graça put her mouth very close to the mike, her lips brushing the metal with every word. Through the sieve of that microphone, Graça's voice was both sweet and malicious. It winked at you. "I like mutts," she growled, and you knew she was not talking about dogs, but men. She wasn't one of those forbidding tango singers, who treated their songs like marathons, their notes like hurdles they leapt over. Graça sounded like she was having fun, like she and the listener were sharing a great night out on the town.

The process of making a record was the same every time: the master disk was made right there, in the studio, with shellac and carnauba wax. One disk, with two sides, A and B, could be made in twenty minutes. After Graça and the boys recorded side A, the producer rubbed his hands.

"You have another original number?" he asked, excited. "I'd planned to have you play a stock marchinha for the B face, but let's see what you got."

Graça turned to Vinicius. "What about Dor's other song? The one about the air you breathe."

"It's too slow for you," I called from the back of the room. We'd only ever performed that song—my song—with me singing it.

"We can up the tempo," Vinicius said. "Try to make it in three minutes. Let's give it a try?"

The technician nodded and began the rehearsal. On cue, Graça purred: "Here I am, Love. Always by your side. I buy your food. I make your bed. I place the pillow under your head."

In our rodas my voice was a plea, making the song tragic. But in the studio, Graça's voice made the lyrics playfully malicious, almost threatening: "What would happen, if I were to leave? No one notices the air they breathe."

Between a few lines of the song, Graça gasped little breaths in time to the band's faster beat. Her inhalations were smooth and quick. Her exhalations bore a hint of pleasure. She'd made the song better than I ever could.

After just a few bars, the producer smiled and clapped his hands, approving "Air You Breathe" as the B side. Ten minutes later, my first song was recorded, though my name was nowhere on the record. When the producer asked for a name, Graça and the boys didn't hesitate.

"Sofia Salvador and the Blue Moon Band!" they replied, almost in unison, as if they'd been practicing forever.

A untie Ciata's was riotous that night. Graça and the boys performed our recorded songs again and again. Tiny found two cabaret girls to sit on his lap and kiss his neck as he played. Kitchen, Bonito, and Banana snorted so much sweet flour that they played their instruments frantically, our songs moving so fast that it made me nervous to listen to them. Little Noel eventually passed out under a table. I envied him.

I did my best to guzzle our entire stock of beer and cane rum in an attempt to stir myself into elation. We'd cut our first record, after all. I'd helped write the songs. Yet I felt satisfaction but not happiness. I'd given up my place beside Graça in the recording studio and she hadn't objected; she'd gone on to sing even better than before. And afterward, as we walked to Ciata's, she'd linked arms with Little Noel. In the roda she'd sat between Tiny and Kitchen and sung without even a glance in my direction, as if the songs and the roda had always only been hers. Only Vinicius seemed to remember me, clapping me hard on the back as if I was a Blue Moon boy.

"We're recording artists thanks to you," he said. "Why don't you come sing? We can't have a roda without you."

I was about to agree when the singing stopped. Graça moved to the center of the Blue Moon boys' circle and held out her hands. Tiny bumped the cabaret girls off his knees and stood, then circled an arm around Graça's waist. They moved to the beat with the fluid, watchful ease of two cats, their hips shimmying in perfect harmony. Bonito whistled. The cabaret girls, annoyed at first, now clapped and cheered. Kitchen ground out the song's beat faster, then faster still, but Tiny and Graça did not tire or misstep. Plumes of dirt rose from the floor around them. Graça tilted her head back and laughed.

I smiled despite myself. Then I looked at Vinicius and saw he was smiling, too. On his face was a kind of dumbstruck awe, as if he'd just set eyes on a mermaid or a unicorn or some other mythical creature forgotten since childhood. I knew that look. I'd seen men in the audience at Tony's wear it night after night. But seeing it on Vinicius? It made something inside me wither and fall away, like the last petal on a flower.

"You look like you're starving," I said, interrupting his reverie. "And she's a steak on a plate."

Vinicius, startled, shook his head. "She's the most selfish person I've ever known. She's impossible."

"Why in hell would we want something that's possible?" I asked.

Vinicius blinked, then backed away, claiming he needed the restroom. He walked quickly inside Ciata's.

"Where's the Dinosaur running off to?"

Graça slid beside me, her chest glistening with sweat, the underarms of her dress dark.

"He's sick of all this. He's probably going to throw up," I replied.

Graça stared at me, her smile rigid. "We're trying to celebrate, you know."

"Then celebrate."

"It's hard when you're over here in the corner, frowning like a fucking nun at a whorehouse."

"Everyone's paying attention to you, not me. It's what you always wanted, isn't it?"

"Stop boohooing," Graça said. "Be happy for once in your life. I didn't steal the record from you."

"You didn't lift a finger to keep me on it, either," I said. "So much for saving each other. It's fine—I don't want to be on a common Carnaval marchinha anyway."

"What do you mean, common?" Graça asked.

"Easy."

"Well you wrote it, sister."

"You got that right. And I'm not your sister."

The music had stopped. The yard was quiet. Red splotches bloomed across Graça's chest. "No, you're a goddamn wet rag! You're as fun as a cemetery. You smell like fucking marigolds! What a bore you always are."

I forced out a laugh. "Everybody bores you because you're such a star. And then you know what happens? Everybody leaves you."

Then I stumbled out of Auntie Ciata's yard and into the street.

I roamed Lapa until I found myself at the shuttered storefront of La Femme Chic. I rang the buzzer. Upstairs, a light came on. I took off my beret and combed my hair with my fingers. The door's peephole slid open. The bolt turned and Anaïs stood before me, holding a metal pitcher of water.

"I thought you were a drunk playing with my buzzer. I was going to douse you."

"I am drunk," I said.

Anaïs used her free hand to fidget with the flaps of her robe. It was a flimsy silk affair. The lace of her slip peeked from under the robe's short hem.

"I should pour this on you," she said. "To make you go away."

I thought of Tiny, of his charm, of his confidence. I smiled. "You want me to go away? I haven't seen you in ages."

Anaïs stared over my shoulder. "Where is the other one?"

"She's not here."

"Well, that is a change. You are never without her, or that musician."

"Vinicius," I said. His name made my mouth pucker.

"You are here alone?" Anaïs asked.

"No," I replied. "I'm with you."

Anaïs laughed and opened the door. I followed her upstairs.

Her flat was tiny but elegant, with a bouquet of flowers on the windowsill and a radio in the corner. A thick curtain divided the main room from the bedroom.

"I would offer a drink, but I do not think that is a good idea," she said.

"Coffee?" I asked, and Anaïs looked puzzled, as if she hadn't quite understood my request.

She turned to the stove and put a kettle to boil. She was barefoot. Her robe barely covered her thighs. Her legs were long and smooth; I pictured her in the bath, shaving them with a man's razor.

"I do not let students up here," she said, facing me again.

"I'm not your student," I replied. "You told me I couldn't sing, remember?"

Anaïs's smile disappeared. "I did not say such a thing. I said your voice would not withstand the pressures of the stage."

I shook my head. "Same thing."

"Do you hold a grudge against me? I am sorry. I know you want to sing for a crowd, but I think it is best you know the truth."

"Is it?" I asked.

"Some wants are like fashions, Dores," she said, taking the kettle from the stove. "They change with time. Yours will as well."

"What if they don't?" I asked. "What if they only get stronger?"

I looked at her hands and remembered how they'd pressed against Graça's stomach. How her thumb had traced my mouth. Her slip was pink with straps as thin as guitar wire. I imagined how easy it would be to pluck those straps from her shoulders. I moved toward Anaïs, getting so close that I could smell her: a mixture of soap and coffee. Then the bravery I'd pretended to have suddenly vanished. I stepped away. Anaïs caught my hand.

"Now you are afraid of me?" she said, smiling. "Do not be."

She leaned into me, her mouth pressing against my neck, my earlobe, my jaw. Then she slid her lips across my cheek until our mouths met.

Men and women all have lips, teeth, tongues. Technically there should be no difference between one person's kiss and another's, since both use identical parts. But this is like saying a song is simply a collection of notes on a page, and that the same song will sound alike even if played by two different musicians. In reality, each musician gives the same notes distinct lives. Kisses are no different.

On that night and many after it, Anaïs made me realize that I, too, could be wanted. That the desires I felt could be shared and even reciprocated; that they did not have to be locked away to wither inside myself. It was a frightening discovery at first, but I wasn't afraid for long.

MEANT TO BE

I don't want to be
the sun that lights your days.
Oh no, my love.
The sun is much too far away.

I'm the towel that dries your skin, wet from the sea.
I'm the handkerchief that drinks your tears.
I'm the pillow that collects your pleas.
I'm the mosquito, drunk with your blood.

Tell me I'm not necessary! Tell me I'm a fool! Tell me you can do
without me, even for a day. And this is what I'll say:

You're the seed, I'm the hands that plant you.
You're the roots, I'm the dirt that surrounds you.
You're the bullet, I'm the barrel that propels you.
You're the fruit, I'm the knife that parts you.

Tell me I am not necessary! Tell me I am a fool! Tell me you can do
without me, even for a day. And this is what I'll say:

You are not you
without me.
And everything we are,
together,
is what we're meant to be.

There are very educated people who insist that samba came from the hills, from the poorest, most unfortunate neighborhoods in Rio. This is true. But it is also true that it came from lucky orphans like Vinicius, from street toughs like Kitchen, and from gentle souls like Noel. It came from romancers like Tiny and shy men like Banana and Bonito. It came from spoiled Little Misses like Graça, and from nobodies like me.

Try to trace samba back and you will find no one origin. Try to inventory its key players, and you will never have enough room on your list. Samba came from masters and slaves, from parlors and slums, from cities and plantations, from men and women. You cannot trace its origins so why try? Why not just sit back and listen to the music?

Samba does not abide simplification and neither should people. In Lapa, no one dared insist they were one thing or another. If, heaven forbid, someone went around proclaiming, "I am a woman," or "I am an Indian," or "I am a man who likes men," they would be considered either crazy or untrustworthy. To place such a definition upon oneself meant you had simplified yourself to the point of absurdity.

In Lapa, people did what they did in bed and didn't talk about it afterward. As long as murder or children weren't involved, no one much cared. Nearly every Carnaval, our own Kitchen would sneak off with some handsome buck to celebrate, and no one dared make him feel like less of a man for it. The fact that my adventures went beyond Carnaval's four wild days was different but not unforgivable. They were, however, still considered adventures—risky, out of the ordinary, and temporary—even by me.

Those of us who grew up in Lapa's bohemian streets and hated definitions were nevertheless required, over the course of our lives, to create some kind of explanation for ourselves. From the very beginning of our lives we must define ourselves as girls or boys. Later, we become good students or bad, artists or businesspeople, pretty or homely. We call ourselves lawyers or shop clerks or musicians or singers. We turn into husbands or wives. Each new definition stacks itself on top of all of the previous ones. And suddenly, you are smothered under the weight of them. At the end of your life, you can be described in one tame little sentence placed at the opening of an obituary: former kitchen girl, former singer, former songwriter, former lover, former wife, former friend.

Then there are the definitions others created for you, or perhaps you inflicted upon yourself but didn't mean to. These aren't in any obituary, but are whispered at the service. I have read some of what biographers, so-called intellectuals, and mean-spirited reporters have written about me. (Their works were never really about me, of course. To them, I was a bit player in Sofia Salvador and Vinicius de Oliveira's story.) I was the slave-driving manager, the ambitious friend, the failed singer, the other woman, the copycat who stole Sofia Salvador's revolutionary samba style to use as her own, the suspect, the wrench in the gears of the Blue Moon Band, the Sapphically inclined hanger-on, the Big Foot, the Gillette razor, the confused girl who couldn't decide what she wanted or with whom she wanted to do it.

Anaïs made me an eager student, ready to test my skills. To my surprise, there were several wives of Victor record producers who secretly enjoyed my company. There were others, too: butterfly girls, barmaids, tanned beach bunnies, prim little store clerks. They were all Lapa girls, so they weren't afraid of me; and if they were afraid it was a good fear, an excitement they couldn't resist, an experience that made them feel daring and safe at the same time. With me, there could be no morning nausea, no secret trips to the doctor, no claims of "appendicitis." I gave them every satisfaction that a man could (if not more), without any of the dangers.

There were men for me, too. At first, my being with a man was driven by curiosity. What was it like? How was it different? What made Graça so damn enamored of them? My first was not a skilled teacher like Anaïs, but a nervous and gangly bartender. Our time together was quick and relatively unpleasant. Afterward, I felt disappointed and annoyed, but not enough to completely disregard an entire sex! I have always been stubborn; I certainly did not ignore men after that, I simply chose more wisely.

There is a myth that men want to dominate and women want to submit. This is what we see in films and read in books, and though it may be true for some, it is not true for everyone, and certainly not all of the time. I detest generalizations, but I have found that men have a refreshingly simple physicality about them. Sex with a man is about arriving at a set destination. If you are lucky, or skilled, you arrive together. With women there are incremental shifts of desire—some subtle, some intense—that rise and fall and don't depend on reaching an endpoint. Women are circles, men are arrows.

"Dor's a Gillette," Tiny liked to joke. "She cuts both ways!"

Despite their wisecracks, my bandmates understood me more than others did because they understood samba. In the roda, some nights we craved simplicity. Other nights, we wanted to lose ourselves in that pulsing circle of music. The songs we played depended on our moods, and on the people we chose to play with. What did not change, for me at least, was the maddening rush of excitement and need that came before each roda. Each song was a conquest. Each note an act of love.

MEANT TO BE

There was a moment in Lapa, just before sunrise, after the cabarets closed and visitors returned to the safety of their neighborhoods, when the only sounds you heard as you walked through dark alleys were the night's last rodas—their voices gravelly, their melodies slow and sad. These were the secret songs, the rough cuts not meant for the light of day. These were the songs you played when all other tunes had already been sung, and the night came down to this: no more drinks, no more friends, no more laughing girls, no more cigarettes, no more food in your belly or water in your cup, just you and a guitar player, alone in the darkness, forgetting everything but your voices and the words to a song inside yourself that you'd always known but could not share, until that moment. Sometimes there are unsuspecting listeners: a new mother awake at her window; a couple tangled in bedsheets; or a young girl in a beret and trousers, her hands in her pockets, her mouth raw from kisses, her body deliciously sore in places she was always told never to touch. She stops and listens to the roda's lament as if her life hangs in the balance. As if everything she has experienced so far in her brief existence—every beating, every lie, every shame, every rush of love, and every triumph (though there have been few of these)—has conspired to bring her there, to hear a song no one else is supposed to hear. It enfolds her. Music—like a green field or a warm bed—is a place where she can always retreat. It is a home like no other.

I remember that walk after my first night with Anaïs. I listened to that music and felt each lovely ache within me, and I wanted to always feel this close to myself. But I knew that such closeness couldn't last. The song ended. The roda finished. Daytime Lapa woke.

I ran inside a bakery, paid for coffee, and sat by the window with my little notebook and pencil. I tried to write what I felt. There was a rush of words and rhymes that felt paltry and hollow. Nothing did justice to what I'd felt that night—how I'd been consumed by another person and, in that consumption, I'd had my own desires met and accepted. Was this what Graça meant, that morning on the beach, when she'd said she wanted to feel real? Had those knuckle draggers given her this feeling? Is that why she returned to them each night?

I put down my pencil, angry now. Graça had this sensation for months now and hadn't shared it. She was always ahead of me. And why had those stupid fools given Graça such feelings? Why had she chosen them and not me? My time with Anaïs faded and Graça came, as always, to the forefront. I wanted to tell her about my night, in part to brag and show her that we were equals now, but also to better comprehend what had happened. Graça would listen. She would understand. Like that moment after our first concert, when she'd told her mother why I was upset: the song was trapped inside me. Graça had known because she'd felt it herself.

I gulped down the rest of my coffee and closed my notebook, ready to rush home. Then I remembered our fight. We'd fought many times before, said ugly things to each other, been vile and petty. Fights were storms I expected us to weather, but Graça would always extract her revenge for my comments. There would be a price to pay—she might not listen to me or, worse, make my experience with Anaïs feel silly and cheap. Just as Graça had the power to give moments life, she could just as easily crush them.

I considered avoiding our boardinghouse. I could stay in the bakery, or crawl back to Anaïs's shop. I could find Vinicius, ask him for a pillow and a spot on his floor to sleep. Later, we could write songs. But the thought of telling Vinicius about my night made my cheeks burn. Telling him felt impossible, not because I was ashamed of what I'd done but because of Vinicius himself. He was older. He was no stranger to women; I'd seen them fawning over him as he played guitar. Telling him about my night would be admitting to my inexperience and youth. To him, I'd seem like a dumb kid when I wanted to be seen as an equal.

So I gritted my teeth and walked to our boardinghouse, telling myself all the while that Graça wasn't the only one allowed to live there. When I put the key in the lock, it did not turn; the door was open.

The shades were drawn. The bed was empty, its sheets rumpled. The room smelled of perfume and cigarette smoke.

"I thought you'd ditched me for good."

I jumped, then turned to see Graça in a chair in the corner, hugging her legs. Her hair was tangled. The soles of her feet were as black as a street urchin's. She sounded stuffed up, as if she'd caught a cold.

"How long have you been home?" I asked.

"What the fuck do you care?"

I sat on our bed. How I wanted to rest my head on the pillows and disappear into sleep! I regretted that bakery coffee.

"I drank too much last night," I said, as a kind of apology. "We all did."

"That's what Vinicius said," Graça replied. "He walked me back after you disappeared."

The cigarette smell was familiar now. I bunched the bedsheet in my hands. "He came up here, with you?"

Graça smiled. "Yeah, but I kicked him out. I wanted to wait by myself. I wasn't sure you'd come back."

"I took a walk."

"That was a long walk."

I could have lied at this point, but I felt a desperate need to tell Graça the truth. Not because I felt she deserved it, but because if I didn't tell her, somehow my experience would feel less real.

"I went to Anaïs's place. I woke her up."

Graça's body relaxed to the chair. "To argue with her about lessons again?"

I shook my head. "We didn't argue. We didn't talk much at all."

Graça squinted, as if trying to work out a difficult calculation in her head. Then her eyes widened, and she smiled. "She kicked you out after. She wouldn't let you sleep cheek to cheek?"

"She has work in the mornings. It's not like we're married. It was just some fun."

"Was it fun?" Graça asked.

I stared at my palms. "It was like when we first saw the city, when we were on the ship, coming into Guanabara. Remember? It felt like this brand-new place and, at the same time, like we'd known it all along. Like we were always supposed to be here."

Graça nodded. "And here we are."

She pushed herself out of the chair and placed herself next to me, weaving her fingers through mine.

"I got into a whopper of a fight after you left," she said.

"Who with?"

"Vinicius, who do you think?" she replied. "He was looking for you. I told him we had a fight, and he started acting all high-and-mighty, saying I'd run you off and how I had to keep my big mouth shut." She rolled her eyes.

"But he took you home," I said. "He came up here to be with you."

"He wanted to see if you were here, crying your heart out because I'd hurt your feelings. As if you'd do that. As if he even knows you! The big bandleader, trying to make everybody behave. Well, I told him he wasn't the leader of us."

I looked at our hands, wrapped together. "Us."

"You weren't on that record . . ." Graça began.

"And I probably won't be on the next one, either," I interrupted. "I'm not cut out for singing."

"But I still need you," Graça said.

"To iron your dresses? To do your hair?"

She squeezed my hand tighter. "I need you to be on my side."

"Against who?"

"Everybody, the whole world."

"The world will eat us up. That's what Nena said."

Graça laughed. "I want it to swallow me whole."

M y Mutt" and "Air You Breathe" played every hour on the radio for months on end. Across Rio, girls began to call their boyfriends "mutts." The Lux soap company ran newspaper ads saying, "Use Lux Shaving Balm to keep your face as smooth as a baby's, even when you're her favorite Mutt!" And when people bought record players for their homes, "My Mutt" was the first record everyone put on their turntable.

We played so many gigs after the record's release that I'm not sure how we survived on so little sleep. The thrill of success—of being admired and wanted—fueled us all, even me. Cabarets, jazz clubs, little show houses—they all wanted us on their stages. Well, they wanted Sofia Salvador and Blue Moon. I stayed backstage, humming along, tapping my feet, noting every shift to every song's tempo or rhythm when the boys would improvise just for fun. Being backstage, huddled in the dark, surrounded by dusty beams, wires, and props—all of the things the audience was never supposed to see because it would ruin the illusion of the performance—was like being in the kitchen of a Great House. That was where all of the chopping, washing, scraping, bleeding, sweating, and preparation occurred for hours on end, all to create the artifice of ease and luxury for those at the front of the house. Part of me felt at home in the dark and utilitarian world backstage. Another part felt a gnawing desperation at being thrown back into the shadows. But there were consolations I held dear: Graça had rejected me but would not replace me; my voice was not on their records but my words were in Graça's mouth.

I wrote many songs in the weeks after the release of "My Mutt." The girls and boys I left behind each morning reappeared in my lyrics. "Peeling the Onion" was so obviously about undressing a girl it was comical, but its double meanings were too hard for Gegê's dull censors to spot. There were lighthearted sambas about handsome bartenders; party marchinhas for Carnaval about making love to a costumed sweetheart in a dark alley; tearjerkers about summer romances gone too soon; angry ballads about being left behind. Vinicius made the melodies, of course, but the only songs he was capable of writing by himself in those weeks were down-and-out love songs.

Vinicius's melodies contained a terrible longing. The notes he played began expectantly—clean and crisp—and then slowly became frustrated, moving lethargically and sounding deeper, as if they had no bottom and you might fall right through them, into nothingness. I heard all of this in his playing, but didn't question the source. I didn't want to know. Whatever rose from within us and floated to the surface as Vinicius and I worked, we never analyzed or picked apart. We simply followed the music, even if it made us afraid. During our writing sessions, Vinicius and I were braver than in our actual lives, in part because whatever we confronted in the music, we did it together.

Victor wanted our songs so badly, it opened its studio to us anytime. Each night, after Sofia Salvador and Blue Moon played their gigs,
we made our way to Ciata's for our roda, which we never missed, no
matter how late it was or how tired we were. We'd refine one of our
three-minute sambas in the roda and one of us, usually Graça, would
smile and say: "It's good. Let's record it."

"Nah," Vinicius said.

"Oh, come on, Professor!" Kitchen teased, his words slurring.
"Dor, get that producer on the telephone! Let's go cut a record!"

That's how easy it was for all of us to agree back then.

A bleary-eyed producer met us at Victor's recording studio. Despite
our drunken antics, as soon as the clock started and the producer
turned on the mikes, we were all in service to the music.

When I think of those early mornings when we headed to the recording studio, stumbling arm in arm through Lapa, giggling and
tripping over ourselves, I feel so much affection for Graça and the boys
that it's hard to breathe. Sure, I wasn't a Nymphette. I wasn't Lorena
Lapa. I wasn't a singer on a record. I wasn't part of the act, and never
would be. But the miracle of our rise—of my rise—wasn't lost on me.
We were a hit. My songs were on people's lips. And all of us—Graça,
Vinicius, the Blue Moon boys, and me—were together, making music
simply for the sake of making it, living a rare moment when we could
be both successful and genuine sambistas.

We didn't know what real success was, of course. We blindly signed
away our songs to Victor for a pittance, and in return we got radio play,
which got us gigs. We made enough money to pay rent and satisfy Madame Lucifer each week, with enough left over to give Vinicius and the
boys their fair cut. We were all still eating rice and beans every day, and
the boys couldn't give up their day jobs, but this was no disappointment. It was, in our naive eyes, a dream come true.

We weren't the only ones living this dream. After the success of

"My Mutt," record labels assembled a dozen other groups just like ours, with the novelty of a girl singing lead vocals. RCA had Jeisy and the Beats. Odeon had Nina and the Highlights. Parphalon had Valdette and the Folklorists. And, along with us, Victor had Aracy and the Hep Cats. They all looked like us, too: the bands dressed in suits, the lead singers like schoolgirls in white shirts and wide skirts. But their sambas were nothing like ours: biting, aching, tragic, and funny all at once. Most of the sambas that played on the radio after "My Mutt" were exactly like those singers posing as schoolgirls: drab, safe, and completely phony. Aracy Araújo's song "The Cat's Meow" was a blatant copy of "My Mutt," but it didn't matter—the song quickly got airtime and Aracy competed with us for gigs.

Before we knew what hit us, our songs lost their constant rotation on the radio. We began to play fewer and fewer shows; cabarets had their pick of popular samba songstresses and their bands. Arriving at Victor's recording studio before dawn, our good moods were often cut short when we found three other samba bands outside, in line, waiting to record their next hit. It was disheartening, to have the tiniest taste of the sweetness of success and then to have that sweetness diluted to the point of insignificance. With fewer gigs, Graça and I went hungry so we could make rent and pay Madame L. For two weeks, we were late with our payments to him. Then, one afternoon, Madame L.'s messenger boy arrived at our boardinghouse. I steeled myself for an order to visit Madame L. in his office. Instead, the boy had another request.

"Meet him at the corner, outside his place," the boy said. "And dress fancy. Madame L. says no trousers for you, and not too much makeup on the pretty gal. And you're supposed to bring the other guy—the bandleader. And tell him to wear a good suit."

"Where are we going?" I asked.

The boy shrugged. "He said you're his guests."

———

I t was past midnight. In the glow of gas streetlamps, Madame L.'s
sharkskin suit shone as if it was wet. Graça, Vinicius, and I followed
him far past Carmelita's Alley and wound our way into a neighborhood
I didn't recognize.

Madame L. whistled, which made me less nervous; perhaps this was
simply an excursion and not a punishment for late payment. Vinicius
was with us, after all, and he didn't owe Madame L. a centavo. These
were the things I told myself as we moved in a line through unknown
streets until Lucifer finally stopped at a rusted metal door. "Here we
are," he said, and knocked.

A peephole slid open. Then several bolts were turned and the door
creaked wide. A muscular youth—no older than Graça and I—greeted
us. His eyelashes were so long and thick, they nearly touched the arch
of his eyebrows. He wore a tuxedo.

"Just in time," the youth said.

We walked into the empty office of an abandoned factory. The
youth guided us through dark corridors until there were voices and
light. The cramped hallway opened to a vast, smoky warehouse filled
with tables and chairs. Men in tuxedos and women in beaded gowns—
people who should have been at the Copacabana Palace—filled the tables and crowded the bar. Upon closer inspection, I saw that several of
the elegant women had Adam's apples bobbing at their necks. Some of
the tuxedoed men had full lips and high cheekbones. Waitresses (or
were they waiters?) wearing jaunty police costumes darted from table to
table, the glasses on their trays rattling. Onstage, a band played samba.

As soon as we were seated, Vinicius asked: "What are we doing
here?"

"We're being entertained," Madame L. replied before ordering a
bottle of sugarcane rum.

The band quickened their pace. Several couples joined the crowd on the floor. Graça swallowed her drink, uncrossed her legs, and stood. "Dance with me, you oaf," she said, and tugged Vinicius from his chair.

She'd borrowed an evening gown from Anaïs: a long silk frock with a nipped waistline that looked as if it had been poured onto her. Graça and Vinicius joined the cluster of couples near the stage. Vinicius was clumsy, staring at his feet and bumping into the dancers around him. He sighed, then pulled away from Graça. He began to leave the floor but Graça gripped his arm. They both stood very still, the only ones who weren't moving. Graça whispered in his ear and Vinicius stared at her, incredulous. Then a smile slowly spread across his face, brightening it. I'd never seen him look so happy, not even after we'd written our best sambas.

I grabbed my cocktail glass and emptied it in one swallow. Madame L. refilled it and pushed the glass back toward me.

"How long did it take for that to happen?" he asked, nodding at the dance floor where Graça and Vinicius now moved in perfect unison.

"What?"

"The bandleader and the singer," he said. "What a tired old story! I'd hoped your act would avoid it, but we're all animals, aren't we?"

I felt the room tilt. On the dance floor, Graça's hair was plastered to her head. Vinicius's shirt stuck to his chest.

"They aren't together," I said.

Madame L. laughed. "Not yet. Your Graçinha doesn't let good sense prevail over whatever she wants in the moment. She doesn't take the long view, does she? You're more that type."

He refilled my glass again.

"What type?"

"The type with ambition."

"Graça's got more ambition in one hair on her head than all the fools in this club."

"She's got needs," Madame L. said. "Ambitions have planning and thought behind them. Needs are just instincts we feed. And they're always hungry, querida. Needs make us into buckets with holes in them."

The band stopped playing. A spotlight hit the beaded curtain.

"I promised we'd be entertained," Madame L. said. "Here it comes."

The dance floor emptied. Graça and Vinicius returned. We sat in silence, the air heavy with cigarette smoke. Then the curtain parted and a man appeared. His skin was as dark and shining as a plum's. His arms were roped with veins and muscle. He wore a headdress of blue and purple feathers, and his dress was studded with pearls and clasped over one shoulder. His face and body were dusted with a glittering powder that sparkled under the light, as if he had just emerged from the sea and was beaded with water.

The band played. The performer strutted and sang. I was dazzled by his movement, his costume, the sheer size of him, the hypnotic force of his energy. He moved away from the stage and into the crowd. Men, women, waiters and waitresses danced enthusiastically alongside him, as if in a trance. I closed my eyes. Without his image before me, the performer's effect was lost—his voice was average, his band members not professionals. I opened my eyes just as the act finished and the club's patrons fell back into their chairs.

"What a number!" Graça said.

Madame L. nodded. "Onstage you must be a dream. And you must make people fall into that dream with you."

"If you've got talent you don't need make-believe," Vinicius said.

Lucifer laughed. "Everyone needs make-believe. Talent only takes you so far. You all know this firsthand, with those copycats stealing your gigs."

"Those other bands won't last," Vinicius said, glancing at me. "Our songs are better."

Graça crossed her arms. "My voice is better."

"Neither is good enough to keep you cats working," Lucifer replied. "You think little girls listening to you on the radio know the difference between Sofia Salvador and Aracy Araújo? Shit, I don't even know the difference. You cats might've been the first and the best, but that doesn't mean shit if no one knows you. You need to find something those other bands can't ever copy. You need girls across Rio to want to dress like Sofia, act like Sofia, sound like Sofia, but never actually *be* Sofia. Sofia Salvador's got to be impressive. She's not a schoolgirl, she's a dream. She's got to burn herself so deep into people's memories that if any tramp singer tries to copy her, it'll look pathetic."

Graça nodded. "I won't be lumped with a bunch of floozies that can't even hum a tune."

"What matters is our music, not our looks," Vinicius said. "You need to believe in your talent, not in some costume. Come on, Dor, talk some sense into her."

Graça laughed. "I'm center stage, not Dor. I'm who people see. You and the boys can wear your boring tuxedos but Madame L.'s right: I have to be different."

Vinicius stood. "And I have to get some air."

He left through the curtained doorway. Graça sighed.

"He's got to be on our side, or the band won't be," Graça said. "Dor, go talk to him? He listens to you."

Madame L. smiled as if I'd suddenly become the evening's entertainment. I stood and made my way through the curtain.

In the alley, Vinicius paced and smoked. Seeing me, he held out his cigarette and I accepted, smoking half before speaking.

"There're samba girls on every corner now. Sofia Salvador needs to be different."

"Real sambistas don't need costumes," Vinicius said, still pacing. "We're not some vaudeville act. I want people to know our songs, Dor!

When I'm dead, I want people to remember our music, not how we looked playing it."

"How can people know our songs if they never hear them in the first place?" I asked. "We're the best in the city, and we're being drowned out. We need something to set us apart."

Vinicius snorted. "A gimmick."

"No, a style. Something to keep us in people's memories."

"If our music doesn't set us apart, then we don't deserve to be playing," Vinicius snapped. "And if people can't appreciate our songs for what they're worth, they don't deserve to be listening."

"So you get to decide who's deserving and who's not?" I asked. "Who's good enough to hear us and who's too dumb? You're as bad as those wet cats at Copacabana Palace. You're a goddamn snob."

Vinicius snatched back his cigarette. "You don't understand, Dor."

"Then maybe I don't deserve to hear your music, either? Maybe I shouldn't be in your precious roda."

"You didn't grow up playing samba. You and Graça hear it for a few months and think you can change it to suit yourselves."

I drew a sharp breath, as if I still had his cigarette between my lips. "We want to make it better. To make it ours. Not play the same damn songs over and over, or be like you and write tearjerkers every damn day because you're pining."

Vinicius's chest rose and fell as if he was short of breath. He looked away from me. "She's a wreck waiting to happen. I've had prettier girls. And I've sure as hell had nicer ones."

"Me too."

"You're better than all that."

"All what?"

"That tomcatting you do."

I laughed. "No one lectures Tiny about being 'better than all that.' You congratulate him."

"Because Tiny enjoys his nights out."

"And I don't?"

Vinicius shook his head. "I'm not the only one pining around here."

The building's brick wall met my shoulder, warm and rough. I closed my eyes and let it hold me as I leaned. In front of me, Vinicius leaned, too, so we were mirrors to each other, eye to eye in that poorly lit alley. He fumbled for another cigarette.

"What did she say to you in there?" I asked, my voice a whisper. "On the dance floor. How'd she make you stay with her?"

Vinicius shook his head. "She said she'd take care of me, like she always does when we play together onstage. It's just . . . it's funny because she's right. I trust her up there, onstage, more than I ever do out here, in life. When we play together, she's different. All her selfishness just goes away. Poof! She gives everything. Everything inside herself; she's not afraid of it, and neither am I. And I know she's not just giving it to me—she's giving it to everyone out there listening. If she puts on some costume, she might not be the same when we play together. She might not give herself up like she does now. And I don't want to lose that feeling, Dor."

Vinicius looked at me, afraid, like a child caught stealing. I wanted to punish him and, at the same time, wrap him in my arms.

Not long ago, I'd basked in Graça's intoxicating generosity onstage. She challenged you without malice, making you a better performer, making you reach deeper within yourself, just as she reached. And what she brought out of herself seemed like an offering she made only to you—not to the dozens or hundreds who also watched her alongside you. This, not singing, was Graça's talent: making a person feel special in her presence when, in fact, you weren't special at all. Vinicius felt this as sharply as I did. A shared affliction can rope two people together tighter than any physical bond. But envy also welled up inside me, bitter and insistent. The stage was where Graça felt most real, and Vinicius got to share in the thrill of that reality with her. And, conversely, Graça got to bring our songs to life with Vinicius in a way I never could with him, in our writing roda.

"At least you get to be onstage, together," I said.

"I miss you up there," Vinicius replied. "You made me feel safe, somehow. Like every show wasn't going to be the end of me."

"But being safe's no fun, is it?"

Vinicius gave me a sad little smile. I returned it.

I slipped my hand into Vinicius's, finding his thumb and stroking the callus on its fingertip, the skin so thick I wondered if he even felt me there, moving my thumb against his, back and forth. How many songs had built that callus? How many guitars had it already outlived? A great heat rose from the pit of my belly and bloomed into my chest. Vinicius straightened. Could he feel this heat, emanating from me?

I was prepared for him to make a joke, or pull away, or maneuver us back inside. I was not prepared to feel his hands—those large, callused, guitar player's mitts—press against my hips. His fingers dug into my sides and pulled me toward him. I didn't know if he would hug me or kiss me, and I felt both petrified and thrilled, wondering which it might be.

Behind us, a door creaked open. A shaft of light brightened Vinicius's face. He squinted. His hands quickly fell from me. Too quickly, as if he was ashamed of people seeing us in any kind of embrace, friendly or otherwise. I felt as if I'd stepped back into the ice-cold showers at Sion School—my body rigid, my chest so tight it was hard to breathe, but my mind suddenly clear. Two couples stumbled from the club and walked past us. The young bouncer held the club's door open.

"You two coming back in?" he asked.

"Yes," I called, then turned to Vinicius. "A costume's just a set of clothes. If you really want to keep her, you'll give her what she wants. Or she'll find someone else who will."

"Dor, wait," Vinicius pleaded, but I didn't let him finish. I was already halfway through the door.

We were, all of us, strivers. Vinicius wanted his music to be remembered. Graça wanted to be known and, through this knowing, loved. And Madame L. and I strove for a similar goal, though I wouldn't realize it until many years later, when I visited him in prison: both of us refused to be cast away by a world that had little interest in keeping us. I can't moan about my lot, given how far I've risen. But I can state facts: I was born a girl with skin a touch too dark, nearly thrown into a cane field to die like a useless animal. I had no family, no money, little looks, and a tendency to enjoy both women and men. Some, like Graça and Vinicius, are never required to question their existence. But I have always had to prove my worth. Madame L. fought to prove his worth, too, just using different methods. Madame L. held a stake in our success not simply because he wanted to fill his pockets—he could do that selling sweet flour and girls—but because he saw in Sofia Salvador and Blue Moon a glimmer of what Graça, Vinicius, and I also saw: the possibility of transformation, and of escape. So while he was a danger to us, he was also a benefactor, helping to transform a schoolgirl into a dream, and then putting her in a contest where she would annihilate either her competition or herself.

After our night out, Madame L. paid a visit to our producers at Victor Records. Every record company in Rio—Columbia, Parphalon, Victor, and others—had been asked to nominate an act for Rádio Mayrink's annual Showcase, which would be broadcast live to all of Brazil. Victor had chosen our rival Aracy Araújo to perform two songs. After Madame L.'s visit, Aracy was limited to one. Sofia Salvador and Blue Moon took the other three-minute time slot.

The Showcase would be in the once shabby Urca Casino, known to be worn and moldy, its plaster ceiling stained from leaks and its chandeliers missing crystals. But Urca had been bought by Joaquim Rolla and immediately closed for renovations. Some speculated that Urca would be transformed into the swankiest casino in Rio. Others called Rolla a con man, and predicted that the renovation would be abandoned because of money woes. Either way, the casino's transformation was shrouded in mystery, making all of Rio curious about its grand reopening, and the Mayrink Showcase quickly became the hottest ticket in town.

In the weeks before the show, Graça and Madame L. sketched pages of possible costumes: evening dresses with ruffled skirts and feathered collars, dramatically drape-backed gowns with scarf point hems that would sway as Sofia Salvador moved across a stage. Madame L. hired seamstresses to make these designs a reality, but the ruffled and feathered gowns overwhelmed Graça's tiny frame, making her look like a child who had raided her mother's closet. In the end, they commissioned a cherry-red evening gown for Sofia, and a set of brand-new tuxedos for the Blue Moon boys. The clothes were expensive, which meant we'd borrowed a hefty sum from Madame L. to look presentable for the Mayrink show. All of us felt pressure to make it a success; Graça and I most of all.

In the hours before the show, five Blue Moon boys squeezed into taxis along with their instruments and, in the cars' trunks, a stack of neatly folded tuxedos. The boys waved good-bye to me and Vinicius on the sidewalk outside my boardinghouse. As soon as they left, we ran upstairs, where Graça was taking her sweet time in the bathroom. She'd disappeared that entire afternoon, insisting she needed privacy before the show. I knocked on the door.

"There're dressing rooms at Urca," I said. "You don't have to get dolled up to ride in a taxi."

"Just shut up!" Graça yelled back.

There was wildness in her voice, a desperation that made her words a plea rather than a command. Vinicius and I glanced at each other.

"Open the door," I said, my voice as gentle as I could muster.

"I can't."

There was a hiccup, then a sob. Water ran in the sink.

"Graça?"

"Oh, God! I want to die!"

My heart drummed in my chest. I thought of Riacho Doce, of the river, of Graça in her mother's driving coat, rocks heavy in her pockets.

"Open the goddamn door!" I yelled.

The lock clicked. Graça sat naked on the closed toilet, her face streaked with tears, the skin around her eyes puffy. Her hairline was red and raw, as if she'd scrubbed it with steel wool. Above that, where her soft brown curls used to be, the hair was platinum blond and as stiff as the bristles of a broom.

"What did you do?" I breathed.

Vinicius pressed behind me. "Shit," he muttered.

I grabbed a towel to cover Graça's nakedness, though she didn't seem to care who saw her. She gulped, then stared at the ceiling. "I wanted to be different! I wanted to look like Greta Garbo! It was supposed to be a surprise."

I leaned against the bathroom sink, afraid I might be sick. We had ninety minutes until Urca's curtains lifted.

Awkwardly, as if moving a mannequin whose limbs might fall and break, Vinicius and I carried Graça to bed and coaxed her into a robe. Then I ordered Vinicius downstairs to phone the only person who could help us.

Anaïs arrived ten minutes later. Upon seeing Graça, our teacher shook her head. She slapped Graça's hand away when she tried to scratch her scalp.

"You cannot have it bleed," Anaïs said.

"But it itches like hell," Graça whined. "I've washed it ten times!"

Anaïs removed a tin of aloe vera paste from her bag and slathered it across Graça's head. Globs of white-blond hair clumped between Anaïs's fingers, leaving bare patches across Graça's scalp. When she'd finished, Anaïs stretched a shower cap over Graça's head before turning to Vinicius and me.

"If we dry and style that hair, it will all fall out. It is burned to a crisp, and so is her scalp," Anaïs said, then turned back to Graça. "It takes three or four sessions to dye hair like yours blond! How much peroxide did you use?"

Graça fell back on the bed and covered her eyes with her arms.

"You will have to cancel your show," Anaïs said.

"We can't," Vinicius replied. "The boys are on their way to Urca. I won't leave them in the lurch."

On the bed, Graça laughed through her stuffed nose, producing a series of clicks and gasps. "The boys are all you fucking care about," she said.

"They shouldn't pay for your stupidity," Vinicius replied.

"Don't call her stupid," I said, my voice echoing across the room.

Graça smiled.

"We can't cancel," I said to Anaïs. "If we don't show up, no one in Rio will hire us again."

"And that won't matter because Lucifer will slit our throats," Vinicius said.

"Then you need to find a new singer," Anaïs replied.

Graça sat up.

"No one knows our material," I said. "We rehearsed a new song."

"You know it," Vinicius said.

My hands felt fat with blood; my fingers twitched as if each had a heartbeat all its own. I nodded to Anaïs. "She said I shouldn't be on-stage. She said my voice can't handle it."

"Well, here is your chance to prove me wrong," Anaïs said.

In one swift leap, Graça stood. "I don't care if I'm as bald as a baby's ass. I'm the one who's singing tonight."

"I knew that would get you up," Vinicius said.

"It was a trick?" I asked.

Vinicius's amusement disappeared from his face. "I was trying to help. I thought . . ."

A joke. That's what he believed the possibility of my singing alongside him and the boys was. I felt a stab of embarrassment so sharp I winced. My hands balled into fists. I was back in Riacho Doce's mill during harvest, where the heat seared your face and those great, foaming vats of liquid sugar threatened to overflow and maim anyone near them. Graça knew that mill, too.

She shoved Vinicius aside and stood in front of me, smelling of peroxide and aloe. Slowly, as if she feared I might buck, she put her tiny hands over my fists and gripped them tightly. Then she came close, her face nearly touching mine, like we were back in our shared bed trading secrets.

"Hey, Dor?" she whispered. "Look at me. That's it. Don't be mad at him, it's all my fault. I messed things up real good this time. But you know how much I want to sing up there, on that fancy stage. You're the only one in the world who knows. At least one of us should get to do it, right? I don't want to be a joke up there. I don't want people to laugh at me. I need you."

I took long, deep breaths, the way Anaïs had taught us. I felt the warmth of Graça in front of me, her mouth close, her breath even with mine.

I need you.

I'd become what I'd never dreamed of being, what no one dreams of being: I'd become necessary, like a bolt in a lock or a screw in a great machine.

I looked up.

"Can we get one of your hats on her?" I asked Anaïs. "The biggest, showiest one you've got?"

Anaïs shook her head. "No singer wears a hat on a stage. It is disrespectful. And no hat will hide her entire head. Only a shower cap will do that. Or a turban. And only Baianas wear turbans."

Graça's eyes met mine. There was, in that moment, a kind of telepathy between us—the kind that appears only after a decade of shared experience forges the deepest knowledge of the person in front of you. We thought of Carnaval. Of Auntie Ciata. Of the Salvador docks. How glorious the Baianas were. How regal.

It was madness, of course. But what else did we have?

For Urca's grand reopening, Joaquim Rolla hired a fleet of water taxis to ship tourists from twenty cruise ships to the new casino. Light-haired, sunburned men and women crowded the casino's atrium, twice the size of Riacho Doce's mill. Flowering white bushes were trimmed into perfect squares, like giant sugar cubes. At the end of the atrium path were massive stone columns marking the entrance to the Grill Room.

Instead of the traditional velvet curtain, the Grill's stage had a curtain covered in thousands of round mirrors, each the size of a coin, that shimmered like a waterfall and would part to reveal whatever artist was behind it. Tourists packed the Grill Room's worst tables. At the best ones—closest to the stage—were the kinds of moneyed and powerful citizens Rolla had promised Mayrink he would deliver. Most had come out of curiosity: to see what kind of gaudy monstrosity President Gegê's rumored friend had built with money made of dubious origins. Rolla's hope—and ours, too—was to turn the curiosity of Rio's elite into acceptance, even wonder.

From my place near the stage, I stared numbly at the audience. The young socialites wore headpieces with little jewels that dotted the centers of their foreheads. Their gowns were so elaborately beaded, I wondered how they could walk under the weight. Beside them sat their mothers and grandmothers, wearing fur stoles despite the heat. (Rolla's newly installed refrigerated air machine was fickle and cut on and off all night.) Tuxedoed record executives and department store moguls squinted at the act onstage. Violinists, a piano player, and a man with a cello accompanied a thick-necked soprano as she sang an aria from a Brazilian opera commissioned by Old Gegê. The president was not in attendance, but several of his most trusted advisers were.

My stomach turned; we were the third samba act in the show, sandwiched between a magician and Aracy Araújo, that copycat. She, of all people, would close the entire showcase. She was supposed to be the folk act that the crowd would remember.

Graça and Anaïs were locked in the tiny Urca dressing room, too small to fit all three of us. The thought of Graça leaving that room made me queasy.

Before going to Urca that night, we were like thieves, grabbing Graça's red dress and stuffing into a pillowcase every piece of costume jewelry she had collected. Then the four of us rushed to La Femme Chic, where Anaïs gathered a bolt of thick red taffeta, some milliner's wire, and a handful of pins. Vinicius helped us carry these belongings to Urca, but he had no clue what we planned to do with them.

Backstage at Urca, a nervous little man ran back and forth, making sure each act was ready for its debut. Ten minutes before our curtain call, Graça was still locked in her dressing room with Anaïs. The Blue Moon boys appeared, looking dapper in their blue tuxedos. Vinicius had slicked back his thick mane, showing off his sideburns and sharp cheekbones. I couldn't look him in the eyes.

Onstage, the busty soprano left and the magician now commanded the audience's attention. Near the Blue Moon boys and me, the talent manager dabbed his forehead with a hankie and then waved it in the air as a signal to us that we would take the stage next.

Behind me, I heard the click of high heels. Vinicius gasped and used my shoulder to steady himself. Little Noel nearly dropped his drum.

Graça's red evening gown was strapless, with a heart-shaped bodice. The gown's skirt swelled from her waist like a bell. On her wrists were every bracelet and bangle she owned. Her lips were bright red. Her eyes were no longer puffy or pink. Her burned head was hidden under a swirl of red taffeta that Anaïs had expertly tucked and pinned until it rose up in a turban.

Graça raised her arms and smiled. "What's the matter, boys? Haven't you seen a Baiana before?"

It was not Carnaval, a holiday when the risqué and dangerous were celebrated. It was a day like any other in Brazil in 1938, when a woman dressing as a Baiana onstage—not as a joke or a costume, but as a powerful, beautiful kind of dress—was unthinkable.

"What game are you playing?" Vinicius asked, then faced me. "That's your solution?"

Graça's arms dropped. Her bracelets clattered. "This is no game."

"Miss Salvador!" the stage manager called, weaving past the Blue Moon boys and me. When he saw Graça his eyes grew so wide, I thought he was having a nervous fit. I think the man would have been less shocked if Graça had appeared naked. He swallowed hard before speaking. "I won't be able to allow this."

Graça's smile disappeared. "Why in hell not?"

"This is a refined house!" the stage manager said, his voice high. "We have diplomats in attendance. We have the president's cousin at the front table! We are expecting attire that's a bit more—"

"Boring," Graça interrupted.

"I was going to say 'ladylike,'" the stage manager said, his cheeks flushed. "But maybe you northeastern *matutas* don't understand that."

"You saying she doesn't look like a lady?" Bonito yelled, startling us all. Our soft-spoken cuíca player breathed hard, his hands in fists at his side. "Are you saying my mother and sisters aren't respectable when they dress like this?"

I turned to the stage manager. "Give us a minute?"

"A minute's all you've got," the manager said. "If she's not decent by the time that magician's finished, I'm pulling your act."

"Decent?" Graça called after him. "I'm more covered up than those broads in the crowd."

Vinicius sighed. "We've only got three minutes to win them over. They're going to spend the entire time paying attention to the fucking outfit, and not the music. If we won't change her clothes, then we need more time out there."

He and Graça looked at me. Vinicius was right; one song would never be enough time for Graça to charm the audience into accepting the Baiana and then forgetting her, to focus on Graça's voice and our music.

"I'll get you more time," I said.

"How?" Kitchen asked.

"Doesn't matter," Graça interrupted. "Dor will do it. So are we shaking those stiffs up, or not?"

The Blue Moon boys exchanged looks. Tiny shrugged. "Fuck it all to hell," he said. "Let's make their jaws drop."

There was a scattered round of applause. Then the MC announced: "And now some popular folk music! Straight from Lapa's hippest clubs, we now present Miss Sofia Salvador and the Blue Moon Band!"

From behind the mirrored curtain, I saw guests whisper and shrug. The stage manager made his way toward us, his face as red as Graça's gown. Before he could snatch her back, Graça ran onto the stage. The boys followed her.

I caught Vinicius's arm. "Whatever happens out there, or back here," I said, "just keep playing."

He paused, then kissed my cheek and stepped through the mirrored curtain.

There was, at first, an eerie quiet. Graça's bracelets clanged and chimed. The Grill Room's many mirrors seemed to sap all of Graça's color, making her pale. The boys and Vinicius arranged themselves in a semicircle behind her and began to play. Graça's first notes came out shaky. The instruments overpowered her. Graça's face instantly registered the shock of hearing her voice so weak, but she did not falter or begin again. She kept singing.

Every audience—even the most refined—looks forward to risk. Risk that there will be an error, that the performer's talent will not reach the bar set by the song itself. So the singer must play with losing control, but never truly lose it. In order for Graça to do this, I had to buy her time.

O ther acts congregated behind the curtain to gawk at Graça and the boys onstage. I pushed my way past them and ran back to the dressing rooms, barging into five rooms before I found her. Aracy wore the same schoolgirl's white blouse and wide skirt that Graça once wore, but the top buttons of her shirt were open and her face was thick with makeup. She faced the mirror and dabbed a powder puff across her cheeks.

"You're in the wrong place," she said, eyeing me.

"No," I replied. "You're the one I'm looking for."

"I've heard about you," Aracy said. "I don't go that route, sister."

I plucked the powder puff from her fingers. "You're not my sister."

Aracy tried to grab the puff back. I moved it from her reach. She tried again. I moved it again and then grabbed Aracy's wrist.

"I'll scream if you try something on me!" she said.

"Be real quiet and I won't break anything," I said, twisting her wrist.

"I've got to get out there," she said. "I'm closing the show."

"Not tonight you're not," I replied, and pushed her away. The dressing room door had a flimsy lock. I turned it, then grabbed a chair and wedged it under the doorknob.

"What're you doing?" Aracy asked.

I stood in front of the chair. "You can give me a private concert."

Aracy charged at me, aiming her painted nails at my face, my neck. The elegant little fascinator Anaïs had made me for the show went crooked, its pins tugging at my hair. I grabbed Aracy's forearm and twisted it behind her until she cried out. Then I turned her around, her back to my chest, my other arm around her in a bear hug. We both faced the mirror. Aracy's lipstick had smeared. There was a red streak across the yellow silk of my gown.

"My band will look for me," she said. "And the stage manager, too. I'll tell them you kidnapped me. They'll break down this door."

"You're going to tell them you're real sick," I said. "And you can't come out." She twisted and bucked in my arms again and I held her, like Old Euclides used to hold down injured donkeys at Riacho Doce. After a few seconds Aracy, like those donkeys, tired. I looked at the dressing room clock; Graça and the boys would be improvising a second song by now.

There was a knock at the door. I could feel Aracy's chest rise and fall under the weight of my arm. I tightened my hold.

"Madame Lucifer is my friend," I whispered, staring at Aracy's reflection in the dressing room mirror. "You ever hear of a club owner called Little Tony? I don't want to see what Madame Lucifer would do to your pretty face if you make a peep right now."

Aracy stared at me in the mirror. The knocking continued. When she finally spoke, her voice was soft. She did as I'd ordered, telling her band that she was sick, and to go away. The knocking stopped. Aracy tilted her face toward mine.

"You're a Big Foot," she said. "I'll tell everyone you forced me."

Big Foot. I'd heard the slur before, just never aimed at me. My arms felt very heavy. I tightened my grip on Aracy.

"Forced you?" I said, attempting to laugh. "I'll tell everyone what a wild time we had together in here. So wild, you forgot to go onstage. We'll see how your fans feel about a Big Foot singer."

Aracy was quiet after that, and her silence made the minutes feel like days. My arms burned and cramped. My legs shook. But I held Aracy until I was sure the show was over. All the while I imagined Graça and the boys onstage, waiting for the MC to direct them off and, when he didn't appear, how they would look at each other and play the first notes of their next song without guilt or hesitation.

Anaïs watched their entire set from the wings. Later, she told me how, after those first few rocky notes, Graça's voice relaxed. She moved her bracelets in such a way that they became instruments. She swayed and shimmied near Vinicius. She used the tone of her voice to challenge him to play quicker, then coax him to go slower. Vinicius never lost track. He played his seven-string guitar, and that extra string added a deep bottom to his playing. Those low notes buoyed Sofia Salvador, helping her voice rise higher and brighter. And the audience heard this wide spectrum of sound and it did not sound dissonant or odd, but like a perfect dialogue.

Waiters stopped their service. Coat-check girls congregated in the Grill Room's dark patches. Somewhere in this crowd a pair of hands clapped in time to the music, then another. Graça's eyes darted toward this noise. She sang louder, danced faster. By the middle of "My Mutt," it seemed as if the whole room had let out a great breath of relief. A few of the society ladies tapped their fingers on the tables. Some of the gentlemen shook their heads and smiled. I can imagine them thinking: *What pluck this little bird has! What charm!*

The show closed. Sofia Salvador bowed. The crowd cheered and stomped their feet until the entire theater shook beneath us. Aracy and I felt the vibration as far away as the dressing room. I loosened my grip. Aracy wrenched herself away.

"You won," she said. "It's over."

The applause stopped. There was music again—an encore. I pulled the chair out from under the knob and flung open the dressing room door. Aracy was wrong: nothing was over. We were just beginning.

E veryone in Brazil who'd tuned their radios to the Mayrink Show-case that night heard Sofia Salvador bring the house down. And, it seemed, all of Rio wanted to see her in person.

We became exclusive players at the Grill Room. The ambassador of Spain came to see our show and kissed Sofia Salvador's hand afterward. Their photograph appeared in the national papers. Rolla paid us enough to make us feel rich, even though we weren't. We paid Madame L. back for our fancy clothes. The boys bought nice suits and ate better meals. Graça and I rented a swanky room complete with a claw-footed bath-tub. The day after the Mayrink Showcase, we went to a beauty parlor and lopped off Graça's burned hair. She wore hats until her bald spots grew back, and after that she skipped around Lapa looking like a beau-tiful, rascally pixie.

The more success we had, the smaller our world became. Cafés and bars became tiresome places for us because young musicians bom-barded Graça and the boys with requests for favors and loans. We couldn't go to any beach or cabaret in the city without getting mobbed by Sofia Salvador's fans—male and female alike. Every fashionable girl in Rio wore Sofia Salvador's signature red lipstick, until Sofia changed hers to mauve, then coral, then electric pink. Her hair remained pixie short and very blond. Sofia Salvador quickly ditched the turban, in part because Bonito and Banana had asked her to, out of respect for real Baianas, and in part because Graça couldn't stand the thought of being an imitator. Her dresses grew more like pillars than like bells, their slits higher up her thigh. Their colors were ones you'd find in a jungle, not in an elegant theater: banana-leaf green, butterfly-wing blue, passionflower purple. She was a chameleon: tiny, colorful, and constantly changing. Her fans and competitors ruthlessly tried to keep up.

By 1940, Auntie Ciata's yard was no longer safe. Samba bands competed for gigs, record deals, and radio play. Good songs were a commodity, and, Lapa being Lapa, there was no shame in eavesdropping on another band's roda, memorizing their songs, and then running to a studio before dawn to record the tracks as your own. This was how lesser bands stole several of our sambas, and forced our rodas out of Ciata's and into cramped boardinghouse rooms. We made some of our biggest hits in those rooms: "Crying for You," "Sweet Moreno," "My Nêgo," "Just a Little Taste," "Win You Over," "Ache in My Heart."

There were still dozens of good samba bands out there, but none had a person dedicated to making them great—except ours. If a stage floor was too slick, if someone tried to skimp on our fee, if they did not provide the band with hot water and face towels, if a dressing room was dirty, then I set things right. Cabaret owners, recording technicians, talent managers, rival bands, and all sorts of other small-minded Lapa nincompoops who hoped to take advantage of Sofia Salvador and Blue Moon called me names behind my back: Guard Dog, Vulture, Bitch, Big Foot, and worse. People thought they were clever with their secret insults but I always eventually heard what was said about me and, to their great dismay, I wasn't upset. Not outwardly. I recalled the names that people had called my mother—what had she done to deserve them? She'd been a child forced to endure the attentions of the Little Senhor and his friends. She'd refused to starve after being kicked out of the Great House and became a cane cutter. She'd refused to be married. She'd refused to be shamed. So they called her names out of fear, and made her well-known. I did not sing onstage beside Sofia Salvador like I'd once dreamed of doing, but I earned my own kind of fame.

I set things right within the band, too. When Tiny, Banana, and Bonito argued over a cocktail waitress, I got the girl fired from Urca and brought three stunners backstage after our show—one for each of the boys. When Little Noel got pneumonia, I convinced Joaquim Rolla to pay for the casino's fancy doctor to care for him. Mostly I settled daily riffs between Graça and Vinicius. When he chastised her for being lazy or questioned her taste in music, I spent our taxi rides home building her up again, showering her with compliments, and poking fun at Vinicius the way we had with those long-forgotten knuckle draggers, calling him "Dinosaur" and imitating his scowling face until Graça cried with laughter. When Graça riled Vinicius on purpose, calling him "old man" or telling him his hearing was going bad, I took Vinicius on walks along Urca's beach to calm him, listening as he called her unreasonable and selfish, and then working those grievances into lyrics we could use later, in our songs. I was, like Kitchen in our roda, the one who kept the band's beat steady, and who guided Vinicius and Graça into a delicate harmony.

I t was in the middle of a performance at the Grill Room when one of Urca's bouncers informed me that we had a visitor.

"He says he's Miss Salvador's father," the bouncer said.

I remembered the day, long before, when the growling automobile had made its way for the first time into Riacho Doce and I'd felt both panic and curiosity. I stared into the dark backstage corridor and told myself: this is a trick. The man was a fan eager to meet Sofia Salvador, or an agent from a rival casino trying to outbid Urca.

"Send him back," I replied.

The man who made his way toward me was too short to be Senhor Pimentel. His hair was gray and thin, his brow deeply furrowed. But when he turned for a moment to the side, confused by the labyrinth of dressing areas and props closets, I saw the sharp Roman profile. And, in the middle of his chest, the diamond sugar cube glittered.

"You've grown, Jega!" Senhor Pimentel said, and smiled as if we were old chums. His eyes scanned my high heels, my trousers, my suspenders and silk blouse.

"I'm not Jega."

Senhor Pimentel swayed closer. I smelled a sweet rankness, as if he'd been pickled in rum.

"Seems like everyone has made-up names around here. What do you call yourself now?" he asked.

"My name's Dores. Like always."

"Is that so? Well, Dores, I saw my Graçinha in the papers, shaking hands with an ambassador. She had that ridiculous thing on her head, and more makeup than a decent girl needs. But I knew it was her. I'd recognize my Graçinha anywhere."

We could hear Sofia Salvador and Blue Moon singing the final song of their act. Once they got offstage, they'd have thirty minutes to rest and change clothes before going on again.

"It took you a while to come looking for us," I said.

"For her," Senhor Pimentel corrected. "Everyone thought she was dead. And for a time, I would've rather she'd been dead than living as some cabaret girl. Or worse."

"And look at us now: in a fancy show. It's the perfect time to find us."

Senhor Pimentel smiled. "We hear her on the radio sometimes, in Recife. No one knows it's her, and I don't tell them. Her mother would roll over in her grave if she saw her dressed like some voodoo woman, on a stage in front of important people."

"So you came to scold?" I asked.

"Every girl needs a father to guide her," Senhor Pimentel replied.

The stage lights brightened and pulsed, illuminating the backstage corridor more than before. The elbows of Senhor Pimentel's suit were shiny with wear. The lapels of his jacket were frayed. The tie beneath the sugar cube pin was mottled with stains.

"How's the sugar business?" I asked.

His eyes met mine. "The market's not what it was. The smart ones diversified. Graça was right to leave. What would she have done? Married another planter who would have gone broke?"

"That's what you wanted her to do."

Senhor Pimentel shook his head. "I wanted to give her an honest future. Love blinds you when you're a father. You wouldn't know about that, being what you are."

"What's that?" I asked.

Senhor Pimentel shrugged. "Discarded. Don't take offense now, Jega! You couldn't help it. It's what your lot do: pop out children and then leave them for us to feed, clothe, send to fancy schools. You're a lucky one. Not every patrão would've been as kind as me."

"I was lucky to have Nena," I replied.

Senhor Pimentel looked pained. "She was a good old girl."

"Was?" I asked, staring at his craggy face.

"Nena fell over one day in the kitchen, not long after you two disappeared. I called in a doctor for her, she was special to me, you know. He said it was her heart."

The heels of my shoes seemed to give out beneath me. I stumbled and reached for the dark wall. There was a wooden beam; I braced myself against it. I'd wanted to send Nena money to show her we'd succeeded in Rio, but I hadn't even written a letter or given her a sign of life. In part because I was selfish and young, and in part because I'd been afraid of being caught by the man who now stood before me. He was not the handsome, menacing Senhor of my memory but a small man in a ragged suit. Who was the real Senhor?

The show ended. Graça and the boys filed backstage, giddy with exhaustion. She saw him then, and there was nothing I could do. Senhor Pimentel yelled "Graçinha!" and opened his arms.

Graça stopped. Her smile disappeared and her face became like a mannequin's—placid and unreadable. I knew better than most that Graça had a profound capacity to wound, and an equally astonishing and unpredictable ability to dole out kindness. In that moment backstage, I wondered which would win out.

Senhor Pimentel's arms fell to his sides. "It's me, Papai."

Graça eyed him. "It took you long enough."

The Blue Moon boys stared, confused. In the front of the house, we heard laughter and chairs scraping. The Grill Room's audience headed back into the casino; Sofia's shows were short enough to get people drunk and happy, but not so long as to keep them from gambling their money away.

"You saw the show?" Graça asked.

"Not yet," Senhor Pimentel replied. "I came straight back to see you."

Graça blinked as if startled from a long sleep. "We go on again in thirty minutes," she said. "I need to rest."

"Maybe you can get me a front-row seat?" Senhor Pimentel asked.

"Do you have a tux?" I interrupted. "They won't let you out front without one. There's a dress code here. It's a respectable place."

Senhor Pimentel's expression darkened and it was as if I was back in the old parlor, face-to-face with Riacho Doce's master, bracing to receive my punishment. But just as quickly the Senhor closed his eyes, and when he reopened them, his face lit up in a smile.

"I'll watch my girl from back here, then," he said. "With you, Jega."

Vinicius and the boys glanced at me, curious. I looked down at my silk blouse, at my trousers with their crisp creases running along each leg, at my expensive heels. None of them seemed to belong to me. It was as if I was a stagehand who had put on a main player's costume and, just before curtain, I'd been unmasked.

WITHOUT REGRET OR VIRTUE

Each time I swim in the ocean,
I think of our night on the beach.
How you ran along the sand,
your body just beyond my reach.

Each time I wade into the water,
I feel the waves' gentle hits.
I think of how I finally caught you,
how you tried to resist my tricks.

Each time I dive,
I think of how our mouths met.
How like the tides we moved,
until we couldn't tell water from sweat.

Each time I crawl back to dry land
I think how like an animal I was, loving you.
And I wish we would've drowned that night,
together, without regret or virtue.

Together,
without regret or virtue.
Together,
without regret or virtue.

If remembering tells us who we are, then forgetting keeps us sane. If we recalled every song we'd ever heard, every touch we'd ever felt, every pain no matter how small, every sadness no matter how petty, every joy no matter how selfish, we would surely lose our minds. I learned this after Graça died and I spent time in a Palm Springs clinic too fancy to be called a nuthouse. You see, I felt all of my memories very keenly—almost as if I was reliving them—and I drank in the hopes of wiping them away completely. My memory, however, was quite stubborn. It was Vinicius who eventually had his slate wiped clean.

It began innocently. He would look at a clock and be unable to decipher the time. Or I'd find him frozen in the middle of a room in our Miami house and he'd laugh and say that, for the life of him, he couldn't find his way to the kitchen. He'd be embarrassed and frustrated, so I'd pretend to forget things, too, and we'd laugh about growing old.

If you forget something completely, there is no missing it because you aren't aware of its existence anymore. But if you forget something and *know* you've forgotten, well, that's where suffering arises—not in the loss itself, but in the awareness of loss. You grieve without knowing what you're grieving for.

They say when you grow old, you return to the places you loved as a child. Vinicius played piano in movie houses when he was a little boy; his aunt stood nearby and if he even glanced at the screen, she'd slap the back of his head so hard his ears rang. Despite this, Vinicius adored the movies.

When he began wandering away from our house on Miami Beach, the first place I looked was the movie theater nearby. I'd find Vinicius in the middle of an empty row of chairs, watching the show. I'd sit with him and smell buttered popcorn, and the cigarette smoke from Vinicius's clothes. Then I felt his arm pressed against mine in the dark as we waited for the movie to begin, and suddenly it was 1940 again, and the two of us were back in Rio at the Odeon theater.

That year, Vinicius and I caught a picture nearly every day. They were our escape from samba's vicious competitiveness, from Senhor Pimentel's stifling presence in our lives, and even from Graça herself. Together, Vinicius and I gaped at Rhett Butler carrying Scarlett up winding stairs. We laughed ourselves to tears at Chaplin playing the Great Dictator. Our jaws dropped and we clasped hands when Dorothy entered a Technicolor Oz.

Movies had none of the snobbishness of the theater, or the opera, or the Copacabana Palace. The movie house was noisy and crowded with every color and class of person. The films themselves—most out of Hollywood—had scrappy heroines full of ambition and pluck. Of course, any character from south of the United States was always a bandit, cantina tart, or mustachioed villain; Vinicius and I avoided those kinds of films at all costs, so as not to break the spell of the movie house.

What we could not avoid were the newsreels before shows. Hitler invaded Poland, Denmark, and Norway. Mussolini's fascists declared war on Great Britain and France. There wasn't yet a war between the United States and Germany, but relations were frosty. At home, the newsreels called Old Gegê "the Father of the Poor." He required neighborhood samba clubs to formally register as samba "schools," or they were not allowed to play in Carnaval's parades. He banned sambas from having wind instruments because they were too foreign, creating the samba school mantra: "If it blows, it don't go." And so Carnaval, once a chaotic street party, became an official competition, where every song had to be about Brazil's greatness. We had rubber and steel, after all, which both Germany and the USA badly wanted. So Old Gegê and many of his cronies flirted unabashedly with Hitler and Roosevelt, seeing which suitor would win out.

Little by little, the newsreels at the Odeon theater began to portray the USA as "Uncle Sam"—a rich, jaunty uncle that would help Brazil in its fight against communists. Years later, I learned that those newsreels were actually produced with the USA's help, as part of the Office of the Coordinator of Inter-American Affairs. In my middle age, after I sobered up, I received calls from academics writing papers about Sofia Salvador and her part in the Good Neighbor Policy's propaganda machine: Was she a victim or an agent? You see, Uncle Sam could not afford to have hostile neighbors in the same hemisphere. So, while Sofia Salvador and the Blue Moon Band sang on Urca's stage, blissfully clueless of the workings of the world around us, a young Nelson Rockefeller persuaded the American president, Roosevelt, to get friendly with his South American neighbors, Brazil especially. But how could the U.S. president reach out to such countries—places considered dangerous and dirty by most American citizens—without risking his credibility? How could U.S. voters suddenly see former enemies as good neighbors? Through the movies, of course! This was how powerful movies were back then: by 1940, Washington, D.C., ordered Hollywood studios to find more Latin characters for their pictures, and to make them likable. So began a feverish search for South American talent.

All of this was happening while Vinicius and I sat in the Odeon, dumbly believing that our greatest enemies were other samba bands and Senhor Pimentel.

In life there are countless firsts and even more lasts. The firsts are easy to recognize; when you've never experienced something before—a kiss, a new style of music, a place, a drink, a food—you know exactly when you are encountering it for the first time. But lasts? Lasts nearly always surprise us. It's only after they've disappeared that we realize we'll never again have that particular moment or person or experience.

When Vinicius was sick, there were countless lasts: the last time he could drive a car; the last time we could travel; the last time he picked up his guitar and could actually play it; the last time he spoke English before reverting completely to Portuguese; the last time we went to the movies together.

It was in that Miami Beach theater near our house. Vinicius and I sat, side by side, watching the screen, where a cartoon for children played. I felt him draw his arm away from mine, and shrink back into his chair.

"Where are we?" he asked.

"At the movies," I said, turning to him. He stared at me, his eyes as wide as a child's. The screen's light flickered across his wrinkled face, making plain the transformation of his expression from confusion to fear. Vinicius put his forearm up over his eyes, as if dodging a blow.

"I'll play! I promise I'll play!" he yelped.

"Vinicius?"

I reached for him. He flinched, backing farther into the armrest on the other side of his chair.

"I'll play! I'll play! I was only watching for a little bit!"

"It's Dor. I'm not your auntie."

Vinicius whimpered and crossed his arms over his face.

The movie continued on the screen before us but neither of us watched. I told myself that it was dark and therefore easy to mistake me for someone else, someone frightening. Even when the film ended and the lights rose, Vinicius remained paralyzed in his chair. Panic sliced through me. Our memories are labyrinths and it's easy to assume that Vinicius's illness made him lost inside his, but that's not true. His maze wasn't becoming more complex, it was simplifying. Superfluous routes were closing off, unimportant paths disappearing. He didn't know he was "the Father of Samba," couldn't recognize neighbors, couldn't fathom how to operate a blender, didn't recall a word of English. But his Portuguese was perfect; he recalled every note and every word of our songs; and he asked for Graça and the boys dozens of times each day. Everything essential to Vinicius had remained. But this fear of me—was this his essential memory of who I was? He knew all of my misdeeds and forgave me for them, but had he erased them from his memory? Or had they returned in that dark theater to haunt us both?

Vinicius curled more tightly into his chair. The usher entered with his dustpan and broom, and I shook off my previous concerns for more practical ones: How would I get Vinicius to leave the theater? How could I convince him to go back home?

When every rational thing we know is wiped away, what are we left with? The rational mind forces us to define, to categorize, to separate: you are this, I am that; your love is this kind of love, mine is another; you are real, while you are a memory. Music is never rational. It works in wholes, not in pieces. I remember well when a scholar showed Vinicius sheet music to our songs, he laughed and handed the pages back. *That's just a transcript, man,* Vinicius said. *That's not the real conversation.*

So there, in that half-lit movie theater, I sang to him. Quietly at first, like when we wrote in cafés, or later, on film sets. I'm not sure why I didn't sing one of our more recent songs; instead, I sang "Without Regret or Virtue," a tune we'd written in 1940, during our year of movies and escapes, our year of lasts and firsts.

And Vinicius? He did exactly what I'd hoped he'd do: he took his hands away from his face, opened his eyes, and listened.

WITHOUT REGRET
OR VIRTUE

Happiness is not an end point. It is not a long-hidden treasure marked with an X on a map. It is not a reward, handed to you after years of diligent service. Happiness is like being in your mother's womb—warm, safe, buoyant—with no inkling of when it will end and why. During those whirlwind months of success after the Mayrink Showcase, we floated through our days in awe of our good fortune. We believed we'd made it. We believed that we'd transformed ourselves into successful performers, yet remained the same little samba band. We believed that we could shut ourselves away from thieving sambistas, overzealous fans, and opportunistic musicians and simply have one another, and our music. Then things began to change.

I'm the only living member of the Blue Moon Band. Being the last of my kind is lonesome, but it has its privileges: I'm the one who tells our story now. And in my version, our naive happiness began to drain away as soon as Senhor Pimentel found us.

"What does he want?" I asked Graça after her father had been in Rio a few days, sharing a room with Vinicius because men were not allowed in our boardinghouse.

She shrugged. "Who cares."

"You should. He could call the police and drag you back to Riacho

Doce any minute to marry you off. He sure looks like he needs a rich son-in-law."

"There's no more Riacho Doce," Graça replied without emotion. "The bankers took it. The workers left him. Even if he wanted to drag me back, there's nowhere to go back to."

I felt Graça's words as sharply as I would a slap against my cheek. Riacho Doce—its vast fields, its cutters' shacks where I was born and where my mother had died, its Great House where I'd labored and spied and listened to music, the schoolroom where I'd learned about words and rhyme, the narrow hallway where Graça had pinched me and I'd slapped her on our first meeting—all of it gone. I didn't know if the mill and the buildings would be razed, but in my imagination they were destroyed, and this inflicted a terrible sadness on me, one that made me ashamed. What a fool I was, to love what was never mine! And to feel betrayed by it—by a place!—for being sold and for sending us the worst of itself: Senhor Pimentel. He'd invaded Lapa, our new home where we'd managed to remake ourselves, and served only to remind us of the trapped girls we once were.

"So he's staying for good?" I asked.

Graça released a satisfied sigh, as if she'd just eaten a ten-course meal. "He didn't think he needed me around, but now I'm all he's got. Now he'll see that I never needed a husband to make me respectable. He'll see I'm really worth something."

During Urca shows he lurked backstage, introducing himself to every waiter, lighting technician, and stage manager as "Sofia Salvador's father," until the casino workers began greeting him as "Senhor Salvador." After shows he swept into Graça's dressing room, ignoring everyone else, and complimented her beauty, her brilliance, her poise. When he was sober enough to sit in on our middle-of-the-night rodas, he broke all of our unspoken rules: talking during songs, interrupting to support Graça's opinions on a new tune, applauding enthusiastically after Graça sang.

Caught in the barrage of his praise, Graça softened to him, but not completely. Try as he might, Senhor Pimentel wasn't used to our bohemian life, and carried with him at all times the weight of his disappointment. His face darkened each time he had to eat a plate of rice and beans. He grew gloomy and petulant when he had to stay backstage because he didn't have a tuxedo and therefore wasn't allowed to socialize in the casino. And when he saw our boardinghouse for the first time, he couldn't disguise his disgust.

"You live here?" he asked, staring at our building.

"What'd you expect?" Graça replied. "Catete Palace?"

Senhor Pimentel flushed. In the past, he might have punished his daughter for speaking to him this way, and Graça knew it. She squared her shoulders but her father's harsh words never came. Senhor Pimentel was smart enough not to anger the sole person who could butter his bread.

"I was expecting something a bit more . . . private," he said. "One that doesn't have you sharing space with factory workers."

"We've got our own bathroom," Graça replied, her cheeks pink.

"Of course you do," he said, placing a hand on Graça's shoulder. "But you deserve a palace for all of your hard work! Every weekend you play that fancy casino. You're making that Rolla fellow a rich man! You're lining the record company's pockets. But what are you getting in return?"

Graça tilted her head, considering his question.

"We buy all of her costumes," I said. "She has a new one every week. And we split everything with the band, fair and square."

"And with Madame L.," Graça said bitterly.

"Who's she?" Senhor Pimentel asked.

"Our partner," I replied.

"She's getting a hell of a deal! What does she give you in return?" he asked.

"Help, when we need it," I replied.

Senhor Pimentel looked again at our building. "Well, it sure looks like you need it."

That morning, as we lay down to sleep after a long night of shows, Graça turned her back to me and wept. When I placed a hand on her shoulder, she elbowed me away.

"They're tearing down all the houses in Copacabana and making apartment buildings with elevators and hot-water plumbing," she cried. "Why can't we live in one of those?"

"One day we will," I said.

"One day I'll be dead."

"You're singing every night. You're on the radio every day. Every girl in the city copies you. Isn't that what you wanted?"

Graça turned to face me, her knees hitting mine. "I'm barely twenty and I'm already one of the oldest samba girls out there. Sure, I've got Urca and the records we've cut, but all those younger bitches—Aracy and the rest of them—they're catching up fast. Every time I change my hair or my outfit, they change theirs to match. I try to stay a step ahead, all the time, and it wears me out. I can sing circles around those girls, but that doesn't matter. People will get bored with me after a while. They always do. And when that happens, what'll I have? A rented room and some old costumes?"

"You'll have me," I whispered. "And the band."

Graça stared at the ceiling. "Those boys will leave me as soon as something better rolls around. Vinicius, too. He lies and says he doesn't care about the shows. He says it's all about the music. But he only says that because a samba man is *supposed* to say that. A samba man can't have ambition. But I know he loves playing for those big crowds. I can feel it, when we're up onstage, it's electric. You know, when Vinicius and me are onstage together, it's like a dream. I wish we never had to wake up."

"So that's what you want?" I whispered. "To be onstage with him, forever."

Graça sighed. "I want to stop fighting for the same damn scraps as every other band: a few casinos, a few piddly radio slots. There's got to be more out there, Dor."

The bedsheet felt as coarse as sandpaper against my skin. I kicked it off, leaving Graça and me uncovered. Surely the entire time we'd lived in Lapa, we'd been observed and judged by those around us. But the trick was, we hadn't felt it. Not until Senhor Pimentel reappeared, and then it seemed as if our successes were constantly being weighed against our failures. Graça and I had thought our lives were magical and bright, but seeing them through Senhor Pimentel's eyes made them seem shabby and smudged, as if we hadn't actually arrived at the promised land but were peering at it through glass covered in fingerprints.

I t's said that necessity is the mother of invention. I'd argue that spite is its father. How many songs, poems, palaces, paintings, books, and enterprises have been made as retribution for a slight, a heartbreak, a careless word? Creation is a form of vengeance against a disbelieving world.

The more Senhor Pimentel disapproved of us, the more he complained about our food and lodging and long hours, the more he needled Vinicius (his reluctant new roommate) about Blue Moon taking a cut of Sofia Salvador's earnings, the more we wrote. Every afternoon, Vinicius and I took in a movie to clear our heads, and then sneaked back to one of our rooms to make music. For a little while at least, we forgot about shows and money and Senhor Pimentel. I suppose

Vinicius and I convinced ourselves that we could always find this solace with each other, if we only shut away the outside world. But inevitably, the world crept in.

One afternoon, as Vinicius and I labored in my room over a particularly stubborn song, he stopped strumming his guitar and asked: "What's wrong?"

"This won't cut down to three minutes," I replied.

"So we play it in the roda."

I shook my head. "It's good. I don't want to waste it."

"The roda's not a waste."

"Why are we giving our songs away?" I asked.

"We're cutting records and people are listening," Vinicius replied. "That's what you wanted."

"And Victor rakes in the dough. How much do you think they make from 'My Mutt' every Carnaval?"

"That's just the way it goes," Vinicius said, and shrugged.

"What if it doesn't have to go that way? What if we owned the songs? What if we cut our own records?"

Vinicius laughed. "You can't own a samba. Samba's like a bird. It flies around Lapa, heck, maybe it'll even get around the world one day! And it tells people a story—our story. If it's real good, it gets inside people's heads. Inside their memories, Dor! Can you believe that? It'll remind them of a good time, or a sad time, or somebody they loved, or their home. That's some magic. You can't own that."

"Yeah, and you can't eat it, either. Or wear it. Or live in it."

"We're not starving, Dor. And I'm happy as a clam where I'm living."

"A clam with a roommate," I said.

Vinicius shook his head. "At least Graça's grateful. She hasn't picked a fight with me since he moved in."

"And that makes it worthwhile?"

"Give him enough rope, and he'll hang himself soon enough."

"Or he'll hang one of us," I said.

The door opened. Graça stood at the entrance, wearing a flowered dress and a beret. "Don't look so thrilled to see me," she said.

"You skipped your lesson?" I asked.

Graça plucked the beret from her head and tousled her white-blond pixie cut. "Papai says I don't need lessons. He says my voice is perfect the way it is. Why do I need a hat-maker teaching me how to sing? Shove over."

She bumped Vinicius's shoulder with her hip. He sat on the edge of our bed, his guitar next to him. He scrambled to move the instrument before Graça sat, her arm pressed against his. "Sorry to interrupt your date."

Vinicius blinked. "This isn't a date. We're not here to enjoy ourselves."

Graça laughed. "So you two sneak together every day to be miserable!"

Vinicius looked at me, panicked.

"This is serious," I said. "We're working."

"Seems like you're chitchatting," Graça said.

"We were taking a break," Vinicius replied. "But I think we're done for the day. We hit a wall."

"Well, I'll help you bust through!" Graça said. "Let's hear it."

Vinicius and I looked at each other. Graça stiffened.

"I've got ideas, too," she said. "You two aren't God's gift." She stretched out a hand and grabbed the notebook from my lap. "You still have this old thing? I remember wanting one, too. But you were always better than I was, at school at least. So let's hear what you've got."

Graça passed the notebook back to me. Vinicius held his guitar in his lap but did not play. I flipped through my notebook, trying to make sense of the words I'd scribbled earlier that morning.

How many times had I imagined Graça witnessing our writing sessions? I'd pictured Graça sitting quietly beside me, impressed by how well Vinicius and I worked together, and realizing for the first time that not all important moments occurred with her on a stage. My imaginary Graça sat, docile and entranced. But the real Graça drew us into her orbit, making us pay attention to every sigh, every crossing and uncrossing of her legs, every bitten fingernail and faraway stare. She upset a balance we didn't know existed, until it was gone.

I skimmed a few lines from my notebook and cleared my throat. "I was at the beach the other night and I was thinking about the waves," I said. "About how they move. And I thought we could write about a couple in the sand, and how they're moving."

"Like those waves," Graça said.

Vinicius brightened. "Yeah. Dor thought we could use the same rhythm—growing, crashing, repeating—as the couple gets more and more—"

"Tangled up!" Graça interrupted. "So they aren't a couple anymore, they're . . ."

"A wave," Vinicius breathed, staring at her.

They looked at each other a beat too long, as if they'd shared some great secret.

I slapped my notebook shut. "The censors will never let it through."

"Fuck the censors," Graça said. "I like it. That's what matters."

"This isn't a dress in a window," I snapped. "Your liking it doesn't do a song any damn good. We're trying to understand it—to see what it could be."

Graça's face was pale. Her eyes were as wide and glassy as they'd been on that afternoon, years before in the Great House corridor, when I'd hit her across the cheek. And I felt the same triumph, and the same fear.

"I guess I forgot my place around here," Graça finally said. "You and Vinicius are the talents, I'm just the birdbrain that sings. That's the way it's always been, hasn't it, Dor?" she said, and nodded at my notebook. "Even Mamãe knew you had the smarts and I didn't."

"It's not about smarts," Vinicius said, his voice soft. "You're meant to be center stage. But when we write, the song's got to be the center of attention. We've got to disappear completely. We do what's best for the music, not for us. Dor and me, we're good at disappearing. Let us do the dirty work, and later, in the roda, you polish it with the boys when you sing."

Graça stood. Her mouth was a thin line. "I'm skipping the roda tonight."

"You can't skip," I said.

"Why not? You two don't need me," she said. "Besides, I'm taking Papai to get fitted for a new suit over in Ipanema, at the Duartes'."

"In the middle of the night?" Vinicius asked.

"They're staying open special, just for Sofia Salvador."

"Those tailors make Gegê's suits," I said. "Where are you getting the money to pay them?"

Graça smiled. "Papai can't dress like a pauper! It makes me look like an awful daughter."

"You're nobody's daughter around here," I said. "That's why we ran away."

"We ran away to sing onstage," Graça replied. "So I'll stick to the limelight, where I belong. And you two geniuses can keep this writing business to yourselves, it's as fun as having a hangnail."

She stood, tugged her beret over her hair, and left.

Weeks passed and one fancy suit became two, then three, then five, each handmade with Portuguese linen and silk linings, all with a tiny metal nameplate on the inside collar. The plate had a number on it, which the tailors used to record the sizes and preferences of their customers, among them senators, casino owners, and President Gegê himself. Madame L. informed me that Graça had stopped by his office looking for a loan, and he'd given it. A day later, Senhor Pimentel appeared at Urca wearing a tuxedo with mother-of-pearl buttons, which allowed him to escape his backstage confinement and hobnob with guests between shows. I took the opportunity to talk to Graça, in private, in her dressing room.

"I know you borrowed money."

"Congratulations," she said, dabbing sweat from her face. "You're a real detective."

"You can't spend what we don't have."

She turned to face me, her bracelets rattling. "I work my ass off every night, and all I do is line other people's pockets. I should get some perks, too."

"The only one getting perks is your father."

"Important people are in the casino. Papai needs to make a good impression."

"For what?"

Graça shrugged. "For me."

Some days later, as we packed up to leave Urca for the night, Senhor Pimentel strode backstage in his new tux and announced, as if he were a master of ceremonies, that he'd gotten Sofia Salvador an important invitation.

"The Lion's son wants you to play a private show, at his home! You're the guest of honor!"

Graça covered her mouth with her hands. Vinicius glanced at me.

"Guest?" Kitchen asked. "You mean we're not invited?"

"Of course!" Senhor Pimentel replied, forcing a smile. "They're expecting all of you."

Leôncio de Melo Barroso, known throughout Brazil as "The Lion," owned nearly every newspaper and magazine outlet in the country. He was close friends with President Gegê and anyone else who bolstered his business, while his enemies were the subjects of scandalous articles—true or not—in his newspapers. He was scrupulous about keeping himself out of the public eye, but his influence was so far-reaching that, after his shocking divorce, the government passed a bill that allowed him sole custody of his children. "If the law is against me, then we'll have to change the law," the Lion bragged. His home was the largest mansion in Santa Teresa, and so heavily guarded that few were allowed inside its gates. The Blue Moon boys and I didn't object to the private show out of sheer curiosity; who wouldn't want to catch a glimpse of the Lion in person? Still, I wasn't enthusiastic about the show because Senhor Pimentel had arranged it and I hadn't.

The Lion sent a private car to fetch us in Lapa. Senhor Pimentel wedged himself into the seat between Graça and me. The diamond sugar cube glimmered in his tie.

The car wound through the hills of Santa Teresa until we reached a stone fence taller than most houses. As the iron gate creaked open and shut behind us, Graça held her father's hand in her gloved one. Instead of wearing one of the colorful gowns she always wore to perform, Senhor Pimentel had convinced Graça to wear a black dress and a single strand of pearls, as if she was attending a funeral and not putting on a show.

I looked out the window and watched as we drove up a winding path lit by gas lanterns. Then there was a massive hill, blacker than the night sky. Atop it, as if floating, sat a building that resembled a museum or a theater, massive and columned, its walls covered in handpainted Portuguese tiles that gleamed in the lamplight. A stone path led up the hill and to the front door, but the car lumbered past it and around the hill, to the back of the house.

A line of garages, each with a car inside, sat open. Uniformed men and women scurried between lit doorways. Nearby we heard the insistent, deep-throated barks of dogs. The car stopped. The driver left his seat and opened our door, which faced the service entrance.

Graça tugged her hand from her father's. "I thought I was the guest of honor, not some maid."

The Blue Moon boys eyed one another, then quickly left the car.

"You're a samba singer, not a countess," Senhor Pimentel snapped. "This is what you wanted."

Graça looked at me, a mix of panic and anger on her face. I reached over Senhor Pimentel and grabbed her gloved hand.

"You want to walk through the front door?" I asked. "I'm right behind you. We'll go there now, together."

Senhor Pimentel took hold of her wrist, his hand below mine. "You're the entertainment. Going in through the front, having the butler announce you, will spoil the effect. Don't embarrass me."

Graça bowed her head as if praying. Then she slid free from both of our grips and left the car. Senhor Pimentel and I quickly followed, each of us grasping for the door, as if whoever got to Graça first would influence her decision. But her mind was already made up. Outside, Graça gave me a sad smile and made her way to the kitchen door.

The service entrance was on the lowest floor, carved into the hill that held up the house. The kitchen itself was larger and more modern than any I'd seen, tiled from floor to ceiling like a hospital. But its steamy air, smelling of garlic and onion, returned me to Nena's kitchen in Riacho Doce. I could not meet the eyes of those cooks and kitchen girls who watched, starstruck, as we shuffled, single file, through their domain. Graça kept her eyes forward and held her chin up as if she was wading neck-deep in water. Only the Blue Moon boys nodded and smiled at the kitchen girls.

We followed the head housekeeper through a maze of narrow halls and up dimly lit staircases until we reached a door. On the other side was a room as wide as a soccer field. Above us, a gilded ceiling glittered with electric lights. In front of us were rows of golden chairs with embroidered seat cushions, all of them empty.

"The Senhores and Senhoras are having after-dinner drinks in the parlor," the housekeeper announced, as if we were her staff. "When they are finished they will retire here, to listen to you. Be ready for them."

Vinicius and the boys removed their instruments from their cases. Graça closed her eyes and performed voice exercises. I went to the back of the room and sat in one of the golden chairs. Senhor Pimentel took the seat beside me, his leg pressing against mine.

"It must feel remarkable: a person like you sitting in a room like this," he said.

"I've seen better rooms."

Senhor Pimentel laughed. "In that casino? This is a private house, Jega! The money up north was a drop in the ocean compared with what's here in Rio. Graçinha was right to leave. She's always had good instincts, it's just a matter of guiding her."

"Like you guided her these past few years?" I asked.

The Senhor's mouth twitched. He forced it into a smile. "Graçinha's forgiven me. She understands I couldn't bankrupt the mill on a search that would've been futile."

"And you lost the mill anyway."

"Fate lost Riacho Doce," he said. "The price of sugar lost it. And it grieves me terribly. It was like losing her mother all over again. My family goes back to the first Portuguese, Jega. They planted Pernambuco's first cane. Graça has a noble lineage. Better than most of these silly guests she'll sing for. Better than the Lion himself. She's not some workhorse. My girl's a Pegasus! She's got wings! But now she's tied to the plow like a common mule."

"She works the best stage in Rio."

"The Copacabana Palace is the best stage in Rio, and she's not booked there because they have standards. How long will this samba fad last?" he asked. "Until Graça's looks go? Until her voice coarsens? Then where will she be—trapped in a rooming house with you, cutting little records and playing shabby clubs all of her life? You've got this closefistedness about you, Jega, this idea that everything is scarce in the world and you've got to take what you can get. That's natural for your lot, but not for my Graçinha. She needs someone with a bigger vision. She needs someone who thinks beyond making the next milréis. Graçinha has a splendid voice. She should sing the right kind of music with proper musicians, not with that band of malandros. She needs to be in rooms like this one, or onstage at a grand theater playing for the classes, not the masses. She needs an international tour, a contract with a reputable record company, her name on a line of fur coats! You've gotten her this far and—believe me—your pluck is impressive. But you're not going to get her any farther, Jega. You dress like a newspaper boy. You drink. You argue. You run around with girls. It's unnatural. If my Graçinha wants a reputable career, if she wants to fly to the moon, she can't be associated with such things."

Fly to the moon. Those words belonged to Graça, not to him. "Has she talked to you about this?" I asked. "Does she know you're telling me to jump ship?"

"Graçinha? She can't decide what color shoes to wear on a walk down the hallway. But my girl's always had ambition. She'll make the right choice between us. You'll see soon enough."

"I didn't know there was a choice."

"There isn't," Senhor Pimentel said, and leaned his shoulder against mine, his mouth close to my ear as if he was about to share a shocking bit of gossip. "I'm her father. I'm her guardian. It's my duty to shield my innocent girl from opportunists, from bands of sambistas, from gangsters and Big Foots. It would be an ugly business if I went to the police and the courts. We both know who'd win."

The room's front door opened. Graça and the boys stood at attention. There was laughter. Women wearing massive jewels and gauzy gowns floated into the room, some on the arms of men, some alone. Tuxedoed men, young and old, held snifters of brandy and joked as they made their way to the front chairs.

"The show's going to start," Senhor Pimentel said, and nodded to the door. "You know the way out, Jega."

It took all of my effort not to hit him. I closed my eyes and imagined what Graça would say if I beat up her dear, sweet father right there, in the Lion's ballroom, in front of our host and his guests. A fight was probably what Senhor Pimentel wanted, so he could win Graça's sympathies and get me kicked out of the Lion's house. But Senhor Pimentel was not the first to underestimate me, and he wouldn't be the last.

"Don't hold your breath," I said, dizzy with rage.

Senhor Pimentel smiled, then rushed to greet the guests one by one, as if he was the host of the party. Then he introduced his beautiful daughter, Sofia Salvador, ignoring the Blue Moon Band.

How many hundreds of shows had Graça and the boys performed with me watching in the wings? For large crowds and small; in dives and mansions, casinos and cabarets; for drunks and nobility, they all blur together now into one prolonged performance that I play in my memory again and again, a record on repeat.

She'd start off sweet, her voice a little naughty, the songs pure fun, as if she'd found you in the middle of a crowded party and decided to flirt. Then, very slowly, she moved into another set of songs, romantic ones. Her voice was a whisper, then the softest little moan. She was confiding in you, she was asking you to take her home for the night. And just when you thought you had her figured out, she'd signal to the Blue Moon boys and shift the tempo and sigh and shake her head and cradle the microphone and begin a series of slower songs, sadder ones. Little by little, she'd bend the song's notes, stretching her voice until you felt nervous for her—it was too high, or too low, and surely she would not be able to sustain it. Her body shook with the effort. She closed her eyes, she clenched her hands, sometimes she even knelt before you. And you, and everyone around you, would hold your breath, afraid she would crack and shatter in front of you. But then she would stand, her voice so full and lush it surrounded you like a warm bath, and you knew she would not break.

When Sofia Salvador finished a show, applause wasn't an obligation but a release. Without even realizing it, you'd held your breath and tensed your body while she sang, as if you were afraid that even the smallest movement would startle her away. But as soon as she bowed and thanked you, every emotion she'd dredged up inside you was suddenly clamoring to be let loose. How could you not clap, howl, whistle, and call for one more? One more! Please, just one more? And, of course, Sofia Salvador always relented. She did that night, in the Lion's mansion.

She sang until my feet ached and my dress pinched. Until the room's many lights made my eyes blur. And when Sofia finally finished, her chest glistening with sweat, her hair matted and her eye makeup a runny mess, that noble crowd clapped and wiped their wet eyes and swarmed toward her as if they all hoped to hug her at once. For what felt like hours those ladies and gentlemen congratulated Graça and the band, and even Senhor Pimentel, who, beaming and red-cheeked, accepted their handshakes and praise as if he was a new father just out of the delivery ward. I could have walked into that tight circle of guests and musicians. I could have forced my way inside and made them acknowledge and congratulate me as the writer of her songs, as the oil that greased the gears of Sofia Salvador and Blue Moon Band. But what is recognition when it's not freely given? A concession. An allowance, doled out in measured doses by those who have the power to give it. Senhor Pimentel was right: there was a closefistedness about me. Only the fists were not mine; all my life I'd pried open fingers to get my due. That night, I was tired. For once, I wanted things to come easily or not at all.

G uests blocked the hidden door that led to the maze of servants' passageways. I slipped out the room's real door and into a wide hall. My heels click-clacked against marble floors. I had the panicked idea that a maid or butler would hear me and think I was an intruder traipsing through the house. I moved faster, my steps louder. Finally I found the massive front door, made from wood so thick I had to use two hands to pull it open. Outside, gas lanterns hissed and sputtered. I grabbed the hem of my gown and wobbled down the stone path.

I looked up at the Lion's mansion; each window blazed as if there were a party in every room. Graça was behind one of those windows, laughing, accepting compliments, charming each guest into dizzy adoration. Those guests were the high-and-mighty of Rio society, not Lapa's Little Tonys or Madame Lucifers or Urca Casino's Joaquim Rolla. They controlled an entire country, not a piddly neighborhood. Maybe my vision was too small, my grasp too tight. Maybe I was a hindrance. Maybe I was never a salvation but a stone in Graça's pocket, weighing her down and dragging her under.

I'd get the Lion's driver to take me back to Lapa, and if he refused I'd walk there myself. I imagined stumbling down Santa Teresa's winding hills, past its gated manors, under the arched aqueducts, and arriving at our boardinghouse by sunrise, if I arrived at all. I contemplated visiting Anaïs but quickly changed my mind. With her I was always the student, intent on pleasing my teacher. That night, I did not want to please anyone. I thought of the line of fancy cars near the Lion's service entrance and the many bored chauffeurs who would appreciate my company. I thought of my fancy gown hiked up to my waist, my legs wrapped so tightly around one of those drivers that he'd gasp for breath as he pushed on top of me, and I'd jeer at him. I'd tell him he was a disgrace. I'd slap him and order him to push harder, to pummel me into that leather seat until I was ground into nothing. Until I disappeared completely.

I need you on my side.

Against who?

Everybody. The whole world.

The world will eat us up.

I slumped onto the steps and covered my face in my hands.

When I finally stood, I couldn't remember which direction led to the garages with the guests' gleaming cars and their chauffeurs. I bumbled around the Lion's grounds, my heels sinking into a gravel path that grew darker and more narrow. There was a smell so sharp it made my nose wrinkle; I felt as if I'd stumbled into a dead-end Lapa alley where drunks relieved themselves. I heard a snarl.

My neck tingled. An animal growled, deep and steady, like a motor revving to life. I stepped back. The gravel crackled under my feet. Then barks exploded so loudly and violently I could feel the force of them pushing me backward. I heard myself gasp. My arms covered my face and I braced for impact. The barking continued, louder and wilder, but I felt no sharp teeth, no wet muzzles.

I lowered my arms. In the hill's shadows were the bars of a kennel. Three mastiffs as massive as donkeys snarled and yapped, squeezing their faces between the iron bars. Their teeth shone. I took another step back and their barking stopped. They sniffed the air. Their tails wagged so forcefully that their bodies shimmied. One of the dogs whined, opening its mouth so wide a child's head could fit inside it. Behind me, gravel crunched.

"They get riled by trespassers," a man said. He wore a tuxedo and carried a metal pail. His white hair looked blue in the night.

"I'm not a trespasser," I whispered.

"Dressed like that you are. This is the servants' area."

His tux was impeccably tailored, his white tie a perfect bow. On the hand that held the metal pail was a ring with a stone as big as a gum ball.

"Then you're trespassing, too," I said.

His eyes were stern. They assessed everything around him like a thief or a prisoner might, making sure there was always a quick escape. With his free hand, he removed a handkerchief from his jacket pocket and held it in my direction. I suppose he thought the dogs had upset me. I thanked him and wiped my eyes and nose.

"You're from Pernambuco," he said, pointing to his ear. "You kept your accent. I'm from up that way, too, but I learned how to speak like the Cariocas. They don't respect you otherwise."

The pail swung in his hand. The dogs whined.

"You're with the band?" he asked. "A wife? Girlfriend?"

"God forbid," I replied.

His eyes glimmered now. "Her music's good. Maybe even great. But don't tell her I said so."

"I didn't see you upstairs, at the concert," I said.

"I was in back like you. I don't hobnob," he said, then stepped past me and near the kennel's bars. The dogs jumped and scampered. He lowered a hand into the pail and removed a fistful of glistening scraps. Then he held his hand out, palm up, and put it between the bars. The animals pressed their muzzles gently to his palm, as if licking a wound. The man dipped his hand into the pail again and again, all the while tutting and shushing and whispering to the beasts.

"There, querida. Yes . . . oh, too fast! Don't guzzle, my love . . . yes, there."

Watching, I felt embarrassed, as if I was prying.

"Everyone's loyal when you feed them filet mignon!" the man announced, holding the pail toward me. "You want to try? They won't bite."

I shook my head. He went back to feeding.

"What do you do for that Salvador girl?" he asked. "Other than linger in dark corners?"

"I write her songs."

He flung the empty pail to the ground with a clatter. His palms and the white cuffs of his tuxedo shirt were covered in dark smears. He put his hands between the bars again and let the dogs lick them clean.

"So you put the meat in her act," he said.

"Pardon?"

"The songs. What good's a singer if she's got nothing to sing? You give her substance. My son's the samba lover. He goes to Urca every week to see your girl play. He's starstruck. Me? I've never been musically inclined. I'm more of a movie man, myself."

"You watch pictures?" I asked.

"The snobs around here say movies are gauche. They wouldn't be caught dead at the cinema. But me? I'm as gauche as they come! I go to Cinelândia once a week—they let me sneak in the back of the Odeon for free and sit in the projection booth. Know why?"

"No."

"Those pictures wouldn't be imported without me. Or the news-reels. We make those, you know. Splice a few photos together, add narration, and boom! You've got a story, even if it's not news at all." He removed his hands from the kennel. "You guessed who I am yet?"

"You're not the night watchman."

He held out a hand to me, the fingers still wet from the dogs' licking. His black eyes glimmered, amused to see if I'd shake or not. I stepped forward and clasped his hand in mine. He gripped me roughly, squeezing until the bones of my fingers hurt, scanning my face as if hoping to catch a glimpse of pain or shock. I squeezed his hand right back.

"Come upstairs with me," he said. "You don't belong down here. The guards will let the dogs loose soon, and these old girls can't tell the difference between a lady and a thief."

"Is there a difference?" I asked.

He allowed himself a smile. It lasted so long that I found myself inching backward, worried he might've taken our little talk as an invitation to a kiss, or worse. When he finally spoke, his voice was low, as if he didn't want the dogs to hear us.

"You ever meet any gringos?" he whispered.

I shook my head.

"I've got a few in high places that might like your gal's act. Maybe I'll send them your way, over to that casino you all play in, and let them take a gander at her?"

"We'd appreciate that," I said. "She's not meant to play casinos forever."

"You stay in the same place too long, you'll either starve or get eaten," he said.

Then the man held out his arm, as if escorting me out of a dark corner and onto a dance floor.

The Lion and I were kindred spirits. I was not, as some have claimed, his informant, though his newspapers did get exclusives with Sofia Salvador. At the time, every entertainer and politician was in the same boat: if you didn't work with the Lion's newspapers, they smeared you. And I was not his friend; he did not have those. But the Lion and I shared a common trait: we'd elbowed our way into places where others believed we didn't belong.

He'd been born to a drunk, traveled to Rio alone at ten years old on the back of a donkey, and made a living as a newspaper boy before becoming a magnate. This kind of social climb might've been common elsewhere, but in Brazil in the 1900s, it was as rare as a comet that burns across the heavens every hundred years. If you're trapped in the muck, below even society's lowest rungs, you are kept there by the weight of others, clambering on top of you, using you as their stepping-stone. Moving upward isn't simply a matter of gumption—to climb the ladder, you must be willing to clear the path. You must be willing to push and hit, and yes, even smother anyone who blocks your rise. For those who called the Lion and, on a much smaller scale, me ruthless and grasping, I ask you: What would you have us do? Stay silent in the muck and endure, as others did before us, until we were pressed so far down we were buried alive?

That first night by the kennels, the Lion took a shining to me, yes, but he also knew that it wouldn't hurt to forge a partnership with an up-and-coming samba star; someone he could slap on the pages of his papers when news was slow; someone he could dangle in front of his gringo associates at the new Office of the Coordinator of Inter-American Affairs. The Lion's motives weren't obvious to me on our first meeting, but a few weeks later, he made good on his promise to send OCIAA officials eager to implement the Good Neighbor Policy to our Urca shows. Those officials got word to Chuck Lindsay, a North American talent agent who'd visited Rio, and who invited us to a late dinner aboard the passenger liner *Normandie*.

That night, as we bounced over the bay's waves in a water taxi headed for the enormous cruise ship, I smiled widely at Senhor Pimentel and tried to contain my excitement. I'd gotten us a meeting with a talent scout from Hollywood! No samba band had ever been considered for the movies. Who had the small vision now?

The Blue Moon boys laughed and joked during the choppy ride. Senhor Pimentel scowled. Graça sat beside Vinicius with her eyes shut tight.

"This gringo expects us to eat dinner after this ride?" she said, holding her stomach.

Senhor Pimentel placed an arm around his daughter's shoulders. "What civilized person eats at this hour?" he asked. "It's a crime to keep you up after doing three shows in one night. You should be resting, not going to sign autographs for some tourist."

"He's not a tourist," I said.

"No, worse—he's a movie man," Senhor Pimentel replied, shouting over the taxi's motor. "What will he ask her to do? Play for the drunks at the Odeon?"

"What's wrong with the movies?" Vinicius asked.

Graça opened her eyes.

Senhor Pimentel smiled. "It's a different caliber of audience. I'd think you'd want to move up from Urca, not down to the lowest denominator."

"Shit, I'm lower than low," Tiny shouted. "I love those pictures. Can you imagine being on-screen, twenty feet tall, playing for the world?"

Banana laughed. "All the dames in Brazil will get to see your giant cavaquinho, brother!"

"Most have seen it already," Tiny said, and winked.

Senhor Pimentel shook his head, disgusted.

There's a difference between wealth and opulence. The first time I understood this distinction was on the *Normandie*. Chuck Lindsay's private dining room had marble-topped tables, mahogany columns, and walls covered in mirrors. The mirrors amplified everything about the room—its size, its lights, its occupants. So it seemed as if there were a dozen chandeliers instead of only two, and fifty diners instead of only eleven: Chuck Lindsay, his translator, myself, Graça, Vinicius, the Blue Moon boys, and Senhor Pimentel.

Mr. Charles Lindsay was gray-haired and affable, like a father in the movies, only better dressed. He wore a tuxedo, like the Blue Moon boys.

"I'm not sure which of you kids are waiters, and which are part of the band!" he said, smiling.

Hearing the clipped, nasal tones of English returned me very suddenly to Senhora Pimentel's bedside, where I heard her soft voice speak that language to Graça and me in the hopes that our young brains would soak it up. And mine had: I recognized a few of Lindsay's words, but not all. His translator—a college boy from Rio—hesitated before relaying Chuck's unfortunate joke to us in Portuguese.

The Blue Moon boys and I forced laughs. But Graça stood stone-faced beside her father. Her red gown had a long slit in the front that revealed a wide, tan thigh, its muscles so pronounced I was surprised her stockings had not ripped. Chuck Lindsay attempted to draw her out with conversation but Graça sighed and crossed her arms, the way she used to when she was bored with Bruxa's lessons.

"Mr. Chuck says you have a marvelous stage presence, Miss Sofia," the boy translated. "He says he likes the way you move your hands when you sing. He says it is quite charming."

Graça gave the tiniest of nods, then looked out toward the boat's deck as if contemplating escape.

"Thank you," I said. "She's entertained people from all over the world. Diplomats and presidents, too. There's no crowd she can't please."

"Well, I don't think she wants to please *every* crowd," Senhor Pimentel piped in. "She's an artist, not a good-time girl."

Graça blushed. The college boy hesitated again, longer this time, before translating. Chuck Lindsay raised his eyebrows, then proceeded as if he'd heard nothing at all. Our conversation continued, only it did not feel like a dialogue but an exhausting game of telephone mixed with charades. By the time our meals appeared we'd all tired of talking. Graça picked at her food. Chuck Lindsay stared at her in the same way Nena used to judge girls before hiring them, calculating how strong their arms were, how soft their hands were, and how well they would do in her kitchen. Twice I caught Mr. Chuck's appraising stare aimed at me. Before anyone had finished their dinner, Graça pushed away her plate, removed a cigarette and lighter from her clutch, and began to smoke. Mr. Chuck coughed and smiled at her, as if humoring a child.

I had to steer very carefully. Graça, when in one of her moods, was like a wild creature, free from the rules of logic or politeness. If I chastised her behavior, or if I told her to stop smoking, she would only behave worse and smoke more. If I tugged her outside, she would kick and scream, without any thought to preserving her dignity or mine. She had to believe something was her idea, her desire, before she would ever do it. One simply had to guess what it was Graça truly wanted, and do it first. She could not abide being in second place.

I removed my napkin from my lap and stood. "Excuse me," I said to the translator. "I'm feeling woozy. I'm going to the deck for some fresh air. Please keep eating."

Chuck Lindsay's vast, private deck wrapped around the top of the ship. Below, passengers chattered in languages I could not understand. Beyond the harbor, Rio sparkled. The city's beaches were well lit but its hills blended into the night sky. Christ the Redeemer, small and glowing upon his perch on Corcovado, was a floating blur of light.

I heard heels click against the deck. I closed my eyes, savoring my victory: Graça pressed beside me in the darkness.

"Give me a cigarette," she ordered.

"It'll change your voice," I replied.

Graça plucked my cigarette from my hand and took a long, slow puff. "Maybe that's what I need—a change."

"You're acting like you need a spanking."

Graça laughed. "And wouldn't you love to give it to me?"

I snatched my cigarette back. "That gringo could put you in pictures. You could be the next Marlene Dietrich. And instead of turning on the charm with him, you're acting like a spoiled brat. You're ruining this for yourself and for the boys."

"Maybe I'm tired of being charming. Maybe I don't want to be in pictures."

"Since when? Since your papai says they're low-class? What do you want to be now—some fancy opera singer?"

Graça looked out at the bay. Waves moved toward shore, their crests iced in moonlight.

"Sometimes I think you should've sung on 'My Mutt,'" she whispered. "You should've been Sofia Salvador, not me. You've got the will for it."

"But not the talent," I said.

"We can't have it all," Graça replied. "Every time that Chuck speaks English, I hear Mamãe. It's like she's a ghost in the room. Papai said she would roll over in her grave if she saw me in a two-bit movie, playing some cantina tart. She wanted a daughter who was elegant, not some piddly samba singer."

My hands gripped the ship's railing. I shook my head. "Senhora Pimentel loved music. She gave us those records. She took us to that fado show. She put us on this path. She wouldn't be mad that we followed it. She'd be proud."

Graça wrapped an arm around my waist and rested her head on my shoulder.

"When we were kids, I had this fantasy," she whispered. "Not about showbiz. Not even about singing. I wanted to be magic, Dor. I wanted to step in front of a crowd and be everything to them, even if it was just for a few minutes. Now I think: a few minutes is too short. What if I'm singing to the wrong crowd? The kind of crowd that'll ball me up and throw me away on some greasy movie house floor? What if this samba business is a fad, and when people look back they'll laugh at me for singing these songs, instead of singing something respectable? Or what if no one remembers me at all?"

I held her tightly against me. The last time we were on a ship in Guanabara Bay, I was pathetic, skinny Jega. That night at the Lion's house, Senhor Pimentel had conjured Jega again: I wasn't good enough to be a singer; I wasn't beautiful—not in the conventional sense; I wasn't a woman—not in the way people expected me to be; I wasn't a help to Graça or to anyone. Those beliefs always existed inside me—they still do—but I'd managed to contain them, to make them small and meek when confronted with my new self. But upon his return, Senhor Pimentel had given them strength. That night on the ship, I realized he'd done the same with Graça. He'd exalted her when he first returned, and then, little by little, he'd picked at her old wounds, brought up her old doubts, made her question the self she'd remade. Who are we, if not the people we imagine ourselves to be? Who was Graça without her audacity? Who was I without Graça?

"You remember that fado dame we saw in Recife?" I asked her.

Graça nodded, her hair brushing my chin. "She's probably stuck in some dive now, singing for peanuts."

"It doesn't matter where's she's at!" I yelled. "To me, she's always on that stage. She's always magic. And that's how I'll remember her."

"Me too," Graça whispered. And then she began to say the words to a song we'd never forgotten:

"At the end of my street,
   the ocean laps,
   the ocean laps.
   Above it I see a piece of the moon,
   a sliver of my destiny."

I sighed, my breath hot against Graça's hair. I began to say the song's words, too, remembering them exactly as Graça remembered. Our voices rose, little by little. We began to sway together like two drunks at the end of a long night. Graça's voice skipped ahead of mine, higher and more melodic. But melody can be bare and lonesome without a harmony, without a few supporting notes adding richness and contrast, like the background of a painting or the set in a movie. So we did not try to keep up with each other, but sang in our own way, together.

"Where is my destiny?
   Where is my home?
   Will I never have a place in this world?
   Will I always be alone?"

When we finished, there was quiet. The chatter on the deck below us had hushed. The clinking glasses and conversation in the dining room behind us had stopped. We heard only the waves lapping against the ship, and then, from the deck below us, clapping. We looked over the rail. Men and women smiled up at us, applauding. One man jammed two fingers in his mouth and whistled. Graça giggled and waved. Behind us, there was more clapping. Chuck Lindsay smiled and applauded, along with the Blue Moon boys.

"Mr. Chuck asks you to come inside," the translator said. "There is a piano."

I held fast to Graça's waist. We had, for a moment on that deck, returned to our girlhood selves, singing together in front of the record player. I knew the moment would last only as long as the song, but I was still disappointed when Graça laughed, nodded, and unhooked herself from me. She headed toward the door, toward Lindsay and Vinicius and the boys, until Senhor Pimentel appeared. Graça stopped. Her father stood beside the others, but his expression was not one of surprise or amusement. His face was a rigid mask of rage. Graça took a small step back, afraid.

It was that step that made me see what I'd been blind to before: the choice between me and Senhor Pimentel wasn't up to Graça. It wasn't even a choice. Never having a parent myself, I'd been naive to think I could compete with the man who had held her on his lap, dispensing and withdrawing his affections as he saw fit. Even the law was on his side: as long as the Senhor was alive, he would own Graça like a farmer owns a cow and he could sell her talents as if they were meat. He would not assert his ownership outright, knowing that Graça would buck against such authority. No, he would do much worse—he would make her afraid. He would wield his affections and his disapproval and make her doubt herself, her talent, her accomplishments. He would separate her from Blue Moon, and from me, until he was the only soul left to guide her.

Judge me if you'd like. Say that I was as bad as Senhor Pimentel in my struggle to control Graça. Maybe this is true. I've had many lonely years to wipe the dust from old memories, to reexamine them, to turn motives around and around, looking for the truest one. What I eventually did, I did out of fear. But I also did it out of love.

So that night, when Graça took a step back, I placed a hand on her shoulder and pushed her forward. "Go on," I ordered. "Get in there and knock them dead."

Inside, I watched her sing. I watched Senhor Pimentel stew. I watched Chuck Lindsay scoot to the edge of his chair as he listened to Graça and silently calculated her worth. I stayed quiet as we bobbed back to shore in the water taxi. I resisted Vinicius's offers to tell him what was wrong. During my few, precious hours of sleep that day, I dreamed the same dream over and over: Senhor Pimentel in Riacho Doce's parlor, pretending to strike me and then laughing in my face. And when I woke early, I made sure not to disturb Graça as I put on my clothes and left to find Madame Lucifer.

On the shelf behind his desk were ten trophies from Lapa's Carnaval Costume Contest; Madame L. had won first place every year he'd entered. I stared at those trophies—with their winged bronze women aiming swords at the sky—and blurted everything about Senhor Pimentel and his speech to me at the Lion's house.

When I finished, Madame L. offered me a glass of water. Only when I'd finished drinking did he speak.

"Success is like honey. It can attract the bees but brings out the rats and the flies, too. The way I see it, Miss Dores, we have a problem. And we have to decide if we're going to deal with it the Lapa way or the Santa Teresa way."

"What's the difference?" I asked.

"You played at the Lion's place. You saw his neighborhood. Up there, everybody's polite as can be. In Santa Teresa they wait things out. They sit in their mansions and write letters to make their threats, and then they have tea and wait for their problems to run away from them. Your Graça came from people like this. Her daddy is betting he can scare you and then wait you out. But you and me, Miss Dores, we're not from that set of people, are we? You and me, we can't afford to wait."

"I can't kick him out," I said. "He'll go to the police, or to some judge, and say Graça's his ward. And then he'll kick the rest of us out."

Madame L. nodded. "What do you want, then?"

"I want him to leave us alone."

Madame Lucifer and I looked at each other across his desk. I was frustrated by his silence and slightly unnerved by it, too. But I would not look away from him, and I would not speak again until he had. We were taking stock of each other. Or, more accurately, Madame Lucifer was taking stock of me. It was a different kind of communication, where words become both useless and dangerous.

"I never turn my back on a true friend," he said, minutes later. "But you have to ask for my help."

My tongue felt gritty and dry in my mouth, as if it was coated in sand.

"Help me," I said, and as soon as I did, a great heat rose within me and swelled into my cheeks, the tips of my ears, the top of my skull. I was back in Riacho Doce, hiding in the dark, watching men hold torches to the cane. It was the only way to get a good harvest, the only way to root out the snakes and scorpions hiding inside. The cane needed to burn so that it could grow back stronger. Of course, once you set something alight, there are no guarantees. You can put up breaks, hills of sand, roads as wide as two trucks. You tell yourself that it can be controlled, monitored, hemmed in. But fire jumps. It moves. It dances. Like any force of nature, it has no scruples, only need.

Madame L. nodded. "Let's have a drink together—the three of us. And make sure her daddy has his bags packed."

The next night, while Graça and the boys performed at Urca, I snuck away and met Senhor Pimentel for drinks. The fact that he accepted my invitation without hesitation or curiosity showed how confident he was in his own plans; I suppose he believed I was going to argue for my right to remain at Graça's side.

Before we met for drinks, I'd asked Vinicius for the key to his apartment, which he still reluctantly shared with Senhor Pimentel. Vinicius hesitated before handing me the key.

"You forget something there?" he asked.

"My notebook," I said without looking him in the eye. "I can't find it. I thought I might've left it at your place."

I told the matron at Vinicius's building that he'd forgotten an instrument and had sent me to fetch it. She'd seen me come and go with Vinicius before and let me upstairs without argument. Inside, I stepped carefully inside the space Vinicius had curtained off for Senhor Pimentel. Under his cot, I found the small, scuffed valise Senhor Pimentel had brought with him from Recife. My hands shook as I opened the armoire he and Vinicius shared. I froze once when a car honked its horn on the street below, and again when the building's pipes rattled. I was, suddenly, Jega again, rifling through the Senhor's things. I had to stop, close my eyes, and tell myself to think clearly.

I filled the valise with a few dress shirts, cuffs, ties, and two new suits that Graça had bought him. I added a pair of shoes, his tin of hair pomade, and his shaving kit. Finally, I found an envelope stuffed with money and put that in the suitcase, too. Then I snapped the valise shut and carried it to a taxi downstairs.

Madame Lucifer had suggested the bar, although Senhor Pimentel didn't know this. The dive was in far-out Ipanema, near the lagoon. It was very late and the bar was empty except for an unshaven bartender, and a burly pair of men who resembled our former Nymphette fans at Little Tony's. I ordered a beer and sat in the corner. My tabletop was sticky. I placed the suitcase on the floor between my feet.

Before long, Senhor Pimentel ambled in. The burly men glanced at him, then away. He wore a dove-gray suit, the linen so fine it was practically sheer. The diamond sugar cube was a brilliant dimple in the middle of his silk tie. Senhor Pimentel smiled and sat across from me, then motioned to the bartender, who ignored him.

"This a place you frequent?" he asked, his smile gone.

"My first time here, actually."

Senhor Pimentel looked longingly at my beer. I wrapped my hand around the warm glass.

"Well, here I am," Senhor Pimentel said. "What do you want?"

"I'd like to talk," I said.

Catching sight of the suitcase at my feet, Senhor Pimentel's smile returned. "You running away, Jega?"

Madame Lucifer arrived. He tipped his hat to the two other men and glided to our table. "Miss Dores," Lucifer said. "I'm glad we can all have a drink together before we head out."

Senhor Pimentel examined Madame L., no doubt noticing that, except for the colors, their suits were identical, made by the same tailor.

"Who the hell are you?" Senhor Pimentel asked.

Madame L.'s smile remained wide but his eyes narrowed. "You didn't order a drink for our friend, Miss Dores?"

Madame L. held up two fingers. The bartender immediately poured two rums and delivered them to our table. Senhor Pimentel stared warily at the glass in front of him.

"You should drink," Madame L. said. "I'll wait."

"Wait for what?" Senhor Pimentel asked.

"Until you finish."

Senhor Pimentel looked at me, then at Madame Lucifer, then back again. "What's the story here, Jega?"

"Jega?" Madame L. said, and laughed. "Who on earth is that? I don't see any jegas around here. But I do see an ass."

Senhor Pimentel rose. Madame L. barred his exit from our table.

"Finish your drink," Madame L. ordered. "You'll need it."

"For what?" Senhor Pimentel shouted. "Get out of my way."

Madame L. sighed, bored. Behind him, the two men rose from their stools and stood on either side of Lucifer. Senhor Pimentel quieted.

A lifetime later, Vinicius and I went to a bullfight in Seville and when I saw how swiftly and gracefully the matador stabbed the long, barbed sticks into the bull's shoulders, I thought of that bar and those men, how quickly one of them produced a bottle of rum from behind his back, cocked his arm, and smashed it over Senhor Pimentel's head.

I covered my eyes. Glass skittered across the bar's tiled floor. The front of my dress was wet with rum. Madame Lucifer muttered, "At least it's clear," and wiped his lapels with a handkerchief. The bartender had disappeared. The two men heaved Senhor Pimentel from the floor. His eyes flickered open, then closed. At his hairline was a deep scarlet gash. Senhor Pimentel's head bobbed forward. Red droplets pinpricked his linen suit.

My foot was slick inside my shoe; my beer, knocked over in the scuffle, pooled on the table and dribbled onto my feet and the suitcase, forgotten under the table.

The men stood on either side of Senhor Pimentel and wrapped his arms around their necks, as if they were drinking buddies escorting a friend home—a wealthy friend, in one of Rio's finest suits. The sugar cube glinted between the folds of his loose tie. I snatched up the suitcase.

"Wait!" I called, startling us all.

I blocked the men's path. Madame Lucifer glared at me. Before I could speak, he reached forward and tugged the sugar cube from Senhor Pimentel's tie and held it in his fist.

"There's no waiting now," Madame L. said as his men dragged Senhor Pimentel out of the bar and into the night.

I took to my bed. My head ached as if I'd spent the night drinking, when really I'd scurried around Ipanema throwing the contents of Senhor Pimentel's forgotten suitcase into rubbish bins—except the envelope of money, which I'd stuffed under my mattress. I imagined Madame L. and his men dumping Senhor Pimentel on a freighter bound for Recife. He'd wake up disoriented, his head pounding, his wallet empty and blood polka-dotting his suit, and maybe he'd recall what happened the night before, maybe not. Maybe he'd think he'd been robbed on the way to the bar. But eventually, he'd realize that it was no coincidence that he was on that boat, bound north. He'd look for something he could trade with the captain to make him turn the boat around. He'd look for his precious diamond pin, and wouldn't find it. Lucifer had taken it precisely to prevent Senhor Pimentel from bartering his way back to Rio. This is the story I told myself, even though I knew it wasn't true.

Senhor Pimentel didn't return to Vinicius's apartment the next day. Graça thought her father was on a bender at first, until Vinicius knocked on our door and said that Senhor Pimentel had cleaned out his closet. At Vinicius's apartment, Graça inspected the empty hangers, the open drawers. Graça rifled through them, seeing what was gone and what wasn't. Then Graça sat on Senhor Pimentel's unmade bed and covered her eyes. She wasn't crying, just still. Vinicius and I sat on either side of her. After a few minutes she spoke, her hands still over her eyes.

"He didn't take his favorite suit," she said. "He took the money."

"You gave him money?" I asked.

"Never mind," Graça said, taking her hands away from her eyes.

"How much money was it?" Vinicius asked. "Maybe he's trying to get the farm back?"

"It wasn't a farm," Graça snapped. "It was a fucking plantation ten times the size of Lapa. He couldn't buy it back even if he wanted to." Graça craned her head back and stared at the ceiling. "I know he was a drunk old snob, but I liked having him around. It was nice to have someone on my side."

"We're on your side," I said.

Graça shook her head. "Not always. Most of the time you're on each other's sides. But Papai was always in my corner."

"Because you paid him," I said.

Graça glared at me. "So what? It was still fucking nice."

Then she heaved herself from the bed and locked herself in Vinicius's bathroom.

"Did you find your notebook?" Vinicius whispered.

I thought of Senhor Pimentel's suitcase stuffed into a trash bin. I thought of Madame L. and those men, dragging him through the bar's doorway. I forced myself to stare Vinicius square in the eyes.

"No," I replied. "It wasn't here."

Five days later, a police lieutenant and an officer appeared backstage at Urca. A body had been found in the lagoon. The corpse was badly swollen but it wore a suit made by the city's best tailor. Thinking the dead man could be someone important, the normally uninterested and bumbling police questioned the tailor, who looked in his records and matched the number on the suit's metal nameplate to his client Sofia Salvador.

"Tailor said he made suits for a relative of yours," the lieutenant, an older man with a thick mustache, said. "We'll need you to identify the body."

Graça stumbled into her dressing room and closed the door. The Blue Moon boys stood along the room's edges, quiet; none of them liked or trusted police. That left only me to deal with the officers. I grabbed Vinicius's arm.

"Go check on her," I said. "She can't be alone."

Vinicius obeyed, disappearing behind Graça's door.

"You can see Miss Salvador's upset," I said to the police, my stomach in so many knots it was hard to stand upright. "What happened to the man, in the lagoon?"

The lieutenant shrugged. "Drunks fall in all the time. We pull one out every other day if you can believe it. This one was better dressed than most."

"Even the rich can't hold their liquor," I said.

"Especially the rich," the lieutenant said, a faint smile creeping across his lips.

"I'd hate to have the newspapers bothering Miss Salvador during a time like this," I said. "If you could keep this low-profile, she'd be grateful to you and so would the casino. They always pay off-duty officers to advise them on security issues."

"Newspapers are a bunch of gossip rags," the officer said. "I don't even look at them."

I handed the officers front-row passes to Sofia Salvador's next five shows. I thought of the driver who'd stolen an extra loaf of sweet-flour bread and then disappeared back when Graça and I were still Lucifer's delivery girls; I thought of Little Tony, his face forever disfigured. And I imagined the sugar cube pin on the shelf in Madame L.'s office, alongside his many trophies. As soon as the police left, I ran into the band's bathroom and vomited.

After our trip to the morgue, Graça, Vinicius, and I went to Lapa's best undertaker. With the money I'd given her—the money I'd taken from Senhor Pimentel's envelope—she bought a velvet-lined coffin and space in a posh mausoleum in Rio's Saint John the Baptist Cemetery.

"Where'd you get all that dough?" Graça asked as we left the undertaker's.

"I've been saving it," I replied.

"For a rainy day, I bet," Graça said, staring out the taxi window.

Despite the fancy burial, the funeral itself was a simple affair, with only the Blue Moon boys and a handful of friends in attendance. Anaïs was there along with Graça's dressmaker, and Madame Lucifer.

The service was at eleven a.m., which was earlier than Graça and the Blue Moon boys had been awake in months. They all stood, bleary-eyed and solemn in the noonday sun as Senhor Pimentel's casket was slid into the tomb, as if he was being stored away for eternity in a drawer. Graça wept like one of her movie heroines, her shoulders shaking, her makeup perfect under her black veil. Vinicius held one of her hands while I held the other.

When the service was over, Vinicius took Graça back to our boardinghouse to rest before playing Urca. Chuck Lindsay would be in the audience again that night, and she insisted she'd rather be onstage than cooped up in our apartment. I stayed behind to tip the cemetery's caretakers and say good-bye to our guests.

"You are too skinny," Anaïs said, resting her gloved hand on my cheek.

Despite the heat she looked glamorous and lovely in a tight black dress and veiled hat. If she had asked me to run away with her in that moment, I would have gone without hesitation. But she simply lifted her veil and planted a kiss on my mouth before bidding me good-bye.

Anaïs and the dressmaker chatted near the cemetery entrance, both waiting for Madame Lucifer. He stood before me in a black suit and lavender tie. A fedora shaded his face from the sun.

"I don't understand what happened," I said.

A few meters away, two cemetery workers cemented the edges of Senhor Pimentel's tomb shut. Madame L. glanced at them.

"A funeral happened, Miss Dores. I think you need to get out of this heat," he replied.

"I wanted him to leave," I whispered. "That's all."

My eyes stung. I wiped them with the heel of my hand, wetting my gloves. Madame L. put an arm around me. He smelled of sandalwood and starch.

"You've got to keep your head, friend," he said, his voice low and soft. "Times like these, it's easy to get confused. We're partners. We both care about Graça. We both need her to be a great success."

"I didn't need this," I said.

Madame L. sighed. "Do me the favor of not acting surprised. When have we ever done things in half measures? Me and you, we make hard choices so others don't have to. We get things done, sometimes not in the nicest of ways, but it's the result that matters, Miss Dores."

His grip on my shoulder was firm. The next day there would be four perfectly round bruises where he'd held me.

But that day, I rode in the backseat of his Lincoln with Anaïs as we zigzagged down hills and back into Lapa. They dropped me in front of my boardinghouse, where I went inside but did not climb the stairs to our room. Graça would be there, asleep in our bed or, worse, awake and in need of consolation. Facing her in the days after Senhor Pimentel's death had been difficult; every look she gave me felt searching and suspicious. Every question she asked felt loaded with a weight I could not bear. This was why I'd left Vinicius to calm her when the police appeared, to prop her up at the morgue, and to take her home after the funeral. That day, I needed Vinicius myself. I checked to make sure my little notebook was in my purse, then left our boardinghouse and walked quickly to his.

The door to Vinicius's room was locked. I knocked. Inside there was shuffling. His voice. Voices. The door opened.

Vinicius stood on the other side, still in the dress shirt and slacks he'd worn to the funeral. The shirt's collar was open, too many buttons undone. His tie was gone. He'd never liked ties and took them off as soon as he could. His hair—floppy and too long, and usually slicked into the pompadour he'd taken to wearing—was mussed. A black lock fell into his eyes. His lips were pink and raw-looking.

"Dor," he breathed.

"I thought we could write."

Vinicius nodded but made no move to let me inside. Behind him, I heard the creak of bedsprings. Over his shoulder, I saw Graça. She wore her black funeral dress, but it sagged strangely at the bust. Her eyes were still puffy. Her feet were bare and dangled off the bedside, barely reaching the floor. She wiggled her toes; her stockings were off.

"She didn't want to be alone," Vinicius said.

"I'll go," I replied, my voice too loud in my head, as if my ears were stuffed with cotton.

Vinicius caught my hand gently. "Later, we'll meet at the roda."

"Sure," I mumbled.

"I'm beat," Graça purred. "Zip me up, amor. I'll go with her."

Vinicius glanced at me, then moved toward Graça. I looked away, staring at the floor, its tiles cracked. I heard the crunch of a zipper's teeth grinding closed. Graça sighed. There were whispers. The wet clicks of kisses. Then she was beside me, stuffing her black stockings into her purse, her perfume sickeningly sweet. I had the urge to run away, down the stairs, across the street, through the alleys, and never stop. Graça hooked my arm in her own and suddenly we were out on the street, squinting in the afternoon sun.

"Don't be mad, Dor. I know you're surprised," Graça said. "I was, too, at first. Well, a little surprised—I'd always suspected he liked me, but he was too hardheaded to admit it. After Papai . . . that night, when the police came, Vinicius was there, holding me. It was like we'd had a door between us this whole time, and then someone opened it and let him through."

It's the result that matters. That is what Madame L. said and what I told Graça years later, during our last, terrible argument. It's always easier to think that your intentions are just as important as the outcome, but this isn't true. The outcome is everything. The outcome is what you live with.

SAMBA, FOR A TIME YOU WERE MINE

For a time you were mine.
My love, we played so well!
I held the curve of your guitar,
I coaxed rhythm from your agogô bells.

Your pandeiro drum
had the smoothest skin.
And in the moan of your cuíca,
I forgot every sin.

Well, I made a mistake,
and thought you were my creation.
Oh, Samba! Oh, Samba!
Now you're another's inspiration.

I traveled far away from you,
to a land of ice and snow.
I courted Rumba, Fox Trot,
Jazz, Swing, and Tango.

No matter where I landed,
no matter how many trips,
the sweetness of your melody,
was always on my lips.

When I sought you out again,
you weren't at any destination.
Oh, Samba! Oh, Samba!
Now you're another's inspiration.

There is no one left who knew me in my youth; no one to resurrect the tall, dark-haired lapa of a girl I used to be. I do not imagine myself as being young, but I am still startled by the woman who faces me in the mirror: her spine curled like a shrimp's, her skin as mottled as porridge. Her hair is so thin, you can see bits of scalp. She squints. She does not even look quite like a *she* at all, but like a collection of bones in an ill-fitting sack of skin.

We are, all of us, trapped in bodies that cannot contain us. We are defined by these bodies and their parts. People's voices can only go so high or so low. Their fingers can only stretch so far across a series of strings. Their lips and tongues vibrate only so fast against a metal mouthpiece. And even the finest instruments have shortcomings: a string can only be stretched so taut, a plank of wood carved only so thin, a sheet of metal bent only so far. But the music in our minds can do anything. It can hit any note, move at any speed, play as loudly or as softly as our imaginations allow. In the deepest, purest parts of our imaginations there is no male or female, no bad or good, no villain or hero, no you or I. There is only feeling, and the exhilaration of feeling.

When I remember our songs, this kind of purity returns to me. In my memory, I replay our sambas and it's as if we are speaking urgently to someone we hold dear, giving them a message that is important, its delivery flawless. When I remember our music, there is the delicious perfection of fantasy, and also fantasy's emptiness. To truly experience a song, you must actually hear it. So I faithfully put our records on my turntable, and listen to Noel's tamborim drum occasionally drowning out Graça's voice; Kitchen's percussion competing with the soft melody line; Vinicius starting a song too hard on his guitar and making us lose the gentle moan of Bonito's cuíca. If there was perfection, it was only in my imagination. But those imperfections return me to cramped studios and long nights, to that slippery, unknowable magic that occurred when we sat in a circle, without pride or expectations, and found a groove that we could ride into the morning. The real music always returns me to the girl I once was. It is treacherous for this very reason.

I tremble when I slip *Samba, for a Time You Were Mine* out of its album sleeve, but I drop it onto the turntable, let the needle fall, and brace myself. It is a strange kind of devotion, like I am lashing myself with my own belt.

Riacho Doce doesn't exist anymore; I've made calls. The fields are owned by a conglomerate that bulldozed the Great House and the mill and the chapel to make room for more cane to make ethanol and rum. Machines are the harvesters now. There is no burning. There is no trace of the Pimentels or of anyone who worked in the fields or the house. This gives me no solace.

Does he come to me at night, like a ghost in the movies, leaving puddles around my house, his fancy suit soaking wet, a gash on his head and fish in his pockets? That would be easier to bear.

We all carry our burdens differently, and in ways that surprise us. The choices we make, in life as in the studio, are never isolated, though they might appear to be as we are making them. Nothing stands alone—no note, no melody, no beat, no decision—they all flow together in the end. They must.

Why do I listen to these songs that make me tremble, make me weak, make me feel like I am being held underwater and cannot come up for air? Because I prefer them to that voice that speaks—even now—calling me Jega, hissing that I will be found out, that I am nothing but a messed-up kid, that I have nothing to give, that I am a hindrance and a hanger-on. His is a whisper so low that, for a long while, I believed it was my own. So I cut every record. I booked every show. I filed every copyright. I signed every contract. I befriended gossip columnists. I negotiated with agents and studio heads. I guaranteed that Sofia Salvador and Blue Moon made every call time and went to every premiere, even if I had to drag them kicking and screaming. I cleared every path with the grim determination of the best cane cutters. I heard only the parts, not the whole.

SAMBA, FOR A TIME
YOU WERE MINE

Graça and Vinicius showed all of the common and irritating signs
of early coupledom. They found excuses to touch each other:
wiping a crumb from the corner of a mouth, patting a leg, fixing a tie,
straightening a hat. Every trivial discovery about each other (You sleep
on your side! You don't like coconut milk, either!) brought with it a
rapture between them, as if they'd just discovered the secrets of the
universe. They walked arm in arm through Lapa as if floating through
a fog and, during rodas, they stared at each other like only the two of
them existed. They created a private language between them—a set of
cues made up of smiles, raised eyebrows, pats, and the biting of lips that
the rest of us saw but could not decipher. Onstage, this language in-
creased. Sofia Salvador still danced and sang, but her focus had shifted.
Her audience sensed this and, like Blue Moon and me, spent the entire
show feeling as if they were watching a private dialogue in a code they
couldn't crack. Afterward, Graça and Vinicius raced into the dressing
room, locking the rest of us out.

The Blue Moon boys had varying reactions to Graça and Vinicius's
pairing off. The Brothers—Banana and Bonito—made jokes at the
couple's expense. Tiny was inspired, and romanced cocktail waitresses
and cabaret girls with impressive fervor. Little Noel was brokenhearted

and began drinking heavily. Kitchen was stoic, like an elder statesman who knew trouble was coming but wasn't about to warn anyone.

And me? I was annoyed that Vinicius skipped our songwriting sessions or, worse, brought Graça along and made doe eyes at her the entire time instead of truly working. After Urca shows no one except Vinicius went into Graça's dressing room, and I wondered who was helping her remove her Sofia Salvador makeup—slathering cold cream over her face and neck, and then carefully wiping it away with a hot towel and rubbing her skin with witch hazel, like I used to do. Staring at the closed dressing room door, I wondered if Graça had taken on this task herself, or if she had Vinicius do it. They left our rodas arm in arm and went back to Vinicius's place, where he'd sneak Graça inside. I did not go back to our empty room but hit the town. I'd wake in some stranger's bed, or on the floor of one of the Blue Moon boys' rooms after they'd let me crash there, my head throbbing, one of my eyes swollen shut and my hand unable to close from some bar fight or other. A few times I woke on the beach outside the Copacabana Palace. I'd be barefoot—how many pairs of shoes did I lose in those weeks?—with sand in my ears and stuck to my cheek, and I'd stare up at the Palace's white towers and think: *It's only a matter of time.*

I believed I knew Graça and Vinicius better than they knew themselves. All of her life, Graça was never stingy with physical affection; she thrived on it. With friends and lovers alike she sat on laps, planted kisses on cheeks, danced too close, whispered in ears, held hands. At first, after being lavished with such attention, you might believe there was a bond between you and her. And there was; Graça was sincere in her affections but she cast them widely. Everyone was special to her, which made no one special. The sooner you realized this, the better. Now, if she decided to suddenly lavish you and only you with her attentions, you might feel as if you were different. As if you had won her. In order to keep this fixed attention, you would give in to her demands.

You would serve her, and by serving her, you would take away any fear she might feel: of rejection, of disappointment, of betrayal. Stripped of fear, desire becomes comfort. And comfort was something Graça could get easily and from anyone. By giving her exactly what she wanted, you'd lost her for good.

So I waited for the moment when Graça would use me as an excuse to get away from Vinicius, dragging me into the dressing room instead of him and saying, *Oh boy, do I need a break from that old sock.* Vinicius might pine for her, but in the end his pride would win out, and eventually he'd come back to our afternoon song sessions with more melodies than ever, and we would all laugh at their little romance. Life would return to how it was before, only better because, thanks to me, Sofia Salvador and Blue Moon were going to be movie stars.

This was the story I told to console myself, even as Graça and Vinicius made a show of kissing each other on the SS *Uruguay*'s deck, as crowds of cheering fans and government-approved photographers watched from Rio's docks.

In her black dress, pearls, and black turban, Graça looked more like a chic society girl than the crowd's dear Sofia Salvador. After Senhor Pimentel's burial, Graça insisted on wearing black every day, even to Sofia Salvador's farewell celebration at Rio's port. A few days before our trip she'd dyed her hair coal black; Graça was a mess because of it. "I look like a vulture!" she'd wailed, and nearly canceled our trip to Los Angeles. I moved to console her but it was Vinicius who'd held her, told her she was the most beautiful vulture he'd ever seen, and convinced her to pack her bags for North America.

Going abroad wasn't a hard choice. The Blue Moon boys and Graça were bored playing Urca shows and living in the bubble of their fame. We were all tired of recording song after song for Victor, like every other samba band. And, after Senhor Pimentel's death, we were ready for a change of scenery, me most of all. Every time a waitress or an overzealous fan rapped on the band's dressing room door, I froze, wondering if it was police. Alone in our little boardinghouse room, I could not sleep, wondering if Madame Lucifer would appear at my door and warn me to change my name and move to Buenos Aires to avoid being caught. They were exaggerated fears, born of guilt and watching too many Hollywood films. Still, Senhor Pimentel's sugar cube remained in Madame L.'s possession, and I felt exposed by that diamond pin as if it was a weight in my own pocket. So, when Chuck Lindsay proposed a bit part for Sofia Salvador and Blue Moon in a picture called *Bye Bye, Buenos Aires*, we all jumped at the chance.

It was a turn of events that, months earlier, would have petrified me: giving up fame and steady income to travel into the unknown. We'd make a pittance on that first film—fifty dollars a week plus lodging—but Chuck said this was common. The studio was testing us out, seeing if we could hack movie work. While we were away, Madame L. wouldn't receive his weekly cut of our earnings, but he was excited for our trip; he knew a golden goose when he saw one. Even if we made only one successful picture, upon our return to Brazil every casino and cabaret and recording company would pay top dollar for Sofia Salvador and her Blue Moon Band, Brazil's greatest exports! Madame L., like the rest of us, like the entire nation, believed our stint in Hollywood would be not only successful but also temporary.

The majority of the *Uruguay*'s passengers were North American tourists who could not comprehend the hubbub. They stared, confused, at our little group as we waved and blew kisses to the crowds.

"Who's famous?" a tourist beside me asked in English. "What's happening?"

I was proud of myself for understanding. In the weeks before our departure, I'd taken an English-language course in part to prepare for our time in the United States, and in part as a distraction. Instead of waiting in vain for Vinicius to show up to our songwriting sessions, I shifted the focus of my afternoons to relearning the language Senhora Pimentel had taught me long ago. Aboard the *Uruguay*, I believed my hard work had paid off.

"We are great artists," I said, in English, to the pale woman beside me.

"Painters?" she asked.

I shook my head and explained that we were sambistas, sent north to conquer Hollywood! We would sing and dance in a real movie for Twentieth Century-Fox studios! My voice, in English, became high-pitched and unfamiliar. My tongue grew tired after just a few minutes of conversation. How startled I was to see the look of confusion and sympathy on that American woman's face! She nodded and quickly darted away. I felt graceless and dim-witted. Above us, the ship's horn blared. Below us, the crowd cheered even louder.

It was not a massive group, but large enough to merit attention. Some waved Brazilian flags. Some held signs that read "We love you, Sofia!"

We would be the first Brazilian act to be in a major motion picture, a fact that the Lion's national newspapers and Gegê's Department of Propaganda touted for weeks before our departure. If before Sofia Salvador was simply a well-known Rio samba star, after the announcement of our U.S. trip, she became a national symbol, a valuable export. All of Brazil was counting on her to succeed.

I remember standing alone on the deck and watching Brazil disappear from view. The sun set. The ship chugged forward, as if moving through syrup. There was no moon, making it hard to distinguish the ocean from the sky. Looking out onto that immense blackness I felt a dizzy euphoria, as if I had been fasting and had forgotten any symptoms of hunger. Graça and Vinicius's little tryst seemed to bother me less. Rio, with its jutting hills, its gaudy cabaret lights, its mansions and slums, its casinos and fancy theaters, its grubby assortment of Madame Lucifers and Lions and Senhor Pimentels, was behind us. Now there was only our band and our music.

The ocean bucked and swayed, making the giant ship rise and fall beneath me. I held stubbornly to the rail, intent on keeping my excitement alive, but the same seasickness that plagued me on my first boat ride years before, on our way to Sion School, found me again. I huddled in my cabin and did not leave until Graça found me, days later.

As soon as I unbolted the door she darted inside, swift as a cat.

"You look like hell," she said.

I crawled back into my berth. "I didn't ask you to look at me."

She placed a tin of crackers and a water pitcher on the table, already strewn with cigarette butts and empty glasses. Thankfully the porter had replaced my sick bucket, which sat empty beside my berth. Graça nudged it aside with the toe of her shoe, then gave my leg a hard push.

"Shove over," she said, and squeezed beside me on the tiny mattress. I turned my back to her. She curled into me, her knees fitting into the backs of mine, her chest against my back, her arm nudging under my own and wrapping around my waist. I smelled rose perfume and the powdery residue of her cold cream. I shut my eyes tight.

"Did you and Vinicius fight?" I asked. "Is that why you're crawling in here?"

Graça stiffened. She unwound her arm from my waist.

"You both think you're so smart," she said. "Always using fancy words and asking questions, but not to me. He never asks me anything. We don't do much talking."

How many times had I pictured the two of them together, behind that locked dressing room door? What a treacherous gift the imagination can be—one minute a blessing that grants you escape, the next an enemy you must fight off for your own survival.

I turned to face her. "What do you want him to ask you?"

"If I'm scared," she whispered. "About leaving. About Hollywood."

"Are you?"

"No one knows me on this boat. In the dining room the gringos look at me and the boys like we're not supposed to be there. Like we should be cleaning their cabins, not sitting next to them at dinner. The captain hasn't even visited our table to say hello to me."

I smiled. "He's probably busy steering the ship."

"Stop it," Graça snapped. "You're acting like Vinicius, making fun of me. Sometimes I wish . . ." She shook her head and turned her body to face the ceiling, squeezing me harder against the berth's wall.

"What?"

"That Papai was still here."

I felt very warm, as if I might need my sick pail.

"If he was still here we wouldn't be together," I said, "on this boat. He wouldn't let you go to Hollywood. He'd have you singing opera at a tea party for some rich bitches in Santa Teresa."

"At least they'd know me," she said.

"Sure they'd know you—some ex–samba singer trying hard to be respectable. Some little planter's daughter trying to win them over with her pretty voice. You'd be a novelty. Worse—you'd be a joke. You know what rich people hate the most? People trying to copy their own game. And you know what scares them? Someone with real talent doing something unexpected—doing something they didn't even think existed. You know why? Because suddenly they see this whole world of music and people and talent that's not there because of them. They didn't make it or pay for it, and they can't buy it or control it. And this scares the shit out of them."

Graça blinked, startled.

"But I don't want to scare people, Dor," she said. "I want them to want me. Not in a going-to-bed kind of way. I want them to hear me sing and, for a little while, forget everything else. They don't have wives or husbands or kids or jobs. They just have me. I'm everything to them, but they can't ever have me. So they'll never get bored with me, they'll never make fun of me, they'll never think I'm plain or useless or stupid. I'll always be perfect to them because I'm stuck in their memories, and every time they think of me, they make me all over again. You can't help but love something you made yourself."

"That's not love," I whispered.

"Oh yeah? How would you know?"

Her arm pressed against mine and my skin felt painfully tender, as if I'd been sunburned. "I wouldn't."

"Well, *I* think it's love," Graça replied. "That's what counts."

"And Vinicius?" I asked. "What does he think?"

Graça shrugged. "He loves his music. He talks about it like it's some kind of religion. If I wasn't a singer—if I didn't sing his songs—he wouldn't even give me the time of day."

"They're my songs, too."

"You and him are two peas in a fucking pod," Graça said, frowning.

I found her hand and wove my fingers through hers. "After we cut 'My Mutt' you told me to stop moping and be happy, be excited. And you were right. I turned what should've been a great day into a pity party. I was only thinking about what I'd lost, not all the things we'd get. So I'm telling you the same thing about Hollywood: be happy, be excited. We're going to make a movie! You're going to be twenty feet tall on screens all over the world! There's nothing to be afraid of."

Graça stared at the cabin's metal ceiling. "If the movies don't work out, it won't matter to you or Vinicius because you'll have your writing and your rodas. But what about me? If those Hollywood gringos hate me, I won't be some great export, I'll be a dud. Aracy took over my show at Urca. If I don't nail this movie gig, I won't get that show back. I won't get any shows. Seems like the higher up we get, the worse the fall. For me at least. What net have I got?"

"You don't need one," I whispered. "I'll catch you."

Graça laughed. "You and Vinicius'll be so busy with your songs, you won't even see me hit the pavement."

When the *Uruguay* slid into New York Harbor, my trousers were baggy and my belt sagged on its first notch. As I stared into the cabin's mirror and applied a coat of lipstick, I saw my sharp cheekbones and the angular lines of my face, and realized that I, too, had a kind of beauty, though it was severe. As I made my way to the ship's deck where we'd all agreed to meet, Tiny whistled upon seeing me. The other Blue Moon boys laughed and slapped my back, teasing me about my seasickness. Vinicius smiled so widely it was difficult to ignore him as I'd done the past few weeks.

"The Sphinx finally rises!" he said, holding his arms out to hug me. Graça, dressed all in white with an ivory turban covering her vulture hair, swept between us.

"You made it," she said, as if our arrival was an appointment I could have easily missed. She wrapped her arm around mine and did not release me until we were walking, single file, down the ship's gangplank.

Seeing the great city of New York, I felt as if a brown film coated my eyes, making everything sullied and dim. The city's gray buildings were clumped close together. Wind blew easily through my cotton coat. It was November and I had never before felt such cold. Our travels, I realized, were just beginning.

A Fox man met us at the port, stuffed us and our trunks into three yellow cabs, and sent us to Penn Station, where we boarded a train to

Chicago. There, numb with fatigue, we filed onto the famous Super Chief train to Los Angeles.

What I remember most from that train ride was the food. After thirteen lean days at sea, I ate like a starving animal: cottage fried potatoes, Kansas City sirloins, fresh trout, Romanoff caviar, eggs, salads, rye bread rolls. *Oh, North America!* I thought as I sopped up the last bits of gravy from my plate. *Land of luxury!* The Pullman porters made sure to always give us the most secluded spot in the dining car. I'd believed they were being gracious—we were a loud bunch, always celebrating— and other diners perhaps wanted peace and quiet. After we'd disembarked in Los Angeles, however, I discovered that it wasn't our noisiness the other diners objected to, but our looks. The Super Chief was not a segregated train by rule, but there were unspoken customs from which the Pullman porters—so tactful and kind—hoped to shield us.

When I think of the eight of us—Graça, me, Vinicius, Little Noel, Tiny, Kitchen, Banana, and Bonito—on the train, admiring the Super Chief's linen napkins and silver finger bowls, making toasts to our success, speculating excitedly about which movie stars we might see, I think of a group of children playing games in a narrow and luxurious house, unaware of the larger workings of the outside world.

I remember our arrival in Los Angeles vividly not only because it was a new place, but also because it felt like we were new people there— different people. We were no longer the seasoned crew of famous musicians we'd been in Rio, but unknown kids learning how to make our way into Hollywood's roda. In the beginning, this didn't diminish our excitement but added to it.

Twentieth Century-Fox assigned a young blond man to greet us at Los Angeles's chaotic and enormous Union Station. We'd learn, weeks later, that real movie stars were greeted at the more picturesque Pasadena Station. But on the day of our arrival we were blissfully ignorant, and we followed that young and cheerful Fox assistant through sheets of rain and piled—sopping wet—into two black cars with tinted windows. The blond separated us: Vinicius, Little Noel, and Graça in one car; Tiny, Kitchen, Bonito, and Banana in another. The Fox boy studied me—eyeing my face and my expensive traveling dress with its matching emerald jacket—before guiding me to Graça's car. The dark automobiles plodded slowly through the storm and into Los Angeles, like a funeral procession on its way to the plot.

Our car had the Fox boy inside it, and he took us to the Plaza Hotel on Hollywood and Vine. The place billed itself as a luxury hotel for "stars in transit." Its lobby had windows covered by red damask curtains, a ceiling tall enough to comfortably fit a giraffe, and carpets so thick, my heels sank two inches into their pile. Graça's eyes sparkled. She removed her wet gloves and elbowed me.

"Tell the Fox kid I need a powder room. I can't face the press looking like a wet rat."

Before I could formulate how to translate Graça's request into my stilted English, the Fox boy began to speak loud and slow:

"Fox will cover you for one week—the length of your shoot. After that, you'll have to find other digs. There're plenty of rooming houses in the city. The sooner you get a used car, the better. L.A.'s a big town if you have to walk and take the bus everywhere. Here's a bus schedule," he said, pressing a brochure into my hand. "Give yourselves ninety minutes to get to the studio. Call time is six a.m. sharp. I'll go check you in now."

I stared blankly at the bus schedule in my hand and tried to arrange what I'd understood of the boy's speech into a coherent thread. Before I could translate it, Graça spoke.

"Where're the reporters?" she asked.

I shook my head. "There are none."

"Where's the other car?" Vinicius asked.

Little Noel nodded. "The boys should be here by now."

I relayed their question to the Fox boy as best as I could. The blond's smile wavered. He replied with a long string of words, of which I could only decipher: *Another hotel. The Dunbar. Swell place.*

"The boys don't speak a lick of English," Vinicius said, running a hand through his soaked hair. "They should be here, with us."

Graça balled her wet gloves in her hands. "Dor, tell this Fox kid how big we are in Brazil," she commanded. "We might be nobodies here, but the least they could do is put us up together. We'll share rooms if we have to; they can pack us in tight."

The Fox assistant stared coolly at us, our room keys in his freckled hand. I cleared my throat.

"We stay all together," I said to him. "The other boys? Here?"

The blond boy raised his eyebrows, as if I'd just asked him to undress in front of me. "Hotels around here don't let certain kinds stay," he replied, his voice low.

"Kinds?" I asked, though I already suspected what he was implying.

"Negroes," he replied.

The word exists in Portuguese. It is not pronounced *knee-grow* as the Fox boy said in his nasal voice. We say *neh-grew*, though most times we don't even pronounce the *r*. It is usually just *neh-goo*. And although it can mean the color black it also means other things. Meu nêgo—my friend, my lover, my brother, my sweet one. In our circles this word was said with great affection. But we weren't blind or stupid; the logic of lighter being better wasn't alien to us, but how it was expressed and enforced in Hollywood came as a surprise.

As sambistas in Brazil we always rode freight elevators, used service entrances, and lived in neighborhoods like Lapa. The difference was we did these things together, as a band. Movies led us to believe that, while the USA might be strict on such matters, Hollywood itself would be a bohemian town where anything was possible and where everything goes. We'd soon learn that the real Hollywood was a business, with a few mill-white men calling all the shots.

The Fox boy muttered some kind of good-bye and pressed the room keys into my hands. I looked back at Graça, Vinicius, and Little Noel. "There are rules," I said. "The boys can't stay here."

Vinicius slumped onto a nearby settee. Little Noel lit a cigarette. Graça tugged her wet gloves back onto her hands and faced me.

"Get us a taxi," she ordered.

Twenty minutes later, we were parked in front of the Dunbar Hotel's arched entranceway. The hotel was, we learned, the home for black performers who entertained white Los Angelinos but could not sleep anywhere near them. Built in a Spanish style we'd come to recognize as a Los Angeles trademark, the hotel had flagstone floors and an impressive colonnade decorated in an art deco style and topped with an enormous crystal chandelier. The Dunbar had its own restaurant and barbershop, and a nightclub called the Showboat. That was where we found Kitchen, Tiny, Bonito, and Banana, having drinks and listening to a bebop trio onstage.

During our long journey to L.A., we'd all taken turns imagining our first night in Hollywood. We'd believed Hollywood was a magical place with the best bands and the rowdiest clubs. It was the capital of entertainment! We thought we would be able to relive our wildest Lapa nights. But on our actual first night, as we sat in the Showboat Club and attempted to get staggeringly drunk, we learned that moviemaking did not allow for late nights. Every club, including the Dunbar's, closed by eleven. In Hollywood, the only real parties occurred on Sunday afternoons—when the studios were closed—and even those ended no later than midnight.

By ten-thirty it was last call. The band played a slow number. Tiny, Banana, and Bonito had found girls to flirt with. Kitchen gestured enthusiastically to a fellow musician at the bar, attempting to mime a conversation. Graça and Little Noel swayed across the dance floor. I sat alone, at a little table in the back, until Vinicius found me.

"This place is better than ours," he said, sitting in the chair next to me, his leg pressing against mine. "It's sure better than our rooms back in Lapa. If they're going to keep us separate, at least they do it in style."

I emptied my drink and banged my glass back onto the table. Vinicius eyed me.

"How long are you going to give me the silent treatment?"

"Until you have something interesting to say."

"She speaks!"

I rolled my eyes. "I'm surprised you let her out of your grip. I was beginning to think we'd have to peel you two apart before filming tomorrow."

"She complained I was stepping on her toes and shoved me away," he said, nodding to the dance floor. "She's picking fights. It's because she's nervous about tomorrow, about filming. She won't admit it, but I can tell. I'm nervous, too."

I looked Vinicius in the eyes. "All you have to do is play our songs. They've never heard good samba before, and we're going to knock all their blocks off. When we're done out here we'll be the most famous samba band there ever was. We'll show everybody."

"Show them what?" he asked.

"That we're not some fad. That we can't be cast aside like we don't matter."

Vinicius put his callused hand over mine. "I didn't plan on this happening with Graça."

I pulled away. "But you always wanted it to. Did you invite me to those first rodas at Ciata's because you hoped she might come along, too? Was that your idea?"

"No," Vinicius replied, and looked away. "Maybe? Shit, Dor, I don't know. Does it matter now? I've never been able to write on my own the way we write together. You got me away from all those old songs. You and me, we're making something brand-new."

"We aren't making anything," I said. "You act like Graça's the only person that exists in this world."

"And you don't?" Vinicius asked. He grabbed my hand, tighter this time. "Cut me some slack, Dor. You know how I feel. You're the only one who knows."

I stared at his pompadour, his thick sideburns, his eyes so dark and shining they looked like pools of liquid, and remembered the first time I'd held his stare as he played at Little Tony's club. This time we were not separated by a stage and a crowd; he was not the performer and I was not a dumb kid in the audience. We were on the same side, to-gether.

Neither of us noticed that the club had grown quiet, the band had stopped, and Graça stood at the edge of our table with her arms crossed. Vinicius's hand flew from mine. The club's lights brightened.

"Party's over, kids," Graça said, and took Vinicius away.

The sun was barely rising the next morning when we reached Twentieth Century-Fox. Upon entering the studio gates, we spent another half hour trying to find our film set. Fox was a city in itself—it had an air-conditioned administration building before air conditioning was common; a massive warehouse where furniture, cos-tumes, and props were stored; a security force with fifty officers; a dentist's office, a clinic, an electrical plant, a beauty parlor, a research department, a cafeteria, a school. Anything you needed could be found on the studio lot, which was what Fox wanted; time away from the studio was considered time lost.

Our film was *Bye, Bye, Buenos Aires*, and would be made in Technicolor, a novelty back then. The plot was the same one used in most of Sofia Salvador's films over the years: a buxom North American gal heads to a foreign land, meets the man of her dreams, quarrels with him, and then, by the end of the film, they are in each other's arms. The action takes place in cruise ships, racetracks, hotel lobbies, and glamorous nightclubs. It's in these clubs that Sofia Salvador and the Blue Moon Band appear.

Although set in Argentina's capital, *Bye, Bye, Buenos Aires* was actually filmed on sound stages in California. The real Buenos Aires had automobiles, glamorous men in Savile Row suits, wide sidewalks and tidy parks. But in Fox's film, Buenos Aires was a backwater town resembling a hacienda and, in it, the Club Argentina. Fox had built an entire nightclub, painting it white, adding enormous Greek columns, and hanging a blue backdrop with stars painted across it. Tiny crosses of black tape were stuck to the set's fake stage, pinpointing where Graça and the Blue Moon boys were required to stand and perform two of our most popular songs: "That Girl from Bahia," and "What's She Got (That I Don't)?" We believed that our first film shoot would be no different from a show at Urca, except, of course, for the cameras.

At six-thirty a.m., Graça, the boys, and I were on set drinking coffee like it was water. The set was a closed hangar and airless. Two dozen stationary fans ran at full speed, but the room still felt muggy. Three large black cameras on metal bases were arranged around the stage—one in the center, two on each side. Ladder-like pillars held large spotlights that flooded the stage, making the white backdrop blinding. Just before filming, production people ran about, shouting and turning off every fan in the room.

Sofia and the boys were bit players, not yet worthy of Fox's many resources, which meant that they did their own hair and makeup and wore their own outfits: the boys in tuxedos, and Graça in her red Baiana-inspired gown with shoulders exposed and a slit up the front of the wide skirt, revealing her legs. Her hair was still black and in its pixie cut, her lipstick bloodred, her earrings massive and dangling.

At the director's cue, Graça walked to her taped mark onstage, her enormous platform heels knocking against the wooden floor.

"Stop!" the director growled. "Leo! Glue some felt to the soles of her shoes. I can't have her clopping around like a fucking horse."

After wardrobe took her shoes and returned them, Graça and the boys were once again ordered to their marks. Everything went quiet. The cameras began to click.

Apart from the movie's crew, the club was empty. There were no waiters milling about. There was no clinking of drink glasses, no velvety haze of cigarette smoke. There was no laughter, no chatter, no applause. Graça had to pretend there was, though. She had to smile and sing as if hundreds were watching her. She had to wag her finger at an imaginary man in the front row, then wink at his lady friend. Near the end of her first song Graça stood at the stage's edge, her chest swelling up and down, beads of sweat shining on her upper lip.

"*Cut!*" the director interrupted. "Get some goddamn powder on her."

A makeup woman appeared, forced Graça to lift her arms, and powdered her face, chest, and armpits.

"Miss . . . uh . . . Salvador, try it again," the director shouted. "Without walking past your marks on either side of the stage. And don't wave your fingers in front of your face. We need to see your face. Jesus! Does she even understand what I'm saying?"

Movies—we quickly learned—weren't live shows. Every drop of sweat had to be wiped away, every loose thread cut, every outside sound muffled. Graça could not dance as she normally did, sweeping back and forth across the stage. She had to stay on her marks, then twist herself toward the camera. The Blue Moon boys had to smile, but only with their lips closed. A hairdresser had to trim Vinicius's hair so it would not fall into his face while he strummed his guitar. Three of the boys stood on either side of Graça, stiffly playing their instruments, making sure not to move too far apart or too close together.

After five hours, only one of our songs had been filmed all the way through. Graça had worked longer stints before, but always with an audience to cheer her. Without a crowd's applause, there was no way for Graça to gauge how well she was doing. On that silent set, each song felt as if it had fallen flat. And just as Graça would hit her stride and begin to feel confident and comfortable, the director would cut her off: the lights were too bright, her earring was crooked, a set piece was smudged. At first, I believed the director's name was Zanuck. Everyone on the set whispered this name, and always in a fearful way.

"Mr. Zanuck won't like that."

"Zanuck will be mad as hell when he sees this."

"Mr. Zanuck wants to make sure Miss Salvador's jewelry isn't too shiny for the camera."

In the afternoon, the director balled up a telegram and growled Zanuck's name, and I realized he was not Zanuck after all. Mr. Darryl F. Zanuck, we'd soon learn, was the head of Fox studios.

At four o'clock that afternoon, we took our second, precious break. The boys and I ordered sandwiches. Graça ate a pickle and drank more coffee; she could not sing and dance on a full stomach. Her feet hurt terribly.

We sat in folding chairs just off set. I held Graça's feet in my lap and undid the buckles of her gold platforms. The shoes dropped to the floor with a thud. The strands of gold necklaces and costume pearls around Graça's neck made it burdensome for her to move; the jewelry was heavy, and she had to conserve her energy. She was nearly asleep, her feet heavy in my lap, when a production assistant yelled to us that the director was ready.

Graça looked solemn when she found her mark onstage. But as soon as the room quieted and the camera started filming, she beamed. Her teeth, framed by the freshly reapplied red lipstick, looked shockingly white. Her eyes were wide. Her hands twirled near her face but never obstructed it. Her hips jutted from side to side, making her skirt flutter. Her voice soared. For the first time, I looked away from Graça and at the cameramen, the production assistants, the set designers and prop crew. They smiled and stared at the stage, their eyes glossy as if they'd been drinking during their breaks. One man bobbed his head. Another patted his leg in time to the music and mouthed the chorus, which we'd all heard a dozen times that day. At the end of the song, Graça held her pose and her smile. Then the director yelled "Cut!" and the room once again buzzed with conversation and movement.

Graça limped offstage, unclipping the enormous earrings that swung nearly to her shoulders and shoving them into my hands.

"Thank Christ that's over," she said. "Let's get drinks."

But before we could return to our tiny trailer, the director stopped us. Beside him was a man we did not recognize—his dark hair was mussed and his eyes bleary, as if he'd been woken from a deep sleep. He spoke to us in Spanish, which was much closer to our language than English was, but still foreign. I had to ask the tired man to slow down.

He was an extra on another film set. The director had found him and ordered him to translate. I looked at the director, who smiled and spoke quickly in English. I caught some of his words, and the tired man translated the rest into Spanish, which I converted to Portuguese for Graça.

"What if," the director proposed, "Sofia Salvador not only sings and dances, but has a few lines?"

Graça wrung her hands. "He wants me to speak in English?" she asked.

The extra and I played our game of translation. The director shook his head. Sofia Salvador would speak her lines in Portuguese and her scene partner, the hero's buddy, would reply in English, giving the audience context. Slowly, the director spelled out the scene for us: Sofia Salvador's nameless nightclub character meets the hero's buddy backstage and argues with him. Sofia was a jilted lover, arguing with her unfaithful gringo beau. It would be a five-minute interlude, tops.

"What's the script?" Graça asked. "What are my lines?"

The director laughed when we translated for him. "No script," he said. "This is just an idea I have—a hunch. Just let her talk. No one's going to understand her anyway."

In our trailer, Graça gulped two mugs of black coffee to pep herself up; we'd been shooting for twelve hours straight by then. While we waited for her costar to arrive, Graça practiced different versions of the five-minute scene over and over.

For the first time ever, she would perform on her own, without me beside her or the Blue Moon boys backing her up, and she would do this in front of the harshest audience imaginable—Fox's exhausted crew.

"How'd that sound?" she asked me after rehearsing for the hundredth time. "Do you think a hurt girl would say this without crying? I think she might cry."

That was how Graça interpreted the character—as a girl who was betrayed and angry.

The Blue Moon boys waited outside while a makeup assistant touched up Graça's powder and lipstick. Her platform heels were so tall that she stood at eye level with me.

"If I don't do this right, I'll die right there, on that set," she said.

"It's only a few lines," I replied. "You'll be fine."

"You always do this," Graça hissed.

"Do what?"

"Make everything seem like it's so fucking easy. But it's not," she said, clipping on her enormous earrings. "Singing's easy, but other things? They aren't easy for me like they are for you."

Graça blinked away tears. Before I could reply, a set assistant opened the trailer door and whisked Graça away.

As soon as the camera rolled, Sofia Salvador improvised her lines perfectly.

"You dog!" she said in Portuguese. "You've ruined my life. How could you do this to me?"

Each time she spoke, her male costar interrupted, trying to appease her, saying he was sorry while, at the same time, backing away. The farther away he moved, the closer Sofia Salvador inched toward him—the scene looked like a song and dance. Graça had drunk too much coffee, making her nervous, almost frantic. Near the scene's end their argument became so heated, with Graça shaking her head so fiercely, that one of her giant earrings began to slip, tugging at her lobe until it fell, sliding down her chest and disappearing into the shadow of her cleavage. Graça clapped her hands to her bosom, her eyes wide.

A cameraman chuckled. Another—his face red and his eyes closed—tried to stifle a laugh but could not. Then the script girl broke out in giggles and, in an instant, the entire set vibrated with laughter. Only the Blue Moon boys and I were quiet.

"Cut!" the director yelled. "Come on, people. Let's keep it together."

Some stared at their shoes to suppress their giggles but their shoulders shook. Others looked at one another and smiled like naughty kids disciplined by a headmaster.

Graça looked dangerously pale. She kept her hands over her heart.

"You okay?" her costar asked. "Hey, George," he said to the director, "I think we need a break."

"Five minutes," the director yelled. "Break!"

"Break!"

"Break!"

"Break!"

Production assistants repeated the word across the set like an echo. I ran to Graça. She fell into me and gripped my hand so tightly I nearly cried out. Even in the safety of her tiny trailer, with the Blue Moon boys guarding the door, Graça would not let go of my fingers.

Vinicius circled us, wringing his hands as if he was waiting for Graça to give birth. I could not think of words of comfort. It was the first time she'd ever been laughed off a stage.

Graça let go of my hand, grabbed the trash bin, and vomited.

As she slumped on the floor, still heaving over the metal bin, Vinicius knelt on one side of Graça and rubbed her back. I knelt on the other.

"Oh, God," she whispered. "I ruined everything. They made fun of me." Graça's face crumpled. "How can we go back home now? After this? What'll the papers print?"

I glanced at Vinicius, then ran my fingers through Graça's sweaty hair. "We can fix it. We'll shoot it again, without the earrings. I'll tell the director we want everybody off set."

Graça's breath caught in her throat. Her eyes were smeared with mascara. "Don't make me go back outside," she whispered.

We pulled Graça up from her knees and moved her to the couch. There, the three of us sat side by side with Graça at the center, one of her hands very cold inside mine.

"Let's leave," Graça said. "Please?"

"I'll call us cabs," I replied. "We'll rest tonight and start fresh tomorrow."

Graça shook her head. "No, leave L.A. I want to go home."

"Take it easy," Vinicius said, his voice hushed as if he was soothing a child. "Let's talk with the boys first . . ."

Graça tugged her hand from his. "All you worry about are the goddamn boys."

She turned her back to Vinicius and faced me. She smelled of sweat and vomit and the powder they'd dusted under her arms.

"I want to go home, Dor."

"We can't," I replied. "We signed a contract."

"Fuck the contract!" Graça yelled, then wrapped me in a hug so tight it was difficult to breathe.

"We can make it like it was before," she said. "Just the two of us. Shit, we can go home and buy our own club! We'll work whatever hours we please, and I'll sing whatever I want. And you'll sing, too, Dor. We can be the Nymphettes again, only better. No cruddy costumes. No bad makeup. We'll sing your songs! It'll be a dream. It'll be like our very first night onstage together. Remember?"

She'd chosen me to escape with, even if her plan was a fantasy. If we burned bridges with the Blue Moon Band, and Fox studios, and our American talent agent, Chuck Lindsay, and we sailed back home, we wouldn't have the money to buy our own club. Few in Rio would hire us. We'd be right back where we'd started, but we'd be together.

"I'll tell the boys we're leaving," I announced. Graça smiled, easing her grip on me.

I felt light-headed. I stood and, in one long stride, I was at the trailer door. Vinicius moved behind me. Gently he placed a hand on my wrist.

"Dor," he whispered, so Graça could not hear him. "It's been a real long day. You know she says things when she's tired. Things she doesn't mean. We should get some rest and talk again tomorrow." He spoke in a fatherly tone, as if he was the adult among us and understood things I did not.

I shook my wrist from his grip, angry now.

"You don't know her," I said. "You don't know me."

Vinicius winced. I took pleasure in his reaction. I'd stung him, just as he and Graça had stung me with their inside jokes, their language of touches and stares.

There was a knock on the trailer door. When I opened it, the film's director stared back at me.

"How is our girl doing?" he shouted, smiling. He peeked at Graça, making sure she was still dressed, then forced his way inside. Behind him was the extra who'd translated for us earlier, his eyes fixed on the trailer's floor.

Graça grabbed a handkerchief and wiped her eyes. Her nose was red, her lipstick smeared. The trailer smelled of vomit.

"I apologize for the crew, Sofia," the director said, speaking very slowly. The extra, never taking his eyes from the floor, as if this might alleviate both Graça's embarrassment and his own, repeated the director's words in Spanish.

"I'm sorry you're upset," the director continued. "I am, too. It's a damn shame we'll have to do that scene again. That came out better than I'd hoped. I'm going to call makeup in here to get you beautiful again. And do you think, if we leave it very loose, you can make that earring fall inside your dress again? That was hysterical."

Graça swallowed. I translated from the extra's Spanish, though she probably understood as much as I had: *He likes what you did. He wants you to stay here and do it again, the same way.*

Graça looked past me at the director and, without hesitation, flashed him her widest smile.

"Perfect," the director said. "Zanuck was right about you: you're going to steal the picture. You're a riot."

A joke is a way of dominating a language. You must have timing and fluidity, like a fine musician. None of us—the Blue Moon boys and I—were able to joke in any language but our own. In English, we were quite serious people. This is what happens when you move to a foreign place: either you recoil into yourself, becoming (on the outside at least) a quiet, tense listener, or you make a show of your errors, flaunting them for all to see. Both are attempts to make people comfortable with your otherness. With the first option you make yourself forgettable. With the second, you make yourself entertaining. What choice did Graça have?

Sofia Salvador filmed her speaking part a second time, doing everything she did the first, only amplified: more waving of hands, more pouting lips, more wide eyes. When the director yelled "Cut!" the cameramen, lighting techs, and sound engineers clapped and whistled. Graça smiled, gave a little bow, and then planted a kiss on the director's cheek, leaving the red imprint of her lips for all to see. Her earlier shame and her desperate escape plans were eagerly forgotten, and so was I.

Without a word to Graça or the boys, I limped to the Fox gates and hailed a cab to the Plaza.

Our hotel's bar was, I would soon discover, a hot spot for nameless extras and aspiring starlets. On set, they called those girls "Dumb Doras." These were the nymphs who invaded Fox, MGM, Warner Bros., and other major studios by the dozens each morning to play the parts of coat-check girls, next-door neighbors, nameless clubgoers, and whatever other part required a pretty face and no spoken lines. Some nymphs were tall, others short. Some had waves of chestnut hair pinned up in the latest fashion. Others had hair so blond it was nearly white. Each girl was perfect in her own way, with plenty of penciled eyebrows and creamy, unfreckled skin, and full bosoms balanced above tiny waists.

I'd managed to down three drinks at the Plaza bar before a Dora asked me for a cigarette. She was short with nut-brown hair that fell in carefully tended waves, just like Graça's before her pixie cut. She was Graça's height and build, and wore a dress so tight, it might as well have been a swimsuit with a skirt attached. She caught me admiring her and smiled, revealing a perfect, empty space between her front teeth. I imagined what it might be like to run my tongue across her teeth and into that gap. She was from some western state I'd never heard of before she'd said it: Montana, Wyoming? You could drive right through her hometown and never know you'd been there. That's what she'd told me, speaking slowly and with some pantomime, and I liked her immediately because she came from nothing and nowhere, and seemed completely unashamed of it. Her name felt something like that western town of her birth: deserted, gritty, simple.

"Sandy," I whispered.

She looked back at me and smiled. "God, I love your accent."

An hour later, we were in my hotel room the size of a shoebox. Lights from the hotel's courtyard shone through the window glass, cutting a yellow square on the rug. Sandy's brown hair fell in soft waves to her shoulders. Her frame was small, her legs strong. She smelled yeasty and sweet, like a cake just out of the oven. For what seemed like ages, Sandy stared up at me, studying my eyes. I couldn't tell if she was impressed or having second thoughts. I decided to give her an escape, if she wanted one.

"If someone from the studio sees us," I said, the words hard pebbles in my mouth. "You lose your job. And I . . . It would not look fine for my friend . . . Sofia Salvador."

Sandy smiled. "Are you kidding? The studios don't care what we do, as long as the doors are closed. Girls like us can have a good time together. We just can't do something terribly wholesome like hold hands in the middle of the day. But I don't want to hold hands now. Do you?"

I shook my head.

Her mouth was wide and soft. I tasted the wax of her lipstick, and then, as we opened our mouths for each other, I tasted smoke mixed with peppermint—the kind of red-and-white candy the downstairs bar kept in a bowl. I imagined Sandy rolling the small round candy on her tongue until it dissolved completely.

She slipped her small hands under my shirt. The hotel bed was a twin—nearly as narrow as a ship's berth—and we moved as if we were waves on water, a precise rhythm between us. Her dress had a glittering belt and a zipper down its back, the hard bodice cracking open like a candy's shell. She wore no nylons, only a flimsy pair of underwear that I quickly removed. I cupped my hands to her face, then moved them down her neck to her chest, rising and falling fast under my palms, and then to her soft stomach, and then to her hips, and then farther still, until she'd opened herself to me completely, as slick and as sweet as a papaya wedge that I scooped into my mouth.

"Appreciate what a wonder the body is!" Anaïs commanded during singing lessons. What is song, she taught us, but folds of muscle inside our throats, made supple by being wet, moving against each other neither too fast nor too slow, neither too hard nor too soft, but with the perfect balance of tension and release in order to set free a sound, a song, from within us.

It was an escape, though fleeting. An hour later Sandy was gone and I was alone again.

The Plaza's lobby was empty, its bar quiet. The movie extras and Dumb Doras had gone either home or upstairs to their rooms to prepare for early shoots. I bribed the bartender to smuggle me a bottle of gin and found the hotel's pool.

Outside it was chilly. The air smelled of eucalyptus. In the bushes crickets droned, a thousand gossips sharing the same story. I sat alone in the dark, my feet in the pool's warm water, and stared up at the Plaza, counting its floors until I found the windows to our rooms— three side by side, with little wrought-iron balconies framing them. The balconies were only a few inches deep; like much else in L.A., they were simply for show. My room's curtains were open. Little Noel's were drawn, his window dark. In the room Graça and Vinicius shared, the lights were on. When had they returned from Fox studios?

I lifted the bottle of gin from my lap and took a long swig.

A silhouette, backlit by the lobby's lights, stood on the other side of the courtyard. I recognized the familiar slouch, the wide shoulders, the pompadour. He was motionless in the lit doorway for a while before he dove into the darkness, toward me.

"What are you, a detective?" I asked.

Vinicius sat, cross-legged, on the concrete beside me. "I asked at the bar. I figured you couldn't be far."

I stared again at Graça's lit window. "Why aren't you up there, put-ting her to bed?"

Vinicius shrugged. "I'm in the doghouse. I didn't cater to her whims today like everyone else on earth."

The pool's lights were on. Their reflection shone upon our faces, blue ripples swaying across our cheeks and mouths, making it seem as if we were both trapped underwater.

"I didn't cater to her," I said.

He laughed. "She wanted to skip town and you had your bags packed. You'd abandon us all if she asked you to."

"And you wouldn't? Shit, you already have."

Vinicius shook his head. "I don't want to fight anymore today. Not with you."

I handed him the bottle of gin. Vinicius took a long gulp and wiped his mouth.

"She drives me crazy, too," he said, running his hands through his hair. "Sometimes it's like we're punishing each other—me and her."

"For what?"

"For not being who we want each other to be. She wants me to be like one of those poor bastards in the crowd when she sings—my mouth hanging open, in awe of her all the time."

"And you aren't?" I asked.

"I am, but there's only so much a person can take. I want her to listen to me, to understand me like . . ."

Vinicius placed his hand on my knee. A jolt of heat ran up my thigh, into the pit of my belly. "You have to be better than this," I said, shaking him off. "Both of you."

Vinicius looked confused. "I'm sorry."

"Sorry doesn't do us any good. If we're going to be a great act, we can't ever be sorry."

"I don't want to be an act," he whispered.

"Then what are we doing here?" I asked, looking around the Plaza's dark courtyard. "I wondered today if Senhor Pimentel was right. If this movie business isn't good for her—or maybe she's too good for it. Can you imagine what her dear papai would do if he saw us here, in L.A., if he saw you two, sharing a bed?"

"But he can't see, can he?" Vinicius said, his voice a whisper I could barely hear. "I don't know why he had that accident or how. But if it means we're together, then I'm not sad about it."

The crickets' buzzing was unbearably loud. My head seemed to vibrate.

"Who's we?" I asked. "That's a stupid question, isn't it? You don't even want to write songs anymore. All those afternoons, I waited . . ."

I swallowed hard, trying to control the tremor in my voice. "You think you can just ignore it? You think you can just shove the music aside over and over again like it doesn't really matter? It won't wait for you forever. It can't."

Vinicius stared at the pool, then at me. "Don't go anywhere," he ordered.

He ran inside the hotel and returned a few minutes later with his guitar and Kitchen's extra pair of agogô bells. They were oblong, one large and one small, fused together like fruits petrified on the same vine.

"Here," Vinicius said, handing me the bells and their stick.

"Kitchen won't like me touching these."

"Are you kidding?" Vinicius said. "Kitchen's happy when any girl plays with his agogôs."

I laughed for the first time that day.

"Should I go to the Dunbar and steal Bonito's cuíca?" Vinicius asked, smiling. "You can rub it and make it moan."

"Oh, boy. Just keep Tiny's cavaquinho away from me," I said.

"It's small but powerful," Vinicius replied.

One by one, we gave each of the boys' instruments lives of their own. Then Vinicius hummed a few notes while I half sang, half whispered.

"Samba, for a time you were mine.
My love, we played so well!
I held the curve of your cavaquinho,
I coaxed rhythm from your agogô bells."

Sometimes Vinicius found the perfect note, the perfect rhythm for my words, and when this happened I felt warmth wrap itself around my neck and move down my spine. We continued then, moving in unison, nodding at each other, unsure of what might come next but thrilled at the same time. Sometimes there was a corny line or a false note, and Vinicius and I laughed at our clumsiness. But soon we did not stop or giggle or break the rhythm. In this moment, there was a perfect trust between us. If Vinicius wanted softer, I gave him softer. If I wanted slower, he gave me slower. There was no hesitation, only anticipation. We kept moving forward, perfectly in sync, until we came to a natural finish. Then there was quiet.

Graça's window facing the pool was open now, its curtains wide, its glass parted. The room inside was still lit but without shadows or movement. When had Graça opened the glass panels? How much had she heard? I felt a sense of satisfaction to have her as our audience but also a strange kind of dread—would nothing be mine alone? When one of us gained, did the other always have to lose?

The next morning at Fox studios we were ushered into an office building, where we followed a matronly woman through a maze of corridors. We arrived, finally, at two large wooden doors. Behind them, a lion's skin was splayed across the floor. As soon as we entered, we saw the beast's snarling mouth, its vacant yellow eyes. Around the rug were several oversized leather chairs and a couch as deep as a bed.

The room's walls were covered in framed photographs. I recognized famous faces in the photographs, all posing alongside the same man— he was short and mustachioed, with a gap-toothed grin. The same man stood before us, in the flesh, in that massive studio office. He held a long wooden mallet. (This mallet, I would later learn, was for playing polo, a sport that Mr. Zanuck loved almost as much as making movies.) Beside him stood a tall man whose handsomeness seemed almost alien, as if he had been manufactured on Fox's lot. His toffee-colored skin glowed; his dark eyes were deeply set and sad-looking, as if he was constantly pining for someone. I'd seen his image on movie posters around Fox—Ramon Romero, heartthrob who always played second fiddle to some younger, paler, peppier, and more famous actor on Fox's roster. He nodded at us in greeting.

Zanuck's eyes scanned Graça's feet, her legs, her hips, her chest, and finally fell upon her face. This examination didn't seem lascivious. I could picture Zanuck appraising a potential polo horse this way—studying its form, its stance, its musculature.

"Ramon!" Zanuck shouted, "tell Miss Salvador that she stole the show in *Bye, Bye, Buenos Aires*. I saw the rushes late last night—you nearly popped off the screen, honey!" A pink bit of tongue flashed through the gap of Zanuck's front teeth. Ramon dutifully translated the studio chief's words into Spanish.

"Let me hear some of that Portuguese," Zanuck ordered. Ramon sighed, then reiterated the request for us.

Graça looked at me. "What do I say to him?"

It was the first time she'd spoken to me since the night before in the trailer, when she'd plotted our new life and then immediately discarded it.

"Talk about our trip here," I said. "To the States."

Graça's eyes lit up. She nodded and proceeded to list for Zanuck and Ramon, in Portuguese, all of the amenities of the SS *Uruguay*. Zanuck sat in his enormous chair and smiled.

"Wonderful!" he interrupted. "Listen, Miss Salvador, I'm not going to mince any meat with you."

I looked at Ramon, worried. "He wants her to eat meat?"

Ramon laughed, but before he could explain, Zanuck continued, ignoring us.

"You're different," he said. "Every studio in town's got loads of gorgeous Lupes and Doloreses. Men certainly like them on-screen. But you've got a unique look, with that haircut and that mouth. And you're funny—a real comedienne."

Zanuck took a sip from his drink while Ramon spoke. Then Zanuck suddenly shouted: "I want a photograph!"

His secretary ran from the room and returned with a portable camera. Zanuck heaved himself off of his enormous chair.

"Come on over," he ordered. "Don't be shy."

All of us moved toward Zanuck, who put up his stubby hand.

"Just Sofia," he said.

We did not need Ramon to translate. The Blue Moon boys glanced at me, then at one another. Graça stood beside Zanuck, who wrapped an arm around her waist and smiled. There was a pop and then a flash and, for a moment, Graça disappeared in light.

TURNED INTO A GRINGA

Well, they say I've turned into a gringa,
with cases full of cash
and diamonds on my fingers!

They say I wring my hands all day,
and have no time to chat.
That I can't stand to hear a cuíca play,
and that my rhythm's gone scat.

'Cause I've turned into a gringa,
with cases full of cash
and diamonds on my fingers!

They say I've dyed my hair yellow,
and coconut milk makes me sick.
That I only date wealthy fellows,
and I sign all my checks with lipstick.

'Cause I've turned into a gringa,
with cases full of cash
and diamonds on my fingers!

Why so much venom and spite
aimed in my direction?
When I look into my mirror each night,
I only see Brazil in my reflection.

'Cause I'll never be a gringa.
But a little girl from Lapa,
a simple samba singer.

As a kitchen girl, I believed that fame meant being a voice on the radio—you were nameless and faceless, but you were heard. In Lapa, fame was popularity, and popularity meant being well-liked. At Urca, fame was not likability but fantasy; it was not about you, but what you created onstage. In Hollywood I learned that all of my previous beliefs were wrong.

Fame is longing. Not yours, but the audience's. A star is nothing more, nothing less, than the public face of private desire.

The biggest stars, like the most successful dictators, fulfill countless desires at once. They are our ever-forgiving parents, trusted friends, fierce lovers, loyal siblings, stern teachers, terrifying opponents. They are everything we aspire to and, sometimes, everything we despise. Of Graça's many talents, this was either her greatest or her worst, depending on your outlook: she could sense what a crowd wanted, and mold herself into whatever that might be.

At the cutters' circles she was the Little Miss who put on a show for the lowliest workers on the plantation, making them feel as if she was in their power and not the other way around. At Little Tony's, she was the Nymphette not because of a silly costume and pigtails, but because of her nervous smile and the ardent innocence of her voice. As a samba singer in Lapa she was the gum-chewing, street-smart schoolgirl whom all others copied. As Sofia Salvador, she sensed that Rio craved the idea of difference and danger but not the reality, so she became the risqué Baiana with her jewels and off-the-shoulder blouses, flashing her legs and singing with a snarl about heartbreak. And in Hollywood during the war years she became the Brazilian Bombshell—not a woman or a child but a combination of both, like a fairy or an imp, who was naughty and funny and from another, Technicolor world.

I'll put it this way, for those of you who have never seen her films: if Rio's Sofia Salvador was like a shot of sugarcane liquor—sweet but heart-stoppingly strong, enjoyed by rich and poor alike, and the most Brazilian of all drinks—then Hollywood's wartime Sofia Salvador was a glass of champagne.

No. That's not right. She was not the champagne. She was the fizz.

During the war, North Americans went to the movies to forget the bombing of Pearl Harbor and the vicious fighting in Europe and Japan. For ninety minutes in the movie theater, they could stop worrying over food rations and if they would have enough meat and sugar to last the month. They could bask in the glow of that giant movie screen and forget that Los Angeles's beaches were blocked by barbed wire and patrolled relentlessly by the Coast Guard on the lookout for Japanese submarines. Surrounded by death and uncertainty, North Americans wanted an escape. Who better to give it to them than Sofia Salvador and the Blue Moon Band?

After our first picture, Zanuck ordered that Graça and the Blue Moon boys be subjected to teeth cleanings and bleachings, haircuts, eyebrow pluckings, and facials. At Fox's clinic, a dermatologist performed what they called a "violet ray treatment" on Graça to burn away a layer of skin and make freckles disappear. They performed a painful treatment on her hairline, to make her brow higher. For a full week,

Graça hid inside the hotel room she shared with Vinicius, her face red and scabbed. A studio doctor provided a hearty supply of painkillers, along with bottles of "Blue Angels" and bennies. The former knocked you out at night, the latter pepped you up for long shoots and the endless, hours-long screen tests to make sure every stitch of every costume looked perfect to the camera's eye.

Sofia Salvador and Blue Moon worked a punishing schedule, making a movie musical every three months: *Private Shirley Goes to Rio*, *She's a Doll*, *G.I. Love Ya*, and *Mexican Tango*, among many others. It was hard to keep track of which picture we were working on because the plots were always the same: North Americans venture south of the border, or travel to an army base to entertain the troops, and chaos ensues. The war's rationing of electricity made daylight valuable, so filming lasted from six a.m. to sundown every day of the week. Time dissolved into a series of early calls, fourteen-hour shoots, rehearsals and fittings and promotional appearances fueled by a steady stream of Blue Angels and bennies, until five years passed and we could count on one hand the number of rodas we'd had together, as a band.

Sofia Salvador's image on posters grew bigger with each consecutive film, and so did her speaking parts, but she was never the official star; she was a musical act with two or three numbers at most. We all got better at speaking and understanding English, but Graça was pitiful at memorizing scripts. She often got her lines wrong.

"I just spilled the cat out of the beans," she said in one film. "Scratch my heart and hope two thighs," she said in another.

When she tried to correct herself, the directors stopped her. "Keep going," they pleaded.

Zanuck visited each movie set and ordered Sofia Salvador's directors to film her musical and dance numbers in one continuous take.

"Never cut away from Salvador once she starts to sing!" Zanuck demanded. "No audience shots. No reactions. No close-ups. Have the camera on her whole body for the entire damn number, I don't care if it's ten minutes long."

Some of her musical numbers grew to be fifteen minutes long, and because of Zanuck's orders never to cut away from her, if Graça or the boys made a single mistake, they would have to stop shooting and begin all over again. Because of this, they practiced each number so many times they could perform them blindfolded as a gag for the crew and cameramen. Graça could sense by the heat of the lights on her face where the camera was and whether she had to turn her head even a few centimeters to get a better shot.

Blue Moon wore their own black tuxedos in our first film, but afterward Fox commissioned more colorful tuxes: bright yellow, aqua, purple, and orange to complement Sofia Salvador's dresses. With each film, there were more eye-watering colors and glittering stones, until the Baiana we'd created in Rio became nothing more than a shadow, a ghost in the costumes' ruffles and off-the-shoulder tops. A wide strip of Sofia Salvador's stomach was always exposed. The slit in her skirts grew so long and wide she had to wear colorful swim bottoms. She kept her hair black and in its pixie cut, a style so avant-garde that it was a full three decades before women on the street cut their hair this way. And clipped to Sofia Salvador's ears were those huge, dangling jewels in fantastic shapes: dolphins, hummingbirds and butterflies, apples, strawberries.

She became the face of Lux soap and Pond's cold cream. *The Brazilian Bombshell never rests,* the ads exclaimed, *but even this go-go-go girl stops to use Pond's!* Reporters from *Photoplay* and *Silver Screen* fought for interviews with Sofia Salvador. In each magazine, she appeared in pullout poster spreads that could be taped to walls or above bunk beds in troops' barracks. In one spread, she wore a bikini with two massive sequined pineapples covering her bosoms. In another, she sprawled across a bed of bananas. When Sofia Salvador and the Blue Moon Band appeared at the Hollywood Canteen to entertain troops on leave in L.A., the soldiers gave them standing ovations.

Despite the fact that Graça and Vinicius were still a couple—caught in their fervent cycle of arguing and making up—Fox staged "candid" shots of Sofia Salvador flirting with stars like Ramon Romero and Tyrone Power for the gossip pages. The studio loaned Sofia Salvador clothes, shoes, and costume jewels. During lunch and dinner breaks, Graça demanded buttered lobster tails and French fries delivered to our trailers and Fox obliged. We were not allowed, after all, to sit together—all of us, at the same table—at Fox's Paris cafeteria. And because the Brazilian Bombshell could not be photographed coming and going in a taxicab, Fox gave her and Blue Moon a red convertible DeSoto for daily use. This was common practice in the studio system, where starlets were like prized racehorses—pampered, fed, groomed, and expected to perform until they expired.

I speak of our "punishing schedule" knowing that as we endured costume fittings and dance rehearsals, men fought and died across the ocean, and, there in Los Angeles, legions of women, Mexicans, and citizens with skin darker than was acceptable for the times built planes, filled bombs, and mixed vats of synthetic rubber. And as these workers poured into the city, so did sailors from small towns across the USA. By the summer of 1943, the city's heat and the factories' fumes settled over L.A. like a lid on a boiling pot. All of us were trapped inside.

When the Zoot Suit Riots erupted and mobs of white sailors stalked downtown L.A. searching for boys who looked Mexican to beat to a pulp, a studio PA warned the Blue Moon boys to avoid downtown music clubs for a while. By then we'd moved into a house on a deserted road where only a handful of slow, sad cars from the San Fernando trolley passed. There was a pool the size of an opera stage, and enough bedrooms to house a soccer team. We had few neighbors, so no one noticed or cared that the likes of Kitchen, Tiny, Banana, Bonito, and me came and went as we pleased; plenty of homes in L.A. had live-in staff, after all. By then Brazil itself seemed like a place in the movies: a homeland that remained pristine and unchanging in our memories. Home was our talisman to ward off frustration and fatigue. It was the card we kept in our back pockets. It was our escape hatch, reassuring us that Hollywood was a temporary adventure and its rules, riots, hierarchies, and the indignities it made us suffer would have no lasting effect. We'd become so used to acting out lies in the movies that we began to believe them.

Hollywood, it turned out, was not a roda that we'd ever be allowed to join. It was a vast Great House. Within it, we were granted—temporarily—tolerance and luxury, but the house was not ours and we were not its guests. We were not its servants, either, for those roles were reserved for natives. No, we'd been purchased and shipped in for the sole purpose of entertaining the residents—like a record player, or a radio, or a piano in a parlor—put there to amuse, to lighten the mood, to work tirelessly and without complaint and then, when not in use, to remain perfectly quiet and still until it seemed as if we'd disappeared entirely.

TURNED INTO A GRINGA

The only Sofia Salvador costume I didn't keep sits in a glass case in Rio's city museum. It is a gold-sequined number that wasn't from her films but was worn at a ceremony at Grauman's Chinese Theatre. In the glass case, behind the costume, is a picture of Sofia Salvador on her knees, her hands pressed into wet concrete, while a gang of men laugh around her. In the concrete, Graça's hands are as small as a child's, her feet barely a size six. The Rio museum calls that day a triumph—Sofia Salvador remains the only Brazilian with her handprints and footprints enshrined at Hollywood's landmark theater, alongside the likes of Clark Gable and Ginger Rogers. When I think of that ceremony, I don't see triumph. I see only the beginning of our unraveling.

It was 1945 and the war was winding down, though we didn't know it yet. Fans and photographers jockeyed for positions outside Sid Grauman's Chinese Theatre. (I'd later learn that Fox had hired fans to appear at the ceremony, knowing turnout would be low. Lavish musicals were losing steam to detective dramas, which were cheaper to film. The Walk of Fame ceremony was a way to publicize Sofia's latest movie without paying for ads.) Beyond the fans' area was seating for honored guests and a small stage with a microphone, and at the center of the festivities, cordoned off with velvet ropes, were two slabs of wet concrete.

A band played a fast-paced rendition of "Ai Ai Ai Love You," a song from her latest film. Afterward, Sofia Salvador appeared onstage, flanked by Ramon Romero and Sid Grauman, like two police officers herding their suspect. She wore a chiffon skirt and a padded top covered in so many gold sequins it looked like armor. Sofia Salvador smiled. Flashbulbs popped and hissed. From the front row of chairs, I shielded my eyes. When the bursts of light died and left only smoke, Graça wobbled. Sid Grauman caught her arm, stopping her from toppling onto the wet concrete.

"Cool it with the flashes!" Grauman barked to the reporters.

Graça had just gotten off her tenth stint in Palm Springs, where Fox sent her to a so-called health resort. Graça's L.A. diet of booze, lobster, and French fries made it difficult for Fox's costume department to keep her in midriff tops and pillar skirts. Each of Graça's stays at the resort lasted two weeks, and left her gaunt and vacant-eyed when she returned. The spa's nurses bullied her into eating only soup, drinking only grapefruit juice, and wearing a rubber suit to sweat off her extra fifteen pounds. I suppose she could have dug in her heels and refused to go, but Graça's stubbornness won out over her good sense; she saw each visit as a challenge. "Those bitch nurses!" Graça said. "They didn't think I could do it. But by the end of the week I told them to go fuck themselves—I lost twenty pounds."

Sid Grauman moved to the podium and spoke of Sofia Salvador, reading an approved script from Fox studios that was filled with words like *pep* and *zing* and *va-va-voom*. Next to me, Vinicius sighed. Kitchen looked at his watch. Banana snapped his gum.

After Sid Grauman's speech, Sofia Salvador stepped forward and pressed her platform shoes into the wet concrete. Next, she bent and did the same with her tiny hands. Finally, Grauman handed her what looked like a golden wand. Graça signed the concrete:

To Sid,
Viva Hollywood!
Love,
The Brazilian Bombshell, Sofia Salvador

The crowds cheered obediently. Then there were interviews with at least a dozen reporters.

"Miss Salvador!" a reporter shouted. "Remind the troops: What are your favorite things about the USA?"

Sofia Salvador's eyes lit up. "Ah, hot dogs. Mash-ed pow-tay-toos. And mens mens mens of course!"

There was a wave of laughter from the crowd. Next to me, Vinicius shifted in his seat. Then another shouted question: "How does it feel to be a part of Hollywood history today?"

Sofia placed a hand on her sequined bosom. "How do I say? It is an honor very great. What am I? A little girl from Brazil. And you hold me into your arms here, make me feel special. Very loved." Graça's voice broke. She swallowed hard, then began again. "It is all I have dreamed of."

"Sofia!" a voice called from the huddle of reporters. "Do you have any words today for Brazil?"

The reporter's accent mirrored my own, and that of the Blue Moon boys, and of the handful of other Brazilians we'd met in the States.

"Who is that?" Sofia Salvador asked, searching the crowd of reporters.

A hand went up. I did not recognize the young man's face. He couldn't have been over twenty. "I'm from Rádio Mayrink!" he called out in Portuguese.

"With pleasure I answer your question," Sofia Salvador said, and switched to Portuguese. "My dearest brothers and sisters in all of

Brazil. I am speaking to you from the Chinese Theatre in Hollywood, where I just put my humble hands and feet into cement. It's one of the happiest moments of my life. In this moment, all I can think of are my fans and friends back home, and my dearest city of Rio. You are always in my heart. May God protect you, and may He bring me and the Blue Moon boys back to you someday soon."

Tiny bowed his head as if in prayer. Little Noel nodded.

The young Mayrink reporter smiled. "Will you actually return to Brazil?"

"Of course, why wouldn't I?" Graça asked.

"Because you've become Americanized," the reporter replied.

Graça's smile disappeared. "We are all Americans: North and South Americans."

"Why do you allow the American press to say you are an Argentine or a Mexican? Are you ashamed of telling them you're Brazilian?"

"Of course not! I am Brazilian through and through. It's not my fault these U.S. reporters don't know how to read a map."

"So you're saying the Americans are ignorant about Brazil, even though we're one of their greatest allies in the war? You're saying the USA doesn't appreciate Brazil's existence and sacrifice?"

Graça's mouth opened but no sound came. She took a deep breath and tried again: "No," Graça said. "I didn't mean it like that . . ."

"What do you say to those in Brazil who are boycotting your movies?"

"Boycotting?"

The reporter nodded. "They say you've turned into a gringa."

Graça's eyes moved wildly from the reporter to Sid Grauman, but the theater's owner did not understand what was being asked.

"What's that boy saying?" Chuck Lindsay, our agent, pressed me.

"Do you think you're representing Brazil nobly," the reporter continued, "or are you and your band, as some newspaper critics claim, puppets to the U.S. imperialists?"

"I . . . I don't know what you mean," Graça sputtered.

I found myself standing. The guests seated around me seemed very far away, as if I was looking down from a great height.

"You son of a bitch," I yelled in Portuguese. "Get out of here."

Beside me, Vinicius and the Blue Moon boys stood. Tiny cracked his knuckles.

"I have a right to be here," the Mayrink boy said coolly. "I have a right to my questions."

"He is upsetting her," I whispered to Chuck Lindsay in English, but this was already obvious. Sofia Salvador's face had gone pale. She covered her mouth with her hand. Flashbulbs popped. A Fox representative escorted Sofia offstage.

"Where's Miss Salvador going?" an American entertainment reporter called out.

"To the powder room," Sid Grauman replied. "She gets emotional hearing her mother tongue. You know how women are." Then he nodded at the theater's band, who began to play so loudly that they drowned out the Mayrink reporter, who was swiftly removed by security.

The Blue Moon boys left Grauman's from the front entrance in a Fox studios car to distract reporters from our exit out the back. Kitchen, the best driver among us, took the wheel of our bright red DeSoto while I sat beside him. In the backseat, Vinicius stared at Graça, who huddled near the door, as quiet and wary as a wounded animal.

"I'm not going back to the house," she announced, her voice steely, the skin around her eyes ringed gray from the mascara and tears she'd wiped away.

I glanced at Kitchen. "Should we get a drink somewhere?"

"I don't want to be around people," Graça replied. "Just drive."

We wound through pre-freeway L.A. on a clear night, past the tawdry themed restaurants in the shapes of giant sombreros and Swiss chalets; past the pharmacies and soda shops with their neon lights. Past the empty lot at the end of Sunset Boulevard where a field of poppies grew, the flowers swaying each time a car passed. Then the streetlights practically disappeared as we made our way into the hills. Los Angeles appeared in the valley beneath us, her lights winking and beckoning like a gorgeous girl laid out in front of us.

"Will you look at that?" Graça breathed, staring at the city. "It looks like magic."

Vinicius snorted. "It's all fake. You of all people should know that."

"What do you mean?" Graça asked.

"This place squeezes everything good out of people," Vinicius said. "All that's left is the rind."

"So I'm the rind?" Graça asked. "You sound like that lying Mayrink filho da puta."

"Maybe he's not lying," Vinicius said. "Maybe people hate us back home. I wouldn't be surprised."

"Why on earth would they hate us?" Graça demanded.

"You, with your *pow-tay-toos* and your *mens mens mens*," Vinicius said. "You think that's funny? You think it's dignified?"

"I'm a singer, not a goddamn English expert," Graça yelled. "I'd like to see you get up in front of hundreds of people every day and speak to them in a language you don't even know. You wouldn't have the fucking guts."

The DeSoto lumbered and growled up those twisting roads. Kitchen shot me a look. I turned in my seat to face Graça and Vinicius.

"There're plenty of people worth fighting outside the band," I said. "Let's not kill each other."

Graça's hair was a scruffy mess. Her earrings gone. Her bottom lip trembled. "He wants me to scowl in front of people. He wants me to be serious like you, Dor. If I did that, we'd be on a ship back to Brazil after just one picture."

"Maybe that would've been better," Vinicius said. "Now we can't show our faces back home."

Graça shook her head. Her gold-sequined top looked dull and heavy in the darkness; she slumped under its weight.

"It's easy for you to complain, isn't it?" she said, her voice almost a whisper. "To sit back and judge me for being undignified, or for having too much energy or not enough, or being too samba, or not samba enough. But not everyone thinks like you do. I don't disappoint everybody. There're people that really love me, you know. I read the fan letters. I meet the soldiers at the canteen. And I help them. I make people happy. Maybe my way of making music, of entertaining, is different than yours. But you don't own music. You don't get to say what's real and what's not. And tomorrow I'm driving to the Brazilian embassy and asking the consul for every goddamn newspaper he's saved since we got here. I'm going to read those critics' reviews. Every last one."

Each Sunday the studios were closed, but our Bedford Drive house was always as full as a movie set. Visiting regiments of Brazilian air force pilots played volleyball in our pool. The musicians we met at the Showboat or the Brown Bottle popped in for a swim and then a jam session by the pool. Under the shade of the cabana, heartthrob Ramon Romero and his live-in boyfriend, Clifton, often played cards with Kitchen. A few Plain Janes who worked as secretaries at Disney

Studios lounged beside the pool, laughing at Tiny's jokes and putting on a show of ignoring the few, stunning Dumb Doras—those lovely Fox movie extras—who sunned themselves on the lawn but never dared swim in our pool. In those Doras' minds, it was risky enough just attending our house parties. In L.A. people stuck with their own kind, but at Bedford Drive everyone was invited: black, white, red, brown, rich, poor, man, woman, or in between. We had only one requirement of our guests: you jammed with all of us, or with none of us at all.

Sofia Salvador made only two hundred dollars a week, while the boys earned fifty. It was chump change considering her box-office earnings, but no one ever said Hollywood was fair. If it hadn't been for Sofia Salvador's deals with Pond's and Lux soap—deals that I'd strong-armed Chuck Lindsay into pursuing, visiting his office every day with beauty magazines in my hands and asking why Sofia Salvador couldn't advertise such things—we would've been flat broke.

We paid a fortune in rent for our Bedford Drive house, even though it wasn't palatial by Hollywood standards and it was off the beaten path. Few homeowners rented to a "mixed group" like ours, and the odd one that was willing to take this risk made sure we paid dearly for the privilege of living together. Our tight finances didn't stop Graça and the boys from ordering sixty pounds of steaks each week, delivered right to our back door, for our Sunday parties. The liquor store brought ten weekly cases of their best gin, whiskey, and tonic water. The green grocer delivered crates of limes, oranges, and strawberries. The local pharmacist delivered bottles of Blue Angels and bennies like they were candy, prescribed by the studio doctor. Graça filled glass punch bowls with packs of cigarettes, which were always empty by the end of the day. She even had me order little plastic cigarette holders that said, in gold writing along their sides: *Stolen from the House of Sofia Salvador.*

The Sunday after the disastrous Grauman's ceremony, Brazilian consul general Raul Bopp and his wife sat under our striped umbrellas and drank gin and tonics. In return for the invitation, he'd brought a stack of Brazilian newspapers from the embassy. Some were the Lion's publications, heavily edited by President Gegê's censors. Others were underground papers out of São Paulo that complained of crippling wartime inflation and Gegê's enforced nationalism.

I sat on a lawn chair beside the pool and read those papers, swooning over the familiar verbs, the many-syllabled adjectives, and the speed and ease with which I understood them all. Portuguese was a cool drink on a hot day. I read every headline, every weather report, every obituary, every ad for cold cream and vitamin pills. The papers' more interesting tidbits I read aloud to the boys and Graça, who'd dragged their lawn chairs around mine.

"'Casinos Nationalized,'" I called out. "'All employees must prove they are native Brazilian.'"

"How will they do that?" Vinicius asked. "Does Old Gegê have a blood test for brasilidade?"

The boys laughed. I read on. Getúlio had enforced an eight-hour workday. Getúlio had agreed to real elections, but only after the war. The United States and Brazil were allies, but that didn't make them friends. Getúlio's years of nationalism had finally taken root—Brazil was for Brazilians, not communists or cronies of Uncle Sam.

"What a fucking bore!" Graça said, plopping into Vinicius's lap. Her hand crept inside his unbuttoned shirt. She wore a sequin-covered tunic that glittered in the sun. It was hard to look at her without squinting. "Flip to the arts section!" she insisted.

I obeyed. There, on the section's front page, was the name Sofia Salvador. The article was a review of *My Crazy Secretary*, which had been dubbed into Portuguese and finally released in Brazil months after its U.S. debut. I skimmed the first few sentences.

**What has Hollywood done to our lovely folk songstress? Her
look has mutated into a sequined nightmare. Her songs are
far from being sambas.**

"What's the matter, Dor?" Graça asked.

"Nothing," I replied, and folded the newspaper shut.

"Then why do you look like someone just kicked the bucket?" Graça
asked.

I put down the paper. "Let's have a drink, enjoy our guests. Maybe
we can go shopping later?"

Graça's eyes narrowed. "Since when do you want me spending
dough? Read that paper."

"No," I said.

Before I could shove the newspaper under my arm and lift myself
out of my chair, Graça leapt from Vinicius's lap and snatched the paper
from my hands. She opened to the arts section. Her eyes moved back
and forth. Her chest rose and fell as if she'd just run a race. The newspaper shook in her hands.

"What's it say?" Vinicius asked.

Graça shoved the paper back into my hands. "Read it to them," she
growled. When I shook my head she pinched my chin, as if I was a dis-
obedient child. "Read it out loud," she said. "They deserve to know."

I started at the beginning. It was only when I got to the middle of
the article that my tongue, so dry it felt as if it might stick to the roof
of my mouth and stay there, began to fumble words.

"Louder," Tiny ordered. I glanced at him. His arms were crossed
over his bare chest, his face drained of all humor.

**Her band—once providing a feral authenticity that captivated
audiences—now looks like a bunch of sad, old birds in their
rainbow tuxedos. Are they even playing their instruments?**

Or have they, too, sold their souls to the American film machine? The theater where this reporter watched *My Crazy Secretary* was as quiet as a church, even during the so-called humorous parts of the film. Clearly, true Brazilians were not in on the gringos' jokes, but was Miss Salvador?

Kitchen lit a cigarette. Little Noel took off his apron and left his grilled steaks leaking blood on their plates.

"Feral?" Banana asked. "What are we, dogs?"

"We were," Little Noel said. "Now we're sad birds. I don't know which is worse."

"Birds can fly," Graça said, staring at the pool. "Birds can sing."

"Depends on the bird," Kitchen said. "Some can't do either. Some are only meant to get their asses cooked."

Despite my objections, we picked up the other newspapers and read on.

She gets worse with each film, a critic for the *Jornal do Brasil* newspaper wrote about *Mexican Tango.*

The bigger the earrings, another critic commented, *the lower the taste level.*

If only Sofia Salvador's abilities as an actress could expand as quickly as her waist has, said a scathing review of *G.I. Love Ya.*

Looks like our queen of samba has turned into what none of her loyal fans ever expected, said one paper. *A gringa.*

Vinicius grabbed the newspaper from my hands and ripped it in half. "If I ever see these asshole critics on the street, I'll smash their faces in."

"You won't see them," Kitchen said. "Because we can't go home. We're punching bags in two countries now."

"*I've* turned into a gringa?" Graça said. "Those clueless motherfuckers. They wouldn't know a gringa if she was sitting in their goddamn laps. Do I look pale to you? Do I ever miss a beat when I dance?"

There was only one way I knew to make Graça and the boys forget those reviews, if only for a moment: a good fight.

"Well, your ass sure isn't shrinking," I said. "That's the first sign of being a gringa, so you're safe."

The boys were quiet. Vinicius gave me a startled look. Graça's eyes narrowed. She put her hands on her hips. I steeled myself.

"A flat ass is a horrible affliction," Graça said, and smiled. "You know that firsthand, Dor."

Vinicius ventured a laugh. The other boys quickly caught on.

"Hey! Check me for two left feet," Little Noel said, wiggling his toes.

Tiny snapped his fingers. "Hold on, I've got to make sure I'm not losing my rhythm."

I grabbed my notebook from under my chair.

"What're you writing?" Graça asked. "A letter to the editor?"

"Lyrics," I replied.

The boys fetched their instruments. We made a circle out of lawn chairs, ignored our guests, forgot our food, and, for the first time in many months, started a roda all together. Vinicius moved his chair close to mine. Graça found a seat of her own beside him. He read through the phrases I'd scribbled in my notebook: *Turned into a gringa. No more rhythm. We're all infected with the affliction.*

"I think we need to have a wonky, almost drunk sound starting the song. Like a comedy," Vinicius said.

I shook my head. "It needs a bite. This is our revenge."

Vinicius nodded. "How about we have the cuíca come in hard, so sweet it's almost ominous, and then Kitchen really scrapes the reco-reco."

"Like a snake," I said. "A rattler ready to strike."

"That's it!" Vinicius replied.

Graça slapped the metal arms of her chair. "Are we going to play music in this goddamn roda, or are you two going to yackity-yak all day?"

Vinicius turned to her. "What's the rush? We're all just getting started."

"No. You and Dor are getting started," Graça replied. "The rest of us are waiting on your highnesses to let us in."

Little Noel stared intently at his tamborim drum. The rest of the boys glanced at me. None cracked a smile.

"No one needs an engraved invitation to join," Vinicius said, his voice weak. "We're all in this roda together."

"Could've fooled me," Graça said.

"Why're you picking a fight?" Vinicius asked. "We're doing this song to defend you."

Graça tilted back her head and laughed. "How fucking kind of you two! Too bad I'm not brilliant enough to add a lyric, or even get a word in."

"If you want to sing, then sing for God's sakes," Vinicius said. "No one's stopping you."

"Oh, we wouldn't want to interrupt you two, would we, boys?" Graça replied, her voice ice. "I've turned into a gringa, and this roda's turned into a duo."

"So let's start over," I said, and handed my notebook to Graça. "You pick the words."

She dropped my old lyric book to the ground. "I can write my own words; I don't need yours. I won't pussyfoot around—let's start strong: *They say I've turned into a gringa.*"

Kitchen scraped his reco-reco. Tiny strummed his cavaquinho. One by one the other boys joined in, until together, hesitantly, we found a beat.

The next day, we began filming *Fruity Cutie Girl*, the most expensive musical made by Fox studios, and what would turn out to be Sofia Salvador's last hit.

"The looniest, liveliest, most innovative musical ever!" That's how Fox billed it. But *Fruity Cutie Girl* had the same plot as all other wartime musicals called "backstagers": the characters were in show business and the story revolved around them putting on a performance for the troops. Once again, Sofia Salvador wasn't billed as the star. In every musical there was always a blonde gal who took the lead. The blonde falls in love, she sings the romantic songs, she fights for her man. Girls sitting in the audience wanted to be the blonde, but everyone preferred to watch Sofia Salvador. She wiggled into every scene, with her boy's haircut and bared belly and massive earrings, her legs and arms always in motion.

Movie sets are painfully boring places; even the biggest stars are forced to do an unreasonable amount of waiting in cramped trailers. For the Blue Moon boys and me, that waiting was doubled—the band was only employed to film song-and-dance numbers, and I wasn't employed at all. During those tedious hours, Vinicius accompanied Graça wherever she went, keeping watch over her. The Brothers and Noel played cards. Tiny romanced Dumb Doras. Kitchen rooted out the few other musicians at Fox. And I holed up in Graça's trailer and answered her fan mail by autographing glossy photographs of the Brazilian Bombshell, addressing them to soldiers, farmers, accountants, and teenagers alike. In the beginning of the war several bags of fan mail arrived each day for Sofia Salvador, but by the end, there was one bag at most, and it was always half full.

A week into shooting *Fruity Cutie Girl* there was a knock on the trailer door. Vinicius let himself inside. He wore a purple tuxedo and held his guitar by its neck.

"Graça's not here," I said.

"I know," he replied, his voice low.

"If you're fighting again, don't hide here," I said. "You know how she gets when she feels left out. Better to get one of the boys to give you cover."

"I'm not a kid hiding from his mama," Vinicius said. "I have this tune in my head. I can't get it out."

I stared at the many Sofia Salvadors in a pile of photos before me, their grins devilish, their lips full, their eyes wide. "So tell the boys," I replied. "And Graça. We'll get a roda going tonight."

Vinicius slumped in the chair beside mine. "Come on, Dor. To-night we'll be so tired we won't even want to look at our instruments. Or we'll be so hopped-up on bennies we won't be able to sit still long enough to play two notes. I don't want to wait until Sunday to play. By then, this tune'll run away from me. You know, a wise gal once told me that music won't wait for us. She said we can't ignore it."

They'd trimmed his sideburns at Fox and slicked back his hair. I had the urge to muss it with both hands, to make it like it used to be. In-stead, I put down my pen and asked: "What you got?"

We worked in secret every day afterward on that film shoot. The songs we composed weren't for Sofia Salvador and Blue Moon, but for ourselves. In those tin-can Fox trailers, we couldn't risk making too much noise, so Vinicius strummed his guitar very gently and I kept my voice almost at a whisper. Many great discoveries begin as mistakes, and ours was no different—Vinicius and I unwittingly created a genre thought to be impossible: quiet samba.

Music historians still argue whether it was Sofia Salvador and Blue Moon, or our duo—Sal e Pimenta, as Vinicius and I named ourselves—who were the creators of this radical quiet samba style that would inspire, a decade later, another of samba's offshoots: the soft-spoken bossa nova. I'm not sure why this argument even exists. Follow the music, and you'll find the answer.

On our days off from shooting *Fruity Cutie Girl*, Vinicius and I lied to Graça and the boys. He said he was going on long drives to clear his head. I said I was visiting Chuck Lindsay on business. When these ex-cuses got old, Vinicius and I began sneaking out in the middle of the night, while Graça and the boys slept. We went to a rented studio near Disney and recorded our newfangled tracks.

The shellac used to make records was scarce because of the war, so vinyl was introduced as an alternative. Vinyl was more durable than shellac, and could be mailed internationally without shattering into a hundred pieces. So we secretly mailed our unbreakable masters to Ma-dame L., in Brazil, and he released them to Rio's radio DJs, never mentioning our association with Blue Moon or Sofia Salvador, because that would have doomed us from the start. No, we were something new, something different. The depth and precision of Vinicius's guitar playing—the only instrument we used apart from the occasional reco-reco—made our melodies feel naked and vulnerable. They were not covered under layers of percussion. And my voice, with its gravelly sound and limited range, was perfectly suited to this hushed and slow samba we'd accidentally created. We were Sal e Pimenta, the perfect pair of opposites and each other's only complement.

The star of *Fruity Cutie Girl* was nicknamed "Saint Blondie." Sofia Salvador's costumes were costlier and more elaborate than the blonde's, her musical numbers more complicated, her trailer more lux-urious. Everyone on set knew this, but Saint Blondie still maintained her authority. There were whispers that she was a favorite of Zanuck's, and visited his office every afternoon for a roll on his enormous couch. This meant that even the film's temperamental director was forced to cater to her whims. She kept a swear box on set and every time someone swore, Saint Blondie made them pay a nickel.

"I'm not paying a goddamn centavo," Kitchen said loudly, in Portuguese. "She doesn't know whether I'm talking about the movie or her ass."

"And what an ass it is," Tiny said. "Let's make a bet: by the time filming's over, I'll get Saint Blondie to swear up a storm with me, in the trailer. Shit, afterward we'll even write a song about it."

"I've got the first line," Vinicius said, "*Once there was an Ice Queen who froze off Tiny's tiny.*"

Kitchen held up his little finger. "*Instead of a pinto, now I've got a Popsicle!*"

Saint Blondie looked over her shoulder at us. "Shhhhh!" she hissed.

Tiny winked at her. The starlet's eyes widened. She crossed her arms and stalked off, bumping into Graça on her way out.

"Who put the bug in Saint Blondie's ass?" Graça asked.

"Tiny," Noel said.

"A bug's not what I'd imagined putting in there," Tiny whispered, and we all erupted into giggles, hanging off one another's arms and slapping one another's shoulders, not caring about the crew and cast around us, like the old days.

When we arrived on set the next day, there were signs taped to our trailers' doors, propped on the coffee cart, and stapled to the cork message board outside the set's bathrooms.

This is an ENGLISH ONLY set.
Support our troops! Be a proud American!

That was the day we were slated to film our longest, most complex musical number. The whole musical sequence—all fifteen minutes of it—would be shot using only one camera, which moved on a rail. Once the singing and dancing got rolling, there could be no stopping until the very end.

The Blue Moon boys wore simple black pants and white shirts, open at the necks. Vinicius and Little Noel sat in the makeup trailer for an hour while the artists bronzed their faces and chests. When they emerged, they were as orange as carrots. On a normal day we would've teased the boys for wearing makeup. But on that particular day, we were all digesting the meaning of the "English Only" signs. Instead of teasing, we sat quietly and waited.

Graça appeared beside us. Her dark blue dress was slit all the way up her thigh. Fist-sized strawberries covered in sequins were sewn along the length of her skirt and dangled over her bosom. Two muscular, shirtless extras appeared. Behind them, an animal trainer guided a pair of enormous oxen onto the set. They pulled a cart filled with fake bananas.

"Miss Salvador," a production assistant called. "I'll help you up."

"Where?" Graça asked.

"Here," the production assistant said, pointing to the cart.

"We go there?" Graça asked.

"Oh, no!" the assistant said. "Just you. The band pulls the cart."

We were all quiet. Graça looked at me.

"It says nothing in the script about a cart, about animals," I said to the PA.

"They're perfectly safe," the animal trainer said.

The PA smiled. "Sofia Salvador's hidden in here, in the bananas, and then she'll pop out. It makes her entrance more dramatic. It was Mr. Zanuck's idea. Don't worry about actually pulling the cart, the animals will do all the work," the PA said cheerfully.

One of the oxen raised its tail. A pile of pungent brown nuggets fell onto the set's green carpet.

"I'm not doing this," Kitchen said in Portuguese.

Graça sighed. "It's just an animal, you don't have to be scared . . ."

"I'm not scared," Kitchen replied, his voice raised. "I'm a musician. I don't pull carts."

"We'll never be able to show our faces back home again," Tiny interrupted.

"We can't show them now," Graça said. "What's the difference?"

"It's not so bad," Little Noel said. "It's *supposed* to be a silly night-club act. We saw worse acts than this a dozen times at clubs back home."

Graça nodded. "It's supposed to be over-the-top. Everybody watching will get it."

Vinicius looked at me. "Will they?"

"How's she supposed to know?" Graça said, crossing her arms over her sparkling chest. "Dor's not the goddamn director."

Tiny shook his head. "We're great musicians and they're making us look like oafs. You'd never see an American swing band doing this shit. They'd wear tuxedos and look respectable."

"We can't bail out now," I said. "Especially if it's Zanuck's idea."

"So Zanuck can make us look like chumps?" Kitchen asked.

"He sure can't," said Banana. "Because I'm not doing it."

"Me neither," Tiny agreed.

Graça's face paled. "You think I like this?" she asked, pointing at the giant berries swinging from her dress. "We're putting on a show here, it's all pretend. It might look silly now, but when it's filmed and we're on a movie screen, it'll be different."

"Everything's 'we' with you," Kitchen said. "Until 'we' can't set foot in the Mocambo Club with you because they don't let our kind inside. Until 'we' can't walk on the red carpet when our own movies premiere because the studio doesn't like our looks. Then you're not part of 'we' anymore, are you? Then you're Sofia Salvador, and we're just some band. Well, I'm not pulling a damn cart, even if it is pretend."

"So you're leaving me high and dry?" Graça said.

"We're not leaving anybody," Tiny said. "We're just not pulling that cart."

"It's one minute of one scene," Graça said. "If you can't do this for me, then don't bother backing me up on anything else."

"Nobody's going anywhere," Vinicius said. "Let's all calm down."

"Don't tell me to calm down," Kitchen said. "You're not the leader of this band anymore."

"Since when?" Vinicius asked.

"Since you and Dor made your own band," Kitchen replied.

Vinicius glanced at me, wide-eyed.

"She didn't tell anybody," Graça said. "We're not dumb. We all know you two have been recording behind our backs."

"It's not behind your backs," I sputtered. "It's a different sound."

"One we can't handle," Tiny said.

"No," Vinicius said, running his hands through his hair. "It just sounds better with two people. It's nothing serious. It's just for fun."

"For fun?" I asked him.

Graça laughed. "See, Dor? It's just a little fun on the side. It doesn't mean a damn thing."

"We shouldn't even be talking about this," I said. "You've got a number to film, and you'd better convince the boys to film it with you. I'm not pulling the strings backstage for you anymore."

"Fine," she said, still staring at me. "I'll film it on my own. I'll pull that fucking cart with my bare hands if I have to. I don't need you."

Kitchen laughed. "So that's how it goes? Who's going to play for you? Some gringos?"

Graça moved her face so close to his, their noses nearly touched. "People buy tickets to see me, not you."

"So pull the cart, gringa," Kitchen replied.

Graça stumbled backward. Little Noel caught her in his arms. "Why don't you cool it, Kitchen!" he yelled.

"Are you bossing me?" Kitchen replied, his voice low.

Tiny stepped between them. "Let's take five. I think we all—"

"English only!" a shrill voice called out.

The blonde starlet's personal production assistant walked imperiously toward us. "You're holding up the shoot," he said. "The director will be back in five minutes and you haven't even taken your places."

"This is a private conversation," I said.

"Then maybe you should have it in private and not in the middle of the set," he replied. "If you're going to talk out here, it has to be in English. Can't you read the signs? Or do you people need everything written in Spanish?"

It would've been sensible to ignore him and Saint Blondie, and to focus my efforts on getting Graça and the boys in front of the camera. Years before, that's what I would have done. But we'd been slogging through films in Hollywood for a while by then, and all of our patience was worn thin. So I ignored that filthy little PA and turned to Kitchen.

"Give me fifty dollars," I ordered.

"Why?" he asked.

"Jesus, just give me the money!"

He reached into his pocket, removed a money clip, and handed me a fifty. I ignored the PA, pushing past him and others until I reached the blonde starlet. The woman sat in full makeup and costume, sipping cola from a straw and watching us. Beside her, one of her assistants held the cardboard swear box under his arm. I pointed at it, and then stuffed the fifty-dollar bill inside.

"There," I said, addressing Saint Blondie in nearly perfect English. "Now we can tell you to go fuck yourself as many times as we please."

The swear box story appeared in a Hollywood gossip column without me in it. It was a catfight between Sofia Salvador and Saint Blondie—the hot-tempered Brazilian bombshell jealous of her costar. I was erased from the story as easily as Blue Moon was erased from their scene. And because that version of the story was printed in newspapers, that was how people remembered it ever afterward. No one recalled the "English Only" signs on set. And even though the entire cast and crew had watched me fill Saint Blondie's ridiculous swear box, years later, when biographers of Sofia Salvador and Saint Blondie printed interviews in their books, crew members only confirmed the gossip column's account. I wasn't surprised; it made for a better story and, in the end, that's what everyone wants.

In reality, Saint Blondie accused me of threatening and grabbing her. (I don't recall this; the moments after I stuffed money into the swear box are a blur of raised voices, shrieks, and footsteps pounding across the set.) Whatever happened, Blondie put on an elaborate victim act for the director, saying she feared for her safety. I was ordered to leave Fox and not come back. I was lucky, the director said, that he didn't have me arrested by studio police. He was doing Sofia Salvador a great favor by letting me go.

Before being escorted out, I was allowed to go to our trailer to collect my things; I had nothing important there, but wanted to see Graça. A part of me hoped she would leave with me, without filming the "Fruity Cutie" scene, and bring the entire production to a grinding halt.

Graça stared at herself in the trailer's mirror. She unclipped her massive strawberry earrings and dropped them onto the vanity with a thud. Her eyes flicked toward me.

"There's the hero," she said.

"How's that?" I asked.

"You're giving the boys exactly what they want: an excuse to walk out on me, to not finish what we all started."

"The boys are allowed to stay if they want."

"But they won't," Graça said. "If you go, they go."

"There was a time when you would've congratulated me for what I did back there. I stood up for you."

"Whatever that was, it wasn't for me," she said.

I placed a hand on her shoulder. "You don't have to go back out there," I said. "You don't have to do that scene."

Graça shook me off her.

"We're not kids in Lapa anymore. We can't smash people's faces in, or make the ones we don't like disappear."

Her eyes met mine in the mirror's reflection. I held tightly to the back of her chair.

"If I don't go out there and perform, Saint Blondie and the crew will say we're a bunch of unprofessional animals," Graça said. "That's what they want, you know. They want us to give up. They want to tell everyone that we can't hack it. Well, I'm not giving them that gift. I'm nailing that scene even if it kills me."

"Don't exaggerate. It's a song and dance."

"Well, I'm tired of it," Graça said.

"Well, it's what you wanted."

"Is it?" she asked, then shifted her eyes to stare at her own reflection. "I'm getting fat again. When this picture wraps they're sending me to some clinic in the desert where they starve you and shoot water up your ass to clean out your insides. I'll either come back skinny or dead. But at least when you're dead, you can't disappoint everybody."

An incessant, tinny ringing filled my ears. "You don't disappoint me."

Graça shook her head. "I don't work hard enough. I don't practice enough. I'm ruining my voice with all these cigarettes. I eat too much. I sleep too late. I spend too much."

"I say those things to help you be better."

"I don't want to be better!" Graça snapped. "I want to be who I am."

"And who's that?"

"I don't even know anymore, thanks to you."

"Do me a favor—don't put on this suffering artist act," I said. "You've never suffered a day in your life."

"I suffer every day, knowing what I know."

Graça's chest was splotched red, as if she'd touched a stinging plant.

"And what do you know?" I asked.

"The only reason you're here is because of me," Graça said. "I saved you. I always save you. But you never save me. You only save yourself."

They show Sofia Salvador's "Fruity Cutie" musical scene in film classes, as an example of the era's over-the-top productions. I've watched it myself, dozens of times. Even by today's standards, the Technicolor is shockingly bright. The camera pans across what appears to be water (it is blue carpet) and onto a vast, exotic land (green carpet dotted with satin banana trees) covered with identical girls—all wearing bright blue turbans. As the music gets louder, the island girls dance. The oxcart appears. Walking beside the cart, looking nervously at the oxen, are five shirtless and muscled men the director had scrounged from another shoot.

The only Blue Moon boys on set were Vinicius and Little Noel, who stayed to support Graça through her number but wouldn't appear on film. They stood behind that camera, watching. In the movie, as soon as the dubbed music begins to play, Sofia Salvador pops up from within the oxcart. At that moment, everyone around her—the island girls, the oxen, the muscled oafs—no longer exists; only Sofia Salvador matters.

"Oh, why does everybody always stop and stare,
  the minute I come in a room, or who-knows-where?
  I guess they think that I don't really have a care,
  because I am the Fruity Cutie girl!

"The blond boys always want to see my delicacies,
  they can't believe a girl can carry all of these!
  But I don't let them see my fruits, those sly young fleas,
  because I am the Fruity Cutie girl!"

It is her first and last song performed entirely in English, and completely by herself. She gives the camera a wink and lowers herself from the cart. She plays a xylophone. She swings her arms. She smiles. She slinks in and out of the rows of identical island girls. Two shirtless men lift Sofia Salvador high into the air. (The director was nearly censored for this; some Christian groups thought it vulgar, but the Hays Commission let him keep it in the film.)

"Brazilian senhoritas are so shy and sweet,
  they do not show their fruits to every boy they meet.
  But when we do, it is the very best of treats.
  Because we are the Fruity Cutie girls!"

Sofia Salvador sways and smiles. The camera pans wide. There are walls of mirrors around her, making it look like the original Sofia had multiplied into hundreds, then thousands—a kaleidoscope of color and glittering smiles, moving into infinity. It is an obvious trick, and its obviousness is what makes it genius.

Rumor was that the entire crew clapped after the "Fruity Cutie" performance, except for the blonde starlet, of course. After I left, Graça performed the complicated scene in one perfect take.

B edford Drive was empty. Graça and Vinicius and Noel were still at Fox. The other boys had gone their separate ways—some to the Showboat, some out with girls, some on a drive. Where would I go after my expulsion? Where did I belong?

The only reason you're here is because of me.

I limped up the curved staircase intending to shut myself inside my room. Instead, I saw the door to Graça and Vinicius's master suite was open.

The bed was unmade, the sheets tangled at the footboard. I clicked on the lamps. Graça's closet was nearly as big as the bedroom itself and, at Graça's insistence, painted flamingo pink. The clothing racks were reinforced with braces at each end to bear the weight of her costumes. Part of her deal with Fox was that as a free agent she received less pay, but was allowed to keep her entire wardrobe, costume jewelry included. Now the costumes from each of her dance routines hung from those thick brass racks like the empty husks of some strange, exotic insect— iridescent, rigid, even sharp. I was careful not to run my hands across them as I searched the closet.

On the shelves above the costumes were mannequin heads—faceless and hairless—that wore Sofia Salvador's bejeweled hats, tiaras, berets, and feathered fascinators. And then there was the wall of drawers filled with a tangle of bracelets and necklaces, and her massive clip-on earrings. In the back of the closet, squeezed between shoe racks and lingerie drawers, was a narrow space with her Sunday clothes: a few swimsuits and ten dresses, each identical except for their color. They were simple and made of the thinnest cotton I'd ever touched. Graça wore these dresses only at home, when she wasn't Sofia Salvador.

I looked at my watch: the boys were most likely on their way to getting stupendously drunk. Graça would still be filming her song and dance.

I always save you. You never save me.

Her vanity was a laboratory of creams and tonics, glass vials with rubber droppers, used cotton swabs, balled-up tissues, discarded eyelashes glued to the table's surface like flattened bugs. I let out a long breath and plopped onto Graça's vanity stool. My hat was crooked, its pins tugging at my hair. The side roll I'd tried to wrangle my short, straight hair into was limp, resembling a flattened tortilla instead of a wave. I tugged off my hat. Sofia Salvador's lipsticks were scattered across the top of the vanity, most without their lids. They were not the drugstore brand we'd bought in our early days in Brazil but a fancy kind, in gold tubes, as heavy as jewels in my palm. I rolled one open. It smelled of wax and vanilla.

I glanced at my bare mouth in the mirror, at my stingy lips, their ends turned down. I dabbed the lipstick against them, then closed my eyes and rubbed my lips together. It tasted good and felt quite smooth. I rolled on more, over-lining my lips to make them fuller, like Sofia did. The slash of color was startling. It was a bright coral, more orange than red. I needed to balance it out, somehow. I moved a powder puff across my cheeks and then blotted them with rouge. Inside the vanity's drawer was a set of earrings—clip-on roses, as big as a child's fists. I opened the mouths of their clips and snapped them onto my lobes.

Downstairs, there was a noise. I turned from the mirror, toward Graça's half-open bedroom door. I listened, holding my breath, for steps on the stairs. Was one of the boys home? My heart leapt—was it

Vinicius? Had he abandoned Graça to check on me? I imagined him climbing up the stairs and finding me not in my room, but in his and Graça's.

I sprang to the door and quietly shut it, turning the lock. When I sat back at the vanity, I met my reflection with surprise. The powder made me pale. The circles of rouge were uneven. The lipstick was too bright. My earlobes pulsed and burned under the weight of those roses. I looked like a drunk who had stumbled onto a makeup table. I pressed the heels of my hands to my eyes. The noise downstairs had stopped; it was the wind, or just the old house creaking. Either way, I was alone, and I had been there too long. I slipped off the earrings, took a generous fingerful of cold cream, and wiped away the mess I'd made.

Exile and fame have similar side effects: if you experience either one, your world is made narrow, and the only people you can bear—the only ones who truly understand you—are the ones who are in the same boat.

After filming wrapped on *Fruity Cutie*, a weight pressed upon all of us—Graça, the boys, and me—settling on our shoulders, making it hard to move, to eat, to talk to one another. Our fight on the Fox set had changed things among us and we all sensed it. Each of us felt betrayed in our own way.

We stayed in L.A. together, under the same roof, even after filming wrapped, in part because we didn't have enough money to go home, and in part because our home didn't want us back. We were all bound by the excruciating intimacies of exile and fame.

Three days into our break after *Fruity Cutie*, and before Sofia Salvador was carted off to another fat farm, Vinicius and I had our standing middle-of-the-night reservation at the recording studio near Disney, where we usually laid down our Sal e Pimenta tracks in secret.

But that night, we couldn't bring ourselves to sneak away from Graça and the boys; they'd know exactly where we were going and what we'd do there. It felt undignified.

"We already paid for the session," I said to the boys and Graça, who'd gathered beside the pool. "It'd be stupid to waste it."

So we piled into the DeSoto and, for the last time, all traveled to the recording studio together. There, we made up songs on the spot. We stretched out those songs—playing them slower and slower still—until we couldn't stretch them any further. Graça sang a note until its sound petered out, and then she paused. These pauses are so long that when you listen to the album (the last we ever made together, as a band), you think her voice has disappeared. And, as a listener, there is a moment of panic, a moment when you think: What will sustain this silence, this emptiness? Then you hear Graça take a breath. You hear Vinicius's fingertips preparing to strum his guitar strings. You hear Tiny sniffle. You hear Kitchen let out a small sigh. You hear Little Noel, Banana, and Bonito shifting their feet or licking their lips. It's all there. And we recorded it—even those mistakes—because they were a part of that moment, of those last ballads, of that terrible night sweating together in that cramped and suffocating L.A. studio, where we sat as exiles from our home and now from one another, with only music to console us.

BETWEEN US

Everything was a lark
between us.
Everything was child's play
between us.
Everything was
a silly bet,
a give and a get,
a laugh, a touch, a shared
    cigarette
between us.

Everything was a talk
when all others were
    sleeping.
Everything was a walk
when the beach was dark.
Everything was
your voice,
your smell,
your mouth closing around
    the secrets
between us.

I fell off the wire,
and there was no net.
I dove into the riptide,
and there was no lifeguard.
I drank the poison,
and there was no antidote.
All along knowing,
there could be nothing
between us.

Everything was a song
between us.
Everything was all wrong
between us.
Everything was
a poem,
a prayer,
a plea
between us.

I fell off the wire,
and there was no net.
I dove into the riptide,
and there was no lifeguard.
I drank the poison,
and there was no antidote.
All along knowing,
there could be nothing
between us.

But hope is a talent of mine.
Patience, too.
Waiting isn't hard when there's
    nothing left to do.
Everything isn't lost
between us.
Everything had its cost
between us.
Everything can be
remembered,
and forgotten,
and forgiven
between us.

When I was young, I sat in rodas every day. I listened. I waited. I made a promise to the music: I'll be here, I'll open a space within myself for you. I showed it that I was devoted, and in return it rewarded me with words, with creation itself. There was the passion of a love affair in these moments because the music demanded my time, my full attention, my complete devotion. And so long as I rendered myself entirely to its service, the music allowed me inside itself, immersed in a space where time didn't exist.

Some artists, if they are wise and lucky, can remain faithful to their work—giving it the time and attention it deserves—for their entire lives. Others of us stray. We stop carving out a space within ourselves; we ignore its calls to us; we make excuses. After Graça died I made no music for twenty-five years. Vinicius appeared with his radios, record players, and invitations to clubs, and those helped me to listen again but not to create. There were moments—flashes, really—when I heard a melody in my mind, or thought of words and rushed to write them down. Scraps of paper littered my squalid apartments like fallen leaves.

Then Vinicius dragged me into that Las Vegas studio to record with that young Tropicália buck, and it was like a locked door clicked open within me. Slowly, over the course of months, I began to turn the knob and peek in at the other side. I got a haircut. I began to shower more regularly and eat meals that consisted of more than stale bread and fried eggs. I bought new clothes. I didn't stop drinking—not immediately—but I felt as though I needed it less. I began to join Vinicius on his trips to the recording studio, though I didn't participate like I had that first time. During these months, I felt like I'd returned from a long exile and saw once familiar people with new eyes.

I was fifty-three years old and Vinicius sixty-two. He smoked too much. He had wrinkles on his face and a shock of gray hair in his pompadour. He was handsome in a wounded way that women still adored; every week Vinicius had a new girl in his bed. But although the women were new, the songs were not; without me, Vinicius hadn't written anything new. He'd spent the past two decades playing and recording covers of our old, stale songs.

During one of my visits to that cramped Vegas studio, I listened to Vinicius and a different exiled musician record our same tired tracks but with a Tropicália twist. The result was painfully exuberant, like someone forced to dance samba with a broken ankle.

"You sound ridiculous," I announced.

Vinicius asked the other musicians to leave the studio.

"You're a piece of work," he said. "You check out for twenty years and now you've got opinions?"

"I've always had opinions, I just didn't share them."

"Maybe you were better that way," Vinicius said.

There was a sharp, familiar ache within me, one that rose after years of numbness. For an instant, it was too terrible to bear. My mouth felt dry. I scanned the studio for a bottle of beer, a half-filled glass, anything that might help me. There was only Vinicius—an old man with a gray pompadour and stooped shoulders—smoking in front of me. I grabbed the cigarette from his lips and shoved it between mine.

"It's embarrassing, what you've been playing," I said. "You're too good for it."

"You're the most selfish person I've ever met," he said. "I thought it was Graça, but it's you. It's always been you."

Her name, said aloud, made me flinch. "If it's selfish to tell the truth, so be it. Make me the villain. I'm used to it."

Vinicius stiffened. "You don't get to tell the truth. You left me. Kitchen's dead. Tiny's stroke means he can't play anymore. We can't go home because those military fucks are throwing people like us out of helicopters. Everything's gone to shit, and where have you been through it? Sitting in some dump like a goddamn zombie."

He slumped into a chair and pressed the heels of his hands to his eyes. I knelt beside him.

"I'm here now," I whispered. "You helped me wake up. And it's a good thing, because this music you're playing is real shit."

Vinicius stared at me, his eyes wet. "Go to hell, Dor."

"I can't. It's too far away."

"From what?"

"From you."

Vinicius stood. There was a piano in the studio and he strode toward it, slammed open its bench, and rifled through the scores inside. He returned with a notebook and a pencil nub, throwing both in my lap.

"That's a good line," he said. "Write it down."

I shook my head. We stared at each other like two tigers, waiting for the tiniest shift, the smallest flinch of muscle, as an excuse to pounce. There was a knock on the studio door. One of the production boys popped his head inside.

"You two okay?" he asked.

"Go home," Vinicius said, still staring at me. "Dor and me are going to work. Lock the door behind you."

We sat face-to-face, like in the old days. We started and grappled and stopped and then started again. We sighed, bickered, crossed out lines, crumpled pages in our fists and threw them to the floor. My lyrics were rough and filled with curses. His melodies were stingy and mean with abrupt endings. When we were kids we could've wrestled those tunes all night, but the years had taken their toll on us. After only a few hours we were exhausted, sweaty, and trembling. We had one measly song to show for all of our suffering. We played it again, from beginning to end.

"What do you think?" Vinicius asked.

"I think it's a disaster."

He put his guitar down. His voice shook. "What're we going to do, Dor?"

"Write more. Write them better. Cut a motherfucking record."

"Me and you?" he asked.

"You got better company to keep?"

We worked hard after that, building up our stamina each day. When we wrote, we drank only apple juice and filled trash bins with cigarette butts. After a few months we had more awful songs than we could count, but we also had enough decent songs to fill an album. Vinicius asked those exiled Tropicália boys, with their long hair and tight pants, into the studio to help us record. After we'd cut the final track, one of those boys planted a kiss on my cheek.

"I don't know what you two did to birth this baby, but it's a real monster," he said. "In the best sense of the word."

With the dictatorship there was too much censorship in Brazil for any recording company to be willing to sell our record. In the United States in the 1970s there was little interest in an elderly samba duo. Our later records as Sal e Pimenta would eventually sell and be hailed as cult favorites that paid homage, as critics said, "to a quiet style Sofia Salvador had single-handedly invented in her final show." Even our best work was attributed back to her, but I didn't mind. That first Vegas record—the one Vinicius and I had fought and sweated and toiled over—never saw the light of day. That might have mattered to the young Dores, but to the old one, just cutting a record again was enough. I sat in that Vegas studio and held the master disk in my hands for what felt like hours.

"Isn't she a beauty?" I said, my voice catching in my throat.

Vinicius stood behind me. He placed his large, wrinkled hands on my arms. His chin sat comfortably in the valley between my neck and shoulder, his mouth near my ear. I closed my eyes, remembering a similar embrace. Something rose within me: a heat that began at the base of my spine and radiated up and out. It was familiar and yet changed—not desire but something else, a seed born of similar fruit.

"We have to cut other records, better ones," Vinicius whispered. "You can't disappear again. I need you."

I put down the disk and moved out of his arms. "You know what Graça told me that night, at the Copa? That I could never be magnificent; I just force myself on people who are. Like her. Like you."

"She always said things she didn't mean when she was angry," Vinicius said.

I shook my head. "She wasn't angry. Not that night. I was the angry one."

"You couldn't have saved her. Once she got an idea in her head she always went for it. She never thought about consequences, she only thought about herself. And you always thought about us—me, her, the boys. I know what you did for us. I've known for a long time, I was just too selfish back then to see you clearly."

"And what do you see?" I asked, afraid to look at him.

"A great musician. My partner."

When I look back on our life together (and I call it a life—not lives—because we were so deeply intertwined), I think of us as two athletes in a race, struggling for the same prize. Sometimes Vinicius pushed ahead, sometimes I did. When we married I was fifty-four and Vinicius sixty-three. We were battered, bruised, limping from the course of our race so far, and our prize was long lost in a Copacabana hotel room decades before. But there we were, Vinicius and I, still together, and we saw in each other the youths we'd been once, long ago, and the gentleness we might have forgotten, if we hadn't been together to remind ourselves of it. We shared a bed, among other things, although the rumors are true: over the years, Vinicius had his girls and I had mine. But those unions were sparked by desire, not love. We only ever made music with each other.

BETWEEN US

The end of the war brought the liberation of concentration camps in Europe, ticker-tape parades, GIs and navy boys returning home and kissing girls in the middle of Times Square like a scene in one of Sofia Salvador's Technicolor movies. But behind the color and confetti and song and dance was a grim, festering anxiety that lingered well beyond the war's end. It was as if the world had battled an illness we'd brought upon ourselves—an addiction, really—that lasted for years and left us ravaged and stumbling and exposed the pettiest, basest parts of our natures. Millions were dead. The atomic bombs dropped on Japan had unleashed a technology that threatened us all. The world didn't know if the peace that had cost so much would continue, but America was determined in its gaiety. No matter what, it would smile for the cameras.

In the months after the war, entertainment was all sugar and no spice. America's greatest crooner was forced to sing a song where he barked like a dog. Serious actors were expected to slip on banana peels for laughs. And Sofia Salvador danced and sang in her sparkling skirts and belly-baring shirts, though she moved slower, and her figure was thinner in a gaunt, shrunken kind of way, making her costumes seem burdensome to her. In the very few postwar films she made, Blue Moon is still behind her, though they seem less like a cheerful band and more like bored orderlies keeping an eye on their patient.

A few of the Blue Moon boys were saving up to go back home—or to whatever Brazil had become during our five-year absence. Money was tight because fewer films meant longer breaks from Fox. Banana, Bonito, and Little Noel took gigs composing music for Disney cartoons, hoping to make enough money for three tickets to Rio. Kitchen stopped sleeping at Bedford Drive and began to haunt the clubs on Central Avenue, learning bebop and jazz, and teaching the other musicians elements of samba. Tiny took up with a Disney secretary and we barely saw him. And we all took something to get us through those bleak months after our *Fruity Cutie* fight: liquor, sweet flour, bennies, Demerol, Nembutal, codeine.

We still read the Lion's newspapers, though there were no more stories about Sofia Salvador and Blue Moon; Gegê had taken their place as an example of disappointment and loss. The end of the war brought images of liberation and new democracies in Europe; Old Getúlio couldn't stop this fever from reaching his doorstep. His military men deposed him. His precious Estado Novo was replaced by a new constitution and real elections. Eurico Gaspar Dutra became Brazil's first democratically elected president in fifteen years.

The United States and Brazil were once again fast friends, while Russia became a common enemy. The House Un-American Activities Committee issued subpoenas to suspected communists in the film industry. In Hollywood, there were massive union strikes, followed by claims from the studios that the strikers were pinkos and queers, slurs that became interchangeable. The vice squad raided the Plaza Hotel's bar and arrested Sandy, my old flame, and dozens of other "sapphically inclined" women, dragging them to jail in their evening gowns and stoles. Union strikes suspended Fox's shooting schedule, which put the brakes on our meager salaries. We couldn't pay rent at Bedford Drive.

We talked about selling some of Sofia Salvador's costume jewelry, and maybe picking up a few shows in Las Vegas, which had become a popular venue after the war. The trouble was, Graça refused to go there.

"I'm not playing for a few tumbleweeds in a fucking desert," she declared.

When Chuck Lindsay called us into his office, we steeled ourselves to be dropped from his roster of clients. Instead, he waved a yellow telegram in his manicured hand.

"Aerovias Brasil wants to hire you!" he said, incredulous.

"For an ad?" Graça asked.

Lindsay shook his head. "To ride in a plane from Miami to Rio. It'll be the easiest money you've ever made."

Aerovias was a Brazilian airline that had helped the United States during the war by running cargo flights. In return for its service, Aerovias had been granted the first international passenger flights to Brazil. Air travel was considered exotic and somewhat perilous in those days; passengers had to be reassured. Who better than Sofia Salvador to show potential U.S. passengers that flying could be a party in the skies? And what better publicity could Aerovias get in Brazil than by being the company that returned Sofia Salvador home to face her countrymen? Part of the deal dangled before us was a homecoming show, played in Rio after our arrival. Aerovias would bankroll it, along with the Lion's network of newspapers.

"Where will we play this show?" I asked Lindsay. All of Brazil's casinos had been closed thanks to the new president's anti-gambling law. I pictured Graça and the boys forced to perform in a small Lapa cabaret or in an empty airplane hangar outside the city, as a kind of penance for their rise and fall. Graça must have had the same worries, because before Chuck could answer me, she grabbed my arm and said:

"We're doing it at the Copa. I won't set foot on any other stage. It's the Palace, or nothing."

The Palace, that ivory fortress in Copacabana that dictated taste and style. The place that had shunned us for being a samba band. The place that, years before, Graça and I had admired from our spots on the beach one morning. She'd had a black eye from one of her knuckle draggers, and she'd stared at the Copa and called it her ticket to the moon.

As we crowded in Chuck Lindsay's Hollywood office, I thought Graça's demand was foolish—surely such a request was impossible to fulfill, and Graça's stubbornness would lose us the only gig we'd been offered in months, as well as the possibility of redeeming ourselves back home. Later, I realized she was right to demand the moon and the stars. After the war, the writing on the wall was quite clear: the United States and its studios had tired of Sofia Salvador. Fox's racehorse had been ridden until she was hobbling, and was easily replaced. Technicolor was out, black-and-white was in. Musicals were passé and spy dramas were becoming all the rage. Where did we have to go but home? And when we made our comeback in Rio, we couldn't do it on a small stage with heads bowed. We would do it on the very stage that had been denied us for so long. Graça wasn't after redemption; she wanted revenge, and resurrection.

S he posed with the beaming pilot. She waved and smiled as she ascended the metal stairs into the plane's cabin. She lifted a heeled foot and kissed the plane's metal side as if it was a leading man in a film. She sat in the cockpit and winked for the cameras. She was a subdued version of Sofia Salvador, in a crimson traveling suit with blue piping, to match the Aerovias logo.

"They can't expect me to wear one of my Fox getups—I won't even fit through the plane's door!" Graça had complained when Aerovias expressed disappointment at her insistence on wearing "normal clothes." She made one concession: dangling from her ears like children's toys were specially commissioned earrings in the shape of Aerovias planes, covered in rhinestones.

When we boarded, we were awarded stamped certificates as if we'd already accomplished something just by entering the plane. Sofia Salvador posed with her certificate for the bevy of photographers accompanying us on the flight. Then, as soon as the pilot announced our departure, she slipped behind the curtained section reserved for her and the band, unclipped her enormous earrings, threw her hat on the chair beside her, and ordered a whiskey, neat.

Over the course of the forty-eight-hour flight, we'd empty the plane's supply of whiskey two times over. We flew only during daylight hours. At night, we stopped in Port of Spain and then in Belém, where we slept in hotels while the plane refueled and loaded its pantry with more booze. I'd also brought along a rainbow-colored stockpile of pills—bennies, Seconal, Nembutal, and more—hoping to have enough to get me, Graça, and the boys through our trip home.

The plane ride was bumpy and we were nervous, but not about the flight. This was, we knew, our last adventure together. Kitchen, Banana, Bonito, and Little Noel would remain in Rio when the Aerovias flight returned to Miami. The rest of us planned to be on that plane back to the USA, returning to Hollywood but only temporarily. We had one last commitment with Fox to fulfill, and a house filled with costumes and records to pack up. Where we would send those crates after they'd been packed remained a mystery.

The closer we came to Rio, the more Vinicius wanted to hash out the Copa's set list, and the more Graça avoided him. She left our private area to chat with photographers and Aerovias reps; she retreated into the powder room; she faked sleep. Finally, Vinicius cornered her.

"We can't wing this show," he said. "If we want to go home, and stay home, we have to nail it."

"Do I look stupid to you?" Graça asked. "You think I want to bomb?"

"You're sure acting like it," Vinicius replied. "We don't have a set list. We haven't practiced—"

"I don't need practice," Graça interrupted.

"Oh yeah? How long has it been since we've done a live show? This isn't a Fox set. We won't get a second take at the Palace."

Graça slapped her tray table. Her whiskey tumbler wobbled and tipped. "Can't you be happy for once?" she whispered, glancing at the curtains that separated us from the photographers. "We're riding in a goddamn airplane and getting paid more than President Dutra for it, and you're still complaining? You're as dull as a hangnail."

"And you're a fool," Vinicius said, his voice cool. "We don't know what's waiting for us; I bet you money that Copa crowd wants us to crash and burn. And you don't care. Well, if you want to hang yourself on that stage, fine by me. But don't drag the rest of us into it."

Graça smiled. "How terrible—I'm getting you a first-class trip back home. I'm dragging you onto the best stage in Brazil. What a tragedy. Let me give you a little advice, querido: Don't you worry about me at the Copa. Worry about your little Ipanema show with Dor over there. What's your new band's name again? Ketchup and Mustard?"

"Tuna and Mayo," Tiny called out.

"Oil and Water." Kitchen joined in the fun.

Graça pointed at me with her thumb. "She's the one you should be lecturing. Look at her! She's turning green."

The plane bobbed and shook. I closed my eyes. Before we'd left L.A., Madame L. had telephoned to ask if Sal e Pimenta could squeeze in a little debut show at a club in Ipanema, of all places. We had a small but loyal fan base, many of them younger than us by ten years, who would like to see us in person. Madame L. cajoled: it would be nothing fancy, just a small stage, a few lights, two chairs, Vinicius with his guitar, and me. My voice was accepted (if only by Vinicius and a few naive fans) because of its flaws. If this opportunity had arisen years before, I might have felt vindicated, but in that moment I was afraid and angry at myself for this fear. I pretended, for Vinicius's sake, to be excited and accepted the gig. We would play the night before Sofia Salvador's big Copa show.

"I'm not worried about Dor," Vinicius said as the plane trembled around us. "Our show's just for fun. It'll be easy."

Graça righted her empty whiskey glass. "And you're calling me a fool."

We arrived in the late afternoon, our plane circling Guanabara Bay's blue waters like a bird coasting in a warm pocket of air. The Blue Moon boys, Graça, and I crowded near the plane's small windows. Rio lay beneath us in all of her glory: her curving strips of beaches, her ample hills, her jagged and lush patches of forest. We tried to spot Lapa, Copacabana, Catete Palace, and our fingers left greasy spots across the window glass. Many years later, a young musician would see Rio from the air just as we did, and he would compose a famous bossa nova (that quiet, watered-down 1950s offspring of samba that Sal e Pimenta inspired) about its beauty. Each time I heard that song I was terribly annoyed—we should have been the ones to write about touching down in Rio, and it should have been a samba, not a flimsy, insubstantial bossa, because only samba could communicate the mixture of overwhelming elation and gutting disappointment that a return home inevitably brings.

The airport's tarmac was empty. There were no eager fans, no cheering crowds holding posters with the message: "Welcome Home, Sofia!"

"Looks like we didn't even make the trip," Graça mumbled as the plane's door opened with a hiss. A military motorcade swiftly drove us to the Copacabana Palace Hotel.

"How about a stop in Lapa?" Vinicius said as our black Cadillac sped away from the airport. "For old times' sake?"

Before any of us could answer, our stone-faced escort responded. "That's not on the agenda. We will take you directly to the hotel for interviews."

At the Palace Hotel, we were given thirty minutes to freshen up before being escorted by the Aerovias uniformed representatives to the hotel's ballroom for a press conference. I swallowed two bennies just to stay awake. Graça drank four espressos.

In the Palace's mirrored and gilded ballroom, Sofia Salvador and the Blue Moon boys were escorted to a row of chairs behind a vast table. In front of them were dozens of precisely arranged red velvet chairs, all of them empty. A gaggle of reporters milled about in the back of the ballroom. At their center was the Lion.

His mane of white hair was still full, his eyes still dark and scrutinizing in their gaze. If, in his youth, the Lion might have been cast as a handsome but silent movie extra, in his old age he would have earned a speaking part: the tycoon; the stern head of a sprawling and troubled family; the savvy club owner; the mysterious stranger at a bar who offers the troubled hero a cigarette, then pulls out a pistol and shoots him in the gut.

"You're our host again," Graça said, pressing through the crowd and kissing both the Lion's cheeks. "I'll never forget the night I sang in your home. I'm glad my father was still alive to see it."

He held her arms and gazed at her. "Stunning. I read that you'd swelled up like a balloon but I didn't believe it."

Graça blinked. Her smile widened. "Don't believe anything the press says. You boys lie more than politicians."

The Lion laughed. "Maybe in the United States, querida."

"Liars come in all nationalities," I said.

"Ah, Dores! I'm glad to see you're still loyal to this old showbiz crew. But I hear you have your own band now! What's it called: Oyster and Pearl?"

Graça laughed too loudly. "Dor's a pearl?"

The Lion shook his head. "You're the only pearl in this room. Dores has always been the grit."

Graça smiled. One of Dutra's military boys approached and escorted her to a seat at the center of the main table.

"I'm surprised to see you at such a small event," I said to the Lion as we watched Graça adjust her hat and smile at the Blue Moon boys, who took seats on either side of her.

"This is the biggest event all year!" the Lion replied. "Things are dull as dishwater now that old Dutra and his Little Saint wife run the show. But Sofia Salvador coming home? Now that's a story that sells. I'm glad Aerovias took my advice."

"You got Aerovias to hire us?"

The Lion looked surprised. "You think they'd make this kind of move on their own? It'll be great publicity for them, no matter what happens. Much better than my papers writing stories about how dangerous their planes are."

"And you got the Copa for us, too," I said.

"I aim to give you exactly what you want," the Lion said. "And it was a brilliant idea for a venue; did you come up with it?"

I shook my head. "You wrote disgusting things about her, about all of us, while we were away."

"I didn't write anything," the Lion said. "My reporters do their jobs. Don't tell me you hold a grudge, Dores? I've listened to those songs of yours, I've paid attention to the words. You know what people want to hear."

"What's that?"

"We don't want to hear about someone else's success and happiness, that only makes us feel bad about our own lots. No, we want to hear about heartbreak and failure and terrible loss, as long as they're someone else's."

The Lion nodded toward Graça, then left to find his chair. I had no seat, so I quickly moved to the side of the ballroom, beside the silent line of government representatives and Aerovias men. There were two massive doorways to the ballroom, both of them flanked by military men.

The ballroom smelled of musty drapes and stale coffee. Near the hive of reporters, the Lion whispered to an Aerovias man, then laughed. Sweat prickled my forehead. It was hard for me to keep my foot from tapping. Why had I taken so many bennies? I searched the room for a table with a coffee urn and perhaps a pitcher of water, but there was nothing of the sort. The chief officer of the Aerovias publicity team stepped forward.

"Shall we begin," he said, his words sounding more like an order than a question.

The journalists opened their notepads and uncapped their pens. Without raising his hand, a man in the front row began without objection from the others, as if the corps of press boys had rehearsed beforehand.

"Miss Salvador, how does it feel to be back in Rio?"

Graça smiled. "Wonderful, of course. I missed it very much."

"So you'd forgotten Rio?" the man continued.

"No," Graça replied. "Missing isn't forgetting. How could I ever forget this beach, this sun, this city?"

Another journalist stood and asked: "People are saying you're back in Brazil because you can't get work in the U.S. Is this true?"

The Aerovias publicity man stepped forward. "Now, boys, we agreed . . ."

There was tapping—insistent and without rhythm—that echoed

across the ballroom. The military men on my right and left turned toward me. Several reporters looked in my direction. I realized it was my heel striking the ballroom's shining wooden floor. Graça stared at me; she did not look angry at me for interrupting her press conference, but relieved. In the mass of reporters, a man so young he looked as if he'd skipped school to attend the conference stood and cleared his throat.

"Mr. de Oliveira," he asked, his voice wavering.

Vinicius looked up, startled.

"Do . . . do you think the new sound you created with Sal e Pimenta is a reaction to the war? Going softer with samba's sound and making the lyrics darker?"

Vinicius glanced at me.

"Well, Dores . . . Miss Pimentel—my partner, over there—and I don't consciously set out to work current events into our sound. Samba comes to us naturally, and we try to respect it, to listen to it. But we were all affected by the war, so I'm sure some elements made their way into our sound. Music is a reflection of ourselves, after all."

A few of the reporters stared at me, then jotted notes onto their pads. Graça's cheeks were flushed, her smile rigid. The youth faced me.

"Miss Pimentel, what made you agree to do a show when you've avoided the spotlight for so long?"

At the main table, Graça laughed. "Dor's avoided the spotlight like a bee avoids honey," she said. "I thought this press conference was about Sofia and Blue Moon coming home, not about Ketchup and Mustard, or whatever they call themselves."

A few reporters chuckled. Another stood and addressed Graça. "There are rumors that you've been sent multiple times to a weight loss farm in the United States. Do the Americans want to change your Brazilian shape?"

The skin above Graça's eye twitched. She gripped her hands together so tightly her knuckles turned white. "It was a clinic."

"Were you sick?" the reporter persisted.

"Filming's hard work," Vinicius said, his voice too loud. "She needed a place to rest."

"Those dance numbers look challenging," the reporter said. "Tell me, will your Copa show be a comedy act like your films, or will you actually play samba?"

Vinicius stood. "You're walking a thin line," he shouted. "Ask me again if we're comedians . . ."

Cameras flashed. The reporters scribbled wildly in their notepads. The Lion beamed. An Aerovias representative rushed before the table, clapped his hands, and said the press conference was over—Sofia Salvador and Blue Moon needed rest before their big show. Vinicius took Graça's elbow and helped her rise from her chair. She blinked several times, as if there was dust in her eyes, and held tightly to Vinicius's arm as he guided her out of the ballroom and into the elevator.

"I could sleep until I die," Graça said.

Vinicius cupped his hand to her cheek. "Don't die, amor. We're going to put on a hell of a show day after tomorrow, and you'll teach those assholes who's boss."

Graça looked at me. "It's not my show they care about."

The hotel's bar was strangely empty for a Friday night. Outside, the sky glowed orange. It was high tide on Copacabana Beach. The waves looked as though they were on fire.

The boys and Graça had disappeared inside their suites on the Palace's private penthouse floor. But after all those bennies, the thought of staying inside my room made me nervous; I could barely keep still. Vinicius found me at the bar.

"You should be sleeping," he said, slipping into the seat next to mine.

"So should you," I replied. "You've got a long few days coming up."

"We all do. If the crowd at the Copa is anything like those reporters today, you'll have to peel us off the stage floor, we'll be beat up so bad. You'll spend the rest of the trip nursing our wounds."

"You'd be a terrible patient—a whiner. And I'd be a bitch of a nurse."

Vinicius smiled. "Sounds like a perfect match."

I focused on my empty glass. "Do you think tomorrow, for our show . . . What if the Ipanema crowd's mean?"

Vinicius rested his hand over mine. "That won't be a tough crowd at all. And if they are, hell, there'll probably be so few people there, you and me can take them with our arms tied behind our backs."

I nodded, then rubbed my eyes with my free hand. "Those fucking bennies. I should flush them all down the toilet."

"Want to take a walk?" he asked.

Without a word, we strolled hand in hand to the beach outside the hotel. The evening was cool. Other couples strolled, arm in arm, along the beach's wide sidewalk. What a comfort it was, to blend in with them, to squint, as they squinted, at the disappearing sun. A vendor popped corn in a metal cart. Vinicius stopped, his hand tight around mine.

"Close your eyes, Dor," he said. "Take a deep breath."

I obeyed.

"Smell that?" Vinicius asked.

The evening smelled of popcorn, of salt water, of perfumed girls.

"We could almost be in Rio," Vinicius said.

"We are in Rio."

He shook his head. "Not the one I remember. It feels different now."

"Maybe we're different," I replied.

We were quiet for a while, staring at the ocean as the sky darkened to gray and then indigo.

"It's okay to be nervous about tomorrow," Vinicius said. "You haven't played in front of a crowd in a long time."

"Thanks for reminding me."

"You'll be great. Pretend we're in the studio, just me and you."

He hadn't shaved since we'd left Miami. I slid my hand across his cheek, just to feel the roughness of him. Vinicius closed his eyes, then caught my hand and placed it, gently, back at my side.

"I don't know if I can go back, Dor."

"To the hotel?"

He shook his head. "To L.A. Tiny's going back because of that Disney secretary of his. Graça's going back for her movies and her costumes. You're going back for her. What the hell am I going back for?"

The ocean lapped at our feet. Once, years before, when Graça and I swam in those waters, the ocean was very rough and a wave took me under. It slapped my face and turned me upside down. Water filled my mouth and throat, but when I got my bearings and paddled onto the sand, my stomach felt strangely empty. It was as if I'd been hollowed out by that wave. I felt the same way in that moment, on the beach with Vinicius.

"Graça," I said. "You're going back for her."

Vinicius nodded. "I'm not sure that's reason enough anymore."

"So you'll wait here for us. Until we come home."

Vinicius's brow furrowed. "After the Palace show, there's no more Blue Moon. And hell, if we bomb that show—and we probably will— there'll be no more Sofia Salvador. Not here, anyway. Graça will have to find herself a new act, or stay in L.A. We said we'd only be gone a few months the first time around, and it turned into a few years. If you girls go back north, you won't be home anytime soon. I can't wait here forever."

"So you want a clean break from us?" I asked.

Vinicius took my hands in his. "If I follow Graça back now, I'll be following her all my life. That's how things work with her. You know that, Dor. Whatever she becomes next, I'll be some accessory to it. She'll change and change, and I'll stay the same, like a horse tied to a different wagon. And either she'll get bored with me, or I'll start to hate her. And I don't want to hate her. It'd kill me."

I spotted a bench on the beach's paved path, away from the water. I walked there and sat. Vinicius followed. I kept hold of his hand.

I thought that if I held on in that moment, I could hold on forever: to him, to the boys, to Graça, to the music. I'd never written a song without him. I believed that as soon as Vinicius left us, all creation would stop. All music would stop. And if it stopped, I would dry up like those bouquets of flowers hanging upside down in Graça's dressing rooms. I would become as brittle and thin as those dried petals. I would break apart and turn to dust.

"What about Sal e Pimenta?" I asked. "What about our songs? You're just going to leave them?"

"People in L.A. don't want to hear our kind of music. It only works here."

"We can make them want to hear it," I said. "We can make the whole world want it."

Vinicius stroked my hand with his thumb. "Graça's right: when you don't get your way, you try to force things. There are some things you can't force."

It was hard to focus on his words; the bennies were finally wearing off. "Have you told her you're leaving?"

Vinicius shook his head. "Please don't mention it—not until after the Palace gig. Graça's nervous enough as it is; I don't want to ruin our last show together."

"What about our show tomorrow?" I asked. "You didn't think about ruining that for me?"

"I . . . I'm sorry," Vinicius said, his eyes wide. "I'm so used to telling you everything."

I stood. "It's all right," I said, wiping sand from my trousers. "Like you said, it's a small show. It's not important. It'll be our first and our last."

Vinicius called me back to the bench but I wobbled in the dark, across the sand to the hotel. I looked up the Copacabana Palace's white façade, made blindingly bright by under-lights hidden in the hotel's bushes. A doorman spotted me staring openmouthed at the hotel, and for an instant, I believed he was going to shoo me away. But he smiled, remembering me in my fine travel clothes, and opened the door. Without a word, I backed away and caught a cab to Lapa.

Anaïs was still the picture of elegance in a fitted black dress and red lipstick, but her face looked care-worn and her hair was pinned into two matronly twists. When she saw me at her door, her eyes widened and she folded me into a tight embrace. She held my hand and pulled me upstairs, where another girl my age sat, smoking a cigarette and listening to the radio. The girl offered me a cup of coffee and then stood to get it, as if the apartment was hers. Anaïs blushed and told me the girl's name, but I could not recall it for the life of me. We sat, the three of us, around Anaïs's little table and I nodded at her stories of the war's hardships, the failing hat business and its glorious postwar return. I listened without listening, as if Anaïs was background music I'd heard many times before and kept on for comfort. When she mentioned Sal e Pimenta, however, I perked up. She'd heard all of our new records, getting copies from Lucifer.

"I was wrong," Anaïs said. "You can sing. You just had to find your own way of doing it."

I smiled. "We're playing in Ipanema tomorrow night. I hope you'll be there—you and Madame L."

Anaïs paled. "You do not know? Lucifer has been arrested."

"For what?" I asked.

"For murder."

My ears burned. I gripped my coffee cup hard, so as not to drop it. "What murder?"

"One of Dutra's soldiers," Anaïs said. "Lucifer shot him. The officer called him a bicha in his own cabaret. And now that soldier is dead and Madame is locked in Frei Caneca."

I will admit that I felt relief, not concern.

After a fitful sleep, I woke early the next morning. Before the boys and Graça had even left their rooms, I popped two bennies, made my way to the hotel's entrance, and stepped into a cab. When I told the driver to take me to Frei Caneca, he glanced at me in the rearview mirror and kept glancing throughout the drive, probably wondering what business a woman who stays at the Copacabana Palace has at the city's penitentiary.

The visiting area smelled of raw onions and damp dishrags. A guard led Lucifer into the room, directing him to the rusted chair across from mine. He still had the prim, straight-backed posture of an aristocrat. His uniform was clean, his nails immaculate, and his hair, which he'd always taken great care to straighten and part in the middle, was twisted into a series of thin and elaborate braids that ran from his scalp down to the nape of his neck. He wore a necklace with a small leather pouch at the end; I'd seen such pouches before, at Auntie Ciata's house. The old-timers called them patuás and filled the pouches with herbs, tokens, beads, and other items important to candomblé. I'd never associated Madame Lucifer with the religion, but a stint in prison could make anyone devout.

"I'm glad you came to see me today," Lucifer said. "If you'd waited, I'd be gone. They're transferring me to Ilha Grande."

Ilha Grande, an island just off the coast, was home to one of the most violent penal colonies in Brazil. "Jesus," I said.

"No use calling on him to help me," Madame L. replied. "I guess some of these military boys thought I was getting too comfortable in here. You can buy anything here if you have money saved up, which I do, thanks to you and our Sofia Salvador. So I get to have my little luxuries and the guards look the other way. It won't be the same on Ilha Grande, of course."

"I'll get you a lawyer," I said.

"Don't waste your dollars," Lucifer replied. "Especially ones you don't have. Don't look at me like that! I read the news. You came back because you went bust out in L.A."

"We didn't go bust. We're still selling albums."

Madame L. smiled. "Sal e Pimenta? Your music's good, schoolgirl. But too different to be a hit. Your voice sounds like an old drunk's at a bar. Like you're whispering all your secrets and will regret it in the morning. But I like that."

"We're doing the show tonight, the one you set up at the club in Ipanema."

"That's a young place. And rich, too. Funny, that they like your stuff. But better to have a young audience than an old one. It means you can keep going for a while."

"Vinicius doesn't want to. He's staying here."

"And you're not?"

I shook my head.

"Give me a cigarette, won't you?" he asked.

I opened my purse and removed two from my case. The guards didn't even glance in our direction as I lit one cigarette for each of us.

Lucifer took several puffs while he studied my suit, my white gloves, my gold-buckled pumps.

"Age suits you," he said. "Some girls get better with time." He laughed and shook his head. "When you used to do odd jobs for me, I liked watching you sweep up. You swept that whorehouse floor like you were angry at the dirt for being there. You had ambition, schoolgirl. You'll always have it."

His voice sounded wistful, almost sad.

"When will they let you out?" I asked.

Madame L. tilted his head to one side. "Don't you know, schoolgirl? We're saying good-bye."

"You won't be in Ilha Grande forever."

"Twenty-seven years is a long time in a hard place," he said, then took a heavy drag of his cigarette. "They're finally letting her onstage at the Palace, those bastards. What's she going to sing?"

"I don't know. Nobody does. She's going to wing it, even though she's been wanting to play there all her life."

"And you wouldn't wing it?"

"No. I wouldn't."

"You think she'll bomb up there?"

I thought of Graça over the past year—sleeping more, flubbing her dance moves, returning from the Palm Springs clinic looking withered and lifeless. "No," I said.

"Do you want her to bomb?" he asked.

Our eyes met and locked, the way they had years before, across his desk, when I'd asked for his help. This time, Madame L. was the first to look away.

"Even if she forgets every word to every song, it won't matter, you know," he said. "People will talk about her for it. And they'll keep talking about her for a long time. She's the first of her kind."

"What kind is that?"

"A real star, the whole world over, born and bred right here in Brazil. People here might hate her for it, but they sure won't forget her. I envy her that."

Madame L. threw his cigarette to the floor and crushed it under his sandaled foot. He bowed his head, removed the patuá from his neck, and pressed the little leather pouch into my gloved hand. "We're all settled up, schoolgirl. There's no more debts between us."

Before I could respond, Madame L. spoke again.

"You could make a lot more records with what's in there," he said, pointing to the pouch. "It'll be easy to sell that now. You could make something for yourself, no one else. There's nothing wrong with wanting that. There's nothing wrong with taking what's owed you."

I pushed my chair away from the table.

"I have to go. I have the show in a few hours," I said.

Lucifer nodded. "I wish I could be there, watching you from the back table, like the old days."

I stepped out of the penitentiary and into another taxi that whisked me across town, to the Palace's doorstep. In the car I removed my gloves and pulled open the leather strings that pinched the patuá closed. Inside the pouch's dark mouth, the diamond sugar cube glittered.

The first time I saw that cube was in the Senhor's mill office, where I stood beside Graça while Senhora Pimentel asked for her husband's permission to take us to a concert in Recife. I had no idea what music was and why the Senhora thought we had to hear it; I'd only wanted to take that glittering sugar cube into my mouth and see if it would dissolve on my tongue. How naive I was to believe that something made to withstand centuries would simply disappear within me, as if by the sheer force of my will. And there it was, nearly fourteen years later, heavy in my hands.

At the Palace I did not return to my room but crossed the street, to the beach. My heels sunk into the hot sand. I squinted as I wove around the day's first beachgoers and made my way to an empty patch near the water. The leather pouch with the cube wrapped inside was as hard as a rock in my fist. Madame Lucifer was right—I could pawn that cube and get a stack of bills. Enough money to cut a few records with Vinicius; enough to help me stay in Rio, in a rented room like the old days; enough to escape from that flight back to L.A. I imagined Graça on that Aerovias plane, staring out a window while I stood alone onshore, watching her rise deep into the clouds.

I cocked my arm and flung the pouch far into the waves.

The club in Ipanema was small but orderly: bottles were neatly arranged behind the bar; the tables and chairs were new and identical, not a jumble of found items; and the stage (if you can call a wooden platform the size of a twin bed a stage) was freshly painted black. The fumes still lingered, forcing the club's owner to prop open the front and back doors for air. There were no microphones, no sound systems, and no electrical outlets.

"We'll have to sing louder than we do in the studio," Vinicius said as we studied the space. We'd arrived early, to avoid surprises.

"We don't belt out our songs," I said. "That's not how we wrote them. They're supposed to be quiet."

"Well, we're just going to have to figure out how to be quiet and loud at the same time," he said.

I nodded. A trickle of sweat moved down my side; if I didn't get a hold of myself, I'd be drenched by show's end. I found a seat at the empty bar and asked the owner for a drink.

What are you wearing tonight? Graça had asked before Vinicius and I left the hotel. I'd shrugged. *I can't let you onstage looking like an orphan,* she said, and riffled through my luggage, picking out a pair of black wide-legged trousers with satin piping along the sides and a blouse in beige silk. She'd dotted lipstick on my mouth and pinned my hair into an elegant twist. *There,* she said, and smiled. *Now you're a force to be fucking reckoned with.*

I'd smiled back and felt truly powerful in her presence, but by the time I'd had my second drink at the Ipanema club's bar, the lipstick had worn off and the twist in my hair was sagging.

"We should head backstage," Vinicius said.

People were starting to trickle into the club. Two chairs had been placed on the platform. Vinicius's guitar sat on a stand beside one chair. On the other was a box of matches and Kitchen's pandeiro. I wasn't a great player, but could hold my own. Kitchen had loaned it to me, knowing I'd need to have something to occupy my hands onstage.

Backstage, Vinicius and I sat in the club owner's cramped office, next to a mop closet. Vinicius rested a hand on my knee; I stopped tapping my foot.

"What matters is the music," he said. "It's just like we're cutting tracks in the studio, okay?"

I nodded. My mouth felt as if it had been wiped dry with cotton balls. Vinicius offered me water but I refused; the thought of liquid sloshing in my stomach made me want to vomit.

Heels clicked against the hall's floor. I smelled her before she even set foot in the office—rose perfume, as if she'd bathed in it.

"This joint's sure cozy," she said, then kissed Vinicius on the mouth and me on the cheek.

"I thought you were resting tonight," I croaked, rubbing her lipstick from my face.

"You think I'd miss this?" Graça stared at the mops. "They expect you to clean up afterward?"

"We don't need fancy dressing rooms," Vinicius replied.

"From the looks of it, you two don't need any dressing rooms," Graça replied. "Oh, don't be so sour! I'm joking, right, Dor?"

I held my head in my hands and stared at my shoes. Graça found a stool and dragged it next to me. There was a swish of silk and the waft of roses as she sat and placed her small hand on my back.

"Think of it like a roda," she said softly. "You're at Ciata's with the boys. I've taken a break and you've taken over. I'm sitting at the bar, right behind Vinicius. If you look up, you can see me, okay?"

I nodded into my hands. How many times had I imagined Graça watching me from the shadows while I shined onstage? Now I had my wish but couldn't enjoy it. Perhaps Anaïs was right: I couldn't withstand the rigors of being alone onstage. I wouldn't be alone, of course— I'd have Vinicius. But he wasn't Graça. I'd wanted a double act, just not this one.

I looked up from my hands, prepared to beg Graça to join us, but she'd already left the mop closet.

Out front, there was clapping. Whistles. The club's owner spoke, saying words like *underground, authentic, a new sound,* and some other baloney. Then there was the name we'd chosen: *Sal e Pimenta!* And more claps, more hoots and whistles. Vinicius pulled me to standing and we walked out together, into the stage's weak light. I don't recall how I made it into my chair, tilted to face both Vinicius and the audience. He smiled, waved, said some things that made the crowd chuckle. Then took up his guitar and looked at me.

He played the soft, repetitive introduction to "Between Us." Those first notes were supposed to be like waves, lapping the sand. We'd had that idea in the studio, Vinicius and I. The rhythm would be soft but insistent, a tide of sound.

He played the intro again. Gently, his foot tapped mine. I had to sing; yes. That was my job up there.

"Everything was a lark
between us.
Everything was child's play
between us.
Everything was
a silly bet,
a give and a get,
a laugh, a touch, a shared cigarette
between us."

My voice was soft. Too soft. Vinicius's guitar, the pandeiro in my hands, the patrons shifting in the club's small space, the clink of glasses from the bar—they drowned me out. Sweat prickled my forehead, as if a dozen mosquitoes were feasting on me. I wiped them away. Vinicius looked at me, his eyes wide. He kept playing. There were whispers in the crowd.

"Everything was a talk
when all others were sleeping.
Everything was a walk
when the beach was dark.
Everything was
your voice,
your smell,
your mouth closing around the secrets
between us."

I blinked sweat from my eyes, looking past Vinicius. Graça sat at the bar, her arms crossed, her mouth pinched in annoyance. She moved her thumb up, and mouthed the word "LOUDER." I nodded. Louder. Yes. I closed my eyes and placed a hand on my belly, as if I was once again in Anaïs's hat shop, practicing my singing. My voice rose, scratchy but full, and heavy with loss. I imagined it covering the space and everyone inside like a wool blanket. The noises around me hushed except for the notes Vinicius plucked from his guitar, notes I knew well, as well as my own heartbeat.

"Everything was a song
  between us.
Everything was all wrong
  between us.
Everything was
  a poem,
  a prayer,
  a plea
  between us."

The crowd was quiet but I felt their anticipation and their voracious need, as if each note, each word, each chord was vital to them. And I know exactly how they felt because I'd felt that way when I was twelve years old, sitting beside Graça and Senhora Pimentel in the Saint Isabel Theater listening to that fado singer. She'd made me forget myself, my mistakes, my poverty, my loneliness, my name. Listening to her, I was not Jega anymore. And after hearing her, I could never go without music again. It was not an addiction—addictions can be overcome—it was a necessity. I depended on it. And that was, I realized, what I'd always wanted to be: not memorable, but necessary. For a moment, in that club, I was.

There was quiet. Then clapping. Then cheers. Vinicius smiled and nodded, not approving, but asking: *Another?* I nodded back.

We played for two hours without stopping, and then we played two encores. At the show's end, Vinicius and I stood. He took my hand and kissed it, and I looked past him once again, to Graça. She was not smiling or clapping. She sat on her stool, legs crossed, looking intent, as if she was working out a math problem in her head. Basking in the glow of that show, and in the thrill of our songs made real by having listeners, I believed that Graça was seeing me for the first time as I saw myself in that brief moment: as someone who had arrived nervous and cowering, and had, by way of music, left transformed.

The Copa show was a crossroads, though we all saw our paths differently. The boys were leaving and we, of course, wanted our last show as a band to be a great one, not a failure. But I think all of us secretly hoped that the show would be such a success that the band wouldn't have to break up. That Sofia Salvador would be vindicated and Blue Moon reunited, and we would, all of us, return to how we were before, in the early days. There was another part of me that hoped for their failure, for a fresh start, for an excuse to stay behind with Vinicius (though he hadn't invited me to do this) and become Sal e Pimenta. And Graça? Where was she in these crossroads? Did she want to remain Sofia Salvador, or fail and make a new start as someone else? I realize now that her choices were not so cut-and-dried. In every success there is loss, and in every failure, a gain. Graça knew this better than anyone.

The Copacabana Palace had been renovated after we'd left Brazil. The main stage was round and exposed on all sides. There were no curtains to hide behind, no wings where an act could retreat. To get onto the stage, bands and singers entered through the ballroom's enormous mirrored doors and wound their way past the crowd. This was a performance in itself. The audience sat at silver two-top and four-top tables littered with ashtrays and drinks. Once the performers were finally on that massive circular platform, bathed in lights and surrounded by audience on all sides, there was no way they could be whisked easily offstage. The only way to exit was to wade back into the crowd.

The night of Sofia Salvador's homecoming show, the Copa was filled to capacity—more than seven hundred people sat around the stage and crammed the balconies. There were smiling Aerovias executives and stern-looking government men and their wives. There were newspaper reporters, critics, and samba stars who had stayed in Brazil and were considered patriots. Aracy Araújo sat beside a general at a table nearest the stage. There were entrepreneurs made wealthy by the war, along with representatives of some of the most traditional and aristocratic families in Rio. The Lion sat in the front row. In the far upper balconies were fans from Lapa, Glória, and the city's center; Rádio Mayrink and Aerovias had offered tickets in a raffle to fifty lucky listeners. President Dutra was not in the audience—his wife, affectionately known as the Little Saint, had taken ill. A photographer positioned himself near the stage, alongside several men holding microphones for Mayrink. The show would be broadcast live across Brazil.

There was no "backstage" at the Copa; there was only an unmarked door outside the main stage that led to a white, windowless hallway smelling of bleach and cigarette smoke. The corridor wound into the bowels of the hotel, past exposed pipes, doors marked "Do not enter!" and painted signs leading waiters and staff to the kitchen and bar. One of the doors in this hall opened to a dressing room for performers. In the minutes before the show, the Blue Moon boys looked solemn in their best black tuxedos while I paced and smoked. Graça was nowhere to be found.

When she finally appeared, the beads of her skirt dragged across the floor, making her sound as if she was on rollers.

She wore the costume custom-made by Aerovias for the event—a cropped red satin top; a massive skirt weighing fourteen kilos and hand-beaded in the Aerovias colors of red and blue; red lipstick; her pixie cut, freshly dyed black for the show; and the fist-sized earrings in the shape of roses that she'd brought from L.A. (She'd refused to re-wear the airplane earrings Aerovias had made for her.)

"Fucking skirt," Graça said, when her hem caught on a nail sticking from one of the dressing room's stools. Graça tugged and the skirt ripped. Beads scattered across the floor.

"Let me run upstairs and get your extra skirt," I said. "These beads will keep falling off when you're onstage."

"Let them," Graça said, and shrugged.

"But you'll slip when you're dancing," I said. "You'll fall."

Graça touched my cheek. "I used to hate your gloom and doom. But I'm glad you're around to worry about me. I couldn't do this with-out you."

Later, during the show, I'd learn that Graça didn't plan on doing much dancing. But in the moment, I was so jarred by her affection that I didn't hear the knock on the dressing room door. A stagehand an-nounced that it was time. Then the boys and Graça held one another's hands, forming a circle, with me on the outside.

Being part of an audience is like wading into a pool filled with strangers—you share the same waters, and when someone moves, even slightly, you feel the ripple. Without realizing, you also begin to move, and your movement sends its own signal. During any live perfor-mance there is always an exchange—not only from performer to the audience, but also within the audience itself.

As soon as Sofia Salvador and Blue Moon walked through the seated crowd and onto the stage, I could feel the audience's grim deter-mination. There were a few scattered claps from the Aerovias executives that quickly stopped, as if they'd clapped out of turn and then realized their error. Sofia Salvador smiled.

"Hello, friends!" she called out.

The audience was mute. Graça glanced back at the Blue Moon boys and growled: "Give them 'Turned into a Gringa.'" The boys obeyed.

At the time, I didn't know why she'd chosen that song; I thought she'd lost her power to read a room. The audience wasn't going to make it easy for Sofia Salvador; they would not welcome her back with open arms, but would make her work to earn their praise, and this work would be a kind of apology to them—to all of Brazil, listening on their radios—for having left them. But "Turned into a Gringa" had never been an apologetic song.

Sofia Salvador's voice carried into the balconies. Her skirt littered beads across the stage and her legs moved like two pistons across them, grinding them to dust under her feet. She twirled her hands. She winked at men and women nearest the stage. She smiled and swiveled and batted her eyes. The Blue Moon boys played their instruments with similar gusto. When no one in the audience returned Sofia Salvador's smiles, she became more energetic, but without her normal cheer and elation. Instead, her movements became sharp, her voice icy, as if she was caught in a fight she was determined to finish.

At the end of "Gringa," Sofia Salvador held up her arms, triumphant. Sweat beaded her forehead. Her chest heaved. The gang of Aerovias executives applauded enthusiastically, but quickly stopped when they realized they were the odd men out. Save a few limp claps from the balconies, everyone around Sofia Salvador was quiet. Reporters scribbled in their notebooks. The Lion grinned; failure sold more papers than triumph.

"Anyone have a chair for me?" Graça asked the crowd.

There was icy silence. Finally, one of the Aerovias men gamely lifted his chair up to the stage.

"Thank you, querido," Graça said, and sat.

I stood in the back of the ballroom, near the large doors where the band entered and exited. As soon as I saw Graça slump into that gold chair, I moved to the stage's steps; if she was unwell, I'd carry her away. Graça saw me catapulting toward her and she put her hand out, palm facing me, like a guard blocking my path.

"How about another seat, for my guitar player?" she asked. "He's getting old as the hills and heavy on his feet."

There were a few chuckles. Vinicius looked startled. Another Aerovias man passed his chair up.

"Sit," Graça ordered. Vinicius looked at Tiny, who shrugged. Then he obeyed Graça and sat across from her.

"I want to try something new tonight. Would you all like to see something new?"

There were a few hesitant claps.

"You see," Graça continued, "I get a feeling from this crowd tonight, that you want entertainment. Real entertainment. Not just what you have seen one hundred times before. Well, I live to serve you."

There were whispers. Aracy Araújo wiggled in her chair. The crowd was both intrigued and nervous—myself included. Was Sofia Salvador drunk, or desperate? What would she show us? Would the night be a disaster or a revelation?

Sofia Salvador unclipped one earring, then another, dropping them to the floor beside her chair. She ran a hand through her hair, making it stand oddly on end. With the tips of her nails she peeled off her fake eyelashes and flicked them behind her like bugs. Then she reached into the bosom of her dress and removed a white handkerchief. Instead of blotting the sweat from her face, she placed the white square on her mouth and wiped one way, then the other, again and again, until the cloth was smeared red and her mouth was raw and pink.

She stood, released her mike from its stand, wove the cord away from her feet, and sat. Then, without a nod or a look at Vinicius, she sang in the sweetest of whispers:

"Everything was a lark
between us.
Everything was child's play
between us."

Vinicius looked on in disbelief, then quickly composed himself and followed Graça's lead. Behind them, the boys began to understand the groove and played low and slow, never overpowering the softness of Sofia Salvador's voice.

She sang every song, in the same order, from my Ipanema set the night before. She sang them the way I had sung them, only better. Her voice was smoother, yes, but there was a terrible loneliness inside it, as if she was singing by herself in an empty nightclub and not in the greatest venue in Brazil. She didn't miss a word or a beat, as if she had known the songs for ages; as if they were hers all along, never mine; as if the act she'd stolen from me was not an act at all but a genuine plea to her audience. Only Vinicius and I knew the truth.

She was a different Sofia with her small eyes and smeared mouth—gentler and older. She had stripped herself bare before them. In return, their quiet felt different than before: attentive, curious, a little embarrassed for her.

I stared at her ruffled hair, at her discarded earrings, at the soiled handkerchief beside her foot. She had not asked for a napkin. She had not wiped her mouth with the back of her palm. She'd had the handkerchief ready, waiting, in her dress. And her eyelashes: they had been plucked off as easily as petals from a flower. Her unmasking had been achieved in a few graceful sweeps. That kind of spontaneity took great planning.

At show's end, Graça closed her eyes as if she were savoring some rare delicacy. Then she stood and bowed. The audience was painfully quiet, as if it had rehearsed this silence many times beforehand and was intent on sticking to its original script. Only a few brave souls in the balcony clapped. At the table nearest to the stage, Aracy Araújo, looking dazed, turned to the general beside her and started whispering. Others in the room followed suit, turning their chairs back to their tables, lighting cigarettes, taking long gulps of their stiff drinks, and speaking in hushed voices, as if they'd just witnessed a car wreck and were unsure of how to respond, or if any of the casualties were even worth saving.

Slowly, Graça stepped off the stage. Vinicius held her arm so she would not tumble under the weight of her skirt. She walked with her head high through the crowd, which made a great effort not to watch her leave. I caught many glance up from their drinks and conversations to watch Sofia Salvador's last exit from the Copacabana Palace. The Blue Moon boys trailed behind her, mouths clenched, jaws rigid with fury. Tiny's eyes pooled. When he finally allowed himself to blink, near the exit, two fat tears ran down his cheeks and into his mouth. Before I followed them out the door I looked back at the stage where Sofia Salvador's earrings lay, glittering and discarded, on the floor.

THE END OF ME

Quiet, please.
Quiet's what I need, a
moment to find my way
out of this maze, querida.
You were sugar on my tongue—
sweet grit.
Now you're gone.
Is there sense to make of it?

I'm wandering.
Let me be.
Following a great samba,
that always escapes me.

Walking our old haunts.
Visiting our beginnings.
Watching the pretty girls walk by—
now my head is spinning.
Life's played its greatest trick
    on me:
there are only dead ends left,
you see.

I'm wandering.
Let me be.
Hearing it now, faint but true—
a song I'll never play again:
    you and me,
me and you.

The leaf forgives the tree
for shedding it.
The shell forgives the sea
for crushing it to sand.
Can I forgive myself, amor,
for digging this grave with
    my own two hands?

Quiet, please.
Quiet's what I need.
I've caught it alive
and won't set it free,
until I sing this samba about
the end of me.

There are moments, just before I wake, when I forget where I am. Am I curled on a hard pallet next to Nena? Am I in one of Sion's narrow school cots? Am I in a dilapidated Lapa room or in our Bedford Drive mansion? The possibilities list themselves in my head, and, just by the fact that I can create this list, I know those places and the people who inhabited them are gone from me and from the world.

Vinicius and I bought this house thirty years ago, after we'd married and back when Miami Beach was considered a haven for the elderly and the outcast. Vinicius and I stubbornly believed we were neither. It is a sprawling, many-windowed home with a courtyard and an old Spanish façade and more bathrooms than seems reasonable. It puts the Great House to shame.

When we moved in, there were two trees in the front yard: one large and one small. The smaller one had germinated in a crevice of the other. The small tree's roots wound down the large tree's trunk and its branches up. It wrapped itself around the larger tree in a net of limbs until they looked as if they were bound in an embrace.

"They're dancing," Vinicius liked to say.

Our gardener asked if he could hack the smaller tree away. "A strangler fig," he called it. "No good."

"Let it be," I ordered, and found us a new gardener.

During our first years in this house, Vinicius and I watched the small tree in our yard catch up to the larger one in size and stature. They were the same height, their branches the same width, and they clung to each other tightly, like lovers. Over time, the smaller tree enfolded the other almost completely in its ropy limbs and roots, until all we could see of the older tree was a thick, solitary branch reaching out from the strangler fig's grip.

Vinicius and I had a happy life together in Miami: walking the beach every morning, stopping for cafecitos at the same diner each afternoon, and producing new records. We even toured briefly as Sal e Pimenta, visiting Europe and Cape Verde, playing small shows until Vinicius's memory began to fail him. We never played Brazil. After Graça's death, we never returned home. At first because Vinicius and I were angry about that Copa show and its aftermath. And then because the military boys had taken over the country and either muzzled or arrested artists like us. Vinicius always said we'd go home when Brazil was a democracy again. In 1988 this happened, but by then it was too late. Brazil wasn't even a memory for Vinicius anymore. If he missed it, it was in the same way he missed all of the places and people he eventually forgot: silently, and with tears. Most days he was cheerful, but other days he'd sit in our courtyard and stare at those dancing trees, his cheeks wet and nose dripping. I'd bring him a handkerchief and kneel to wipe his face. If he remembered me, it was as a safe and enduring presence, like a favorite chair or a faithful dog, but not as Dor. I, too, became a blank space for him, wiped clean from his memory.

What endured were the songs. Not our songs from the Sal e Pimenta days, though their melodies were more complex and their lyrics better. No, the songs that stayed with Vinicius, the ones he sang even when he could no longer hold a fork and, later, when words were not available to him, the songs he hummed, were our earliest tunes, the ones we'd recorded in Lapa. He asked me to play those records over and over, and when he could no longer ask for anything and had to go to the hospital, I lugged our record player into his room and played them there. The songs we return to again and again allow us to hear something new in them each time. They are familiar and yet mysterious, like our greatest loves.

"Where's Graça?"

He'd ask for her when he could still speak. And even when her name left him, she didn't.

"Is she coming? When will she be here?"

"Soon," I'd say. "You know how long it takes her to get ready."

This always made him smile.

When words left him altogether, he'd stare at the door, waiting. Always waiting. His face as expectant as a child's. When I appeared in the doorway, he couldn't hide his disappointment.

In tropical forests, competition for light is fierce; the world under the canopy is as dark as dusk. I read this in a book, long ago. I also discovered other, kinder names for the ugly and ambitious little tree outside, the one that forced itself upon the back of the other: Ficus, Banyan, Epiphyte. It's in their nature to grasp, to embed, to grow up and down, all at once. By the time Vinicius died, his face still turned toward the hospital room's door, the original tree outside our house was a withered trunk in the middle of that thriving fig. Today, as I write this, even that dead trunk is gone. The fig is hollow in its center, a circle without a core, but it carries on.

I listen to those early songs now, too. Every night. And I do it for the same, simple reason Vinicius did—not to honor our music or to reminisce about the two of us, but to hear Graça's voice.

THE END OF ME

If you have ever been in a car crash, or escaped a fire, or experienced the sudden, nauseating drop of an airplane as if the imaginary string keeping it afloat has suddenly been cut, or if you've experienced any number of less dramatic but equally perilous incidents—a car stops short and knocks you over; food lodged in your throat makes you unable to breathe; a slip and a fall and that moment before you hit the ground where time seems to lengthen and you steel yourself for the impact—then you understand how, in the moments after, when you realize you've been spared, your sheer relief evaporates and you feel something else entirely. It's in these moments that we're confronted with life's cruel indifference to our survival. We realize that we are at the mercy of forces we cannot fathom; the control we thought we'd exerted over our lives slips like a fish through our hands.

This is how I felt that night, after Graça closed her Copa show.

Before we arrived at the door, marked "Employees Only," that led to the dressing room, a military boy ran behind our group.

"Wait!" he called, breathless. "I don't know about people's manners downstairs, in the good seats, but I thought you were out of sight!"

Without a word, Graça cupped the boy's face in her hands and kissed him lightly on the mouth. Then she opened the employee door and disappeared behind it.

We didn't bother stopping at the dressing room, where a Mayrink reporter waited. A waiter slipped us through the hotel's kitchen, where we found the freight elevator. Inside, the Blue Moon boys were mute. The elevator's iron gate pressed into my back. My head felt like a fragile instrument wrapped in cotton batting.

Vinicius spoke. What did he say? I could not hear, but Graça's expression changed, her face suddenly stern.

"We needed to try," she said.

"No, *you* needed to try," Vinicius replied. "Those were our songs, mine and Dor's. They don't work for you."

Graça crossed her arms over her red top.

"So you two are better than the rest of us?" she asked. "And what about that thing you used to say: 'Nobody owns samba.' Well, I guess you don't believe it. I didn't butcher those songs, I made them better."

The elevator shuddered and whined like a wounded beast, and we were all trapped in its belly.

"Dor? You okay?" Vinicius asked. His voice was muffled, as if I'd pressed a cup to a wall and he was on the other side. I can't remember what I said in reply, but his body slumped, his face fell slack.

"What did you expect me to do?" he asked. "Leave halfway through? Refuse to play? We had seven hundred people watching. I didn't know she was going to do this."

When we finally lurched to a stop at our penthouse floor, the boys left but Vinicius stayed inside the elevator. I almost stayed with him, but Graça pulled me out by the arm.

"Don't ditch me," she said.

She held my hand very tightly during the walk down the long hallway to her suite, as if she knew that if she let go, even once, I would run.

I often dream of Graça's suite at the Palace. I walk on its glossy terrazzo floor past wide sofas and long yellow curtains. In my dreams, the suite's colors are dingy and muted, as if someone had dipped a paintbrush into dirty water and wiped it across the entire scene. It is larger, too—a labyrinth of tables, lamps, and chairs that I wind my way around, attempting to get to the closed French doors of her bedroom, although I do not want to go there. In my dreams I feel a terrifying, heart-stopping dread the closer I get to those curtained doors, yet my feet carry me there anyway, step by step, even as I hold on to the furniture in an attempt to stop myself. When the door is finally in front of me, I tell myself to move away, to run, to step back, yet I reach out and turn the handle. As soon as this happens, I always wake. I am alone in my Miami bed, sweating and gasping for air. Vinicius is no longer here to comfort me. Even when he was, I only pretended to be calmed so that he would fall back asleep. Then I would creep out of our room, knowing I wouldn't sleep the rest of the night, knowing that I'd already opened that door and seen what lay behind it, and this was not a vision I could erase or a nightmare I could wake myself from.

The suite was on the Palace's top level, overlooking the ocean. That night, after the show, the view from the suite's windows was as black as coal, except for the lights of a few boats. They looked like fireflies trapped in tar.

Graça flicked on the lights. The dark ocean disappeared and there was only our reflection in the glass—Graça in her smeared stage makeup and tousled hair, me in the black evening gown she'd called plain, and it was.

Graça covered her eyes and flicked the switch back down. "I'm so sick of lights," she said.

The room went black again. I stayed perfectly still. Only my

breath—quick, ragged from too many cigarettes smoked backstage—
gave my presence away.

"I'll die if I don't get this fucking costume off. It's like carrying an
extra body," Graça said, unzipping her skirt and letting it fall, with a
thump, to the floor.

My eyes began to adjust to the darkness. I watched Graça move
slowly to the bathroom. The faucet creaked and water rushed from the
tub's tap. I dropped my purse; the arsenal of pills inside rattled in their
glass vials. Then I groped my way forward, careful of everything that
blocked my path.

Graça was in her robe. A candle flickered on the stone countertop.
She sat upon the vanity's small stool and tilted her head up. Then she
swiped wet cotton balls roughly across her face, her hands moving at a
frantic pace. Even in the candlelight I could make out the few thin
hairs left in her eyebrows after years of plucking. There were creases
around her mouth, a series of stubborn little wrinkles across her forehead. Graça kept her eyes on me as she worked.

The room grew hot. My gown felt wilted and sticky.

"The tub's going to overflow," Graça said.

I turned mechanically and shut the tap. Steam rose from the water.
My hands shook. Gently, Graça pushed me aside.

She let her robe drop. I turned my back but it was impossible not to
glimpse her in that vast, mirrored bathroom. The pounds she'd lost
again and again in Palm Springs had returned. The tops of her arms
were thick, her stomach meaty. She looked like a woman from an ancient Italian painting, all soft flesh and dimples. She climbed into the
steaming water and sat without hesitation, taking up a sponge and rubbing her arms.

"Are you going to be a mute all night?" she asked. "I'm the one that
bombed out there, not you."

Her spine was like a piece of rope caught under her skin. I resisted the urge to trace it with my fingers, to tug it underwater and hold it there. "Those were my songs."

Graça let out a long sigh. Her breath cut through the steamy air. "So you'll get all the credit for my flop."

The room's heat made my cheeks prickle. "I don't want credit."

"You always want credit," Graça said, and leaned back to wet her hair. Her breasts bobbed on the water's surface, round and pink. I closed my eyes.

"You planned that bit with the makeup, the earrings," I said.

Graça sat back up. "I couldn't keep doing the same old thing. I needed something new. When I saw you, in Ipanema, that was it. You know how important this show was for all of us. It was do-or-die. I needed your act."

"I'm not an act."

"Sure you are," Graça said. "We all are. Everything's an act, from the minute we wake up and open our eyes."

"You can't sing them anymore. I won't let you."

Graça let out a high-pitched laugh. "Nobody wants me to sing anymore."

She pushed herself from the water, stepping out of the tub. Her hair dripped down her neck. She sighed and seemed to deflate, burying her face in a towel and keeping it there for a long time.

Her shoulders did not shake; she wasn't crying, was she? Had she become dizzy? Or was she composing herself, like an actress about to go onstage? These are the questions I asked myself as I stood in that sweltering bathroom. I've had decades to look back on this night, on this moment, to put the pieces into place again and again and wonder how I might have changed them or rearranged them to give us all a different outcome. It is futile, this kind of reminiscing. It is a cruel game with no winner, because I cannot go back to that night. I cannot erase my mistakes. I cannot be kinder, more generous, more understanding. I cannot tell myself to put aside my pride, my anger, my sense of retribution. Now, I see things more fully. I see those many uncomfortable minutes when Graça hides her face in her towel as a kind of plea I did not answer. I couldn't, because in that moment, I thought myself the victim and Graça, the thief.

When she finally emerged she dropped the towel and moved toward me, naked and trailing water with each step. She took my hand in her wet one.

"I've had this awful feeling, ever since *Fruity Cutie*," she said. Shadows from the candlelight distorted her face, making it look as if she was made of putty, melting in the room's heat. "I know Vinicius doesn't want to stay with me. Hell, he's so mad at me right now, he's probably already packed his bags. Singing's the only thing I could ever really do. Every day I wake up and I think, *How much longer?* How much longer do I have to trudge through this fucking life before I can get in front of a crowd again, before I can sing again. I used to be able to wait, you know? The time between shows didn't feel so long. But now? Shit, now a day feels like forever. I just . . . I can't seem to get things right out here, in life. But up there, in front of people, boy do I nail it every time! Except for tonight. Tonight I couldn't make them love me again."

Her voice cracked. The steam made my nostrils burn and no matter how many breaths I took, I felt short of air. I let go of her hand and moved away, across the room, hoping the distance could stop her from winning my forgiveness. I wanted the Graça who'd pulled my hair and fought me in Riacho Doce's river; the one who'd tricked the Sion nuns; the one who'd yelled and cursed and called me names in Lapa. I wanted her meanness, her smallness, her stinging words, her bite. I wanted an opponent, not a victim.

"That was my music," I said. "You should've asked me for it."

She flinched as if I'd shaken her awake. Then her face changed, her gaze sharpening, her features hardening into a kind of mask. And my heart leapt.

"And if I'd asked, if I'd begged you, you think you would've given those songs to me?" Graça said, shaking her head. "I don't want to be rich, or known, or given credit like you do. I want to be magnificent. Do you even know what that means? You've never been magnificent a day in your life. You want to be, but you aren't. So you put yourself around people who are, like me. Like Vinicius. You want everything that's mine, but you'll never get it. You can't. You'll always be Jega in fancy clothes."

We were girls again, meeting for the first time in that empty Great House hallway where everything I'd come to know was changing: the tiny scrap of freedom I'd experienced was being taken away; everything I'd pretended was mine had never truly belonged to me, and never would. And there was Graça, with her cork-colored eyes and beautiful pink mouth, as proof. *Jega.* She'd never before called me that name.

The bathroom was small. My legs were long. In two paces I was in front of Graça. I gave her two gorgeous slaps across the face, my hand bouncing off both of her cheeks. Graça's eyes lit. I curled a hand around her neck, feeling her pulse under my fingers. It would have been easy to squeeze harder, to press all the air out of her as if she was a balloon. Wasn't this the fight I'd wanted?

Graça moved her hands up, toward me, but instead of gripping my hands, instead of fighting to make me let go, Graça placed her hands on my face, cupping my cheeks the way a mother might hold a child's.

"Don't you fucking leave me, Dor," she wheezed. "Everybody leaves me. But not you."

I let go. Graça wrapped her arms around my waist and rested her head on my chest. She whimpered and gasped like a small, hurt animal until the front of my gown was damp. Then Graça, naked, stared up at me with wet eyes, her nose red and her mouth trembling, and I grabbed her again, only gently this time and for a different purpose.

Kiss. To say this word in English, your lips must pull back, your teeth must lock together so that you may press air through them and make a hissing noise. *Beijo* is quite different. To say *beijo*, you must pucker your lips. You must do as the word intends. What Graça and I did as girls in our little Lapa room, those were beijos—soft, wet, hesitant at first and then, slowly, becoming bold. What we did in the Copa's bathroom was nothing like those early beijos of ours.

Graça's teeth clicked against mine. Her tongue was a muscle—hard, probing, intent on prying me wide. I tried to shake my head away but Graça clapped her hands to either side of my face. I tried to catch her, to grasp her into some kind of calm submission, but she was still wet from her bath and slipped under my fingers. She was roundness and muscle, softness and resistance.

It was not as I'd imagined it. How could I not have let myself imagine, from time to time, what it might've been like to kiss her again? In that vast, unbounded landscape of my imagination there were many places I went, and this was one of them. I could not allow myself to visit often because, like walking into a field of uncut cane, I was afraid of losing myself inside or emerging covered in a thousand invisible wounds from head to toe. But there were moments when I did enter, and what I pictured was Graça both amazed and afraid—not of me but of herself, of the extent of her wanting me and nothing else. And all the while there would be a perfect rhythm between us—our breaths, our movements, even our intentions would sync so seamlessly that we would not be able to tell Dores from Graça, Jega from Sofia Salvador.

How faraway this fantasy seemed that night, in the Copa's bathroom! My mind whirred as Graça pressed on, intent, it seemed, at completing a task. *Is this her way of giving me comfort?* I thought. *No, this is her way of getting comfort.* But that didn't seem right either, and all I could think of was her onstage, wiping away her red lips. And the songs. My songs.

I stepped out of our embrace.

"Why are you doing this?" I asked. "Why now?"

Graça put her arms tightly around me again. "Shut up. Just keep kissing me."

I shook my head. "I can't."

She moved her face closer to mine.

"Not now," I said. "I won't."

Graça's nails dug into my cheeks. "Do it," she ordered. "Just take it."

"No."

I stumbled from the bathroom, into the dark, cool air of the suite, taking deep and gulping breaths, as if I'd been trapped underwater.

Graça slumped in the doorway. She wiped her mouth, leaning weakly like a boxer staring at her opponent after receiving a particularly vicious blow.

"So you're leaving," she said, her voice small. "You don't want me."

What could I do but deliver the knockout punch?

"No," I said, "no one does."

I left. My arms ached from our bathroom tussle. My hands shook so badly that I had trouble closing the suite's door behind me. In the elevator, I reached for a cigarette but realized I'd left my bag—and in it my room key, my entire arsenal of bennies and Blue Angels, and my cigarettes—back in Graça's room. For an instant, I thought of pressing the elevator's buttons and going back.

I recalled our first concert in Recife, lifetimes ago, when we were children and yet Graça had not behaved as a child might have. She hadn't ridiculed me for crying, or held me at a distance. She'd given me comfort as no one before or since had ever done. Jega—always kicked and slapped and threatened—had been held and understood. Why hadn't I been able to do the same for her in that bathroom? She'd wanted comfort, wanted to fall into the oblivion of another's body. Hadn't I sought the same kind of comfort so many times before, from so many women and men? Yet I'd denied her, and myself, the pleasure of that comfort.

As I stood inside that Copa elevator with its brass gate and padded walls, I wanted badly to return to Graça's suite. I wanted to hold Graça and shake her, yell at her, tell her what a mistake she'd made. If she'd only asked, I would have given her anything. Everything. But Graça— always the Little Miss—had called me Jega and then commanded me to grasp whatever scraps I'd been given.

Do it. Just take it.

Hearing this order, my choice was already made.

After searching the hotel bar and the backstage corridors, I finally found Vinicius on the beach. He'd walked a little ways from the hotel, to a more secluded spot near the water. Tide was low, the waves only ripples. A massive sandbar extended nearly to the horizon, where the moon sat, round and white like a low-hanging fruit that we could twist and pluck.

"Jesus," he said when he saw me. My hair was unpinned. My gown sweated through. I wore no shoes. I began to take huge gulps of air, but couldn't fill my lungs. I tried harder, my face wet now, my eyes losing their focus. Vinicius caught me in his arms.

Shhh, shh, shhh, he said, and rocked me gently, as if putting a child to sleep.

I didn't want to leave that embrace, didn't want to have to sit on the sand and explain myself. What would I explain? That I was still Jega? That I would always be Jega? That Graça believed I'd always wanted to steal from her, and I had. And she'd stolen from me. We were a pair of thieves, she and I—a perfect pair—always looking for one more thing to take from each other. That night, in her suite, there was nothing left.

I unwound myself from Vinicius and looked up, wondering if I could see Graça's penthouse window from the beach; if her light would be on, or if she'd be a shadow at the glass, staring down at the beach, at us. When I looked up I saw only Vinicius, and he saw me. Both of us wounded. Both wanting the same thing, but never able to fully grasp it.

He bent his head into my neck. The tip of his nose moved from my collarbone upward, taking in my scent. I held tightly to him, afraid my knees would buckle, afraid I'd fall and that the sudden movement might startle Vinicius away. *Shouldn't I want to startle him away?* I thought, and then I stopped thinking altogether.

There is no stubble on a woman's cheek. There is no smell of after-shave or sweat. There is a softness, an exquisite delicateness, to a wom-an's mouth that one will never encounter in a man's. But sometimes you do not want a calm bay—you want a rough ocean. You want to be tossed by waves, to be pounded into sand and rubbed raw, to feel your lungs and body burn until you finally, thankfully, come up for air.

I was twenty-six years old—a child! I wasn't wise enough to be able to weigh my conflicting desires and see which should be fed and which left to wither. I fed them all. And isn't that the beauty and the danger of youth: that reckless ability to feel without asking yourself why, or how, or if that feeling is good or bad for you? What did I truly want in that moment on the beach with Vinicius? I wanted what all of us want at one point or another: to be yearned for; to be the very center of someone's longing—only me, the star of the show.

A chord is three notes struck simultaneously. It is the basis of har-mony and disharmony. I learned this late in life.

That famous young musician who recorded with me in Las Vegas also did me the favor of teaching me about music's more technical aspects. I asked for the lesson. After our recording sessions, he patiently explained to me about chords, pitch, tempo, and timbre, among other things. The more he spoke, the more I realized that he was simply giving names to things I always knew existed. *Harmony. Contour. Melody. Tone. Rhythm. Meter. Key.* I'd spent my life sensing these aspects of music without ever knowing what to call them, or why.

I take great comfort in the fact that music existed before anyone could pin names onto it, and music will exist even when language fails us. And it will fail us; it always does. We think we need words because it is in our nature to define, to decode, to try to understand by piecing things apart and labeling them, like specimens in a museum. A child is born and we give it a name, but it is not the naming that brought the child into being. Our names make us easy to recall, and by recalling we believe we know, and by knowing we believe we understand. Names bring us comfort. It is the things we cannot name that frighten us most.

Here we are then, after so many sleepless nights, and all I've done is arrive at the point in the story where most choose to begin. Why did all those reporters, biographers, and hacks choose to start their stories about Sofia Salvador here? Because death sells books and magazines, and Sofia Salvador's death came too soon, and (for most) without warning.

Contrary to popular belief, I've told this part of the story many times. So many times, in fact, that I vowed never to tell it again. In the days after she died, I repeated the story over and over to police, military officials, the lawyer I was forced to hire, and to the Blue Moon boys, of course. It's infuriating how twelve short hours can come to define our lives and the stories others tell about them. If I wrote a song about us—Graça, Vinicius, the Blue Moon boys, and me—this part of our story should merit only a line. But, like a drum setting the rhythm of the entire melody, it has become the heartbeat of our song.

V inicius found her. Most days I am grateful for this.

He and I fell asleep on the beach, side by side. Without having taken any Blue Angels that night, I didn't fall into the dreamless trance they usually provided. Instead, I dreamed of Riacho Doce. I stood before a sea of cane. Nena was next to me. The cane towered over us. When the wind hit, I heard the cane's stalks scrape one another, like knives sharpening. Behind us, something let out a wail—hoarse and desperate. An animal, wounded? I looked back and Riacho Doce disappeared.

The sun was too bright; I could barely open my eyes. The boning under the satin corset of my black gown pinched my sides. My left hand was numb. I sat up and shook it until it tingled back to life. My head throbbed. Grains of sand crunched between my teeth.

Vinicius and I hobbled into the hotel. It was still very early; hardly any guests were up and about. The Palace's staff stole sideways glances at us as we called the elevator. Inside, we didn't speak or look at each other. Then I stood before my room's door, while Vinicius bid me good-bye.

"I'm going to face the music now," he said.

He and Graça still shared a room. Had he meant that he was going to face her foul temper? Would he leave Sofia Salvador and Blue Moon that morning? Would he tell her about our night together on the beach? Would this be his revenge on her, as it was mine? Who knows. We never answered these questions, even though they seemed vital at the time.

As Vinicius shuffled down the hallway, I stood before my room's door, blinking at the lock. I didn't have my key. I'd have to face Graça, too, if I wanted the purse I'd left in her room. I looked down the hall but Vinicius was gone. Then I thought I was dreaming again, because the wailing I'd heard earlier, in my sleep, came back. Only it was louder now, and coming from Graça's room.

The door hadn't been locked. Inside, it was bright. The curtains were wide open. The French doors were closed. The howling came from behind them. I turned the knob and walked inside.

The bedroom smelled sickeningly sweet, like Lapa's alleyways after Carnaval. Vinicius sat on the floor beside her bed, his mouth open. Graça lay at his knees. The bedsheets were satin and I remember thinking how slippery satin was, and that's why she had fallen out of bed. But why wasn't she cussing or joking? Why didn't she open her eyes? Everything in that room looked familiar but also terribly askew, as things sometimes do in dreams. I wondered again if I was still asleep.

I knelt beside Graça. Something wet and cold seeped through the skirt of my gown, where my knees touched the floor. Vomit—yellow, like congealed mustard—puddled under us. It had seeped under Graça's head, clumping in her hair. A yellow crust dotted the corners of her mouth and coated her chin. Her hand was cold, the fingers stiff.

I heard myself talking, but can't recall the words. When I think back on this moment I see Vinicius's once handsome face, rigid with shock. He'd stopped wailing and listened, intently, to me. Apparently I told him to call a doctor. Not the Copa hotel's doctor on call, but our doctor. One we could trust. Dr. Farias, the man who'd treated Graça during her stint at Urca years before. I didn't know his telephone number but I somehow remembered his address: Barata Ribeiro Street, in Copacabana. I told Vinicius to ask the telephone operator to find him and only him, though I had no idea if Dr. Farias was still alive. The police asked me over and over to recount what I'd said to Vinicius.

How did you know this doctor?

He helped us before.

Helped?

Yes, helped.

In what way?

In a doctor's way.

Why call a private doctor?
She would never let a stranger touch her.
Why did you tamper with the body?
Tamper?
Why did you move her?
Because she was cold. She needed to be warm.
You thought she was still alive?

Vinicius was gone, off to find a telephone. I stared dumbly around Graça's bedroom. On her bedside table was my purse, its mouth open on its side, and my bottles of Blue Angels and bennies sat empty, their caps discarded on the floor.

How many Nembutals, Benzedrines, codeines, and Seconals had I brought on that trip? Fifty? Sixty? How many were left on the night Graça and I fought? I'd taken two Blue Angels on the plane, two bennies on our first day in Brazil. Or did I take more? Did I give the boys some pills on the airplane, or backstage before the show? I've tried to account for those pills so many times over the years—first to police, then to Vinicius, then to myself. I close my eyes and think of those amber vials and try to recall the numbers and colors of the tablets left inside. It's ridiculous, really, the amount of time one can spend fretting over what doesn't matter, and what can't be changed. It doesn't matter how many pills were in those vials when I left her room. What matters is that they were all empty when I returned.

I brushed my hand through Graça's hair. Vomit smeared my fingers. Suddenly I was in the bathroom, wetting one washcloth, then another. I dabbed her face. I wiped her hair and her arms. I cleaned the floor.

I tried to prop Graça to sitting, so I could wash the back of her head. She was heavier than I'd expected. She would not bend at the waist no matter how much I coaxed her, so I somehow found the strength to heave her into bed. I put a blanket on her. Her hair, wet from my washing, soaked the pillow. In the bathroom I found a tube of her red lipstick. Graça never saw visitors without lipstick.

Did you know that the most essential part of any voice is air? Empty space. You must make room for your voice to pour out. Great singers know how to relax their throats and tongues when they sing. They know how to breathe so that they expand their bodies, taking in as much air as possible, sustaining each note for as long as humanly possible. It is air, after all, that makes our vocal cords vibrate. The air we breathe is our voice's food. It is its source.

Vinicius said, later, that as he and the boys ran back down the presidential suite's private hallway, they heard a terrible kind of moan that went on and on, for as long as they ran down that interminable hall. The voice did not die, did not pause, did not stop to catch its breath. Hearing it, Vinicius said, made his stomach drop.

Funny. When I was curled beside Graça in bed, her small, cold hand in mine, I believed I was singing to her.

How long before Dr. Farias and the Blue Moon boys erupted into the suite, ruining our peace? The police report says thirty minutes.

I remember Vinicius squatting in the corner, his hands over his face. I felt Tiny pulling me, gently, from the bed beside her. I could not move. He and Kitchen carried me, curled as I had been on the bed, to the couch. There was shouting. Police. A forensic investigator brought a camera to document the scene.

The photographs were leaked to Brazilian magazines and, later, American ones. In those black-and-white pictures she looks serene in her bed. Her skin is clean. Her lips are dark and glossy. Even in death, she is a star.

In their report, the military police wrote that the deceased was moved from the floor to her bed. It's a detail that biographers and conspiracy theorists like to bandy about. As if it's even important. I was asked many times about the pills I'd left with her: What kind, how many, what for? It was later, after the autopsy, that I'd gotten different questions: Was she upset after the Copa performance? Did I notice signs of mental unsteadiness? Why had I left so many pills in her possession? Why had I left her alone? Had she ever tried to hurt herself before?

There is Graça wading into the dark river, her hand clamped firmly around mine.

I won't go in too deep. And you're as strong as an ox.

And if I'm not?

Then we're both goners.

You'll drown.

I always save you. But you never save me.

That's not the story.

It's the story I want.

You can't do that. That's not how it goes. I could have obeyed. I could have stayed.

If you're not careful you'll stay here all your life.

We'll stay.

I almost feel real.

You are real. To me.

I'm so tired, Dor. How much longer?

Not long now, amor. Not long at all.

Sofia Salvador received a funeral worthy of a head of state. If in life she was an American puppet, in death she became Brazil's beloved victim who had escaped a hostile USA and returned home to re-create herself, introducing a new form of samba only to be tragically cut short from seeing it flourish after her death.

Sofia Salvador could always read a crowd, and she wasn't wrong about the audience at the Copa: those reporters, socialites, government men, and nationalists had been intent on rejecting her. They were like scorned lovers, wanting to punish Sofia Salvador for leaving them and then for returning so boldly. What Sofia Salvador could not see from the Copa's stage—what none of us saw—were all those listening, rapt, to the radio broadcast across Brazil. She could not see them in cafés, bars, and living rooms, closing their eyes to better hear her sing. She could not hear their praise or their applause. No one (except for a few avant-garde patrons of a club in Ipanema the night before) had heard samba done in such a way: so moving, so vulnerable, so in need of acceptance and forgiveness. After the broadcast those many listeners across Brazil held Sofia Salvador's voice in their memories and were ready to accept her back with open arms. This was, in part, why her death was upsetting to so many: they hadn't been able to buy her records again, to wait in line to see her shows, to call her an innovator, to tell her it was as if she'd never left them. They loved her after all; they just hadn't shown it in time.

She was embalmed, a luxury in those days. Her coffin was lined in bronze and covered in the Brazilian flag. A fire truck draped in black cloth carried her through Rio's streets, to the House of Representatives. For two days she lay wearing her red dress and red lipstick, surrounded by flowers, in the House's main lobby, where lines of people shuffled by to pay their respects. The lines of mourners snaked past the Odeon movie house and around Floriano Square. Some mourners were puffy-eyed from crying, some were solemn, some simply curious. There were generals, bakers, police, housewives, socialites, famous disc jockeys. Even Aracy Araújo appeared, wearing a black mantilla over her head and with mascara running down her cheeks. I looked at Graça, waiting for her to sit up and laugh out loud at Aracy, who ignored me but grasped Vinicius's forearm. "How will I be a great artist now?" she asked. "Without the best to compete against, how will I ever get better?"

I wanted to tear that mantilla from Aracy's head and slap her. I wanted to slap every last one of them, powerful and poor alike.

Why hadn't they swarmed the airport to welcome her back? Why hadn't they applauded her that night at the Copa? Why hadn't they shown her this affection when she'd really needed it?

If Graça had died an old woman, having lived a life full of music and several incarnations of Sofia Salvadors, would she have received such love and adoration? Or is losing life more acceptable than losing your youth? And had Graça, always so attuned to her audience, sensed this, and given them exactly what they'd wanted: a star who'd returned to them for her final show; who was always young, always beautiful, and always theirs in their memories? As I sat and watched those mourners edge by, I'd never before felt so much hate.

When they finally closed the coffin, the Blue Moon boys and I carried her back to the fire truck. We stood side by side as we drove slowly past the crowds. Who would have thought there were so many people in Rio? As we edged past Flamengo Beach, Oswaldo Cruz Avenue, Botafogo Beach, and beyond, all the way to Saint John the Baptist Cemetery, people lined the streets. Only, unlike the lines of mourners in the House's dreadfully hot chamber, these were not silent. Some played cuícas, others banged drums, others scraped reco-recos. All of them sang. "My Mutt," "Clara," "We Are from Samba," "Air You Breathe"—there wasn't a Sofia Salvador song they didn't know.

Atop the fire truck, Little Noel cried like a baby. Banana and Bonito propped him up. And then we heard Kitchen's voice—as deep and startling as a siren—join the crowd's song. One by one, the Blue Moon boys and I forgot our anger and our hurt, and we sang along, too. It became a Carnaval like no other. What a shame Graça didn't see it.

M ost of Blue Moon stayed in Brazil. Only Vinicius and, surprisingly, Kitchen returned to Los Angeles with me. Kitchen made it clear that returning to the United States wasn't an act of kindness toward me but one of defiance to Brazil—he couldn't take being there anymore, living beside those so-called fans who had betrayed Graça when she was alive, onstage in front of them, and now heralded her talent after death.

Kitchen moved to Chicago, where he played samba-infused jazz and blues until 1965, when he had a stroke and died in a rented room. Banana, Bonito, Little Noel, and Tiny had some small successes as musicians, but nothing like they'd had with Blue Moon. The bulk of our best songs belonged to the Victor Recording Company, and immediately after Graça's funeral, I hired a lawyer and took Victor to court. The case took nearly a decade to decide but eventually came out in our favor. We were all suddenly rich, but by then I was too numb to notice. I had, in Vinicius's words, checked out.

Those first months after Graça died, when I was still relatively sober, Vinicius helped me pack up the Bedford Drive house and insisted I go with him to Las Vegas.

What was Vegas back then but a new land, ripe with possibility for every singer, gangster, showgirl, musician, waiter, and gambler? Vegas was, during the war, famous for being the place for quickie divorces, where estranged couples stayed at casinos that resembled Old West saloons with sawdust on the floors. The Flamingo Hotel changed all that, with its forty acres of air-conditioned rooms, crystal chandeliers, golf courses, and health spas. After the war, Hollywood became a land of morality and blacklists. Las Vegas was the haven for every star exiled for being a suspected communist or homosexual or both. Vegas was a kind of Lapa in the middle of the desert, but it was not an escape. Not for me.

Memories of my life before Las Vegas were achingly vivid; it was as if the emptiness of the desert revived every smell, every taste, every conversation, every pause, every touch, every emotion I'd experienced in my brief time on this earth. And it was too much. I was a product of those memories and suddenly, like a mother holding its child too tightly to its bosom, they were smothering me.

Before his second term, President Dutra was ousted in free and fair elections. The people used their secret ballots to put old Getúlio back in office. It was around this time that Vinicius appeared, unshaven and red-eyed, sitting beside my hospital bed. My forearms and legs were strapped down; they did this back then, to patients they believed were a danger to themselves. I felt more ashamed of those straps than of the wide ribbons of gauze around my wrists. It was Vinicius who'd found me on the floor of my Las Vegas apartment. It was Vinicius who convinced the doctors to unbuckle me.

After my discharge from the hospital, each time a memory rose in me I reached for a drink.

Getúlio's second spell in office didn't last long. Even in my drunken stupor I kept up with news from Brazil, like a spurned lover sniffs out stories about an ex, hoping to hear of their failures rather than their successes. Despite his flaws, I felt a strange comfort knowing that Old Gegê—the man we'd always called by his first name, and who fought for the presidency since Graça and I were girls at Riacho Doce—was back in Catete Palace. Once again there was scandal, a grab for power, and Getúlio was again on the verge of being ousted, by force, from office. Instead of retreating, he sat at his desk, loaded his favorite pistol, and shot himself in the heart. "I leave life to enter History," he wrote in a note left beside his body. Vinicius told me the news.

"Old Getúlio's killed himself," he said, his hands shaking as he lifted a cigarette to his mouth. I wasn't surprised. For some it's easier to imagine death than to face the person who the choices and burdens of life have forced you to become. But death robs us of many things, including the chance to redeem ourselves.

Sleep doesn't come easily now, if at all. The nurse says I need my rest; I can't listen to my records at night anymore. So I write in secret, or sit in the dark and listen to the murmur of my hospital bed's motor. The bed was installed in my home after a fall I had recently. It lowers itself so that the night nurse can help me onto it like a child.

I close my eyes and listen: my heart sounds sluggish, as if it is pumping syrup, not blood.

I press a button. With a groan and a puff of air, my bed lowers.

"This is it," I say, out loud. "Here goes nothing."

I heave myself up and out.

The night nurse is asleep in the room next to mine, her mouth open, her head tilted at an odd angle. I shuffle past her, as silent as a lizard. When I reach the den, I squeeze through the maze of boxes and clothing racks until I come to the record player. And there, behind it—yes—there it is. I lift the guitar easily, instilled with a strength I didn't have just hours before. All its strings are intact, though probably out of tune. I carry it, like a thief in the night, outside. In the courtyard I find a metal chair and collapse into it, shaking and sweating in the dark.

I can smell the salt air. The strangler fig's leaves—thick and shiny like leather—bump against one another in the breeze. I hold the guitar close. After he forgot how to play it, Vinicius never again asked for his guitar, not even to hold in his lap.

"We can't take anything with us, why keep it now?" he liked to proclaim before he got sick. He allowed many musicians to cover and sample our songs without paying us a dime. "Let them have the music," he said. "We can't keep it when we go."

"Where are we going?" I'd ask.

Vinicius shrugged. "Hell if I know."

Did he mean he didn't know where we'd go after we'd shed these husks of our bodies, or did Vinicius truly think we'd go to hell—the both of us?

Go to hell, Dor.

Hell's too far away.

From what?

From you.

Write that down. That's a good line.

Nena had a saints' altar where she lit candles and muttered requests. Prayer for Nena was bartering: I do this for you, and you keep me safe in return. She never spoke of heaven or of souls. If I'd mentioned such things to Nena I'm sure she would have hit me.

During my year of school the nuns spoke of creation and original sin, of confessions and purgatory and the nine different kinds of angels. Even the goddamn angels had a pecking order! If the nuns' heaven is as petty and mean as our own world, I want no part in it. Not that I'd be allowed through those pearled gates anyway.

It's the result that matters.

Madame Lucifer died in jail, stabbed inside Ilha Grande, but for all of his misdeeds I can't imagine him there. I see him tall and robed and glorious, dancing atop a Carnaval float, forever in motion.

There was, not long ago, a story on the radio about parallel universes, about how time can fold on itself again and again, giving us many versions of our lives, each with a different outcome. Surely there exists the life where I stay with her that night in the Palace. The life where I give her my songs. The life where I open my fists—closed for so long—and understand, before it's too late, what Graça knew all along: When we create, it is not to prove, but to share.

The songs aren't important, I say.

I'm lying, and she knows it. She sees the pain of my lie and the gift of it. A gift always and only for her. And she gives me one in return: I am her only audience now, and she loves me as she's always loved them, finally, and completely.

My chest feels warm and terribly tender, as if I've been stung there. I hold the guitar closer. The metal chair wobbles beneath me.

In Lapa no one talked about heaven or hell; we were all too busy living and playing music. My Lapa's just a place in the history books now, but I let myself imagine it still exists. I strum Vinicius's guitar. Yes. There it is.

Graça and Vinicius and the boys are sitting in Ciata's yard, waiting. The roda can't begin until we're all there—that's the rule—and they've been waiting awhile. I push open the creaky gate, feel the packed dirt floor under my sandals, smell the smoke from Vinicius's Onyx cigarettes. And there they are: Tiny holds his cavaquinho on his soft belly; Kitchen winks; Noel smiles as brightly as a child; Banana nods; Bonito pours me a generous drink; Vinicius's large, dark eyes take my breath away; and Graça—oh, my heart—with her dimpled smile and her impatience. The chair next to her is wide open.

We are all beautiful in our youth. And we are all forgiven. In the roda, there are no grudges that can't be put aside, no wounds that can't be healed. Music is the greatest kind of reciprocity. For a taut string to make sound, it must be pulled from its stillness. The musician plucks the string, and the string expands as it strives to return to its original place. And in this return is vibration, and in this vibration is sound. A song couldn't exist without first having stillness. Music couldn't exist without a steady disruption, and a continuous return to what was, and what can be.

I can hear my heartbeat, yes, and in it, the drums from the cutters' circles. The words to those songs return to me like an ache, words I'd thought I'd forgotten, words that spin tales of infatuation, pain, re- venge, regret, mercy, and, yes, even grace. I look at Graça and she nods to me; it's my turn to start us off. I feel something ancient rising within me: a breath of the impossible, a whisper of a truth I've always known but could not name. I pluck a string and its sound fills the circle.

ACKNOWLEDGMENTS

This book went through many incarnations. Mika Tanner, Deanna Fei, and Cristina Henríquez read nearly all of them, never shying from telling me the truth, never letting me quit, and always being the smartest and most generous readers (and friends) I could ever hope for. My agent, Dorian Karchmar, has been an unwavering advocate and a source of encouragement for fourteen years and counting. Thank you to everyone at Riverhead for giving this book your support and belief. Thanks especially to Danya Kukafka and the amazing Sarah McGrath, whose wise letters and thoughtful edits were my lifelines. Thanks to my copy editors—your diligence helped me bring this book across the finish line.

No mother can be an artist without support from a tribe of women who listen, care, and help clean up life's messes. Thanks to Kate, Bahareh, Logan, Tatiana, Maria (Abegunde), Ashley (Tee-Tee), Ruth, and all of my daughter's teachers and caregivers. Thanks, always, to my first caregivers: my parents, David and Lúcia. Thank you to the readers of this book for being partners in its creation by bringing Dores, Graça, and the Blue Moon boys to life in your imaginations.

My deepest thanks go to the members of my own little roda: my husband and daughter. James, I'm eternally grateful for your calm, your steadfast belief, and your willingness to take this ride through life with me. Emília, meu amor, you were inside my belly when I started writing this book. I'd listen to music as I wrote, putting one earbud in my ear and taping the other to my stomach so you could hear Cartola, Otis Redding, Marisa Monte, Carmen Miranda, Kanye, Tom Jobim, Paulinho da Viola, Édith Piaf, and so many others. Thank you, minha filha querida, for keeping me company back then and now, and for teaching me to improvise, to play, and, especially, to listen.